Cuddies Strip

Rob McInroy

RINGWOOD PUBLISHING
GLASGOW

First published in Great Britain in 2020
by
Ringwood Publishing, Glasgow.
www.ringwoodpublishing.com
mail@ringwoodpublishing.com

ISBN 978-1-901514-88-9

British Library Cataloguing-in-Publication Data
A catalogue record for this book is available from the
British Library

Printed and bound in the UK
by
Lonsdale Direct Solutions

About Cuddies Strip

The true crimes depicted in Cuddies Strip happened as they are described in this novel, taken from contemporary accounts in the Courier, Dundee Evening Telegraph, Sunday Post and other newspapers. The main lines of investigation are also taken from contemporaneous accounts, but details have been invented. All police officers and officials are fictitious and bear no resemblance to the officers who investigated the real crime and solved a difficult case in only two weeks. Lord Chief Justice Aitchison, the presiding judge in the subsequent trial is real, and is famous in legal circles as the first Labour politician to hold the office of Lord Advocate

Publisher's Note

Readers are alerted that the text contains three uses of a racist term that would be completely unacceptable in a modern context. After careful consideration, they have been retained in the text because of their contemporary relevance in a 1935 context..

About the Author

Rob McInroy was born in Crieff, Perthshire but now lives in exile in east Yorkshire. He has an MA in Creative Writing and a PhD in American literature, both from the University of Hull. His doctoral thesis was on the novelist Cormac McCarthy, with whom he continues to have a love-hate relationship.

Originally a writer of short stories, he has won four short story competitions in the past eighteen months (Hissac, ChipLit Fest, Writing Magazine and the Bedford International Writing Competition) and has been placed in numerous other competitions. Cuddies Strip is his first published novel.

His fiction is all based in and around the Strathearn valley in Perthshire.

For my mother, Margaret McInroy

Part One

August 1935

Wednesday 14th August

A Day of Terror

They sat in a triangle of plush grass at the edge of the Cuddies Strip, looking over fields of wheat that stretched towards the River Earn. In the milky-blue of a late-night full moon, the lights of Perth burned low. Love like a moment in time. Danny Kerrigan turned and kissed Marjory Fenwick inexpertly, his hand tentative on her back. She leaned into him, felt him warm and gentle.

'Thank you,' he said.

'What for?'

'This. You're right. This is much better than the pictures.'

'Better than Shirley Temple anyway.'

'Shirley Temple's alright.'

She peered at him pretend-haughtily. 'I think you'll find I'm a lot more alright than Shirley Temple, Daniel Kerrigan.'

Danny grinned. 'Yes ma'am.'

They kissed again, long and slow, each discovering the joy of intimacy. In the distance the clock of Perth Academy struck ten.

'We'd best get back. Your mum'll be starting to worry.'

Marjory stood and wiped grass and moisture from the back of her swagger coat and put her hands in her pockets, hooking out an arm to allow Danny to slip his inside. They walked down the Cuddies Strip towards Perth. Trees hung low around them, beeches and silver birches rustling in the wind as darkness settled over Strathearn. Swifts, hundreds of them, circled in the moonlight. The Strip narrowed and dipped and turned, then opened out again, and they walked arm in arm, laughing, into the gathering gloom.

The stand of whins was so innocuous they didn't even notice it but as they did their lives changed forever. From behind them the evening quiet was shattered by an explosion and Marjory felt a surge of air whistle past her right ear.

'What?' she said.

Danny turned. 'Don't faint here, Madge,' he said. He didn't have time to look at her before a second detonation sounded and he collapsed backwards. The noise of his body crashing into the earth was the most terrifying Marjory had ever heard. He lay with his head and shoulders on the grass by the side of the path and she knelt beside him and stared in bewilderment. There was blood on his face and on his lovely blue sweater and jacket. He stared upwards but made no movement.

Marjory heard a noise and looked up. There was a man standing over her. In her confusion she couldn't imagine who he might be.

'Stay with him,' she said. 'I'll get help.'

She started to run down the Cuddies Strip towards the stile at the bottom which led onto the path back to Buckie Braes and the outskirts of Perth. She stumbled over stones and tree roots and gasped as branches whipped against her face. She could think only of Danny, of getting help, of making sure he was okay. There were footsteps behind her and she turned and saw the man in pursuit. She speeded up and he speeded up and they ran together towards the stile.

As she stepped onto it she felt her foot being grabbed and she was pulled backwards onto the path. An arm gripped her throat and a rough hand was forced over her mouth. She could smell woodsmoke, acrid and stale. Helpless, she was dragged into the undergrowth between the path and the wheatfield. Brambles scratched her legs. Nettles stung her. She felt something being wrapped around her wrists and then a foul-smelling fabric was tied over her mouth. She gagged. She struggled in the darkness, trying to comprehend what was happening.

The man was kneeling on her chest, scrabbling at her clothes with frantic movements. She could hear him panting and she felt his breath on her face. He was pulling at her hands and she realised he was untying them again and for an instant she hoped the ordeal was ending but as soon as her hands were released she felt him tugging her coat. There was grass in her mouth, the smell of soil in her nostrils. Terror overtook her and she fell still, unable to resist. *Never fight back, Marjory*. Her mother's words came to her, uttered often enough. *Never fight back, it just makes things worse.*

He stripped her naked. The object around her mouth slipped off and she screamed but he punched her and gripped her throat and she felt something else being tied tightly around her jaw and she was silenced again. Her hands were re-tied, this time behind her back, more tightly, and she lay crookedly as the body slithered on top of her and began to paw at her, pulling at her breasts, hands rasping across her belly and downwards. Her legs were dragged apart and she felt fingers pushing inside her and the full weight of his body pressed down on her and she closed her eyes and shut down her senses.

Afterwards, she was conscious of her attacker fumbling about for some moments, and then of him running off and then of another gunshot sounding. Nothing felt real. Later, she thought that perhaps half an hour passed before she could move. Her hands were still bound behind her back and there was something tied around her ankles. In a moment of panic she realised how dark it had grown. Then she became aware of being cold, and then of being frightened. She struggled against her bindings and felt movement in the material

5

round her ankles and guessed it must be her stockings. She stretched and bent her knees and felt the stockings slacken and fall off. After a furious struggle with her wrist-bindings she managed to pull one hand free and swung it in the air to relieve the numbness in her wrist. She dragged the gag down from her mouth and recognised it as her own suspender belt. Still dazed, she scrabbled in the blackness for her clothing but could find nothing except her swagger coat. She wrapped it round herself.

'Danny,' she said. She ran back to where he lay and bent over him. His face was covered by a piece of dark-coloured cloth. It hadn't been there before.

'I'll get help,' she said. She wasn't sure who she was trying to reassure. She pushed through the hedge into the field beyond and ran towards Buckie Braes, sobbing as she stumbled among the wheat. 'Help,' she shouted. 'Help.' There was movement on the path behind the hedge and she shouted again and ran for the gate. A man and a woman were walking hand in hand.

'Please, mister, can you help me?'

The couple looked around to see where the voice had come from and saw Marjory standing on the other side of the fence. She was sobbing uncontrollably.

'Are you lost?' said the woman. 'D'you want us to take you back to Perth?'

'There's a man with a gun. He's killed Danny and taken all my clothes.' The words were forced out between sobs that racked her body. 'He's shot Danny,' she repeated.

John Spence pulled her through the spars of the gate and Helen Ewan hugged her, feeling shivers rippling through her tiny body. At first she assumed the girl was only thirteen or so. Clutching Marjory between them, they started to walk towards Perth. All the time, Marjory repeated over and over what had happened, as though trying to believe it herself.

'Did you see what he looked like?' said Spence.

'He had his hat pulled down. He wasn't very tall. I don't know. But he had big eyes. Big, staring eyes. And a red face.'

At Cherrybank, Spence called the City Police from the public telephone kiosk. In the dull gas streetlamps they could see the girl had a handkerchief knotted round her wrist and something – it looked like a suspender belt – tied round her neck. From what she'd told them, she was probably naked beneath the coat.

*

'Kelty,' shouted Desk Sergeant Hamilton in the City Police reception. He replaced the telephone on its hook and waited for the young constable to approach. 'Disturbance up at Buckie Braes. Go and have a look.'

'What kind of disturbance, Sergeant?' Police Constable Bob Kelty was slightly built and unprepossessing. Despite incipient and highly premature baldness, he looked younger than his twenty years. His expression was solemn, his mouth tight.

'No idea. The line was terrible, couldn't hear properly. If it's Cherrybank it'll be drunks or burglars. Or both.'

'I'm due to finish in ten minutes. Is it okay if I stop home to tell Gran I'll be late?'

Hamilton stared at him with exasperation. It was a nanny this new lad needed, not a sergeant. 'Out,' he said.

Bob cycled to his house on Jeanfield Road. 'Gran?' he shouted from the hallway. The house was cold and in darkness. He went into the living room, his eyes gradually becoming accustomed to the gloom, enough to see the shape in the chair by the empty fire.

'Are you no' in bed yet?' he said. 'It's near eleven.'

'And how am I tae go tae bed with no' even a cup of tea for my supper?'

'I left you some cold meat out and some bread. You knew

I was at work, Gran. You could have made yoursel' a pot of tea.'

'As if you care.'

'I'm sorry, Gran. I have to go out again. There's been a disturbance at Buckie Braes.'

'Aye, off you go and enjoy yoursel'. Just like your mother.'

'I'll be back as soon as I can. Will I put the kettle on for you?'

'And burn the hoose doon?'

Bob sighed and retreated through the house to the street. He cycled up Glasgow Road and turned off towards Buckie Braes. When he arrived, there were three people huddled round the telephone box.

He listened as Spence relayed Marjory's story. He looked at Marjory and bit his lip. The girl seemed terrified. She was sobbing and shivering. Bob could handle drunks and burglars but he had only been in the force three months and this was beyond his experience.

'We need to get back to Danny,' Marjory said, pulling his arm.

'We'd best take a look, I suppose,' he said. Across the road he spotted James Drummond, his old janitor from Perth Academy, on his way home from the bowling club. He hailed him and explained what had happened. 'Will you come with us?' he asked.

'I'll need to ask the wife,' said Drummond. 'I live just up here.' They walked one-hundred yards or so in the direction of Buckie Braes and stopped at a small bungalow. The entrance to the Braes was visible at the end of the road.

'I don't want to go back up,' said Helen Ewan.

'You can bide here,' said Drummond. He explained to his wife what had happened and the old woman invited Helen inside. The others started back to Buckie Braes but Marjory stumbled on the pavement and gave a cry.

8

'Hell, lassie,' said Drummond, 'you've nothin' on your feet.'

'He took all my clothes.'

'You cannae go walkin' about wi' nae shin on.' He went into his house and returned a minute later with a pair of boys' shoes. Marjory slid her bloodied feet into them and knew straight away they were too big. She tied them as tightly as she could but still her feet moved freely inside.

'Please,' she said. 'Hurry.' She marched uphill and the three men followed. 'Go through the field,' she said. 'It'll be quicker.' She climbed the fence and jumped into the field and started to run. Her heart was pounding. An acid pulse of fear rose in her throat. She pushed through whins onto the Cuddies Strip and stopped and tried to establish how far she had come and which direction she needed to turn. She broke right and after twenty yards she slowed as she saw the shape on the path.

'Oh Danny,' she said.

Bob placed his hand on her shoulder and gently eased her aside. He crouched over the body and trained his torch on it and felt for a pulse but he could tell by sight the boy was dead. His right leg was fully extended, the left bent and lying outwards across the path. A handkerchief covered his face. He raised it carefully and his stomach lurched and he thought he might be sick. He replaced the handkerchief and looked at Marjory, the hope in her expression, fear emanating from her. He turned to Spence.

'I'm afraid this man is very seriously injured. Run back and telephone for an ambulance. And call the County Police and ask them to attend. The Cuddies Strip is outside the City Police's jurisdiction.' He took him to one side, away from Marjory, and whispered in his ear. 'Tell them it's murder.'

Spence ran off and Bob turned to Marjory.

'It's Danny Kerrigan, isn't it?'

'Yes. Do you know him?'

'Aye, I played fitba with him five nights ago. Is this how you left him?'

Marjory shook her head. 'His face wasn't covered like that.'

'Do you recognise the handkerchief?'

'Yes, it's Danny's. It was in his top pocket.'

'Could it have blown onto him?' asked Drummond.

'No,' said Bob. 'It's been deliberately placed. Look, it's been tucked into the collar here.' Bob took Marjory's hand. There was another handkerchief knotted around her wrist. Her suspender belt was tied round her neck. He inspected the knots on both. He raised her hand and sniffed the handkerchief.

'Did your attacker do this to you?'

'Yes.'

'Do you recognise this handkerchief?'

'No, I've never seen it before.'

'The suspender belt?'

'It's mine.'

'Were you assaulted?'

'Yes.'

'Criminally assaulted?'

'What do you mean?'

'Did he take full advantage of you?'

'Yes.' She explained what happened. Her voice was low now, calmer. She was almost withdrawn. She complained of being cold. Bob wanted to hug her. He didn't know what else to do.

'Should I take the lassie back down?' said Drummond.

'Aye. I'll come by when the County boys get here.'

Alone, Bob inspected the body. It was hard to believe. Hard to understand the completeness of death. He knew that Danny lived with his grandfather during the week and he thought about that knock on Mr Fiskin's door in a few hours, the ruination it would unleash, never-ending and unchangeable. In the distance he saw a couple of torch lights glimmering in the darkness.

'Hello,' he shouted.

'Hello.' A man in a light-coloured suit appeared from the gloom, followed by someone in uniform, and Bob cursed as he recognised Detective Sergeant Braggan and PC Jones of the County Police. Jones was a fine sort but Sergeant Braggan was notorious in both the County and City forces.

'The body's over here,' he said.

'You haven't buggered about with it, have you?'

'No.'

Sergeant Braggan hunched over the body and trained his torch on it. He turned to Bob. 'This is a right to-do, eh?' He lit a cigarette. 'Aye well, it's going to be a long night. We'll get some good overtime out of this.'

Bob stared at the body in silence. 'The assault happened doon there,' he said.

'What assault?'

'The girl that was with Danny when he was shot. She ran off but the killer caught her. Raped her.'

'Raped?'

'Aye.'

Braggan frowned.

*

Inspector Conoboy stared down the hallway as he listened to the news on the telephone. It was twelve-thirty. Weariness weighed on him. His head ached. Murder and rape? In Perth?

He looked into his wife's bedroom. 'I have to go out,' he said. Bella Conoboy turned in her bed and he explained what had happened.

'Poor babies,' she said. 'What a world it's coming.'

He arrived at the scene a little after one. Acting Chief Constable MacNaughton was already in attendance and

Sergeant Braggan was briefing him. Conoboy spotted PC Kelty standing at the back.

'Why, hello Robert,' he said.

Bob gave a shy smile. 'Hello, Mr Conoboy.'

'Inspector Conoboy to you, lad,' said Braggan. He turned to the inspector. 'It seems he was shot, sir. Pistol, I should imagine.'

Conoboy trained his torch on the body and shook his head. 'That's a shotgun wound. Close range. I wonder if it's here.' He grabbed one shoulder. 'Help me,' he said. Braggan took the other shoulder and they hoisted the body upright. 'Lift up his clothing.'

Bob faltered.

'Go on, lad,' said Braggan.

Bob took hold of Danny's jumper and shirt and lifted them up, then the simmet beneath, revealing his bare chest. Conoboy peered at the body and carefully eased something from it.

'A wad,' he said. 'From a shotgun cartridge.'

'It went through the clothing?' said Braggan.

Conoboy nodded and put the wad in his pocket. 'What is the meaning of the handkerchief on his face?'

'I don't know,' said Braggan. Bob made to speak but saw Sergeant Braggan's forbidding expression and changed his mind.

'Do we know anything about him?' said Conoboy

'The City boy does,' said Braggan. He nodded to Bob. Bob didn't reply and Braggan gestured in irritation. Finally, the young constable spoke.

'Danny Kerrigan. We play together for Scone Thistle. He's an outside left. Was.' He stopped. Danny Kerrigan, fast and furious, full of talent. A fair percentage of Thistle's goals came from Danny's sprints down the wing and crosses into the centre. Bob felt the onset of tears and blinked and bent and turned his torch on the ground as though in search of

12

evidence. 'He was only eighteen. Apprentice glazier with McLeod's.'

'Poor boy,' said Conoboy.

'The girl ran off and the killer chased her,' Bob continued. 'Stripped her naked and raped her.'

'Allegedly,' said Braggan.

'Where?'

'Down there.' The night had clouded over and as Braggan led them towards the stile the collective light of their torches did little to penetrate the darkness. They reached a spot where the grass was heavily flattened and showed signs of struggle.

'At daybreak,' said MacNaughton, 'every man on duty. I want this place searched from top to bottom.' He turned to Inspector Conoboy. 'I want this man found. Understand?'

'Yes sir.'

*

'Take off your clothes.'

It took Marjory a moment to react to the doctor who was busying himself with his implements without even looking at her. They were in an office at the police headquarters and Marjory looked at the door, wondering whether anyone might come in. Mutely, she stripped out of the clothes Mrs Drummond had given her, all of them two sizes too big and smelling of stale tobacco. She sat hunched on the couch, hands gripped against her knees. There were smears of blood on her upper thighs. It was one-thirty in the morning and she wanted to close her eyes on this nightmare and will it away. She doubted whether closing her eyes would ever be possible again. Every time she did she was back in the Cuddies Strip, Danny by her side, and that noise, the noise of Danny's body collapsing. She knew, now, that he was already dead before he hit the ground. The deadweight of a body falling, that sound would never leave her. That, rather than the gunshot, was the sound of death.

She looked up at the man who had introduced himself gruffly as Doctor Murphy.

'Pardon?' she said.

'I said what is your age?'

'Seventeen.'

'Address?'

'8, Longcauseway.'

He gripped her jaw lightly and tilted her head. She winced.

'Your mouth is sore?' She nodded. 'Did he hit you?'

'Yes.'

He opened her mouth and looked inside. 'Bit swollen,' he said. 'Nothing serious.' He inspected her body. There was one large bruise on the left side of her neck and three smaller ones on the right. Clear evidence of being grabbed by the throat. A right-handed man. He walked around and studied her back. 'Superficial bruises to the shoulder blades,' he said. 'Scratches down the middle of the back.' He continued the inspection, making notes in his notebook. There were multiple abrasions on both feet, one abrasion on the left knee, scratches on the right knee and superficial scratches on the left thigh and buttock.

'You've been in the wars.'

'Yes, sir.'

He pushed her onto her back and lifted her knees and pulled them apart. Her vagina was red with blood.

'What are you doing?' Marjory said. She recoiled as he slid two fingers inside her and pushed and probed. Her attacker had done the same thing two hours before. It hurt then and it hurt now. The sensations were the same.

'You're menstruating?'

'Yes.'

'Did he physically assault you?'

14

'Yes.'

'Sexually?'

'Yes.'

'Are you sure?'

'Yes.'

'Miss Fenwick, this is a vital question, so I'll ask it again. Are you sure?'

'I'm sure.' She turned onto her side and shut herself off from reality. She could still feel those fingers, that invasion.

'Come along, child. You can get dressed again now. The police will need to interview you.'

'Tonight?'

'Of course.'

Marjory dressed herself once more. The bulkiness of her clothing made her appear even more slight, a dark-eyed foundling physically smaller than her age. She was light-headed, barely able to assimilate what was happening around her. There were police officers everywhere but none appeared to be doing anything practical. The noise of their footsteps echoed through the building. Plain walls lowered over Marjory, made her feel enclosed, small, alone. She shivered into her swagger coat and pulled it tightly around herself as she was escorted through a darkened doorway.

'Miss Fenwick?' said a kindly looking man in a crisp uniform sitting behind a large mahogany desk. He had a neatly trimmed moustache and smiling eyes. He indicated for her to sit in the seat opposite him. 'My name is Inspector Conoboy. This is Detective Sergeant Braggan and you know PC Kelty. May I say how sorry I am for your ordeal?'

'Thank you.'

'You and Danny Kerrigan were sweethearts?'

'Yes.'

'How long had you been going out?'

'Since New Year.'

'Had you planned to go to the Cuddies Strip tonight?'

15

'No. Danny wanted to go to the King's. Shirley Temple was on. I wasn't feeling too well and I didn't fancy being cooped up in a smoky picture house. So I suggested a walk. We just ended up at the Cuddies Strip.'

'Have you been there with him before?' asked Sergeant Braggan.

'Yes. Once.'

'Regular lovers' lane, isn't it?'

'I suppose so.'

'What were you doing there tonight?'

'Just talking. Laughing. Larking about.'

'Did you see anyone while you were walking?' said Conoboy.

'We met a couple out courting. The boy said hello to Danny.'

'Did he greet him by name?'

'Yes.'

'Did you know him?'

'No.'

Inspector Conoboy lit a cigarette. He flicked the match into an ashtray. 'Do you know who did this?' he asked.

'No.'

'Do you know anyone who would want to hurt Danny?'

'Nobody would want to hurt Danny. Everyone liked him.'

'Can you describe the man?'

'He wasn't very tall. Red-faced. Not shaven. A one-day beard. He had a flat nose. Big staring eyes. It's the eyes I really remember.'

'Can you tell me what happened when he attacked you?'

Marjory went through it once more. She spoke automatically, almost disinterestedly.

'Why did he take your clothes?'

'I don't know. To stop me running away?'

'But he left your coat?'

'Yes.'

16

'What were you wearing?'

'A grey skirt and green blouse.'

'What else?'

She looked at him. 'Everything?' He nodded. 'A peach-coloured vest, a pink bra, green suspender belt, two pairs of knickers, an underskirt, stockings. My shoes were grey. I had a red and white necklace with a pendant on it. Danny bought me it.'

'Do you still have that?'

'No.'

'You were wearing two pairs of knickers?' said Braggan.

'Yes. One pink. One green.'

'Did he have wandering hands then, young Danny?'

'Certainly not.'

'So why the two pairs?'

'I wasn't feeling well.' Marjory began to cry. She looked at the inspector. 'Please can I see my mum?'

'Yes, child,' he said. 'You've had enough for one night.'

Braggan coughed. 'We could do with more information, sir. To help the men when they start at first light.'

'They'll be doing a search of the area first, Sergeant. That will take most of the morning, I imagine. Robert, take the girl home. In the morning, come back here. I'll clear it with your superiors at the City Police.'

Sergeant Braggan made no attempt to hide his irritation. Conoboy noticed it, wondered whether to confront him and, instead, walked out of the room. Braggan and Bob exchanged glances.

'Take her home,' said Braggan.

Thursday 15th August

A Day of Initiation

In the hour before dawn, John McGuigan headed east from his tent over the fields of Kirkton of Mailer farm towards Callerfountain Hill. He walked quickly despite the darkness, despite the rain, despite the sack he carried over his shoulder and the shotgun in his hand. He headed deep into the woods, where no light penetrated and the ground was dry and layered with desiccated pine needles. He walked steadily, as though he could see a path through the blackness. After twenty minutes he came to a sloped clearing. Shapes in the gloom indicated entry points to a series of badger setts. He took the sack from his shoulder and opened it and pulled out a pair of knickers. He smelled them and paused before stuffing them back in the sack. He tied the sack and thrust it into a large hole and used the shotgun to force it six feet down. He broke the shotgun in two and pushed the parts into the same space.

'They'll be there a hundred year,' he said.

*

Twenty police officers stood on the Cuddies Strip as dawn rose over Kinnoull Hill. It was raining heavily. It was cold. Miserable. They shifted apprehensively like a herd of cows awaiting the farmer for morning milking. Each man stood within yards of the murder scene, trampling underfoot any vestige of evidence.

Detective Sergeant Braggan barked instructions. Two men were to stand guard on Buckie Braes and turn away sightseers. Four men were to comb the murder scene. A further four were to search by the stile where the rape took place.

'The rest of you I want to search in the woodland over there. Every ditch, every bush, every hole. The bloodhounds will be here shortly but see what we can find in the meantime. Anything that doesn't grow here or live here shouldn't be here.'

And neither should I, he concluded. *I'm not being paid to be in charge of this bloody operation.* Rain dripped from his bowler hat. The trousers of his brown suit were soaked.

*

Marjory Fenwick lay in bed in Longcauseway and listened to her mother's activity next door. She had not slept and her eyes ached and her body ached but she wasn't tired. Her blankets felt heavy. Replaying in her head simultaneously were these new moments of her life, Danny's shooting, the chase, the capture, that, running towards Buckie Braes, the police, inspection, that man touching her, going home, hugging her mother, lying in bed, here, now, this reality, and as she thought these thoughts, time merged so that she was trapped in a continuous present of catastrophe and she wondered how she would ever be able to escape it.

'Please, Madge,' she said. 'Get over this.'

*

Bob Kelty lathered foam on his cheeks and stared at himself in the mirror. Unhappiness stared back. He searched his memory for moments from last Friday's football match, touches by Danny Kerrigan, the last movements Bob would ever see him make. He didn't believe in God or heaven or an afterlife but this, the true nature of nothingness, was beyond his understanding. The sight of his uniform hanging behind the door filled him with dread. Another day of pretence, another futile attempt to be good at something. He dressed slowly and went downstairs to make breakfast for Gran, speculating on what her mood might be.

'Where have you been?' she shouted at him. She was standing in the kitchen in her overcoat and hat and she held an umbrella in her hand. She was clearly agitated. 'We'll be late, you stupid laddie.'

'What for?'

'You ken damn fine I've to be at the doctor's this morning. Come on.'

'That was yesterday, Gran.'

'Eh?'

'Yesterday. Doctor Wishart gave you some pills.'

A baffled expression overtook her face as she tried to remember. She sat down and stared at the linoleum flooring for some moments before going into the hallway and hanging up her coat and hat. Bob put lard in the frying pan and took a slice of bacon from the pantry and slid it into the pan.

Unknown to him, at that moment his future was being shaped in an early morning telephone conversation.

'How has he settled in?' asked Inspector Conoboy.

'Steady,' said Chief Constable Fraser of the City Police. 'He's quiet. Too shy for the police, if I'm honest. I wouldn't have taken him but for your recommendation.'

'I hoped it would be the making of him.'

'He's a loner. Doesn't mix with the other men. And oddly, given how shy he is, he's not really that good with authority.'

'He takes that off his grandmother. Won't be told anything. I wondered, Charles. This case. It's going to be a big one for us. We'll need a lot of resources …'

'You want a loan of Kelty?'

'Until the crime is solved. I could do with an extra pair of hands. And I know Robert. His grandmother worked for me for twenty years. She even brought him to the house in the school holidays. He's had a difficult life and he's retreated into his shell. Perhaps I can bring him out of himself.'

'Very well. He's yours.'

*

'Conoboy organised this, did he?' said Acting Chief Constable MacNaughton. Behind him, arabesques of rain slid down the windowpane of the County Police headquarters in South Street.

'I believe so, sir,' said Bob. 'A temporary transfer until the case is solved. I was told to attend here and ask for the inspector. He requested it personally.'

'And where is he?'

'Sergeant Strangeway said he went to inform the deceased's mother, sir.'

'That was two hours ago. Where is she? Inverness?'

'St Catherine's Road, sir.'

'Are you being facetious, Constable?'

'I don't think so, sir.'

Inspector Conoboy bustled into the Chief Constable's office, shaking rain from his umbrella. 'Sorry I'm late, sir,' he said. He nodded to Bob and Bob smiled back. He pulled off his cap and slipped out of his overcoat and hung it on the coatstand. 'I had to make Bella's breakfast.'

MacNaughton looked witheringly. 'I hope she enjoyed it.'

'Sausage and bacon and egg.'

'Splendid. Meanwhile there are twenty officers brought in on their days off and from annual leave standing about on a hillside in the rain at dawn awaiting your instruction.'

21

'I'll get up there straight away, sir.' He put his cap back on and reached for his mackintosh.

'Don't bother. I've already sent Sergeant Braggan to lead operations.'

Archibald MacNaughton sat at his desk and indicated to Conoboy to sit opposite. He recoiled from the knowledge that Conoboy was now integral to his own advancement. The death of Chief Constable Spiers in July had jolted the small Perth County force. As his deputy, it was natural that MacNaughton was made Acting Chief Constable and it was expected the recruitment process for a permanent replacement would commence within weeks. MacNaughton had anticipated time to demonstrate his seriousness, his organisational nous, leadership skills, investigatory flair. He would lead a steady ship, prove himself capable. Indispensable. The last thing he wanted was a high profile murder case that could go badly wrong. And absolutely the last thing he wanted was Victor Conoboy leading it. They had joined the force within months of each other in 1898 and had made similar progress until eight years before, when MacNaughton had been promoted to Assistant Chief Constable, a role that everyone, the two men included, assumed would be Conoboy's.

'I am going to be taking a direct interest in this investigation,' he said.

'Your experience will be invaluable, sir.'

'Yes it will.' MacNaughton was eight years younger than Conoboy. 'I need to impress on you how important this investigation is ...'

'Indeed ...'

'The Police Committee will be studying our conduct. They will be making important decisions in a few weeks. Finding the culprit is crucial. Do I make myself clear?'

'Abundantly, sir.'

'Dr Murphy's autopsy reports the deceased was killed

with a 12-bore shotgun fired at close range. The girl said it happened just after ten. I want corroboration of that. Secondly, I want to know everyone who was on Buckie Braes or the Cuddies Strip last night. Everyone. And third, motive. Was it a random killing or was Danny Kerrigan the killer's target? My hunch is this isn't a local man. It doesn't feel like it.' A clock on the mantelpiece chimed eight o'clock. MacNaughton waited until it had finished, then motioned to Conoboy and Kelty.

'Dr Murphy confirms Fenwick was attacked but he's got some questions. She might not be as innocent as we think. He's doing the formal examination with Dr Trotter this morning. Speak to her again afterwards.'

'Yes, sir.'

Conoboy and Bob walked into the grand hallway in silence. 'Conference at six,' MacNaughton barked after them.

'Well,' said Conoboy. 'You heard the Acting Chief Constable. Start by checking the lodging houses in town. Anyone new. Anyone strange.'

Bob cleared his throat. He looked around and there was no one but the Inspector close. 'I beg your pardon, sir,' he said. 'What the Chief said, about it not being a local man ...'

'Yes?'

'Well, not to contradict him, but I think it's more likely it *was* a local man.'

Conoboy stopped in the act of putting a cigarette in his mouth. 'Why?'

'The Cuddies Strip, sir. It's the middle of nowhere. You wouldn't arrive at it if you didn't know it was there. So I'm thinking, it's more likely to be someone who knows Buckie Braes. Bird watchers. Poachers. Peeping toms. Tinkers.'

Conoboy lit his cigarette and blew smoke from the side of his mouth. 'Good thinking,' he said. 'Make a start on gun licences. Anyone got one who's known to frequent Buckie

Braes.'

'Yes, sir.' Bob faltered.

'Was there something else?'

'A couple of things, sir.'

Conoboy nodded encouragingly. When Robert's grandmother first brought the child to the house, after the death of his father, he had been almost totally mute. The painful silence lasted three years or more. That Robert could now offer an opinion such as this was greater progress than anyone but Conoboy could have known. 'Go on,' he said.

'Well, sir, the handkerchief. That was used to bind Miss Fenwick's hands. I had a good look at it. There's a laundry mark on it. My gran worked in the Dallerie laundry in Crieff when she was a girl. She's told me about it. They put marks on laundry items to identify which account they belong to …'

'So, if we identify the laundry?'

'Yes, sir. We could identify who the handkerchief belonged to.'

Conoboy pondered. 'Leave that one with me,' he said. 'And the other thing?'

But at that moment Desk Sergeant Strangeway approached. 'If you don't mind, sir,' he said to Conoboy, 'I have an errand I thought the City boy might run for us. A possible sighting in Glover Street.'

'By all means, Sergeant. He turned to Bob. 'Constable, your other point?'

Bob looked at Strangeway's austere expression. 'It's nothing, sir.' He followed the Desk Sergeant to the counter and Conoboy headed for his office. Strangeway turned to Bob. 'What's he got you doing?' he said.

'Checking gun licences.'

'And what are the chances our killer would bother with a gun licence?'

'I couldn't say, Sergeant.'

24

'Well, let's get something clear straight away, City boy. When you're in this station you do what I tell you. Understand?'

'Yes, Sergeant.'

'Why was the inspector late?'

'Making breakfast for Mrs Conoboy.'

Strangeway cursed. 'Biggest case in a hundred years, half the force standing about waiting for instruction, and he's cooking breakfast for the vegetable.'

'Why do you call her that?'

'Because she is. Her laddie was killed in the war, and she seems to think she was the only mother ever to lose a son and she went mad. She's never been seen in public to this day. They say she doesn't even speak, just sits there staring into space.'

'That's terrible.'

'They even say Conoboy has to spoon feed her.'

Bob said nothing. He knew the Conoboys and he knew that wasn't true. Why would people make up such malicious gossip? 'Sergeant,' he said eventually, 'Glover Street?'

'Oh that. I just made that up to get you away from him.'

*

Just after midday, Sergeant Braggan, his suit sopping wet, marched into Inspector Conoboy's office. He was followed by Aggie, carrying a cup of tea for the inspector. Braggan shook his head. The murder was already fourteen hours old and twenty men had spent all morning combing the Cuddies Strip in the pouring rain and they had no evidence except a handkerchief and some shotgun wads. And Conoboy was in his office drinking tea. That was the trouble with these uniformed men – they had no idea about a real criminal investigation. Wasn't Braggan forever saying how they needed a Detective Inspector on the force? Maybe if

25

MacNaughton was made Chief Constable he'd create one.

Before he had a chance to brief Conoboy, Bob Kelty looked around the door. 'Sir, there's a chap in the interview room says he saw Kerrigan and Miss Fenwick last night.'

The hesitancy in Kelty's voice irritated Braggan. In fact, everything about the City boy irritated him. He turned to Conoboy. 'Shall I interview him, sir?'

Conoboy said yes and Braggan rose and followed Kelty out of the office. 'You got something to do?' he said and Bob told him he was checking gun licences.

'Waste of time.' He entered the interview room and sat heavily on the wooden chair facing a nervous-looking man in working clothes.

'Name?' he said.

'James Shepherd.'

'And you saw Kerrigan and Fenwick last night?'

'I can't believe it. We saw them ...'

'We?'

'Me and my girl. Shona. About half nine, walking down Buckie Braes.'

'What direction?'

'We were walking towards Perth, they were heading out to the Cuddies Strip. I said, "Hi Danny," and he said hello and they walked on. I'm probably the last person to see him alive.'

'Apart from the murderer. How did he seem?'

'Happy.'

'And the girl?'

'Her too. They were messing about. Jumping over puddles. Real happy like.'

'Right.'

Braggan was unconvinced by this Fenwick girl. Her story didn't make sense. Why did the murderer let her run all the way down to the stile? He could easily have stopped her at any point. Why did he strip her naked? Rapists don't do that.

It wastes time. Why didn't she scream? Why did he take all her clothes but not her coat? There was more to her than she was letting on.

'Did you know the girl?'

'No.'

'Kerrigan ever mention her?'

'No.'

'How did they meet?'

'No idea.'

Interview complete, Braggan joined MacNaughton and Conoboy in the Chief Constable's office.

'Find anything useful on the Strip, Sergeant?' said Conoboy.

'Two shotgun wads near where the body fell, sir. That's all. I took the decision to stand down the search.'

Conoboy reckoned it was too soon for that but he said nothing. He hadn't been there, after all. 'Do you recall Richard Hamill?' he said.

'We arrested him last year on suspicion of murder?'

'That's the one. He owns a shotgun. Known to frequent Buckie Braes. Malloch's report he bought a box of cartridges last week. Kelty's gone to Meal Vennel to fetch him.'

'Promising, sir.'

'Meanwhile, I wonder about the handkerchief found on the girl's wrist. There's a laundry mark on it. Just here. "M1-2." That is bound to be unique to a laundry service. Find the laundry and we might find the killer.'

MacNaughton frowned. 'I don't see that will do any good. Do you imagine murderers use laundry services?'

'Perhaps not, but it's a tangible lead, sir. It's worth pursuing.'

'Concentrate on the boarding house searches. They're the priority.'

Conoboy nodded and retreated to his own office to ready himself to visit the Fenwicks again. Braggan went to the toilets to dry his trousers. MacNaughton watched them go and slumped into his chair and poured a large whisky from a bottle in his bottom drawer. He downed it in one and poured another. He tried to concentrate but he stared, instead, at the bookcases opposite, at the bound records of Scottish law they contained, the order, the duty, and he continued to stare at them until they blurred into indistinction.

*

Grace Cross wiped the whisky glasses with a none-too-clean dishcloth and placed them on the shelf below the optics. It was nearly lunchtime but the General Railway Station bar was deserted. She emptied the ashtrays and wondered what else to do to negotiate the minutes until one o'clock.

She looked up in surprise as the door from the northbound platform opened and a man entered. There had been no departures or arrivals in twenty minutes and there was no reason why anyone should be approaching from the empty platform. A hunched man entered, rough, in a tweed cap and black jacket and muffler.

'Whisky,' he said. He put a handful of coins on the bar.

'No' a nice day,' said Grace. The man took his whisky without replying and sat in a corner facing the door. He peered at it constantly. There was mud on his boots and trousers. Grace felt a pulse hammering in her throat. This was him, the murderer, here in her bar. Didn't he look like he'd cut your throat without a word? She tried to memorise his appearance, long, squint nose, deep-set eyes, big ears with hair sticking out like thatch. She imagined herself in court, pointing to the man. Him, your honour, I'd know him anywhere.

'You waitin' for the Inverness train?' she shouted. He turned his back on her, still watching the door. It opened and he tensed before relaxing as a man entered, the clack of

28

his peg leg echoing on the wooden floor. The man ordered a whisky.

'Gie me a minute,' said Grace. She hurried into the back and through to the main office, where a railway policeman was reading the *Evening Telegraph*.

'Sid,' she shouted. 'It's the murderer. In the front.' They rushed back to the bar but the man was nowhere to be seen.

'Where did he go?' said Grace to the one-legged man.

'Who?'

She cursed and ran outside, followed by Sid Sheers. They looked up and down Leonard Street but there was no one in sight. 'You go left, I'll go right,' she said. Sid did not seem keen but Grace had already fled and he did likewise, more slowly. Sid searched for ten minutes, Grace for thirty, but neither found any sign of the man.

'He could have got on the 12.50 to Inverness,' said Grace.

'I'll telephone the Inversnecky police,' said Sid.

'It was him, wasn't it?' Sid didn't answer but Grace had decided anyway. It was the most exciting day of her life.

*

'You did all this last night,' said Marjory. Tears welled in her eyes.

'I know. But we have to do it formally now. With two doctors present.' Dr Murphy approached Marjory's bed but she shook her head and rose up.

'Not in here. Otherwise I'll never be able to forget it.'

They went through to her mother's room and Marjory lay on the bed and stared at the ceiling while Doctors Murphy and Trotter began their examination. They noted again the bruises and abrasions Murphy had identified the night before.

'Spread your legs, child,' said Murphy.

'No.'

He gripped her knees and roughly parted them. Marjory

29

gasped and tried to cover herself. As he had the night before, Murphy pressed two fingers deep inside her vagina and the shock of it jolted through Marjory's body. Him, one hand roughly against her knee, the other inside her, pushing, twisting. The other man standing, watching. Marjory felt panic rise in her throat, fought against the urge to scream. The ordeal went on for some moments before Murphy removed his fingers and wiped them on a handkerchief and nodded to Trotter.

'I need to take some swabs,' he said. 'For scientific examination.'

'Why are you doing this?'

'So we can apprehend your attacker.'

'Really?'

Next door, Conoboy sat in the kitchen with Mrs Fenwick, sipping tea. 'How is she?' he said.

'We were up most of the night. She hasn't slept.' Mrs Fenwick was a rotund woman, permanently fidgeting. She wore cheap black spectacles but still squinted at the inspector. Conoboy imagined she was normally jovial, but now strain pulled at her face.

'Did you know the boy?'

'He was that good with her. A real gentle laddie.'

'We need her to take us to the scene. Tell us what happened. Do you think she'll be able to do that today?'

Mrs Fenwick bustled about the kitchen, being busy, doing nothing in particular. 'The sooner we do these things, the sooner we can get back to normal,' she said.

'That's a sound philosophy.'

But the moment they turned into Cherrybank and saw the rise of Buckie Braes, Inspector Conoboy knew it was a mistake to bring Marjory. They might gain better insight into what happened the previous night, but at what cost to the child? They approached with trepidation, Marjory gripping her mother's arm. Mrs Fenwick, looking even more stout in black coat and hat, proceeded stoically. Marjory started to sob and had to be physically supported by PC Kelty.

'It's okay,' he whispered.

Crowds had gathered, a couple of hundred or more, camped out on the Braes and craning to see over hedges and dykes into the Cuddies Strip. As the police entourage passed, word circulated of who the girl in the middle was and a chatter of excitement filtered through the onlookers.

'Everyone's staring at me,' said Marjory. 'Stop them.'

'Don't worry, Marjory,' said Conoboy, 'nobody is allowed further than the stile. Once we're on the Strip it'll be fine.' He checked himself. Fine was not an appropriate word to use to describe that place.

They arrived first at the scene of Marjory's attack and she explained what had happened and where. The quietness of her voice disguised the terror she felt at seeing this place again. Her mother stood aside and stared impassively into the distance. They walked up the Strip to the murder scene. The green of the undergrowth seemed darker in the rain-racked gloom. Water dripped. Trees sighed. It did not feel like a lovers' lane.

Marjory let out a cry when she saw the blood. Her knees buckled and Bob caught her.

'I'm sorry, Marjory,' Inspector Conoboy said. 'But it will help us enormously if you can be brave and tell us everything you remember.'

Mutely, she showed them where they had sat overlooking the fields and how they had walked to this spot, how the first shot whistled past their heads.

'The noise was still humming in my ears as we turned around. Danny said to me not to faint and then the second shot came.'

'Where from?'

'Over there.' She pointed to whins about ten yards away on the right. 'I felt the first shot whoosh past my ear.' She

31

collapsed into tears once more and crouched low to the ground and covered her face with her hands.

'Take her home,' Conoboy said to PC McNab. 'And fetch a doctor. She needs to rest.'

*

Hill Farm of Pitheavlis was quiet in a midday sun that had finally replaced the rain which had fallen ceaselessly since the early hours. The yard was festooned with puddles. A horse looked over a half door into the yard. Conoboy addressed a tall, angular man, his face weathered and lined, the skin on his hands hardened by years of labour.

'Do you work here?'

'Aye. William McDougall, farm hand.'

'Did you see or hear anything last night?'

'Gun shots, fae doon the Braes.'

'What time was that?'

'Back o' ten.'

'How many?'

'One definitely. Maybe two, but I couldnae swear to that. I was hammerin' a magneto at the time …'

'A what?'

McDougall stared at him as though not understanding the question. 'A magneto,' he repeated.

'It's a kind of generator, sir,' explained Bob.

'I see. What happened?'

'I went oot to listen efter that. There was a wee while and then there was another shot.'

'Is it unusual to hear a gunshot at that time of night?'

'No' really.'

'So why did you go out to listen?'

'I thought it was strangely near. Thought somebody was poachin' on oor land.'

'Did you see anybody?'

'Naebody.'

*

By two o'clock a steady stream of sightseers was progressing up Buckie Braes and onto the Cuddies Strip. They queued to stand and look at the blood-soaked grass by the side of the path. A few tried to recreate the scene. Shrieks of incongruous laughter rang out.

William Hodge shook his head. 'Ghouls,' he said.

Fred Kitchen snorted. 'And we're no'?'

'No,' said William vehemently. 'I'm looking for evidence.'

'Aye, right you are.'

'Listen,' he said, 'Madge Fenwick's my cousin. She's a nice lassie. If I can help in any way, I will. That's the only reason I'm here. So either you can help me or you can ogle the murder scene with the rest of them. It's up to you.'

He strode back towards the stile and Fred followed.

'Sorry,' he said. 'But we're no' likely to find anythin'. The polis were here all morning.'

'That lot? I wouldnae trust them to find a whisky bottle in Bell's distillery.' He stopped at the spot where the grass appeared to have been most disturbed and stepped among it and crouched and started to search. Fred followed suit. All the while sightseers trudged past, airing increasingly elaborate theories about the attack.

'They say she was naked under her coat when she got here. That's why they couldnae find any claes,' said one, a balding and overweight man panting with exertion.

'That's absolute rubbish,' shouted William. 'Stop spreading vile rumours.'

'And you know, do you? Were you here last night? Maybe you're the murderer. You seem to know all about it.'

'Ignore him,' said Fred. He stretched forward. 'What's this?' he said. He picked up a broken pendant and a red bead and handed it to William.

33

'Madge has a red and white necklace,' said William. 'I've seen her wear it often.' He took it from Fred and slipped it into his pocket. 'Keep looking. There might be more.'

They found no more of the necklace but a couple of feet away William found a strip of fabric with a piece of lace attached to it and Fred found a large yellow rubber band beneath a tree a few yards from the stile. William pocketed both. They walked back into town and took them to the police station and laid them on the counter.

'You found these at the Cuddies Strip?' said Sergeant Strangeway.

'Aye.'

'What were you doing there?'

'Looking for clues.'

'That's our job.'

William bit his lip. 'Just tryin' to help,' he said. 'I was surprised none of your boys were up there keeping order. Half of Perth's playing amateur detective. There's not a blade of grass that hasn't been flattened to buggery.'

'Well, that'll help.'

When they left the station a large crowd had gathered in South Street, mostly men, milling around and chatting and smoking. A fug of smoke hung in the air. 'What are you doing?' William asked a man leaning against the station window.

'They're goin' tae make an arrest.'

William and Fred tried to get past, but the crowd was perhaps three or four-hundred strong and there was no way through. Even the road was thronged. At Victoria Bridge, traffic was being diverted by a morose looking City policeman in white overalls.

'The town's gone mad,' said William. A loud roar was raised behind them and the crowd pulsed forward. 'Whoever it is, he's in danger of gettin' lynched.'

'I hope so,' said Fred.

'Not if he's innocent.'

Back at the station, half a dozen officers fought to clear a passage. Bob emerged from the crowd with a man handcuffed to him. Both looked terrified. They were jostled and a few punches were swung at the suspect but none connected. Jeers and curses rained down on them. The crowd seethed forwards, everyone determined to get close to the killer. See him. Touch him. Experience evil. The reinforcements surrounded them and guided them into the station and the suspect turned in relief as the door was shut behind them.

'Could you not have just questioned me at home?' Richard Hamill said.

'Quiet,' said Strangeway. Hamill was taken into the interview room and told to sit. Conoboy and MacNaughton looked at Hamill through the doorway.

'Our man?' said MacNaughton.

'Very possibly,' said Conoboy. 'I've arranged for Miss Fenwick to do an identification parade.'

'Well, get that crowd dispersed before she arrives.'

'Yes, sir.'

Half an hour later Braggan and Conoboy sat before the suspect. Braggan glowered at him.

'Richard Hamill,' said Conoboy.

'That's me.'

'I've questioned you about a murder before, haven't I?'

'A year ago, aye. My mate Eddie Pringle. Shot his missus. I sold him the gun. I was completely innocent.'

'But here you are again. Like a bad penny. Being questioned over a second murder.'

'Third actually.' He enjoyed their expressions of surprise. 'I was interviewed about five years ago as well. Stabbing and robbery in Glasgow. I didn't do that either, I'd like to add. Not that I got away scot-free. Fined two pounds for having no tail light on my car.'

'This isn't a joke, Mr Hamill.'

'It certainly isn't. I knew this was going to happen. I said it at work today. Just you wait, I said, I'll be arrested before nightfall.'

'And why did you predict that?'

'I was up Buckie Braes with my shotgun on Monday and I just knew you'd be coming to see me.'

'So where were you last night?'

'At home.'

'Alone?'

'Aye.'

'What were you doing?'

'Listening to the wireless.'

'What was on?'

'There was the Lesley Bridgewater Quartet on the National channel and I cannae stand that screechin' singing so I changed to the Scottish channel. Jack Payne with his orchestra.'

'Well remembered.'

'It was only last night.'

There was a knock on the door and Bob Kelty looked in. 'Miss Fenwick is here, sir,' he said.

Conoboy turned to Hamill. 'We're going to set up an identification parade. Then we'll see.'

'How exciting.'

Hamill followed Sergeant Braggan into an adjoining room. Six men, picked from the crowd outside, stood in a line at the far end. Only a couple of them vaguely resembled Hamill.

'Stand anywhere you want,' said Braggan. Hamill eased himself into the spot second on the right and when they were settled Marjory Fenwick and her mother were brought in. Marjory was turning her hat round and round in her hands. Her eyes bore the same haunted expression as earlier on the Cuddies Strip.

'Look at each man in turn,' said Conoboy. 'If you

recognise your attacker, tap his shoulder.'

She crept forwards and stared at the first man and walked on and stopped before the next man, and then each man in turn. She didn't know what she would do if she recognised him and part of her hoped he wasn't there.

He wasn't.

'I'm sorry,' she said.

'Are you sure?'

'He's not here.'

Hamill made to speak but Braggan waved his finger. Marjory and her mother were escorted to Inspector Conoboy's office and Aggie brought tea and biscuits.

'Hello, Vi,' she said to Mrs Fenwick. 'I'm awfae sorry about all o' this.'

'Aye, Aggie, it's a to-do.'

'How's the lassie?'

'She'll be fine.'

Marjory was accustomed to being talked about. She stared ahead, then looked at the policemen. Nothing felt real. Even when she walked she felt like she was standing on someone else's legs. The world was muffled, distant, confused.

'I'm sorry to make you go through such an ordeal,' Conoboy said to her.

'If it finds the man who did this it'll be worth it,' said Mrs Fenwick. Marjory said nothing.

'We have some items discovered at the scene,' said Conoboy. 'Could you take a look, please, and tell us if they're yours?'

Marjory took the pendant and bead and rolled them in her palm. She sobbed. 'From my necklace,' she said.

'You were wearing it last night?'

'Yes.' She took the piece of fabric and showed it to her mother. 'That's from my underskirt.'

'Are you sure?'

'Aye,' said Mrs Fenwick. 'I've washed it often enough.'

'And this,' said Marjory, holding the rubber band, 'is what I used to keep my stockings up. It's from the confectioners where I work. They're all that colour.' She wiped tears from her eyes and looked up hopefully. 'Is this important? Will it help catch him?'

'It's evidence, miss. We're building a strong picture.'

*

There were only two ways from Nellie Gammon's work at Aberdalgie House to her home in Cherrybank – the long way, down Necessity Brae and into the village from the Glasgow Road, or the shortcut.

Through the Cuddies Strip.

Mrs Moon, the head maid, had arranged for Geordie to pick her up that morning, when news of the murder first filtered through town, but he had taken the master to Edinburgh in the afternoon and Nellie had insisted to Mrs Moon she could walk home alone. Now she regretted it. She half hoped the police would still be there and the route through the Cuddies Strip would be closed. The extra hour it would take her to negotiate the long way would be worth it. But as soon as she crested the hill at the Woodhead of Aberdalgie road she could see the Strip was open. She breathed heavily and tried to persuade herself it was safe. The raped girl was seventeen, probably just a silly lassie. Nellie was twenty-three. She could look after herself.

It was not yet eight but the lour of the day left the Strip indistinct, especially where larger trees combined to form a canopy. She stepped along the path quickly, not looking right or left, fixing her gaze on the yards in front of her. Don't let there still be blood, she pleaded. Don't let me see where it happened, where the boy was killed. Where the girl … Wind soughed above her in the trees. Branches crackled. The grass shifted in waves. Nellie grew hyper-conscious of

38

every sound, every movement. And then – her heart lurched, her ears rang, her fingers tingled – and then she thought she heard a noise. Behind her. Was that a footstep? A breath? She hurried on.

Faster Nellie, faster. Turn around. No, don't. What if someone's there? Best to know. No. No. She was jogging, almost running. *It's okay, it's okay.*

It's not. It's not.

And then she knew there really was something behind her. And when she speeded it up, it speeded up. She slowed. It slowed.

'Oh, God.'

She started to run, stumbling instantly on a tree root, lurching forward, feeling herself topple, stagger, fall, then somehow regaining her balance. She pressed forwards.

'Nell,' came a voice behind her. 'Nell, it's me.'

She recognised it and turned and gave a cry. 'Oh,' she said, and she began to sob. 'Oh, it's you.' She rushed to him and folded herself into his arms.

John McGuigan grinned. 'I saw you from a bit ago. Knew you'd be scared coming through here alone. I've been trying to catch you, but you were running too fast, gal.'

She hugged him close. He allowed her but did not reciprocate. He looked over her shoulder to the fields beyond and a distant tree, splendid in isolation as though it were a silent observer.

'I thought you was the killer,' she said.

He gave a low laugh. 'Oh, there was nothing to be frightened of, really,' he said. 'You'd be okay.'

He was especially pleased with the way he said that. *You'd* be okay. They walked on and reached the stile and crossed over it and McGuigan did not look round. There was no need. It was in his head now.

Friday 16th August

A Day of Sightings

When Bob Kelty awoke, his pulse was racing. It was always the same. Any tension during the previous day would provoke those memories, that fear, and he would be back in Logierait, walking home after speaking with Jeannie Anderson after school. The front door locked – it was never locked. Keeking through the window. His father dead on the floor, blood everywhere, shotgun by his side where it fell from his grip. Bob ran to the farm and raised the farmer and from that moment his life would never be the same again. The visions came less often now, but when they did, they were always with the same intensity. During waking hours, he could, with effort, banish all thought of it, but at night, in dreams, alone, he was at the mercy of the past. He would wake sweating and shouting and twisting in the bed as though still in the grip of that moment.

And now, of course, the past and the present were fused by the shotgun that killed Danny Kerrigan and the shotgun Bob's father had used to kill himself.

'Of all the causes of death,' he said, 'why that one?'

*

Victor Conoboy brought breakfast into the dining room and laid it on the table in front of Bella. He left the morning *Courier* beside her and sat opposite and poured tea.

'You were late home last night,' she said.

'Case conference.'

'Progress?'

He shook his head. 'Nothing certain.'

'What's your main lead?'

'Chap on the Inverness train. And we're checking all boarding houses.'

'Why?'

'MacNaughton's hunch.'

'Surely it's going to be someone local, who knows the Cuddies Strip.'

'That's what Robert said, too.'

'So why are you looking in boarding houses?'

'Local men sometimes stay in boarding houses, too. For extended periods.'

'Perhaps.' She cut a slice of toast in two and raised a piece to her mouth. 'But even more live in their own houses.'

'I know.'

'This is your investigation, Victor.'

'I know.'

'Do you?'

*

Marjory opened her eyes. Sleep was a laborious process, her mind consumed by memory. She could not escape, repeating and reliving every moment over and over in a never-ending loop. Morning came as a relief. At least there was no further pretence of rest. She studied her neck bruises in the mirror. At first, each finger had been identifiable but now the bruising had generalised into a vague purpling of the skin. It was as though his grip was still there but spreading, sliding beneath her skin, invading, possessing. Scabs were forming on the abrasions down her spine. In a week they would be gone.

Which meant nothing.

Her mother was making breakfast when she entered the kitchen. 'I need to go back to work,' said Marjory. 'On Monday.'

'The police said no. Not until they tell you.' She set a cup of tea in front of her. 'They want to see you again. Eleven o'clock. Thon blate bobby came round to ask. Kelty.'

'Oh no, Mum. Please not again. I've told them everything three times now.'

'They just need any information to help them on their way.'

'But I don't know anything else.'

'You might remember. Just think aboot it.'

'I want to be able to not think about it.'

*

The sun was high and there was no prospect of rain. Charles Elder, grieve of Kirkton of Mailer farm, leaned against a fence post and looked out across a field of wheat. 'That's an awfae affair up the Cuddies Strip, is it no'?' he said.

'Aye,' said Sandy Arnott, the joiner. They talked about the crime, whether it was a local man, what direction he would have taken afterwards. Into the woods and away, reckoned Elder. Down into Perth, said Arnott. 'He'll be hidin' in the toon.'

As they talked, John McGuigan traipsed up the rough farm track towards them. They followed his lethargic progress, a slight man, thin as a rake, skin prematurely weathered from outdoor living. Elder winked at Arnott.

'Now then, John,' he shouted to the newcomer. 'What's this you've been up to now?'

McGuigan gave an insouciant smile, lop-sided and lazy. 'Ach,' he said, 'I was up the Strip with my glasses havin' a wee look around. But I was back down by half nine.'

Arnott considered it a curious reply but Elder, deaf as a

42

drunk at last orders, carried on as though the younger man hadn't spoken.

'Any chance of you doin' some work soon? That's four days you've been off now.'

'Aye, I'll be back the morn.'

'Just mind, you dinnae get paid for sittin' on your arse.'

McGuigan gave a wave and sauntered towards the top field. The sun was growing fierce. Graeme Peddie, working behind a dyke, grinned as he saw McGuigan approach. He inhaled heavily on his cigarette and blew out a large cloud of smoke, trying to look older than his eighteen years. Bumfluff ruined the effect.

'You back at work then?' he said.

'The morn's morn. Maybe. Expect you'll be needin' some real hard graft to get you through.'

'Is that so?' They laughed and turned downhill towards the stables. A brace of partridges flew up from a copse to their left. McGuigan tracked their flight with an imaginary gun and sounded off a couple of shots, twitching his arms as though in recoil.

'Have you still got your shotgun?' said Peddie.

'Naw.'

'I was wonderin' about that. Thon murder, wondered whether you'd been up there and accidentally shot the man.'

'I thought you'd be thinkin' that.' McGuigan walked on, making no further comment. Peddie followed.

'Where is your gun?'

'Away.'

'Why?'

'Because I havenae got a licence for it.'

'You didnae have a licence before.'

'Naebody had been shot before.'

'Have the polis spoken to you yet?'

'What for?'

'Havin' a gun.'

43

He turned. 'I havenae. I just telt you.'

*

In County headquarters Sergeant Braggan grimaced at the legs of his brown suit trousers. He'd managed to get most of the stains out but they needed proper dry cleaning. Irritation washed over him again as he recollected the day before and Conoboy's lack of leadership. Braggan had been in the force fifteen years and was concerned by his lack of progress. He had made Senior Constable quickly and was transferred to CID and promoted to Detective Sergeant earlier than most. He was the highest ranked officer in Perth CID and was well regarded, not least by himself. The last five years, though, had been constant frustration. His principal fear, the longer he went without promotion, was that he might be posted to some teuchter area of northern Perthshire where the only crimes were sheep stealing and drunkenness. What he craved most of all, even if it meant a return to uniform, was the role of inspector. But there were only five of them in the whole county. And only one in Perth.

And that was already taken.

'Kelty,' he shouted. 'Since we seem to be your new nursemaids, you may as well earn your keep. We've a report of clothing found in a dump in New Street. Could be the girl's. Check it out.'

Bob tried to deny the trepidation he felt whenever Braggan addressed him. There was something about the man's abruptness, the aggressive rasp of his voice that made Bob nervous. The sergeant reminded him of the dominie when Bob was a laddie at Logierait School, with his shouting and his bullying. Bob fixed his helmet in place and walked out into a gathering of the hopeful and the inquisitive loitering in South Street.

'Any news, son?' said one, a man of indeterminate age,

44

badly dressed and dirty, a tattered cap set louchely on his head.

'We're making investigations.'

'You've nae idea, then.'

Bob ignored him. His mind was on Danny Kerrigan, on the mystery of death, the difficulty of life. Scone Thistle were due to play Luncarty that evening and the whole team, Bob especially, wanted it postponed. Word had come, though, that Mrs Kerrigan was keen for it to go ahead in tribute to her son. It would be difficult.

'Are you Mr Jellicoe?' he said when he reached New Street.

'Aye,' said the street cleaner. 'I was expectin' you quicker than this.'

'Sorry. Can you show me what you've found?'

Jellicoe, a short man with a polio limp, indicated to Bob to follow him down a side passage. 'In this dump, here,' he said. He opened it and pointed to a parcel resting on a pile of rubbish.

Bob lifted it, a bulky piece of sacking, stained and foul-smelling. He didn't want to touch it but carefully opened it and peered inside. The female clothing it contained bore no resemblance to the items described by Marjory Fenwick. Too dark. Too old fashioned.

'Thank you,' he said. He bunched up the parcel and held it in front of him gingerly.

'Is there a reward?'

'In heaven.' Bob blushed, worrying that he had been rude.

*

MacNaughton, Conoboy and Braggan sat in the Chief Inspector's office. Bob stood behind them. 'We have a press conference in half an hour,' said MacNaughton, 'and if I understand you correctly we have nothing to tell them.' He

45

glared at Conoboy.

'We're following up the railway sighting, sir. And ...'

'So, nothing.'

Braggan watched the inspector's discomfort with satisfaction. Just desserts for a man who seemed to think he could lead an investigation by sitting on his arse in his office, drinking tea and being nice to the Fenwick girl. For an instant, a smirk eclipsed his usual, blank expression and Bob, standing at the back, spotted it.

'The handkerchief on his face,' said MacNaughton. 'Have we no explanation for that yet? It's bizarre.'

'We still can't account for it, sir.'

'I can.' Bob spoke without intending to. The room turned to him and instantly he felt blood pulsing in his head, the horror of being the centre of attention. He had tried to tell the inspector about the handkerchief a couple of times but Sergeant Braggan had always got in the way.

'Well?' said MacNaughton.

'It's an old tinker custom, sir,' Bob said. 'A mark of respect. For the dead. They cover the eyes.'

Braggan stared at him incredulously. 'And you knew that? All this time? Did it not occur to you it might be helpful if we knew we were looking for a tink?'

Bob knew his face had turned red. 'It just occurred to me, Sergeant,' he lied. 'This very minute.'

Braggan shook his head disbelievingly. Conoboy noticed Bob's discomfort.

'Well done, Robert,' he said. 'We'll announce this at the conference. See if it provokes any new information.'

*

MacNaughton explained the theory to the assembled press. Blank expressions were returned. Templeton of the *Evening Telegraph* raised his hand.

'Acting Chief Constable,' he said. MacNaughton bristled. He was sure he heard a calculated insult in the way the hack said the word 'acting.'

'If you are now looking for a tinker, does that mean the man sighted at the General Station is no longer under suspicion? Miss Cross's description of him did not suggest he was a tinker.'

MacNaughton gazed sourly at him. 'The individual at the General Station behaved in such a suspicious manner it is incumbent on us to investigate.'

'You mentioned a handkerchief yesterday,' Templeton went on. 'That was used to bind the girl's wrists together. Has there been any progress on that?'

Conoboy intervened. 'We're still examining local laundries. But nothing as yet.'

'However,' said MacNaughton, 'I should stress that is a speculative line of enquiry.'

'Is this killer likely to strike again?'

'At this stage we are still evaluating motive.'

'So should people be afraid?'

'They should be vigilant, certainly. And notify us immediately of anything unusual or suspicious. We doubt that theft was a motive, given that Danny was just a lad. That makes us now think this was a random attack and the killer wasn't in any way connected to Danny or Miss Fenwick. Which makes it harder to solve, of course.'

The conference broke up a few minutes later. Journalists milled about in the hallway, hoping for a private word with one of the officers. Nothing was forthcoming. Conoboy marched across the hall and knocked on MacNaughton's door. The Acting Chief Constable looked up from his paperwork.

'I'm not seeing a pattern, Conoboy.' He spoke dismissively, as he always did to Conoboy.

'We're still examining motive, sir ...'

'Not in the crime. In the investigation.'

'We're juggling leads.'

MacNaughton sighed. 'You're actually investigating the laundry mark idea?'

'Yes, sir.'

'Is there any evidence that it could identify an individual?'

'An individual account with a laundry, certainly. Each laundry uses separate markings for every account ...'

'But if it's from a hotel, say, it could belong to hundreds of people.'

'Hotels wouldn't launder handkerchiefs. They're personal items.'

'You're wasting time and resources on this. Wrap up that line of enquiry. Concentrate on tinkers and gun owners.'

'Yes, sir.' Conoboy returned to his office and sat at his desk and shook his head. The case was building a momentum of its own but he wasn't sure he was still in control of it. Since he'd lost out on promotion to MacNaughton he had gone out of his way to avoid him. It was easier that way. But now they were forced to work together and it was increasingly impossible for Conoboy to deny the fact that his superior officer was, in every way, inferior to him. That knowledge, and the fact he could do nothing about it, weighed heavily on him. He stared out of the grimy window onto South Street.

*

Marjory Fenwick's arrival at eleven o'clock inflamed the crowd outside, occasioning further rumours of arrest. She stepped out of the police car and her mother followed. She bowed her head, avoiding eye contact with the strangers pressing around her.

On the corner of Tay Street, John McGuigan inhaled heavily on his cigarette and threw it to the ground. He stared at Marjory, her face, those worried eyes, the tense body. *I've*

48

been there, he gloated. *I've fucked that.* He had expected it to feel better when he saw her again but overriding any sense of satisfaction was the frustration of failure. He'd fucked her but still the mysteries remained. He hadn't been able to get it all the way inside her and he didn't know why. How it worked. Wasn't the cunt just an ordinary hole? He watched the bitch now, the ride of her buttocks as she retreated into the station, and anger pulsed through him.

'I do apologise for the rabble,' said Conoboy when Marjory was seated in his office.

'We're getting used to it,' said Mrs Fenwick. 'We have them outside our house too.'

'PC Kelty,' said Conoboy. 'See to that. Ask Sergeant Strangeway to arrange for someone to go out there and move them on.'

Bob said he would, knowing that Sergeant Strangeway would do no such thing.

'We have various items of clothing we'd like you to look at,' Conoboy said to Marjory. Bob showed her the sack he had collected from New Street and Marjory shook her head quickly. Garments found in Craigie by a pair of young boys were brought in.

'They're not even women's clothing,' said Marjory.

'No. Indeed. Next, these shoes were found in Elibank Street.' Marjory shook her head again. 'Look at the size of them,' she said. 'I could fit in them twice.' She looked at her mother and then at Conoboy. 'It's a pity you can't find anything that really would fit me. Perhaps if you did I could keep it. I lost two pairs of knickers. I haven't enough to see me through the week.'

'We'll manage,' said Mrs Fenwick quickly.

'By washing twice a week.'

'If that's what we have to do.'

Bob admired the resolution of the older woman. He saw the yearning in Marjory's expression. He gathered up the bundles of clothing.

'We'll keep searching,' said Conoboy. 'Meantime, is there anything else you can tell us about the man's appearance? Every policeman in Scotland is looking for him, I assure you, but any scrap of information you can give us might be vital.'

Marjory shook her head. 'I've told you everything.'

'Excuse me, miss,' said Bob, 'did he by any chance smell of stick reek?'

'Of what?'

'Wood smoke.'

Marjory gave a start. 'Why yes, he did. I'd completely forgotten. How did you know that?'

'The handkerchief, miss, that was round your wrist. I noticed it at the scene. It smelled of stick reek.'

'Well done, Constable,' said Conoboy. 'On your rounds, look out for anyone who might be living rough. Building wood fires.'

'Yes, sir.' For a moment, the nervousness that Bob customarily felt was eclipsed by satisfaction. A brief smile crossed his face. Marjory was watching him and he nodded at her. She smiled back.

As they exited Conoboy's office Mrs Fenwick tapped Bob on the arm. Her voice reverberated around the stone-floored foyer. 'I havenae heard anyone call it stick reek in a long time.'

'That's what I aye call it.'

'Good for you, son.'

Sergeant Strangeway called him over when the Fenwicks had gone. 'You're with the County police force now, boy. You speak properly, d'you hear?'

'Aye, Sergeant.'

Strangeway searched for insolence in Bob's expression but saw only gaucheness. 'Right,' he said. 'I've a couple of jobs for you. First, get on your bike and get out to Bridge of

Earn ...'

'Sergeant Braggan told me to stay in the station, Sergeant.'

'... to see some man the village bobby is holding, thinks could be our man. Then, when he isn't, get back to Dick Currie's pawn shop in the High Street. There's been someone trying to pawn a shotgun.' Bob stared at him. He didn't know how to manage conflicting instructions.

'I told you, City boy, when you're in this station you do what I say.'

'Yes, Sergeant.'

It was about four miles to Bridge of Earn, south and east of the city, in a valley surrounded by the Ochil Hills. On his left was Kinnoull Hill, known locally as suicide hill, where three or four times a year the desperate and helpless would throw themselves over the edge in the knowledge that the unyielding granite beneath afforded the certainty of instant oblivion. Bob tried to ignore it. Suicide was an act he knew too well.

He cycled on. Around him, the fields were ripe, ready for harvest. Birds were sleek on the wing. He spotted a couple of roe deer lurking in a stand of trees, watching. They bolted at some sign of danger apparent only to their perfect alignment of senses. The hedgerows were plush with wild rasps and early brambles. The sun shone. For a few brief minutes Bob escaped into his mind and became the man he was, not the person he portrayed. He whistled as he rode, the sun warm on his back and causing a profuse sweat beneath his helmet. He cycled past Craigclowan to Craigend. There, if he turned right he would reach Kirkton of Mailer farm. Instead, he followed the road, past the Hilton farm, the river Earn looping alongside and doubling back on itself. He reached the bridge over the river and cycled into town.

An angry scene confronted him in the village police station, a suspect outraged into anger and a bobby fearing his dignity was being offended by the suspect's lack of deference.

'Three hours I've been here,' said the man. He was in his forties, about six feet tall, tanned and brawny. He was not remotely like the description of the murderer. Bob asked to speak to the policeman alone and they retreated to the back office.

'Why did you pick him up?'

'He was cycling through town. He's not local. Couldn't give an account of why he was here. I asked his whereabouts on Wednesday night and he couldn't account for them, either. I thought I'd better bring him in.'

Bob nodded to the poster bearing the description of the man they were seeking. 'Does your man look like that?' he said.

'It was dark. She's only a lassie. You cannae trust a lassie's description.'

'It's nothin' like the man.'

'You're a City bobby anyway. What are you doing here?'

'Seconded to personally assist Inspector Conoboy.'

'Is that right?'

'Aye.'

'So what are you doing out here in Bridge of Earn, then?'

Bob nodded to the waiting man in the other room. 'You have to let him go,' he said. 'It isnae him.'

The village bobby sighed and nodded. 'Aye,' he said. Bob gave a surprised smile. Being agreed with was an uncommon occurrence for him.

*

A group of boys were cavorting on the North Inch. Some played leapfrog. Others kicked an ancient football. Others still sat on the grass and chatted. Beyond them, maids and nannies and young mothers promenaded with black prams. Further beyond, the Tay flowed ineluctably towards the coast.

52

Bella Conoboy stood in Victor's bedroom and watched the turn of everyday life in silence. Behind her, the room was dark, solitary. Her thoughts were of Mrs Kerrigan and Mrs Fenwick, two women scarred forever by the pain of injury to their children. All mothers will take any pain on themselves if it spares their children. Mrs Kerrigan and Mrs Fenwick, they now joined Bella in understanding the impenetrable depth of that resolution. Anything. Anything to prevent harm. She turned away, restless, walked through the gloom of Victor's room into the gloom of the house, walked downstairs, well-worn route into the living room, the armchair, the wireless, the novel, the escape from reality, refuge from pain.

She wanted to speak to Mrs Kerrigan. To explain. Explain that blackness isn't black and pain does not hurt and memory can be overcome and sensation controlled.

All it takes is a lifetime.

*

'Now then, Mr Currie.'

'Now then, young Bobby. How's your gran?'

'Bad tempered as ever.'

'Good. Tell her I was asking for her.'

'I will. You've had a sighting, I hear?'

'Aye. Youngish chap. This morning. Labouring class, I'd say. Not smartly dressed. He came in wanting to pawn a fowling piece.' Bob raised an eyebrow. 'Exactly. So I said, "It's illegal to trade weapons, you ken." "Oh," he said, "I didnae realise," but he carried on lookin' at me, as though he was waitin' for me to change my mind and mak' him an offer. Just smilin' at me, ken? So I telt him again. And then he went oot.'

'What did he look like?'

'About thirty. Not too tall. A bit red-faced.'

'Big nose?'

'No. Battered, like.'

'Aye, that could be him. Did he have a hat?'

'Bunnet. Pulled down.'

'That fits. What direction did he go in?'

'Towards the station.'

Bob cycled towards the General Station but saw no sign of the man. He knew he ought to return to base but on impulse he cycled up Glasgow Road and out towards Buckie Braes.

'Look out for anyone who could be living rough,' the inspector had said. There was a campsite the far side of the Cuddies Strip that was regularly used by tinkers as a stopping point on their way to Blair for the berries or Crieff for the tatties.

He left his bicycle at the foot of Buckie Braes and walked up it and down again towards the Cuddies Strip. Panting, he walked its length and crossed over the Dunning road and climbed a rough track. In the trees to the left there was a patch of open ground. A large pit held the remains of a wood fire. He bent and picked charred remains and sniffed them. Stick reek, right enough, but this fire was old. The grass around it was long and unflattened. There was no sign of recent occupation. He stood up and turned and came face to face with another man.

'Who are you?' he said, taken aback.

The man appeared as startled as Bob. He took off his hat. 'Robert Barrie,' he said. The way he was standing made it obvious he was trying to conceal something.

'What's behind your back?'

'Nothin'.'

'Dinnae move.' Bob walked slowly around the man and saw a game bag, already bulging with rabbits.

'I'm guessin' you're no' the gamey?'

'Naw.'

'So what you doin' here?'

'Just oot for a walk.'

'A walk, aye? No' poachin'?'

'No.'

'Is that rabbits in your bag?'

The man turned around in surprise, as though he had no idea the bag was there. He looked inside. Rabbits.

'I found them,' he said.

'Hangin' fae a tree?'

'No. In snares.'

'And was it you put the snares there?'

'Me? I wouldnae ken how tae.'

'But you're fine at removin' rabbits fae them?'

'Oh aye. That's easy.'

'And guttin' them.'

Again, the man looked inside the bag as though to confirm this assertion.

'How did you do that?' said Bob.

'Wi' a knife.'

'So you didnae set the snares. But you just happened to be carryin' a knife?'

'Aye.'

'And a game bag?'

He paused. 'Aye,' he said finally, but his heart wasn't in it.

'Do you come up here to not poach often?'

'Sometimes.'

'You werenae here on Wednesday, were you?'

The man froze. Bob spotted it.

'I cannae mind.'

'Well, let's see if you can mind doon the station.'

'I havenae done nothin'.'

Bob looked at the game bag and then at the man. 'Your address?'

'39 Pomarium.'

'Near Stevie McLagan?'

'He's upstairs fae me.'

'Right. Be at the station at five o'clock sharp. Ask for me. Kelty. Aye?'

'Aye.'

'And get rid of thae rabbits.'

'Aye.'

'An' the snares you havenae got.'

'Aye.'

Barrie sloped off uphill, a trail of cigarette smoke wafting behind him. Bob walked in the opposite direction, back to the Cuddies Strip. PCs Marchant and Armstrong were on their hands and knees in the undergrowth.

'What are you doing?' Bob said.

'Looking for shotgun pellets,' said Armstrong, a rookie who'd been with the force less than a month.

'They winnae be there.'

'Why not?'

'Shotgun pellets dinnae just fall to the ground. Something has to stop them.' He stepped across the flattened grass and lined up the spot where Danny fell and the whins where the murderer was presumed to have hidden. He traced the line to a tree behind them and peered at its bark.

'Here,' he said. Embedded in the bark were half a dozen pellets.

'That confirms where the shot came from,' said Armstrong.

'Aye,' said Bob. 'Well done, lads. Good find. Braggan will be pleased wi' you.'

'That's good. He was a bear wi' a sair heid when we left.'

'How?'

'Partly because you seem to have disappeared.'

'Oh.'

'And partly because we're inundated with sightings.'

'That's good, is it no'?'

'Not this many. There's a man been arrested in Kirkcaldy

56

and they want us to go down and fetch him. There's a bloke in Dunnottar Woods. Someone in Tibbermore. A man ran off in Glasgow. Another one arrested in Anstruther, but he had an alibi. There's still the bloke at the General Station that Inverness police are looking for. The man in the pawnshop. Bridge of Earn.'

'Seems like anyone in the whole of Scotland who looks a bit strange is being referred to us,' said Marchant.

'What's the one in Tibbermore?'

'Someone who hasn't been seen for a few days.'

Bob pondered. Tibbermore was where Marjory Fenwick lived before the family moved to Longcauseway.

'Better get back and face the wrath of Braggan,' he said. He waved and scrambled back onto the strip and strolled back to his bicycle. He checked his pocket watch. He had time to make Gran a pot of tea before going back. He pedalled slowly, making the most of the late afternoon sunshine.

*

That same sunshine was hot against John McGuigan's tent. He lay back in his cot and stared at the fabric above him. He was already hard and he stroked lethargically. He needed to piss but couldn't be bothered and, in any case, the best spunkings came on a full bladder. He pictured the girl, that night, that thing. It still troubled him. He had put his hand down the girl's front and it felt sticky. Blood? How? He hadn't done anything. He had smelled his hand. Musty, strange. Disgusting. It spoiled the moment.

He fumbled in his jacket and pulled out a photograph, Marjory Fenwick smiling a serious smile beneath a tight perm and nervous eyes. He stripped naked and crawled out of the tent. A breeze blew through the trees, slaking his skin. He loved the sensation of fresh air on his testicles and anus. In pale sunshine, exposed should anyone happen by, he crouched over the photograph and imagined and remembered and he improved that memory, removed the blood, allowed himself to come inside her. Staring at Marjory's picture all the while he brought himself to a climax.

*

Dr Murphy took the whisky proffered by MacNaughton and poured some into a tumbler and sipped it. MacNaughton gestured at the paper in front of him, covered in neat, blue handwriting.

'Thank you for your report on the girl. Comprehensive and clear, as always.'

'Thank you.'

'In your view, was she a virgin?'

'There's reason for doubt. The hymen was broken. It wasn't recent.'

'She insists she was.'

'Well, that would cause you to consider anything she might say in a different light, at the very least. In my opinion.'

'Quite.'

'Child that age. Little better than a strumpet.'

'Quite.'

*

In the cramped wooden changing room Bob stripped out of his uniform and put on the blue and white strip of Scone Thistle. The mood was sombre, far removed from the usual pre-match joviality. Eleven players who wanted to be somewhere else got ready.

'Let's win this for Danny,' said Johnny Johnstone, team captain, bricklayer and amateur boxer. The team gave a roar of approval but it was half-hearted and they knew it. They trooped onto the pitch alongside the Luncarty team and

58

stood on the halfway line as the referee blew his whistle and each player lowered his head and Bob Kelty, like all of them, remembered a life lost. For two minutes silence filled his mind and tears filled his eyes. He wanted to be somewhere else. Someone else. A quiet life on the farm, free from all this strife.

It was only later, when he was home and had put Gran to bed and he was playing his guitar that he realised Robert Barrie had failed to attend the station as instructed.

Saturday 17th August

A Day of Remembrance

Bob Kelty was queuing outside the sub-post office when Tam Stobbie opened up at nine o'clock. He bought two ten-bob postal orders and sealed them inside an envelope. He addressed it, dropped it in the postbox and walked home.

A hidden sense told him something was wrong as soon as he entered the house. He knocked on Gran's door loudly and looked in. The bed was unmade and there was nobody there.

'Gran,' he shouted. He ran downstairs and checked the living room and the kitchen and the larder. He went into the garden and looked in the outhouse.

'Not again,' he said. He put on his jacket and ran towards Letham Road. This had happened three times since Easter and each time he had found her trying to make her way back to the house where she'd lived before the war. It had been demolished ten years before and new council housing erected in its place. Gran would get disorientated and lost and bewildered. When Doctor Wishart warned him her condition would deteriorate, Bob didn't believe him, but now it was happening. She'll need to go into the cottage hospital, Doctor Wishart said, and when Bob vowed he would never permit it, the doctor's silence was more eloquent than words. Bob couldn't keep up a permanent watch. She wasn't safe on her own.

In the distance he recognised the green shawl and Gran's shambling presence, her head bowed, legs unsteady as she struggled up Rannoch Road. He caught up with her outside the Cooperative.

'Gran,' he called. She turned and scowled at him.

'What do you want?' she said.

'Come hame, Gran.'

'I nearly am hame.'

He took her arm gently. She stopped and her angry expression was overtaken by one of bafflement, then of disappointment, then of despair. She looked round in confusion at this strange new town.

'I dinnae ken where I am, son.'

*

Victor Conoboy laid Bella's breakfast on a tray set across her knees. He looked tired, she thought. Unhappy. The most important trait of a police officer was to be able to separate the professional from the personal. It was a skill Victor had never mastered.

'Something is bothering you,' she said.

'Just the case.'

'Something specific?'

Conoboy sat at the foot of her bed and stroked her ankle beneath the blankets. 'Dr Murphy,' he said. 'His report. The Procurator Fiscal will use it to argue Marjory wasn't a virgin.'

'But you said she was?'

'That's what she told me and I believe her. But it will undoubtedly be a key line of the defence's case and that means the Procurator Fiscal will want to investigate it. He won't want to be wrong-footed by them.'

'The child needs to be warned.'

'I'm not sure we need to raise the matter with her.'

'If it's going to be raised in court, in front of everyone, in front of the press, it's better she's prepared for it.'

He rose stiffly and nodded. 'You're right, of course. As ever.' He bent and kissed her cheek.

*

Marjory awoke to the sound of birdsong. It would have been beautiful but for a pigeon nearby, insistent in its tuneless dirge. She still felt the grogginess of sleep, and then she remembered.

Today was the funeral.

She had argued with her mother long into the previous evening, determined that she would attend. Her mother forbade it and they went to bed in silence and anger.

She *would* go.

They can't stop me. I'm a grown woman and he's my lad.

She heard her mother trudging down the hallway.

'Marjory, hen, you have to get up. The police are here, want to ask you some more questions.'

She banged her fists on the blankets. 'There can't be anything they haven't already asked.'

'I know, but up you get.'

Inspector Conoboy was sipping tea when she appeared ten minutes later. He smiled at her. 'How are you feeling?'

'More rested, thank you. I think I shall be able to leave the house for a bit today.' She stared at her mother. 'I plan to attend Danny's funeral.'

'That wouldn't be wise, miss. We're expecting a very large crowd. The Procurator Fiscal has ruled the cemetery is to be closed to prevent disruption. I fear you would find it intolerable.'

'But I want to ...'

'I think it would be best if you were to go later, to pay your respects alone. We can arrange that.'

'He's right, hen,' said Mrs Fenwick. She couldn't hide her satisfaction that the inspector was supporting her.

Marjory sank into her chair as though being consumed by it. She glowered at the inspector, knew that she couldn't argue with him, didn't have the courage or the eloquence or the energy. Failure. Failure.

Inspector Conoboy sat forwards. 'Did either Danny or you have a penknife that night?'

'Not me. Danny might have.'

'One was found yesterday by an amateur detective at the scene.' He sucked in his cheeks as though smoking an invisible pipe. Marjory and her mother watched him. He looked around their tiny living room, bright and clean, sparsely furnished. The matter of the penknife was merely a pretext. He needed to raise the question of Marjory's virginity but Mrs Fenwick showed no sign of leaving. He couldn't discuss it with her there.

It could wait.

*

Letters and telegrams arrived throughout the day. Flowers too, ferried into the back bedroom, dozens of wreaths and bunches of roses and lilies. The coffin sat on a trestle, Mrs Kerrigan's wreath of chrysanthemums laid on top. A single word, 'Danny', was written on the card in shaky, spidery handwriting. The house was overwhelmed by silence, broken spasmodically and incongruously by the crooning of a budgerigar in the front parlour. People drank tea, sat, stood, paced, sat again. Smoked cigarettes. Waited. The cruel hours turned slowly.

Bob arrived at one o'clock, cycling past the onlookers and leaning his bicycle beneath the front room window. He introduced himself at the door.

'I'm accompanying the funeral cortège to the cemetery.'

'On your bike?'

'Sergeant Braggan's bringing the car.'

He was invited in and greeted everyone in turn and sat at the piano in the corner, it being the only spare seat.

'D'you want a cup of tea, son?' said Mrs Kerrigan.

'Aye, please, that would be grand.' She retreated to the kitchen, glad of something to do. Bob turned to the others. 'Danny had a fine send-off last night,' he said. 'At the fitba.'

'I'm glad,' said Daniel Kerrigan senior.

'Pity we couldnae win for him.'

'You cannae have everything.'

'That's a fine piano you have.'

'Family heirloom.'

'Is it in tune?'

'Nae idea. How do you tell?'

'Can I?' Kerrigan said yes and Bob lifted the lid and rested his fingers on the keyboard. He played a scale. 'Pretty close.'

'Can you play?'

'Aye. Just self-taught, like.'

'Give us a tune, then.'

'Would you mind?'

Kerrigan shook his head. 'It'll pass the time.'

Bob addressed the keyboard as though in reverence. Music was the only thing that took him out of himself, allowed him to relax. His right hand began a two bar introduction and the left joined in with a mournful rhythm. 'Did you ever sit thinking,' he sang, 'with a thousand things on your mind?' He closed his eyes. 'Thinking about someone who has treated you so nice and kind.' His voice was sweet and mellow, perfect for the stoic emotion of the tune. He sang off the beat, syncopated as though he were living the song and not merely singing it. When he finished he turned round.

Sergeant Braggan was staring at him. His expression was not benevolent.

'I think that's enough of that, City boy.'

'Yes, Sergeant.' Bob stood but didn't know what to do

next and sat down again. Braggan glared and he stood again.

'Go outside and keep watch until we're ready to leave.'

Bob collected his helmet and eased past the watching mourners into the hall. Mrs Kerrigan followed him.

'Thon was beautiful, son,' she said. 'You took me out of myself for a few minutes. Thank you.'

Shortly after two, Reverend Keir arrived, carrying a cross and a vessel of holy water. He was shaped like a barrel and wore spectacles with lenses a quarter of an inch thick. His voice was high and reedy, his delivery fast. He shook hands with each mourner in turn and stood before the coffin and sprinkled it with holy water and began to intone *De Profundis*.

From the depths I have cried out to you, O Lord;
Lord hear my voice. Let your ears be attentive
To the voice of my supplication.

A small, birdlike woman, Mrs Kerrigan hunched in on herself as though seeking to evade the present. Her sobs carried over the sound of the priest and the silence of the house. Daniel Kerrigan Senior patted her back and stared at the wall unblinkingly and tried to empty his mind.

The Reverend Keir led the brief service and at three o'clock Johnny Nichol, the undertaker, supervised the transfer of the coffin to the hearse. Wreaths were piled next to Mrs Kerrigan's, placed on top of the coffin, and two further cars were filled with flowers. It took twenty minutes before eventually the funeral cortège turned out of St Catherine's Road at the start of Danny Kerrigan's final journey. The day was fine, a cornflower-blue sky dotted with white clouds, sunshine dominating. The tribes of Perth lined the route seven or eight deep. Men removed their hats. Women bowed their heads. Children watched solemnly.

'Who are all these people?' said Mrs Kerrigan.

'City folks,' said her husband, 'saying goodbye to one of their own.'

'Nosy parkers gawping at others' misery.' She sobbed again and turned and stroked the coffin. Her poor boy, catastrophically alone.

My life. My love.

My laddie.

At Longcauseway Mrs Kerrigan looked up at the tenement where the Fenwicks lived and saw Marjory staring solemnly down. On the side of the tenement giant advertisements, discordant in this moment of grief, extolled the virtues of Colman's Starch and Nestlé's milk and BSA bicycles. Bass brewed solely from the best. Farola flour. Horniman's tea. They rolled on, up Feus Road and Jeanfield Road to Wellshill, all the while observed by crowds on either side.

Police officers guarding the cemetery entrance opened the gates and quickly locked them again behind the cortège and it came to a halt in sunshine and despair. From outside, people watched. Inside, the legions of the dead lay spread beneath and around. Grass and stone and tranquil air. Among it all a single patch of open ground lay exposed, fresh like a wound.

The pallbearers gathered by the graveside, Daniel senior in the front rank with Danny's grandfather, David Fiskin. In the middle rows were cousins Thomas, James and Charles Fiskin and his uncle John Scotland. Cousins Tom and David Fiskin took the rear. In the hearse Mrs Kerrigan sat paralysed.

'Come Ida,' said Johnny Nichol. 'It's nearly done.'

'It'll never be done, son.' She took her position next to her husband and her father in front of a black oblong of death but she saw nothing of it. Instead, she saw a baby smiling, crawling; a boy running, playing, laughing; a young man shy and diffident, small smile of satisfaction, holding hands with his girl, revelling in her presence, her company, her trust.

She saw the future betrayed.

The priest gave his graveside address as the men lowered Danny Kerrigan into the ground. It looked too deep. Not something for a boy of eighteen. The mourners took turns to scatter earth on the coffin, the noise resounding, sharp like a pain. Danny's grandfather broke down and sobbed and clutched enormous hands to his face. None of it felt real. All of it felt hard. The Reverend Keir gave the final petition before they retreated to reality. 'May his soul and the souls of all the faithful departed through the mercy of God rest in peace.'

The mercy of God, thought Mrs Kerrigan. What was it worth?

*

John McGuigan lay on the grass by the side of the river Earn, halfway between Kirkton of Mailer farm and Aberdalgie House. He chewed a stalk of grass and followed the easterly progress of the clouds. By his side Nellie Gammon slept, enjoying her afternoon off. He turned on his side and stared at her, the movement of her breasts, the shape of her hips beneath a pale yellow dress. A fine-looking girl. She should probably have her teeth out but it was a pretty enough smile.

As though conscious of being observed, she woke and looked up at him. 'It's that boy's funeral today,' she said.

'Aye.'

'Poor laddie.'

'Shouldnae have been there.'

'What d'you mean?'

He lay on his back and stared at the sky. 'If he hadnae been there he wouldnae have been shot. Simple as that.'

'Doesn't make it right.'

'No. But that's just life, isn't it? Things happen.'

'That's a hard way of thinking.'

'It's a hard world.'

She leaned towards him, tucking her left leg over her right. 'I'll be needing someone to look out for me, then,' she said lightly. He continued to stare upwards. She pressed her fingertips to his lips. 'You can kiss me if you want.'

'It's too hot,' he said. He jumped up and pulled off his shirt and unbuttoned his trousers. 'I'm going for a swim.'

'Don't. It's dangerous. Dad always says …'

But he was already in the water, diving flat and low into the current and reaching out towards the centre of the river. He turned and waved and she waved back. He treaded water.

'Come in,' he said, but she shook her head and watched him intently. He looked so confident in the water, strong, brave.

Wild.

Her heart beat faster and she wondered if she would ever be able to tame him.

Or would want to.

He swam back and forth for fifteen minutes and all the time she willed him to come out and rejoin her. Finally, he returned to the bank and hauled himself out and shivered and wrapped his arms around himself. He put on his shirt, the worn cotton clinging to his wet skin. She stared. Wiry. Strong.

She leaned over and kissed his cheek.

'You're a bad boy,' she said.

'I am.'

She held her breath. 'You can be bad with me, if you like.'

'I can be bad with anyone.'

*

The painting on the living room wall, the only such decoration in the whole house, was a landscape, the work of a long-dead cousin of Mrs Fenwick, with hills in the distance and a river running through a shallow valley. Cattle stood in fields. The sky was thick, deep clouds threatening rain. Marjory had studied it hundreds of times and wondered why the artist would choose such an unpromising day. Why not sunshine? Why not something hopeful, or beautiful, or happy? Today, the painting finally made sense. It represented the world Marjory now inhabited. The clock on the mantelpiece told her the funeral would be over. Danny was in the ground. She shivered.

'Cup of tea, hen?' said her mother.

Marjory said yes. She would not cry.

There's nothing without you, Danny, she said to herself. *I'm nothing without you. I want to be with you. Whatever that takes.*

Whatever.

Marjory Fenwick blinked away reality and retreated into silence.

*

'I'd like to speak to Constable Kelty.'

Desk Sergeant Strangeway peered up in surprise. 'That's a first. Who are you?'

'Robert Barrie.'

'And why do you wish to speak to Constable Kelty?'

'He told me to attend the station. He met me up near the Cuddies Strip and wanted me to make a statement. About Wednesday night.'

'You were there on Wednesday night?'

'Aye.'

'And Constable Kelty knew that?'

'Aye.'

'And he just invited you to drop by, at your own

69

convenience?'

'He said yesterday, actually. But I was out.'

'This gets better and better. Right, Mr Barrie, through to the interview room. Someone will be with you directly.'

Strangeway shook his head. He couldn't help liking the City boy but he wasn't remotely suited to the police, to its discipline, the detail, the drama. There had been an article in *The Courier* the other day about what constituted the ideal policeman. Strangeway had read it with incredulity: courtesy, conscientiousness, cautiousness, contentment, comradeship. At the time, he couldn't put his finger on what irritated him so much about that list, but now, thinking of Kelty, it became clear. It was a perfect description of him – a nicer, more thoughtful person you couldn't hope to meet – but was it a description of a policeman? Never in a million years. The characteristics in the list were predicated on harmony. They presupposed conformity. But a policeman needed to operate in discord, anticipate divergence. And that was why Kelty, who saw only the good in people, would never make a policeman. Strangeway knocked on the inspector's door and explained what had happened.

'Let's have a word with him, then,' said Conoboy, making no reference to Bob's actions. He strode into the interview room and introduced himself and invited Barrie to tell his story.

'Me and Jamesie Stewart ...'

'Who?'

'My neighbour. We were oot walkin' on Wednesday, early like. We'd have been at Buckie Braes about eight. We went alongside a field to a stile leading to the Cuddies Strip and crossed it and walked by the side of the field, towards Callerfountain ...'

'Why?'

'Just walkin', like.'

'There's no path that direction, is there?'

70

'Not as such.'

'Funny way to walk.'

'We werenae in a hurry. Anyway, after a while you come to a drystane dyke that divides the field in two. We walked along by the dyke a while. It would be after nine by this time.'

'But it was only eight when you were at Buckie Braes. You wouldn't take an hour to walk that short distance.'

'We was just daunderin'.'

'Were you checking snares as you went?'

'No, sir. Not us. We dinnae do that sort of thing.'

'Continue.'

'Well, as we were walkin' along we saw a man comin' doon the other side.'

'In which direction?'

'Towards the Cuddies Strip.'

'And towards you?'

'Aye.'

'And?'

'So I says to Jamesie, there's the gamey, get doon ahint the dyke.'

'And why did you say that?'

'We was trespassin' on his fields.'

'But not poaching?'

'No, just walkin'.'

He was a small man, in his twenties, weasely and untrustworthy. His hands were callused and dirty. Conoboy tried to put aside his prejudices. 'What happened?' he said.

'We ducked doon, but I keeked up again to see if he was past. He was right close, only a few yards away, and I could see straight off he wasnae the keeper. He was far ower young.'

'And?'

'He walked towards the Cuddies Strip. Then he went into the whins.'

'At the Cuddies Strip?'

'Aye.'

'And?'

'We never saw him again.'

'Would you recognise him?'

'Aye.'

Conoboy stared at him. The weasel stared back, expression merging fear and insolence.

'Did you catch many rabbits that night?'

'I wouldnae ken how to, sir.'

*

Eddie Carcary looked up as the bell on the shop door rang and a bedraggled man entered. He was probably in his late forties and looked like he'd been on the road for some time. His hair was greasy and he had a two- or three-day stubble. His hands were filthy. His clothing too. His boots were covered in dust.

'Afternoon,' he said. Mr Carcary returned the greeting. 'Could I hae tuppence worth of roast beef?' His voice had the reediness of a much older man. His eyes were dull. He was a pitiful sight. Mr Carcary sliced a generous strip of beef and wrapped it in paper and handed it to him. The man unwrapped it and took a bite and chewed quickly.

'I'm awfae sorry,' he said. He shuffled at the counter and dug his hands into his pockets. 'But I've nae money to pay for this.' He handed the half-eaten beef back to Mr Carcary but the shopkeeper shook his head. The vagrant was a pathetic soul, right enough, and on another day he'd have sent him on his way with a bob in his pocket but the murder on the Cuddies Strip still occupied everyone's thoughts. Carcary appraised the man and believed he could pass for the description in the papers.

'Why don't you come ben for a cup of tea?' he said,

indicating towards the back of the shop. The man stared at him for a moment, scarcely believing his good fortune, then followed him into the back.

'Take a seat,' Mr Carcary said. He filled the kettle and laid it on the gas and went through to the shop and on a piece of wrapping paper he wrote an instruction to the police to come at once as he had apprehended a suspect in the murder case. He called for Billy, the apprentice laddie, and whispered to him to take the note to the County Police office immediately. Billy ran off on the greatest adventure of his sixteen-year-old life and Mr Carcary went to make the tea.

*

When Constable Kelty returned from the funeral, he found himself in the strange position of being, simultaneously, chastised and praised.

'Excellent work, Constable,' said Inspector Conoboy.

'Did you not think to mention to anyone you'd found a vital witness?' said Sergeant Strangeway.

He was spared further interrogation as Billy from Carcary's ran in and silently thrust the note into Sergeant Strangeway's hand. The sergeant read it and passed it to Inspector Conoboy. 'One for you, I think, sir.'

Conoboy read it. 'Robert, come with me,' he said, and Bob followed him out of the station, almost flattening Sergeant Braggan as he ran down the steps. Inside, the two sergeants exchanged glances.

'Wild goose chase?' said Braggan.

'Wild goose chase,' said Strangeway.

Strangeway relayed the story of Robert Barrie. 'God knows what he would do if he ever found the murderer. Ask him to tea, probably.'

'I can top that,' said Braggan and he explained about Bob's musical interlude. 'And to top it all,' he said, 'it was

73

some nigger music he was playing.'

Strangeway appraised him but said nothing, and after a moment he walked away.

*

In Carcary's shop the vagrant looked up as two police officers strode in. He set his cup back on its saucer and tried to extricate his finger from the handle. He gave them a rheumy smile.

'Where were you on Wednesday night?' said Conoboy. 'About ten o'clock.'

The man looked at them with a puzzled expression. He looked at Conoboy. Then he looked at Bob. Then he looked at Conoboy again.

'Ask the puppy,' he said.

Conoboy turned to Bob.

'Mr Johnston was in the City Police cells, sir. I arrested him for vagrancy in Skinnergate on Wednesday evening.'

They walked outside and Inspector Conoboy took out his cigarette case. He offered one to Bob.

'Not on duty, sir.'

'No, of course not.'

As they ambled back towards the station, Bob plucked up the courage to speak. 'There was a lead yesterday, sir. Tibbermore?'

'Someone not been seen for a few days,' confirmed Conoboy.

'The Fenwicks used to live in Tibbermore, sir.'

'They did?'

'Yes. So, it seems a bit of a coincidence. This man disappearing now. I wondered, sir, whether perhaps it was someone who knew Marjory.'

Conoboy clapped his hands. 'Let's go and find out,' he said.

'I'm on desk duty this evening, sir.'

'We'll be back in plenty of time.'

Bob smiled. 'Aye, sir.'

Conoboy drove them to Tibbermore in his ageing Wolseley Viper. From the noise of the engine, Bob feared they might not make it back, but he watched with satisfaction as town gave way to country, fields stretching far into the distance, towards the hills that held the valley in their grip. He felt himself unwind.

'How's Mrs Conoboy, sir?' he asked.

'Oh, she's fine. She's been doing a lot of writing recently. That keeps her busy.'

'Has she had anything published?'

'No. She does it for her own amusement.' He paused. 'And Annie's doing very well, too.' He watched with amusement as Bob coloured slightly. Bob and Conoboy's maid, Annie Maybury, had known each other since Bob came to live in Perth and it was obvious to Conoboy that the lad was smitten with her. It was Conoboy's mission to bring them together but it was proving thunderously difficult, what with Bob's nervousness.

'Actually, I worry that she's been working too hard recently,' he went on. 'Maybe you should invite her to the cinema? She'd like that.'

'I'll think about it, sir.'

'Shirley Temple's on at the King's.'

'Not really my thing, sir.'

'No. Nor mine. But the ladies like her.'

'Except Marjory Fenwick.'

Conoboy shook his head. 'It's a terrible thing, Robert.'

'It is, sir. But we'll solve it.'

'There are just so many leads. Which are real and which are false?'

'There's no way of knowing, sir. So we have to check everything.'

'Exactly.'

They drove on in silence and stopped on the High Street in Tibbermore. Smoke was billowing from Miss Mouncie's chimney, despite the near eighty-degree heat outside. They knocked on her door and introduced themselves.

'Heavens, I wasn't expecting a police inspector. It's only Geordie Forbes gone missing.'

'Does he customarily go missing, madam?'

'Not that I'm aware.'

'Then it's worth investigating.' Miss Mouncie invited them into a Victorian living room, dark and cluttered, smelling of gas and cat urine. The heat from a coal fire was overwhelming. Three haughty cats traversed the backs of the chairs. A grandfather clock ticked loudly but otherwise there was no sound. Bob held onto a black sideboard, fearing he might faint.

'When did you last see Mr Forbes?'

'Monday or Tuesday, I believe.'

'And did he say he was going away?'

'No.'

'Would he usually say something?'

'I would think so.'

'Excuse me, ma'am,' said Bob. 'Do you happen to know if Mr Forbes knew the Fenwick family who used to live in the village?'

'Of course. They were my next-door neighbours on the other side.' She indicated to her right. 'Mr Forbes on this side and the Fenwicks on that.'

Inspector Conoboy slipped his index finger inside his shirt collar and pulled at it. 'Do you know if he was acquainted with Marjory Fenwick in particular?'

'Oh yes, he had a soft spot for the child. Everyone did. She was the youngest of the four lassies, a lovely wee thing, so quiet.' She smoothed her hands over her lap and a cat leaped on to it and she stroked it contentedly. 'Why do you ask?'

Inspector Conoboy looked around the room. There were no concessions to modernity. Not even a wireless. No newspapers. The house was a time capsule occupying a different reality from the hustle of 1935.

'No particular reason, madam. Do you know what Mr Forbes does by way of recreation? Hobbies? Interests?'

Miss Mouncie bent forward. She pursed her lips. 'I'm afraid to say he is somewhat too fond of the ale, Inspector. It's one of his failings, God preserve him.'

Outside, they paused and allowed the breeze to wash over their faces. Sweat dried on their brows. Bob rubbed his palms on his trousers.

'That was hot,' he said.

'Enough to make a sinner repent.'

They walked down the High Street and Bob pulled open the swing doors of the Gloagburn Inn and they entered a dark, smoky bar. It was full of Saturday evening drinkers who watched the approach of the police warily. The barman gave a false smile and looked furtively at the optics behind the bar. A regular, not yet drunk, seated at the end of the bar, noticed this unconscious betrayal and smiled at the confirmation of a long-held suspicion.

'We're looking for Geordie Forbes,' said Conoboy. 'Has he been in here?'

'Not for about ten days.'

'Is that unusual?'

'Not especially. Once a week or so he comes in.'

'Have you any idea where he might have gone?'

'I don't know he's gone anywhere. He hasn't been in here. That's all.'

Conoboy turned to the bar and addressed the regulars. 'Does anyone know where he is?' The bar remained silent.

'Does he drink anywhere else?' asked Bob. Again there was silence, and in silence they departed.

MacNaughton's office was dim and the electric light flickered. He sat at his desk, left leg crossed over his right and foot curled behind the calf. He was smoking a cigarette when Conoboy arrived, an hour late for the evening conference. A large glass of whisky was in front of him. He made no acknowledgement of Conoboy's entrance and the inspector stood before the desk. MacNaughton drew on the cigarette and stubbed it into the ashtray.

'Where the hell have you been?'

'I was in Tibbermore, sir, following a lead.'

'What lead?'

'We had notification a man had gone missing earlier in the week. Tibbermore is where the Fenwicks used to live. We concluded there might be a connection.'

'Haven't we been working on the theory the attack was random? Somebody who didn't know the victims?'

'Yes, but I believe this line is worth following up.'

'Perhaps, but did it have to be you who did it?'

'I suppose not, sir.'

'The Police Committee meets in September. I fully expect them to sanction the commencement of the recruitment process for the new Chief Constable. You haven't got time to be gadding about the countryside.'

'No, sir.'

'I'm losing patience, Conoboy. I warned you yesterday I wanted to see some coherence to this investigation. I'm still not seeing it. You're on borrowed time. Do you understand?'

'Yes, sir.'

*

As midnight struck, Bob Kelty lay on his back in the small

patch of lawn at the rear of his house and stared at the sky. It was alive. Every few seconds, lights streaked across it, hundreds of them, meteor fragments careering in and out of Earth's orbit. Who could say how many billion years old they were, residue of past catastrophe ricocheting around the universe into eternity? Bob watched until the early hours, contemplated and failed to understand the vastness of it all, and in this way he felt his cares diminish. Could anything really be so important?

Less than quarter of a mile away, in Longcauseway, Marjory Fenwick lay in her bed and watched the same light show out of her window. She watched the comets trail across the sky and pictured her boy, her Danny, only he wasn't rotting in his grave, he was flying, soaring, living, and she pictured herself flying, and she pictured them flying, just the two of them, flying together into the nothingness of forever.

It was easy.

Sunday 18th August

A Day of Rumours

Morning sun filtered across the cemetery, laying oblique shadows on the ground in front of each gravestone in turn. It reached the area used for current burials, high on the hill looking north over green land reserved for future generations, final resting place of souls not yet born. A fresh mound was overlaid with wreaths and flowers, a wooden cross above it. Surrounding it was a rope, three feet above the ground, staked at each corner. PC Marchant stood watch, preventing souvenir hunters from making off with the wreaths.

'You're up early, miss,' he said.

Marjory explained who she was. 'May I get closer?' she asked. The policeman looked around the otherwise empty cemetery. He raised the rope and allowed her to stoop beneath it, then retreated a diplomatic distance and watched from beneath a swaying yew tree. She was little more than a child, he thought. Fragile.

'Hello Danny. How are you, my love?' Marjory crouched by the grave and rested her palms on the dew-damp turf. The ground all around was flattened by the feet of two-thousand sightseers but here, by the grave itself, Marjory felt alone and at ease. Her eyes were red-rimmed but dry. She wore no make-up, her girlish face fresh in the morning light. Her hair was turning greasy, the tight curls of her perm beginning to separate. She stroked the wreaths as she spoke.

'I hate waking up,' she said, 'because there's a moment

when I've forgotten and then it washes all over me again. And I don't like going to bed because I can't sleep. I just lie there and go over it again and again. It's like I'm still there. Like I can never escape. But in between times I'm getting better. I am. I'm not crying all the time anymore. It's just that I feel … empty.

'We should have been going out tonight. That's going to be hard. The first time we haven't gone out as usual.'

She fought back tears. What would they have done this evening? Shirley Temple was still on at the King's. She'd give anything to see Shirley Temple tonight, Danny by her side, her hand in his, feeling him, warm and comfortable. *Animal Crackers in My Soup.* Instead … Instead …

'I think we would have got married. I know we're only young but I believe it. We were right for each other. You stopped me being too serious. I kept you organised. I'm sure we'd have married. I'm not just saying it because of what's happened. You know me. I'm not fanciful like that.'

She saw a group of four walking towards the grave, early morning intruders in other people's misfortune. She sighed and wiped grass and moisture from her knees.

'I'll come back as soon as I can,' she said. 'I love you.' She thrust her hands into her coat pockets and hurried away, head bowed. Marchant watched her depart and resumed his position by the grave. He saluted the newcomers.

*

Victor Conoboy brought a folded copy of the *Sunday Post* with Bella's breakfast and laid it on her bed. *Perth Police House to House Search*, the headline ran. Bella ignored it and concentrated instead on the world news in the next column. *Talks May End in Paris. Eden and Laval Likely to Go to Rome.*

'Talks about nothing,' she said.

81

'Perhaps, but if Mr Eden can speak directly to Signor Mussolini, he may be able to influence him.'

'You can't influence people who have already made up their minds. The Italians have mobilised a million men. Eight-hundred thousand are already in Africa. This can only end one way.'

Victor Conoboy studied the newspaper, the grainy picture of Mr Eden, looking too young to be a diplomat. His two younger brothers, the report said, were killed in the war. It greatly affected Mr Eden's outlook. If anyone could influence such malign matters, Conoboy reflected, Eden might be the man. All the same, he knew that Bella was right and Abyssinia would be invaded before the summer was over. It was the latest disaster in a cavalcade of despair since the financial crash. The grim inevitability of global affairs distressed him greatly. The world was taking a decisive turn and it would be a generation before the damage could be understood, far less undone. And who could say what would become of the intermediate generation? He worried for them.

They talked of yesterday's progress in the case, the Tibbmermore lead, MacNaughton's reaction.

'You were right to investigate it,' Bella said. 'It might be important.'

'Tell that to MacNaughton.'

'Bring him here and I will.'

Victor laughed. 'I think you would.'

'You know I would. And so should you. You have to stand up to him.'

'I was never very good at that.'

She sighed. 'I can't criticise you for it. I'm the same. I can stand up for anyone but myself.' She dropped the newspaper on the bed. 'And talking of standing up for yourself, young Bob was speaking to Annie again yesterday.'

'Excellent.'

'Not really.'

'He didn't ask her out?'

'No.'

'I told him to.'

'Tell him again.'

*

Wattie Barwick left the Skinnergate hostel after a breakfast of a dry roll and weak tea and headed for the South Inch, in front of the South Church. He liked Sundays. Sabbath passers-by were more generous than those on weekdays and it was possible to collect enough to last three days or more. Today promised sunshine, too. If he could bag a good spot near the Walter Scott statue he would be in position to greet folks on their way into the kirk. They always gave more on the way in, as though making atonement in advance of their weekly engagement with the Almighty.

'You.'

He turned and cursed as two City policemen walked towards him. He gave his name and age and address, litany of identity much rehearsed.

'Where were you on Wednesday night?'

'Same place I told you the first time you asked me. And the second.'

The elder of the two policemen, an emphatically moustached man of around fifty, clearly unbelieving, gripped his coat by the shoulder. 'Which was?'

'Tay Street.'

'Whereabouts in Tay Street?'

'Opposite the Methodist church, watching the river.'

'Why?'

'Why not?'

'Can anyone vouch for you?'

'A couple salmon, maybe. Other than that, not a soul on this Earth.'

83

The policeman transferred his grip to the back of the tramp's arm, above the elbow. He cringed at the layers of grease and grime. 'I think we need to ask you a few questions. Come with us.'

'Ah, come on, fellas. That's the third time I've been arrested for this.'

'Is it really? Well, we'll no doubt have the paperwork to prove that back at the station.'

They stood either side of him and marched him towards the City station in Tay Street. Walking towards them, morose and intense, on his way to the County station in South Street, was Bob Kelty.

'Wattie,' he said.

'Do you know this man, Bob?' said the elder policeman.

'Arrested him on Thursday afternoon on suspicion of the Cuddies Strip murder. He was arrested again for it on Friday, weren't you Wattie? What are you doin' with him?'

'Arresting him on suspicion of the Cuddies Strip murder.'

'He didnae do it. The hostel can vouch for him.'

They looked at their suspect, implausible vessel of their hopes of success and advancement. They sighed.

'On your way.'

*

'There are sightings coming in from all over,' said Sergeant Strangeway. 'So many we can't respond to them all. We have to prioritise …'

'We have to check each thoroughly,' said Conoboy. 'Our colleagues in forces throughout Scotland have considered these to be worthwhile leads and it's our duty to investigate them.' Strangeway stared ahead grimly. 'Let's go through them,' Conoboy said definitively. 'The man on the bus?'

'Stirling to Muirhead bus,' said Strangeway. 'Reported by a member of the public. He answered the description.

Looked shifty. Staring eyes.'

'That could be our man.'

'It could be half the male population of Stirlingshire, sir.'

'Send Marchant to Stirling bus station, see if anyone recollects the man.'

'Yes, sir.'

'The pawnbroker man?'

'Ah,' said Braggan, 'he's been found. McNab tracked him down to a farm the other side of Bridge of Earn. Mr Pettigrew, farmhand. He told us the gun had been in Malloch's for a week for repair. He only picked it up the day he tried to pawn it. Which was the day after the murder.' He paused and stared at Conoboy. 'Mr Malloch confirms it. A dead end, sir.'

'Not a dead end. A possibility eliminated. Keep dismissing all possibilities, eventually you'll be left with only one lead, and that will be our man.'

'That may be, sir,' said Strangeway, 'but there are an awful lot of leads and there aren't many of us.'

'So we keep working at them. Now, the railway man.'

'I think we need to close that line of enquiry, sir. It's completely cold.'

'Our colleagues in Inverness?'

'Nothing, sir. We don't even know he took the Inverness train. No one saw him get on it.'

'Well, he can't have just disappeared.'

'I'm afraid he has, sir.'

'Who's covering this?'

'Jones and Armstrong.'

'Keep them on it.'

'I had hoped to move them onto …'

'Another couple of days.'

'The description Miss Cross gave doesn't even sound like our man, sir. She says he had a big nose. The Fenwick girl said our man had a flat nose.'

'We'll review it tomorrow.' Conoboy rested his hands on the desk. Resources were stretched. The County Force was small, not equipped to cope with major investigations. He was the only inspector in the city and Braggan was the only sergeant in CID. He knew Strangeway was right to seek to prioritise but in all conscience he couldn't abandon lines of enquiry before they had been exhausted. The very fact the train man had disappeared was suspicious, surely? It needed to be explained. He sat back. 'Now, what about the house searches?'

'We've done all of Cherrybank and we're working downwards into town,' said Braggan. 'Glasgow Road, Jeanfield Road, Glover Street. Nothing as yet, but as you say it's all about working methodically and eliminating false leads.' Braggan flashed a smile that convinced nobody. 'I've been thinking, sir.'

'Yes?'

'The girl's story needs looking into. I have my doubts about her.'

'She was definitely attacked.'

'Yes.' Braggan didn't believe the Fenwick girl was complicit but, even so, her story didn't ring true. And the girl herself aroused his suspicion. Perhaps she was just a bit slow but he found her hesitant manner and lack of descriptive ability unusual. At times she seemed almost detached. 'I remain sceptical,' he said.

'I know. But you have no proof. Nothing she has said has been proved wrong.'

'The virginity.'

'Dr Murphy is not categorical on the matter.'

'I just think we should look into her a bit more.'

'When is the Procurator Fiscal likely to precognosce her?'

'Tomorrow.'

'Then we need to interview her before then.' *For her sake*

as much as ours, he thought.

'I'll have her brought in, sir.'

*

McIvor from *The Courier* and Templeton from the *Evening Telegraph* shared a joke in the front row. MacNaughton watched them balefully. Neither had written positive features about him in the weeks since Chief Constable Spiers's death. McIvor had been using *The Courier* for years to wage a campaign against him. MacNaughton was certain of it. Neither journalist made eye contact now. The man from *The Scotsman* limped in, leaning heavily on his cane. A methodist lay preacher, MacNaughton understood. Not to be trusted. What was he doing here on a Sunday, anyway? Shouldn't he be communing with God? Half a dozen more journalists sat with notebooks in hand and MacNaughton was growing accustomed to their faces but couldn't remember yet which newspapers they represented. The one on the right, tall and with unfeasibly black hair, was English, a syndicate man who sold stories to the regional presses which revelled in a good murder. People who couldn't point to Perth on a map were devouring news of the Cuddies Strip murder as though it had happened in their own back yard.

'Gentlemen,' said MacNaughton, spreading his arms. Lord Kellett, chairman of the Police Committee, sat to his right and Conoboy to his left. 'Thank you for coming. It's fair to say this is the most complex murder investigation in Scotland for over a century.'

He had no basis for such an assertion but it sounded good. He had a headache, a constant thrum of tension he could not escape, even in sleep. Every night he dreamt he was having a headache and when he awoke he was more exhausted than when he went to bed. Sun shone through the rear window directly onto a patch of flooring in front of him and the glare

87

from the varnish hurt his eyes.

'Investigations are ongoing,' he said, 'but at this stage we are no closer to an arrest. We have concentrated to date on people with shotgun licences, on people who are known to frequent Buckie Braes, and on people resident in town lodgings. House-to-house enquiries have been conducted from Cherrybank into town. Over five-hundred people have thus far been spoken to. We are in contact with forces throughout Scotland and a number of interesting leads are being pursued, but as yet there is no firm evidence pointing us towards the culprit.'

The man from *The Scotsman* tapped his cane on the floor. 'I understand that a reward is to be offered for information leading to the capture of the criminal?'

Lord Kellett raised his hand. 'If I can answer that,' he said. 'There has been no meeting of the Police Committee since the crime was committed and none is planned until September the 15th. There has been no opportunity to discuss any reward.'

'Lord Kellett,' said McIvor from *The Courier*, 'is there any truth in comments that another force will be brought in to lead the investigation?'

MacNaughton pursed his lips. Odious man, pursuing his own agenda. He wants me out.

'Again, there is no truth in that,' said Lord Kellett. 'The County force are making excellent progress in this very difficult case.'

'Yet by the Acting Chief Constable's own admission there is no prospect of an arrest.' McIvor sat forwards, clearly enjoying MacNaughton's discomfort.

'The Acting Chief Constable has detailed the comprehensive and impressive list of investigations that have been undertaken. We are at a very early stage in a complex case, but I assure you all steps are being taken to unmask this fiend.'

'If there are no further questions, gentlemen,' said MacNaughton, rising from his chair, 'I would like to return to my investigations. We will reconvene tomorrow. Good afternoon.' He strode out of the conference room into his office and closed the door, opened the bottom drawer of his desk and pulled out the whisky bottle.

*

'How are you?' said Inspector Conoboy.

'I shall be glad when people stop interviewing me.' If only she could wake up in six months, thought Marjory. In a different Perth. As a different Madge. Her mother's bulk pressed against her. The inspector's office was wood panelled, brown and stark, with only four small photographs hanging on the walls. Each included the inspector, either on his own or posed with a small group of other men, always in uniform. Never smiling. He had been handsome in his youth, Marjory thought, with deep-set eyes and a granite-like face and a moustache larger than he had now. He seemed smaller altogether now, somehow.

'Mr Fiskin, Danny's grandfather, has told us that he gave Danny ten shillings on the day of the murder.'

'Yes, for the pictures.'

'Did Danny spend that money?'

'No. We didn't go.'

'So he still had that money? Are you sure?'

'Yes. It was in his pocketbook. He showed me it.'

'When?'

'That night, when we were sitting at the Cuddies Strip. He opened his pocketbook and showed me. The ten-bob note was there, and some loose change, and some photographs.'

'Did you see the photographs?'

'Yes.'

'What were they?'

'The one I remember was of me.'

'Where did he get it?'

'I gave it to him on my birthday. It was taken at Boots.'

'Can you describe the pocketbook? It's very important.'

'It is?'

'Yes. Because there was no pocketbook and no money on his body.'

'He was robbed?'

'It seems so.'

Marjory fought back tears. It shouldn't matter. With everything that had happened, this should have been trivial. Instead, it seemed like yet another intrusion. She told him the pocketbook was brown kid leather. 'Quite new. His grandpa gave him it for Christmas. It had his initials on it.'

'Would there have been anything else in his possession that night?'

Marjory didn't think so, but she wanted to be certain. 'He probably had his asthma inhaler. And he often wore a chain. A snake chain, with a locket on it.'

'He definitely had those with him?'

'Not definitely.'

Conoboy nodded and made some notes in large, spidery writing. He smiled at Marjory. 'Tomorrow you will be precognosced by the Procurator Fiscal. Do you know what that means?'

Marjory shook her head. Her dark eyes watched Conoboy closely, scrutinising him as though in search of some hidden truth.

'Precognition is where the Procurator Fiscal formally gathers evidence to assess whether it is sufficient to bear scrutiny in court.'

'I'm only telling you what happened. How could it not be sufficient?'

'He will wish to reassure himself that your testimony is credible and complete. He will wish to assess whether there are gaps or inconsistencies. He will wish to assess your character.'

'My character? I'm not the one who's done anything wrong.'

'Once the murderer is found, Marjory, he will be tried in a court of law. You will, of course, have to take the stand. You will be the primary witness.'

'And you think my character is failing?'

'I didn't say that.'

'As good as.' Marjory felt a sting of anger. Her mouth was tight. She fixed her gaze on Conoboy.

'The Procurator Fiscal will want to know whether there are any factors in your history which might be pertinent.'

'Such as?' The girl was staring at him in bewilderment. Her tiny face was strained and creases lined her eyes. She held her hands tightly in her lap.

'You've told us you were a virgin,' he said.

Marjory looked at her mother. 'That's right,' she said.

'Is that the truth?'

'Of course.'

'Are you sure?'

Marjory opened her mouth but no words emerged. Finally, she hissed, 'Yes.'

Conoboy explained about Dr Murphy's statement, the conjecture about the already-broken hymen. 'I must advise you that this is an area I expect the Procurator Fiscal to explore.'

'Why? What does it have to do with Danny's murder? My rape?'

'It's a question of credibility. In court.'

'If I'm not a virgin they won't believe I was raped?'

'If you aren't but maintain you were.'

'But I am. Was.'

'That's what the Procurator Fiscal will wish to discuss.'

'And how can I prove that?'

Conoboy patted her hand. She retracted it and sat with her hands in her lap once more. Contained. Fearful.

'I really don't understand,' she said.

'No,' sighed Conoboy. 'I'm not sure any of us do.'

*

In early evening sunshine John McGuigan picked his way through the thick whins on Callerfountain hill. He arrived at a spot where the grass had been previously flattened and settled himself in place. He replayed the previous afternoon with Nellie, the way she had leaned over and kissed him.

'You're a bad boy,' she had said. 'You can be bad with me, if you like.'

McGuigan felt himself harden at the memory. He squeezed his penis. She would have let him. She wanted it. He could have done it. Fucked it.

From down the hill he heard voices, male and female, and raised his telescope to his eye and began to search until he saw a couple making for the benches at the side of the path. He started to watch. He reached inside his trousers but already he knew this wasn't going to be exciting enough.

Things had changed.

*

Strangeway watched the old woman limp down the station steps onto South Street. He handed the bag of clothing she had brought to Bob.

'Put that in the museum,' he said, indicating with a jerk of his head the room at the rear where they deposited any unusual items. As Bob departed, Braggan arrived at the front desk and picked up the newspaper Strangeway had secreted there.

'Looks like the Tallies are really going to war,' he said.

'Aye. Still, you can't believe for a minute they'll make much of a fist of it.'

Braggan smiled in agreement. 'They're deserting in their droves to Switzerland, I hear. Christ, a war between cowards against niggers. It could go on forever waiting for one of them to figure out how to win it. Mind, I expect Eden will try to talk them out of it.'

'I hope so.'

'I hope *not*. Abyssinia's the only place in Africa not ruled by the white man. It offends the natural order of things.'

Bob returned from the museum before Strangeway could reply and, besides, there was nothing to say. There was no getting away from it, Braggan was a boor.

'City boy,' Braggan shouted. 'I've got a job for you.'

The smirk on Braggan's face suggested it would not be one Bob would appreciate. 'Two lads have just reported a man peering into windows in Canal Lane and James Street. Quite what he expects to see down there is anyone's guess. Unless it's inbreeding. See if he's still there and, if he is, send him on his way.'

Bob looked at Strangeway and the desk sergeant nodded slightly. Bob fixed his helmet to his head and hurried outside. His secondment had lasted four days and it felt much longer. This was an alien place. Strangeway's sarcasm and Braggan's aggression were wearing and it was a relief to escape the station. By the time he arrived at Canal Lane it was growing gloomy. The sound of children's laughter echoed in the otherwise quiet evening. A strict demarcation of the sexes was in force, the boys playing football and the girls hopscotch. Blackened tenements rose high above them. Gas lamps threw a pale pool of light across a narrow, gravel road. Everywhere else slid into shadow. The air was still warm.

'Are you the lads who came to the station earlier?'

'Aye, sir.' A short boy, scrawny, wearing thick spectacles,

grinned up at him. His foot rested on a battered football.

'Is the man still around?'

'Naw.'

'He's in Charterhouse Lane,' said another boy, younger, perhaps eight or nine. He should have been in bed. He wore a dilapidated sleeveless pullover pocked with holes and a pair of grey, ragged shorts. His socks were held up with garters that were visibly too tight. His boots were a size too large. 'My sister telt me,' he explained.

'Charterhouse Lane?'

'Aye. Have you caught the murderer yet?'

'An arrest is imminent. Just you wait and watch.' Bob adjusted his helmet and walked towards Charterhouse Lane. Behind him, the children scattered and ran, witnesses bearing exciting news.

Bob walked through an opening into a small, enclosed lane. Terraces rose above him on either side, stone stairways curling up to the first floors. Old animal byres, some still in use, were on the ground floor. The cobbles gleamed in the yellow light of the street lamps. Bob saw the man at the far end of the lane. He did not appear sober.

'What are you doing?' said Bob.

'Nothin',' said the man. He was in his twenties but balding even more than Bob. His suit, probably older than him, was once blue but was now an indeterminate dust colour. Beneath it he wore a frayed shirt with no tie and his shoes were scuffed and worn. He did not give the impression of possessing much in the way of brain power.

'I've had reports you've been keekin' through windaes.'

'What for?'

'You tell me.'

'I've no' done a thing, Constable, honest I havenae.'

Bob stared at him. His eyes were dull and lifeless. He stank of alcohol. 'What's your name?'

'Bert Quinn.'

'Where you from?'

Bob was aware of a hubbub behind him. He turned and saw around thirty locals approaching. Behind them, another wave advanced. He looked up. People were hanging out of windows. Shouts filled the air.

'Auchtermuchtie,' said the man.

'Eh?'

'I'm frae Auchtermuchtie.'

'What are you doin' here, then?'

'Tryin' to get hame. I was with my cousin, Joe Considine. We were in the Scott Street bar. He buggered aff and left me there. I got lost lookin' for the bus station.'

Bob could barely concentrate for the noise. There were over one-hundred people now, perhaps nearer two-hundred, watchful, jostling to get closer.

'What's happenin'?' said Quinn uneasily.

'I've nae idea. Look, get yerself back to Auchtermuchtie as soon as you like. The bus station's this way. Follow me.'

They set off and the crowd parted but immediately closed up behind them and began to follow.

'You gonnae arrest him, Constable?' shouted a woman in a black shawl.

'Naw. I'm takin' him to the bus station.'

'Aye, right.'

'I am,' he said, but the crowd were in no mood to be dissuaded. He saw the ragamuffin boy holding his father's hand. He saw the boy with glasses. He replayed the earlier conversation in his head.

'I never said,' he said, but stopped. 'Look, there's no' goin' to be any arrests. The lot of you, go home.' He and Quinn walked off. The crowd followed all the way, chanting and cheering as though they were embarking on a grand social outing. They followed them up James Street and into Canal Street. By the time they arrived at Hospital Street they were singing. When they reached the bus station at Leonard

Street there were hundreds of them, marching and singing in unison. People hung out of windows and cheered them on for the entirety of the procession. Sporadic fights broke out, drunks egged on by greater drunks.

'Funny town, this,' said Quinn as he jumped onboard a brown and yellow bus. He sat in the front seat and wiped condensation from the window and watched the crowd watching him.

'Aye,' said Bob.

Monday 19th August

A Day of Heat

Bob stood over the chipped Belfast sink of the station toilet and stared at his reflection in the mirror. He ran a comb tentatively through his hair, as though seeking not to disturb it. He checked the comb's tines, pulling off loose hairs and depositing them in the bin and ran his hand across his scalp and checked the hairline. Gran had been difficult that morning, aggressive and argumentative, and he had toyed with the idea of staying at home to make sure she didn't abscond again. The thought of spending another day at the County headquarters did not appeal.

'Just get on with it,' he said to his reflection.

Sergeant Strangeway called him as he emerged. 'That Pied Piper impersonation last night,' he said. 'Five-hundred people following you halfway across Perth. Funny how that blew up.'

'They assumed I was going to make an arrest.'

'And why would they assume that?'

'I don't know, sir.'

'It's not as if you would have said that's what you were doing, would you?'

'No, sir.'

'Not even to a bunch of kids.'

Bob felt a sweat rising on his brow. 'No, sir,' he repeated.

'Because if I had evidence you did, even as a joke, and you caused a major public disturbance, I'd have you shifted

97

back to the City Police before your arse left my boot. Conoboy or no Conoboy.'

'Aye, sir.'

Strangeway threw down his pencil. 'On your way.'

'What do you want me to do, sir?'

'Whatever you like. Just get out of my sight.'

*

The man seated before Marjory was tall and thin and frightening. Thick-rimmed spectacles were perched on his nose. He glared at her and introduced himself as Mr Harman.

'I am precognoscing you on behalf of the Crown. Your evidence will be recorded and used to establish whether criminal proceedings can commence. It is essential you explain everything as fully as possible.'

'I have.'

'With respect, child, you have not. There are gaps in your statement. There are inconsistencies.'

Impatience overtook Marjory's face. 'I've told the police everything the best I can remember. It was dark. I was frightened. It all happened so quickly.'

'Your attacker. You have given different descriptions of his height.'

'He was a bit taller than me. Not as tall as Danny.'

'And red-faced? Or not?'

'Flushed.' Marjory could not understand why this man seemed so angry with her. He treated every response with scorn. His expression oozed disbelief. Marjory's instinct was to retreat. Succumb.

'You allege you were sexually assaulted. Raped.'

'Yes.' She took a breath. Dizziness overtook her and she gripped the handles of the chair and planted her feet on the floor. This had happened to her before, about a year before, when her granny and grandad died within days of each

98

other and she panicked that everyone she loved was leaving her. She struggled now to maintain concentration. It felt as though the world was sliding sideways and she was falling in the opposite direction. She focused on Mr Harman.

'Do you maintain you were a virgin before that night?'

'Yes. But I don't see what it has to do with anything.'

'You've never lain with a boy?'

'No.'

'Have you had other boyfriends?'

'No.'

'Believe me, if there are, the defence will find them.'

'There's nothing to find.'

'Did you know your attacker?'

'No.'

'Are you protecting someone?'

Her voice rose in pitch and volume. 'I didn't know him. I'd never seen him before. He killed my boyfriend. He raped me. What reason would I have to protect him?'

'When you were attacked did you resist?'

'At first. Not at the end.'

'Why not?'

'Because I was scared. He was stronger than me. He was on top of me. I couldn't do anything.'

She was close to tears. Harman put down his fountain pen and reached for another cigarette. He studied her face. She was frail and timid, the sort who could become overwhelmed by life. She had endured an ordeal, to be sure. But what, exactly?

*

Nellie Gammon knelt and scraped the last of the previous day's ash from the grate and slid it into the pail. She stood and stretched, enjoying the sensation of blood flowing back into her legs. She carried the pail to the kitchen and laid it at

99

the back door for collection.

'Hey, doll.'

She cursed and continued as though she hadn't heard him, washing her hands and drying them on a grimy towel.

'Lookin' fine the day,' Dougie Fisher leered at her.

'This is how I look every day.' She bustled past him and picked up a basket of dishcloths for the laundry. Dougie Fisher was twenty-one and gormless, employed as a kitchen hand because his mother was related to Mrs Moon. Throughout the year he had worked at Aberdalgie he had made the same cack-handed approaches to Nellie and nothing she said could persuade him of her lack of interest.

'I do think you're fillin' up a bit. That rump gets tastier every day.'

She slammed the basket down with exasperation. 'Look,' she said, 'leave me alone or I'll tell my lad and he'll sort you.'

Dougie hid his surprise behind a broad grin. 'Didnae ken you had a click,' he said.

'Aye well, I do, and he's a lot older than you and bigger than you and stronger than you and if you dinnae stop pesterin' me I'll see to it you find out just how strong.'

'Does Mrs Moon ken aboot your strong lad?'

'No.' Nellie blustered. 'What would it have to do with her?'

'Oh, nothin'. It's just she likes to ken what's goin' on wi' a'body. I dinnae suppose she would like it if she found out you were seein' a lad and hadnae telt her.'

Nellie waved him away irritatedly but he was right and she knew she'd made a mistake telling him about John.

'Never mind,' he said. He hovered over a block of cheese under a glass dome on the kitchen table. He stared at her and lifted the lid and cut a corner off the cheese with his penknife. He put it in his mouth and chewed, staring at her all the while.

'It'll be our wee secret, won't it?'

Nellie stared back for a moment, then gathered her washing again and stormed outside to the laundry.

*

Malcolm Harman knocked on Acting Chief Constable MacNaughton's door and entered without waiting. MacNaughton covered a momentary agitation by reaching for his cigarette case. He offered it to Harman and they both lit up.

'I've finished the precognition of the Fenwick girl,' said Harman.

'And?'

'It's a very strange case. So much of her story is remarkable, almost incredible. And there are inconsistencies. Minor ones, but all the same. I don't think she's very bright.'

'Is she reliable?'

'I think she's honest enough.'

'She still claims she was a virgin.'

'She may well have been.'

'That's not what Murphy thinks.' MacNaughton drew heavily on his cigarette and blew out smoke through his nose. He picked an invisible thread from his tunic.

'I've arranged a professional examination,' said Harman. 'Professor Mathieson from Glasgow University. Next Monday.'

'As you see fit.'

'It could be germane to the court proceedings. Such things matter to juries.'

They sat in silence for some moments. Cigarette smoke swirled above them.

'You should know I've had the Home Office on the telephone,' Harman said. He registered MacNaughton's concern. 'They're very keen to see progress.'

'As are we all.'

'Indeed. They're pressing me to give an answer about whether or not there's a case.'

'And?'

Harman pondered for some moments. 'The case is viable,' he said. 'If you can find a culprit. But we don't want the trail to go too cold, Archibald. The Home Office …'

'No,' MacNaughton said. He stared out of the window.

*

Marjory was tired and irritable by the time she got home. The smell of fried mince pervaded the house and her mother was fretting with the living room curtains. There was a letter for her on the hallway table, addressed in unfamiliar handwriting. She studied it curiously. Her mother hovered as she opened it. Inside there was a single sheet of paper with neat, childish writing. 'Buy yourself something nice.' Alongside it were two ten-bob postal orders. She looked at her mother in confusion.

*

Arthur Hill sat forwards in the wooden chair, hands clasped tightly. For four days he had argued with Dottie about telling the police what they'd seen.

'It's not important,' he said.

'That's up to them to decide,' she replied.

'I could implicate myself.'

'Don't talk soft, Art, I was with you the whole time.'

'They'll want to know why I waited so long to come forward.'

'Then don't delay any longer.'

Eventually Dottie ground down his resistance. He wore his best suit and tried to look more mature than he felt.

'Mr Hill, what can you tell us about Wednesday evening?' Sergeant Braggan's hostile expression suggested he anticipated precious little from the interview. Arthur Hill was taken aback, immediately regretting submitting to Dottie so easily. Not that argument ever made any difference where she was concerned. He concentrated on the other man, the inspector. He seemed more friendly.

'I was out walking on Buckie Braes with my girl, Dottie Chalmers, about half eight, heading towards Callerfountain. Just enjoyin' the view, like.' Braggan raised an eyebrow. Hill swallowed. 'We met a couple of chums of mine, the Dickson brothers from North Muirton and we were chattin' to them for half an hour or so.'

'Long chat.'

'They're grand lads. Lots of stories. Anyway, while we were talking we saw a couple of youngish looking lads, early twenties, maybe. They were creepin' behind a dyke, hidin'. "Oho," I said, "there's a pair of peeping toms and no mistake." We watched them for a bit and they were still hidin' ahint the dyke.'

Braggan listened with ill-concealed disinterest. If they were to round up all of the peeping toms on Buckie Braes they'd need to double the size of the prison at Friarton.

'And then we saw another lad coming in the opposite direction. From Callerfountain. He went towards the Cuddies Strip and disappeared into the whins. Dave Dickson said, "And there's another one" and we all had a rare laugh at that.'

'What time would this be?'

'After nine, maybe. The Dickson brothers went back to town and we carried on uphill for a bit but we realised we wouldn't make the top of Callerfountain and back before dark so we turned around. We got back to Buckie Braes about ten o'clock, and I heard two gunshots. "Damn fool," I said to Dottie, "shootin' rabbits at this time of night." About ten minutes after that I heard a third shot.'

'You're sure about that?' said Braggan.

'Aye.'

'And that would be what time?'

'About quarter past ten.'

'Well thank you, Mr Hill. That ended rather more usefully than it began.'

Hill rose, unsure whether to be pleased or offended. He settled for relief.

*

'So which one's your room?' They stood in the baking heat outside Nellie's house in Cherrybank, a new council semi-detached with a long garden and shared central path leading to the front doors of either house.

'Top left,' said Nellie. 'Why, are you going to sneak up in the night and have your wicked way with me?'

John McGuigan grinned. 'As soon as I get a ladder.'

'There was a ladder at Aberdalgie House. But it disappeared.'

'Aye,' he said. 'I ken. And I ken where it's hid.'

'Where?' She laughed and took his hand and swung it.

He pulled away from her angrily. Why did she always want to touch? Forever pawing at him. He gripped her jaw tightly, suddenly angered by the docility in her eyes, the fear in her expression. 'Stupid girls shouldnae ask stupid questions,' he said. He let go and walked on but he realised she had stopped and he turned round. He forced a smile. 'Come on,' he said, and she followed.

They climbed through Buckie Braes, enjoying the cooler air beneath the shade of the trees and stopping at the wooden bench halfway up the western path. Instinctively, McGuigan looked uphill, into the bracken, into his hideaway, but saw no activity within. Too hot even for peeping toms.

'Hottest summer in twenty years,' he said. 'So they reckon.' It was the first time he had spoken since the confrontation. Nellie, thinking his silence had represented continuing anger, latched on to this communication with relief.

'It's too much. I can't even sleep at night, it's so hot.'

'You should try a tent, gal. Nice and cool.' He bit his lip, rebuking himself. That sounded like an offer. Stupid bitch would want to take him up on it. He stood up and walked on and she followed, climbing uphill to the edge of Buckie Braes and skirting round the Cuddies Strip towards Callerfountain. They walked alongside the dyke running uphill from the Strip and passed the old beech that dominated the skyline.

McGuigan pointed and Nellie followed the line of his finger and saw two partridges having a dust bath in a shallow hole created by a plough months before. They spread their wings and splashed in the dust, turning round and round in obvious pleasure.

'Partridges love bathing in the dust,' he said. 'Sparrows do too, but they're partial to a water bath as well. Partridges wouldnae.' They walked on, uphill and round the edge of the farm, skirting the moorland on the slopes of Callerfountain. The sun continued to beat down on them. Nellie was growing uncomfortably hot but didn't like to say. Suddenly, McGuigan stopped and she stopped, too, trying to see what he had spotted.

'What?' she whispered.

'That grouse.'

'Where?' She scanned the shallow hillside but could see no sign of any wildlife. He pointed and she saw it, almost concealed, about twenty yards away.

'Isn't it frightened?' she said.

He nodded. 'It should be, aye.' It was unusual indeed to get this close. He walked on slowly, watching the bird all the time. When he was closer than ten yards from it he knew something was wrong. He waved his arms. The bird did not move. He shouted. Still, it did not move. He picked up a clod of dried earth and threw it. It landed a few inches from the bird but still it didn't move. He walked towards it and stood over and studied it. It was seated on its nest but its head was limp, cocked to one side, a single eye staring sightlessly towards the sun that had killed it.

'Heatstroke,' he said. He picked it up. Beneath were three eggs. He picked them up and put them in his pocket. 'Couldnae leave its eggs and just baked to death in the sun.'

'Poor thing.'

'Senseless beast.' He held the bird by the legs and turned and started to walk back the way they had come. 'That's my tea sorted anyway,' he said.

Invite me, Nellie thought.

He didn't.

*

Bob sat in the reference section of the Sandeman Public Library. He had been planning to come here since Saturday and wasn't sure how to do it surreptitiously. Now, Strangeway had given him permission to do what he wanted and he intended to do just that. He was surrounded by telephone directories, from which he carefully annotated the numbers of laundries into his notebook. It took him two hours. The vagrants and tramps who used the library as a daytime refuge eyed him warily, resentful that they had to be on their best behaviour for so long. When he had finished, he replaced his helmet and nodded to the librarian, a young man carrying too much weight, and gave a salute to the rows of watchers in the newspaper section. He whistled *Jenny Dang the Weaver* as he skipped down the marble steps and exited onto Kinnoull Street and turned towards County Place. He knocked on the door of the police box overlooking the junction of South

Street and Scott Street. It was empty. He closed the door behind him and sat down before the telephone and opened his notebook and spent the rest of the day telephoning laundries. A man unaccustomed to speaking, by five o'clock his throat was sore and he still hadn't finished all the numbers in his book. He had nothing to show for his afternoon, but he felt a glow of satisfaction all the same. When he returned to the station, Inspector Conoboy greeted him and explained Hill's evidence.

'It certainly corroborates the time,' Conoboy said. 'And three shots for certain. That's more definite than McDougall's statement. As for the peeping toms, I doubt they're worth pursuing.'

'If they were peeping toms, sir.'

'What do you mean?'

'What time were Barrie and Stewart on the Strip?'

'About eight, I think.'

'I wonder if the lads Hill believed were peeping toms were actually Barrie and Stewart, out poaching. The timing's not far out, and Barrie was being deliberately vague about it.'

'And he also mentioned a man coming towards them and disappearing into the whins.'

'Exactly. Which Hill has now confirmed. I think it's more than likely that the man in the whins is our culprit, sir.'

Conoboy stared for a moment, then nodded. 'Robert, I do believe you're right.' Bob beamed. 'I think the Acting Chief Constable should be told.'

Bob hesitated. 'Perhaps wait until we have something more substantial, sir. It's only a sighting …'

'A second sighting.'

'Yes, but …'

But Conoboy had gone.

He finished his explanation to MacNaughton. MacNaughton didn't speak for some moments.

'It's useful,' he said at length. 'It helps build a picture

of that evening. But I want to know what progress you've made.' He lit a cigarette and crossed his right leg over his left. 'I was with the Procurator Fiscal earlier. The Home Office are taking a keen interest. They want result, that's what he said to me. What fresh leads have we?'

'We've interviewed a couple of hundred people today, sir. The same yesterday.'

'That's not a lead.'

'We've placed the murderer at the scene of the crime.'

'With respect, the murderer was always at the scene of the crime. Otherwise there would have been no crime.'

MacNaughton sighed. There was something about Conoboy, his posture or lack of presence or his general disposition, that irritated him beyond measure. 'Anything else?' he said.

'No, sir.' Conoboy rose and turned and MacNaughton watched Conoboy's retreating shape. He opened the bottom drawer of his desk.

*

Late evening sun glinted through the window of the County police station, showing up streaks in the glass and sections which had not been washed. Sergeant Strangeway vowed to have it out with Bill Gillespie about that next week. He looked up from the counter as a small man in a tweed suit entered, smiling, and introduced himself as Mr Herrick. He was carrying a heavy rifle.

'I found this in a field in the Glasgow Road and I reckoned, with the murder and all, you ought to see it.'

Strangeway knew immediately this was not the murder weapon. It was like no weapon he had ever seen.

'You haven't walked all the way through town carrying that thing, have you?'

'Aye. It caused a bit of a stir.'

'I should think it did. You're lucky you didn't get lynched, man. A crowd'll gather to watch someone tying their shoelaces right now. Could you not have put it in a poke?'

'I didnae have a poke big enough.'

Strangeway picked up the rifle. It was rusty and probably useless. The loading mechanism was jammed. He bent forwards and studied it closely. There was writing engraved on it and he held it to the light.

Waffenfabrik
Mauser AG
Oberndorf 1917

'Do you think it's the murder weapon?' Herrick asked.

'Not unless the murderer's a Boche left over from the war.'

'Pardon?'

'This rifle is from the Great War, sir. A German rifle.' Strangeway detected an element of exaggeration in Herrick's look of surprise.

'How on earth could that have found its way into a field in Perth?'

'You tell me. Perhaps someone put it there. Who had it and knew he wasn't allowed it.'

'Would you not be allowed to keep one of these?'

'What do you think?'

'I doubt it can fire, even. Probably harmless. It would make a nice ornament.'

'Well, I tell you what, if Kaiser Bill doesn't come to claim it within six months it's yours.' Herrick looked briefly hopeful but Strangeway gestured with his thumb. 'Hop it.' He watched the man depart and yelled for Kelty.

'Take this to the museum and add it to the collection. And don't drop it.'

Bob took the rifle and made to raise it to his shoulder.

'Don't even think about doing that, City boy.' From outside he was aware of a growing commotion, a clamour of voices and running feet.

'What now?' he said. He approached the front door, followed by Bob. 'Get away with that ruddy thing. You'll start a riot.' Outside, he saw Marchant trying to park the patrol car by the kerb. He rolled it to a halt and pulled the handbrake noisily and got out and walked round to the rear door. He opened it and a man stepped out and the crowd surged around him. Yells of 'That's him,' resounded around South Street and the throng pressed closer. The man appeared startled by his sudden notoriety and shrank towards the patrol car.

Marchant turned to him. 'On your way,' he said.

'Much obliged,' said the man, but he showed no willingness to depart and face the crowd. Strangeway sighed and pulled open the station door and ran outside.

'Marchant?' he said.

'I was patrolling up at Cherrybank and I saw Mr Harrogate behaving suspiciously on the Glasgow Road. I questioned him about the murder. He had a cast-iron alibi so there was nothing further to do but he said he had hurt his leg and could we give him a lift back into town.'

Strangeway looked at the man, and at the crowd gathered around him, and at Marchant.

'Right,' he shouted, 'Go home, you lot. This isn't the man. There will be no arrest tonight.' He waved at Mr Harrogate. 'You. Limp off.' He turned to Marchant. 'You. Inside.'

He shook his head and retreated to the sanity of the station and debated what oddity Glasgow Road might throw up next.

*

110

The evening was still hot, too hot for a shawl, and Marjory's scalp was prickly and uncomfortable beneath it, but it remained a necessary precaution. She walked, head down, across the North Inch towards the Tay and sat on a bench overlooking the sleek water. Half a dozen ducks and a couple of swans swam past. Immediately above the water was a fog of midges, black and silver in the evening sunlight. An occasional splash of water suggested a trout rising to catch them but Marjory never managed to spot one, seeing instead only ripples in the water left in its wake. A single magpie landed on the grass near her and walked stiff-legged towards the bushes by the river.

'Good evening, Mr Magpie,' Marjory said quickly. No more bad luck, please.

'Good evening, miss.'

Marjory gave a start and turned to see a man walking past. He raised his hat. 'I'm sorry,' he said. 'Did I give you a fright? I hope you didn't think it was the magpie answering you.' He gave a gentle laugh and Marjory smiled in return. 'Grand evening,' he said. 'Too hot earlier, but it's lovely now.'

'Aye,' said Marjory. She had a vague feeling she recognised the man and she was waiting for the now customary 'aren't you …' line, ready to jump up and run off, but the man gave no indication of knowing her. He talked casually, relaxed and friendly, never stepping any closer towards her, never asking anything personal. After five minutes he raised his hat again and said goodnight and walked off. Marjory watched him go, thankful for the brief interlude, the intrusion of normality.

Richard Hamill sauntered away, whistling to himself. The girl still looks haunted, he thought. Such a shame. What a bonnie lass.

*

111

The Conoboys' living room was dark and cluttered, the furniture old, mahogany, solid against the walls. Bookcases lined the wall opposite the window, collections of poetry, ancient history, philosophy, myth. *The Waste Land* lay on the side table beside Bella's chair, much read, worn, the spine broken. Mellow light escaped from an electric standard lamp beside the fireplace. Rudy Vallee and his Orchestra played *Home* on the phonograph. Bella would have preferred it performed slower, allowing the underlying mournfulness of the melody to emerge. *When Shadows Fall* ... It was beautiful, a call of return to all life's prodigals, the wanderers and discoverers, the lost and the dead. She cradled her pendant in her hand, stroking its surface with her thumb, seeing as though in the clear light of reality the face of the boy in the photograph concealed within. He would be thity-four now. As long had elapsed since his death as the extent of his life. Seventeen years alive, seventeen dead, and, in between, a no-man's land, beyond help and reason, hope and time. The pain was undiminished. It would never cease, not until her own last breath, and even then who could say?

'This tune makes me think of Tom,' she said.

'Let me turn it off.'

'No. It's okay to think about him. I like it.'

Bella thought about him too much, that was what Victor believed. He would never say so. He would never say Tom made his choice and died as a man on account of it. He would never say that Bella should stop torturing herself about his decision. Because she never would.

'You've said nothing about your investigation tonight. Is it not going well?'

Victor shook his head. He reached for his tea but it was too hot and he put it down again. 'You were right. The Procurator Fiscal has ordered another examination of Marjory.'

'Another? What on earth do they expect to find?'

'Exactly.'

112

'I want to meet her.'

'I don't think that's possible.'

'Of course it is. They haven't taken the case from you yet, have they? Have Bob bring her tomorrow night. That will give him and Annie a further opportunity to meet, as well. Who knows? We might resolve that issue, too.'

'If you're sure. It won't be too much of a strain for you?'

'Have her brought.' She picked up *The Waste Land* and began to read and the conversation ended.

Tuesday 20th August

A Day of Suspects

The noise of dozens of pairs of feet reverberated through the high-windowed conference room, intensified by the wooden floor and wood-panelled walls. Five rows of ten straight-backed chairs faced a table at the front. Gradually, the press took their places. MacNaughton wondered when interest would begin to wane. And when they would turn on him.

'No,' he said in response to Templeton of the *Tele*'s inevitable question. 'There is no prospect of an imminent arrest.' He studied the room. Blank faces stared back. These people had no vested interest. Their concern was only to generate sales for their newspapers. Parasites.

'We now believe robbery to be the motive. A brown pocketbook was stolen from Daniel Kerrigan's body. It had his initials burned into it. It contained a ten shilling note and sundry loose change. There were a number of photographs, including a portrait of Marjory Fenwick. We believe his asthma inhaler was taken, and a snake chain with a locket. We are anxious to trace any of these items.'

Oliver from *The Scotsman* tapped his cane. 'Has the murder weapon or clothing been found?'

'We have a theory that the murder weapon may have been hidden in one of the wheatfields to the south of the Cuddies Strip. It will not be possible to search until the crop has been harvested ...'

'Even in a murder investigation?'

114

'We are in discussion with the farmer. As for the clothing, apart from the fragments I have previously mentioned, no additional items have been found.'

Templeton waved and MacNaughton acknowledged him. 'You mentioned previously a penknife found near the scene. Has this offered any clues?'

'Unfortunately not. It transpires the penknife was dropped by one of our officers during the initial search.'

Laughter rose in the room. MacNaughton stared ahead in silence.

'Is it correct that the Glasgow force have offered assistance?'

'That is all I have to report at this stage. Same time tomorrow, gentlemen.'

*

Lord Kellett entered the Chief Constable's office without knocking. 'You seemed irritated out there,' he said.

'The press,' MacNaughton said. 'They're against us.'

'I don't get that sense.'

'Templeton of the *Tele* and the man from *The Scotsman* in particular.'

Kellett lit a cigarette. He'd known MacNaughton for many years. Never liked him but always believed him steady enough. The man in front of him now was strained, his eyes tired, his skin sallow. He was under pressure as never before. It was illuminating.

'How do you think the case is going?' Kellett asked.

'I think we're making strong progress.'

'I do, too.' Kellett noticed the relief in MacNaughton's expression. 'But I've had Sir George Gray on the telephone. From the Home Office.'

'Yes, sir?'

'Very keen for results.'

'So I gather.'

'There's an election coming. Maybe even this year. Next spring at the latest. It's imperative the National Government is re-elected. For the stability of the country.' He frowned. 'There are malign forces afoot. The world financial situation. Revolution's in the air. People take advantage. Communists. Fascists. People who don't have the country's interests at heart.'

'Indeed, sir.'

'People like that feed off instability. Uncertainty. Public dissatisfaction. It breeds discontent with the status quo. The public back the wrong horse, vote the wrong way. Look at Germany. We can't allow that here.'

Fascism was on the rise, Gray had told him. Mosley could conceivably take power. Kellett recoiled from that. He had been in Germany, knew what was happening there, the terrifying totality of the state, the perilous status of the individual.

'The Home Office are particularly keen for this case to be solved quickly,' he said. He raised his hand to prevent another platitude. 'And if I can't evidence strong progress they will bring in another force and I will be unable to prevent it. Do I make myself clear?' He walked to the door and turned back. What he wasn't clear about himself was whether or not another force's help might be desirable. The agitated man in front of him did nothing to assuage any lingering doubts. 'Find a suspect,' he said as he left.

*

In Muirhead, Lanarkshire, Joseph McHendry braved an early morning squall to take Bess for a walk. She skittered about behind him, crazy spaniel, intent on investigating every tree and hole in the wood. McHendry yelled but she paid no heed.

116

There was a rustle to his right and McHendry was startled to see a man emerge from the woods. He looked like a tramp, unshaven and dishevelled in an oversized trench coat.

'Got a light?' the tramp said.

'Aye,' said McHendry. He reached for his matches but the man lunged towards him, hand raised, and McHendry fancied it held a razor. He sidestepped and ducked and came up at the man, trying to grab his arm. They wrestled, McHendry holding the man's arm outstretched, the razor now clearly visible. McHendry could hear him panting, smell his breath. Fear overwhelmed him and gave him strength, courage borne of panic. They struggled for some moments before the man broke free suddenly and bolted back to the woods, heading for the same gap from which he had emerged. McHendry blew out hard and bent and rested his hands on his knees while his heart pumped in his chest and his ears rang. He was certain he had come face-to-face with the Perth murderer. Bess sat at his feet, wagging her tail.

'You were a lot of good,' McHendry said.

*

Meanwhile in Newburgh, Aberdeenshire, Mrs McCann was polishing brass in the kitchen when the doorbell rang. She wiped her hands on her pinny.

'Yes?' she said. Before her was a man of perhaps thirty, a vagrant, with several days' growth on his face and hair lank with grease.

'Beg your pardon, but could I have a piece?' he said. 'I'm fair hungry.' His voice was husky. He smelled of woodsmoke.

Mrs McCann considered him. Mr McCann had told her last night he'd seen evidence of someone eating their turnips. This must be the man.

'Where are you from?'

117

'I'm trying to get to Aiberdeen. I've been dodgin' the polis.'

'Why?'

'Their sort and mine, we dinnae get on. Could I have a piece? Wi' jam. Or cheese. Or a bit biled ham, maybe?'

She positioned herself behind the door. He certainly looked as though he needed help. It was Mrs McCann's practice to help those less fortunate than herself. But there was that awful murder in Perth. It didn't do to be careless.

'Wait here,' she said and closed the door and locked it. She prepared a piece with cold ham and one with cheese and wrapped them in paper and took them to the man.

'I'm that hungry,' he said, 'what I really need is a hot meal first, and then some more bread for the road. If you wouldnae mind.' He stared at her, challenging her, and she felt a stab of fear. Mavis, what have you done? She slammed the door and the vagrant tried to intercept it but she managed to close and lock it before he could.

'Kindly go away,' she shouted through the door. 'I'm telephoning for the police.'

*

Meanwhile in Dunfermline, police were called regarding a suspicious-looking character wandering in Linburn Road. He was sitting on a garden wall when they arrived, a man in his twenties. He was clean shaven and freshly laundered but the sole of his right boot flapped forlornly, revealing a callused foot.

'Who are you?' said the policeman.

'Bert Ward.'

'You from round here?'

'Perth.'

'Perth, aye? What are you doing here, then?'

'Looking for work.'

'In a residential street?'

'Odd jobs.'

'Were you in Perth on Wednesday evening?'

'No, I was in the jile.'

'The jail?'

'County Prison. Ten days for theft. Couldnae afford the one-pound fine.'

The policeman laughed. 'If that's true it might be the best break you've had in a while.' Bert Ward looked confused. 'Aye, come on, let's get back to the station and check you out.'

*

Sergeant Strangeway replaced the telephone receiver in its cradle. 'They seek him here, they seek him there, they seek that killer everywhere. Is he in Glasgow, is he in Fife, will I be after him the rest of my life?'

'Another sighting?' said Braggan.

'Fourth today. This is a good one. Travelling salesman on the Inverness train got arrested for drunkenness at Aviemore. They searched him and found women's undergarments in his case. He swears they're his but the Inversnecky force think they might be the Fenwick lassie's.'

'Don't tell Conoboy, for God's sake. I've no more men to send out.'

'I'll ask them to post them on.'

'And I'll add them to the clothes mountain. We had another pair of shoes this morning from Elibank Street.'

'What is it with Elibank Street and shoes? That's the third pair.'

A young woman entered the station, clutching a bag to her bosom. She gave a nervous smile.

'Good morning, miss,' said Strangeway.

'I'd like to make a statement, please. About the Cuddies

Strip murder.'

'Would you indeed? Sergeant Braggan, would you please try to locate the inspector? Just look for an untamed gander. He'll be in the vicinity.'

*

'Could you tell me your name and age, please?' said Conoboy.

'Elizabeth Gray, nineteen.'

'And there's something you wish to tell us?'

'I was on Buckie Braes on the night of the murder. I work at the dairy farm at Oakbank and I was walking home after work, about nine o'clock. I saw a group of people standing talking, two men and a man and woman. They waved and walked in opposite directions. The two men came towards Buckie Braes and the man and woman went out to Callerfountain.

'Then in the field above the Cuddies Strip I saw another man on his own. He was creeping about in the whins and I didn't like the look of him so I turned away sharply.'

'Did you see his face?'

'Only from a distance. He was ordinary height, quite slim, I think. He had a bunnet on his head and a dark-coloured jacket. That's all really. I don't know if it's important but I thought I ought to tell you.'

'Yes, miss. I rather believe it is extremely important.'

*

Bob was trying to negotiate the crowd in South Street when he felt a tap on his shoulder. He recognised the man facing him but couldn't place him.

'The other night,' the man said, 'you were in the Gloagburn.'

'Enquiring about Geordie Forbes, aye,' said Bob. He recognised him now as the man who was seated at the end of the bar. 'Why, d'you ken where he is?'

'Nae idea, son. But the Gloagburn isnae really his local.'

'No?'

'No. Mostly he drinks in the Old Ship Inn.'

'On the High Street?'

'Aye. If anyone kens whaur he is, it'll be Kenny Mackie, the barman there.'

'Thanks.' Bob studied him for a moment. 'Could you no' have telt us that the other night?'

'An' hae folk thinkin' I would clype tae the polis?'

Bob cursed. 'We're no' bad people, you ken.'

The man looked Bob up and down with a sardonic smile. 'Aye, you're a fine lad.' He turned to go. 'That's why I telt you.'

*

Bob reported the news to Conoboy. 'Marvellous,' he said. 'Come on. I need to go and see Marjory and then we can go and investigate.'

'Sergeant Braggan …'

'To hang with Sergeant Braggan, Robert.'

'My thoughts exactly, sir.'

They took the rear entrance to where Conoboy's Wolseley was parked and they pulled out onto South Street into the throng of watchers.

'Have they no work to go to?' said Conoboy.

'Not all of them, no. There's a recession.'

'Yes, they're grim times, to be sure. There's talk of an early election.'

'Not too early, I hope.'

'Why?'

'I'm not twenty-one until December. Before then I won't

get a vote.'

'Capital! It's quite a landmark, your first vote. Have you decided which way you will go?'

'I'm very taken with Mr Lloyd George's new deal, sir.'

'Surely not, Robert.' Conoboy shook his head. 'We don't need "new deals." We just need sound management. There are no quick cures for the troubles the world is in. Beware people who pretend to have all the answers.'

'I do, sir. But I like the Liberals' message. Peace, trade, employment, social reform. That sounds a grand ticket, to me.'

'It is. I can't argue. But the Independent Liberals will be wiped out at the election, I guarantee it.'

'That's no reason not to vote for them, sir. If it's what you believe in.'

Conoboy smiled. 'Yes,' he said. 'Have the courage of your convictions. Well done.' They drove on and Conoboy summarised Miss Gray's evidence. 'We now have verification of everyone on the Strip that night. Marjory saw Shepherd and his girl. Arthur Hill told us about Barrie and Stewart and the Dickson brothers, and now Miss Gray confirms that Arthur Hill and Barrie and Stewart and the Dicksons were there. They all confirm each other's stories.'

'And they all saw the man in the whins.'

'Exactly. Our murderer.'

'Our culprit, sir.'

'Pardon?'

'He committed two crimes, sir. Rape as well as murder.'

Conoboy reflected. 'Quite right.'

Outside Marjory's tenement in Longcauseway Conoboy reached behind for his cap. 'I'm inviting Marjory to supper tonight,' he said. 'I'd be obliged if you could bring her.'

'At your house, sir?'

'I do have a life outside the station, you know.'

'Yes, sir. It's just … Will Mrs Conoboy be there?'

'Of course.' Conoboy's hand rested on the door handle. 'I'm well aware of what they say about her in the station. You know as well as I do it's rot.'

'Yes, sir.'

Their feet echoed in the cold stone stairwell as they climbed the steps to Marjory's house. 'When you bring Marjory, I'd be grateful if you would wait until she's ready to go home. I thought, perhaps – Annie is on duty tonight. You could sit and chat with her.'

Bob felt that spike in his stomach. He didn't know what it was precisely – excitement? Desire? Fear? Dread? Perhaps some bastard combination of them all. Annie Maybury was the bonniest lass he had ever seen. She was the only person who spoke to him in those difficult early years when he was wee Boabby Kelty with his funny accent and a father who blew his own brains out. Then, loneliness helped overcome his shyness. Now, the idea of spending the evening alone with Annie filled him with terror. What to say? How to behave?

'Think of it as being on duty,' said Conoboy. 'Be civil to the lass. Talk to her.'

Mrs Fenwick invited them in and they waited in the plain living room for Marjory. She acknowledged the inspector and the shy constable and sat opposite them with her legs tightly together and her hands clasped in her lap.

'I have some more clothing for you to inspect.'

'Goodness, you could open a shop with it all.'

Conoboy opened a large sack and brought out pieces one by one, shoes, blouses, undergarments, two dresses, a skirt. Marjory shook her head each time. By the time they had finished she was crying.

'Make this end,' she said.

'I'm trying, my dear.'

'I do wonder whether possibly you might try harder?'

Conoboy studied her face. Those eyes, dark and wide,

they seemed dead, lost. Conoboy fancied that normally they would have a lustre that was dazzling. They would make her beautiful. She had the prettiest smile. He'd seen it only once or twice, and then only briefly, but it was enough for him to discern the true nature of the girl.

'I feel like I'm being accused,' she said.

'Not by me, I assure you.'

'Nobody believes me.'

'I do.'

'The Prosecutor Fiscal doesn't. The other policemen don't. People outside. They make comments. I can hear them. I can see them staring at me. I can't even go to Danny's grave and chat to him because there's so many ghouls there.'

'Still?'

'*The Courier* reckons there's been over five-thousand visitors so far, sir,' said Bob.

'Interest will fade soon,' Conoboy said. 'I promise.' But he was not convinced it would. Whenever events like Danny's murder occurred, people seemed to gain vicarious excitement simply through proximity. It was why they had to contend with so many false witnesses and hoax confessions. 'Now,' he said, 'I would like to ask you to my house tonight. Just a spot of light supper. My wife is most anxious to meet you.'

'Me? Why?'

'I've told her all about you and she's most insistent on being introduced. Robert will pick you up at 7.30, if that is agreeable?'

'What should I wear?'

'Whatever you like. We have no airs in our house.'

Marjory and Bob exchanged glances, recognising in each other the fears that resided in themselves.

*

Conoboy pulled up on the High Street and they ducked beneath the lintel of the Old Ship Inn. It was smoky inside and full of ageing men playing dominoes, talking, drinking, staring into space. Conoboy introduced himself and silence descended.

'We're looking for Geordie Forbes,' he said. 'Has he been in recently?'

The barman shook his head. 'Geordie? Not likely.'

'Why?'

'He's in France.'

'France?'

'Visiting his sister. I got a letter from him the day.' He fished in his jacket pocket and pulled out a creased letter and handed it to Bob. Bob checked it. It was signed Geordie Forbes and postmarked France on August 10th. Four days before the murder. He showed it to Conoboy.

'Thank you,' said the Inspector. They retreated from the bar and the chatter that had been silenced recommenced. Laughter echoed as they opened the doors of the Wolseley.

'Keep following the leads ...' said Conoboy.

'... And eventually the truth will emerge.'

But Conoboy was far from certain. We're drifting, he thought.

*

'Sergeant,' said PC McNab. 'We've just searched Kerrigan's bedroom again. We found these.'

He placed on the table in front of them an asthma inhaler and a snake chain and locket. On top of these he placed a brown pocketbook with DK burned into the leather.

Braggan stared at them impassively. 'No photographs or money?'

'No, it was empty.'

'The pocketbook that Marjory Fenwick insisted Danny

125

Kerrigan was carrying that night.'

'Yes, sir.'

'Well done, lad.'

*

Mrs Gammon was frying mince and onions when the sensation she was not alone prickled down her spine. She looked at the little clock on the fireplace. Too early for Nellie. Jack was still on his rounds. She turned off the gas and wiped her hands on her pinny and went to the kitchen door. She paused and returned to the sink and picked up a peeling knife and opened the door and peered into the hallway. It was empty. She stood at the foot of the stairs and looked up. The bedroom door was open. She always kept it closed. She looked at the front door. It was ajar.

She ran down the garden path and looked up and down the narrow street. Walking towards Buckie Braes, head bowed, was a figure, lazy-gaited and hunched. Mrs Gammon watched until he was out of sight and returned to the house and went upstairs but could find no evidence of disturbance.

*

'What do people call you?'

'Madge.'

'Welcome, Madge. Would you like some lemonade?' Bella poured her a glass from a jug on the sideboard. It was cloudy and viscous, chilled. They sat side by side on the settee.

'Goodness,' said Marjory, staring at the bookcase in front of them, 'what a lot of books you have. More than the Sandeman Library, I'd fancy.'

'Victor and I love our books. Do you read?'

'Not a great deal.'

'What was the last book you read?'

Marjory blushed. She could only think of *Milly Molly Mandy*. 'There was one story about children playing on a lake. I can't remember the name.'

'*Swallows and Amazons*?'

'That's it! How ever did you know that?'

'As I said, we like to read.' Bella talked for some minutes about books which Marjory might wish to try and Marjory said she would search for them in the library. They talked about music. They talked about cinema. Gradually, Marjory relaxed.

'I expect you're not sleeping well?' Bella asked.

'No.'

'That takes time, I'm afraid. But it will come.'

'I can't stop going over it in my head.'

'Concentrating on anything else is difficult.'

'Yes.'

'And you feel guilty.'

'I do. Danny was shot dead and I didn't even get a scratch. That doesn't seem fair.'

'The hard truth is that the world is considerably more random than we would like to suppose.'

'We shouldn't even have been there. Danny wanted to go to the flicks. It was me who said no.'

'So you think "if only …"'

'All the time. It won't go away.'

'Does anyone talk to you about it?'

'Only the blasted police. No offence, sorry.' Bella patted her knee conspiratorially. 'It's just that all they want to do is catch me out. They ask me the same things over and over. Did I know him? What did he look like? Was I ...' She faltered. 'And Mum just pretends it never happened. She won't even mention it.'

'So you have to bottle it all up as well?'

'Yes.'

'And what you really want to do is talk about it?'

'Yes.' She dabbed her nose with her handkerchief.

'Tell me all about it, Madge. Everything you want to say.'

Marjory sipped her lemonade and regarded this curious woman. She had the brightest blue eyes Marjory had ever seen and a calm and cautious appearance. Serene. Marjory was sure that was the right word. She felt comfortable in her presence, not overcome by shyness as she normally was. She placed the glass on the table and sat back in her chair and began to talk. Two hours later she stopped.

'Thank you,' she said.

'Whenever you feel the need to talk, about anything, come and see me. I'm always here.'

'I will.'

'On Wednesday, you were at the end of your period, weren't you?'

'How did you know that?'

'May I ask, do you have particularly heavy periods?'

'I don't know.'

'Do you have a great deal of blood flow?'

'I suppose so.'

'Some women don't, you see. Some only experience moderate bleeding. Others have copious discharges.'

'I'm like that.' Marjory took hold of her lemonade glass again and clutched it on her lap. The conversation embarrassed her and she was relieved when the older woman changed the subject.

'Where do you work?'

'Campbell's the confectioners. I work in the office. Filing mostly.'

'Do you aim to be a manager one day?'

'I shouldn't think so.'

'Why not?'

Marjory gave a nervous laugh but the older woman remained serious. 'Well, I only do filing and typing and such.'

'For now. That could change.'

'Do you think so?'

'It's not what I think that matters, Madge. What do you think?'

'I've never wondered about it.'

'Perhaps you should.'

*

In the kitchen Annie made a pot of tea and poured two cups. Conversation did not come readily. Topics were raised and quickly exhausted. Weather. Prices. Bob's gran. Annie's work.

'It must be terribly difficult,' Annie said, 'investigating the murder of somebody you know.'

'Aye,' said Bob. 'When I first lifted that hankie and saw Danny I thought I would be sick.' The room was gloomy, a single bulb in the middle of the ceiling offering scant illumination. A tap dripped into the sink. 'To be honest, I dinnae think I'm cut out for the polis.'

'Of course you are. You're a clever chap, and resourceful, and strong. You'll follow in Inspector Conoboy's footsteps one day.'

'I'm no' sure that's what I want.'

'What would you want?'

Bob was someone about whom assumptions were made. He had always known it. Other people plotted his course and he followed. The dominie at school. His gran. Inspector Conoboy. Bob knew what he wanted from life but had never articulated it. Now, without being conscious of deciding to do so, he spoke.

'What I'd really like is to hae a wee place where I could teach music. The fiddle. Bagpipes. Piano. Guitar.'

'Can you play all of those?'

'Aye.' He took her question as criticism of his plan. She considered it foolish. Him foolish. 'I dinnae suppose it would be awfae secure employment, though. I mean, if I had a family to support.'

'Oh, I'm sure you could make a success of it.'

He stared at her in surprise and found the courage to continue. 'What I thought was, maybe if I ran a wee café or something, and taught music in the back, that would help pay the bills. It would be like haein' two jobs.'

'You've thought it through.'

He became animated. 'I have, aye. I even ken where I'd like to have it. Crieff, it's a bonny wee toon. My gran comes fae Crieff.'

Annie refilled the kettle and laid it on the cooker and lit the gas. 'Will you have a day off on Sunday?' she said.

'Aye, as long as nothing happens with the case.'

'I wondered if maybe you'd care to invite me out for the day? That is, if you have no other plans?'

Bob's heart hammered in his chest. He splayed his hands on his legs to conceal their shaking. 'Aye,' he heard himself saying. 'That would be grand. Maybe a walk up Callerfountain?'

'Aye. Or maybe you could take me to Crieff? I've never been.'

The kitchen door opened and Bella Conoboy entered. Bob stood up.

'Madge is ready to go home now,' said Bella.

'Yes, ma'am,' said Bob.

Bella settled the lemonade glasses on the draining board. She turned to Bob. 'Have you had a pleasant evening?'

'Yes, ma'am.'

She looked at Annie. Annie gave a brief smile. Bella clapped her hands. 'Splendid.'

Marjory was putting on her coat when they joined her in the hallway. Annie followed from the kitchen.

130

'Beg your pardon, ma'am, but I wondered if I could ask Madge something?' Bella raised an eyebrow. 'We know each other a bit. We were at school together. I was two years above.'

'By all means.'

Annie smiled at Marjory. 'I wondered if you'd like to come for a walk with me tomorrow. It's my morning off. I thought perhaps you'd appreciate a chance to do something different.'

Marjory shook her head but Bella clapped her hands again. 'That's a grand idea, Annie,' she said. 'I only wish I could come with you.'

'Why don't you?' said Marjory.

'I find it difficult to get out of the house, my dear.' Bella patted Marjory's shoulder. 'But I know you'll have a lovely time.'

Marjory realised she had somehow committed to going and she wasn't sure how it had happened. She gave a tight smile as Bob led her to the car. She climbed in and he closed her door and walked round to the driver's seat. He pulled out the choke and turned the engine and it caught second time.

'PC Kelty,' said Marjory, 'would you mind awfully dropping me at the cemetery? I can walk home by myself afterwards, it's only a few minutes.'

'I was given orders, miss …'

'I know, and I don't like to ask, but really I want to go and see Danny and I can't during the day because of all those frightful sightseers. I just want five minutes with him.'

Bob drove without replying. He wasn't good at taking orders at the best of times. But now, now he had talked to Annie. And she hadn't laughed at his ideas. She believed him. She had asked him out. Orders? Orders be hanged. If the lassie wanted to be with her lad that was fine by him. He drove to the cemetery gates on Jeanfield Road and drew to a halt.

'Be careful, Madge.'

She thanked him and jumped out of the car and skipped into the cemetery. PC Marchant was guarding the graveside again and he retreated once more to leave her in peace. She sat down by the grave and stroked the grass.

'Hello, my love.' She told him about her evening, about Bella Conoboy. 'She's lovely, Dan. I've never met anyone like her. She understands me. Even better than I do, I think. She's so clever and wise. And she's got me thinking. She says I shouldn't just think about being a secretary. Maybe do an evening class, she said. What d'you think? Oh, it's probably just fancy talk.'

She said that she missed him and she still cried herself to sleep at night and woke up crying in the morning.

'D'you know what I read in the papers today?' she said. 'Shirley Temple's the most popular actress in the whole wide world. What do you make of that? If only I liked her, we would have gone to the pictures and none of this would have happened. Oh Danny, I'll never stop feeling guilty about that.' She lay down on the grave, her head resting beside the wooden cross that still marked it.

'One day, my love, I'll be in here, too. That much I know.'

*

Nellie Gammon put on her coat wearily. Her feet ached and her back was sore from standing. It was gone nine and she had been at Aberdalgie House since seven that morning. Now she had to walk home.

'Good night,' she said to Mrs Moon.

'Straight home, now,' said the head maid. 'Dinnae talk to anyone.'

'I'll not see anyone,' said Nellie but she was not as confident as she sounded. Even after nine days the Cuddies Strip terrified her and there was no pretending otherwise.

The wind was gusting as she climbed the shallow bank to the start of the strip. Dense trees plunged her into darkness. There was rustling in the undergrowth and the leaves joined in as though in conference. It was difficult to see where she was putting her feet. She stepped in a puddle of mud and shrieked in irritation. Come on, she scolded herself. I wish Johnny was here. He wouldn't be frightened. She looked straight ahead when she reached the whins where it happened. Nothing could persuade her to look in their direction. She rushed on and let out a small scream as she thought she heard something moving behind her. That was no rabbit. A deer? Or?

She began to run, following the route that Marjory Fenwick had taken nine days before, the route that she herself had taken eight days before, stumbling over the same exposed roots, struggling with the same low branches.

Behind her, the same man followed.

This time McGuigan kept back, keeping her in sight but not attempting to catch up. Chase was more stimulating than capture. The excitement of that night returned, the adrenalin, the anticipation, the ache of sexual tension. He had only intended on meeting Nellie to walk her home but now, now he was intent on something different.

He wouldn't do it tonight. He wasn't ready.

But he would do it.

Nellie was going to get it, too.

Wednesday 21st August

A Day of Last Chances

Bob Kelty looked at the alarm clock by his bed. Seven. He had a few minutes before he needed to get up to make Gran's breakfast. He smiled. Then he frowned. Then he smiled again. Was he really going on a date? With Annie Maybury?

There was a loud banging on the bedroom door. 'You lazy wee bastard,' Gran shouted. 'Nearly midday and not even up yet.'

'It's only seven, Gran.'

'Bone idle all your life.' She stomped away and Bob sighed and sat up in bed. He looked at himself in the wardrobe mirror.

'Another day begins,' he said.

*

When Conoboy carried in the breakfast tray Bella was already propped up in bed and reading the new Marjory Allingham from the library. He placed a pot of tea by the bedside table and positioned the small table across her knees. Steam rose from a plate of porridge.

'She's a lovely child,' Bella said.

'She has something, doesn't she?'

'She's fragile, though. She needs help. To get through this.'

'I fear so. I fear it may get worse before it gets better.'

Bella nodded. 'Would you mind opening the curtains?' she said. 'Half way.'

Conoboy contained his surprise and crossed the bedroom and pulled the thick curtains apart. Light chased across the room as though in search of areas long kept hidden. Motes of dust flickered in the sun. In ten minutes, Bella's bed would be basking in sunshine. For the first time in who knew how many years.

*

A heavy shower settled over Kirkton of Mailer farm, bringing activity to a temporary halt. Conversation turned, as it generally did in the days following the crime, to the murder on the Cuddies Strip. Sandy Arnott spoke.

'Robert Brown was telling me the polis are trying to make him cut the two wheat fields below the Strip. They think the murderer might have hidden the shotgun there.'

Charles Elder shook his head. 'He wouldnae go that way. Too open. You could be seen from all around.'

'It was dark.'

'It was a full moon. You would still have seen a body walkin' through the fields.'

'He could have hidden ahint the dykes,' said John McGuigan.

'The dykes dinnae run the whole way. Anyway, he'd still have to go through open ground afore he made it to the woods at Callerfountain.'

Arnott agreed. 'He'd have come out of the Strip at the Dunning road. Straight over and into the woods to the west. From there you could get on the low road and no' be seen for hours. Plenty places tae hide a shotgun, too.'

McGuigan shrugged his shoulders. 'Aye. You know best.'

'Anyhow, Robert's adamant. They're no harvestin' that field till he's ready.'

135

Inspector Conoboy shook the farmer's hand. 'Mr Brown, it really is of the utmost importance ...'

'So's my harvest. Another couple days winnae make ony difference to you. It will to me. I need to get the bottom fields done first and then I'll be able to do your fields. Once I start it'll only take a week or so. If there's onything in that field the stookers will find it.'

Conoboy sighed. The brief rain had been replaced by bright sunshine and the day was growing hotter and hotter. He found it wearying. Hard to concentrate.

'Tomorrow,' he said.

'Aye,' said Brown. 'Or Friday.' They parted and Conoboy trudged towards his car.

*

The morning case conference grew increasingly tetchy. MacNaughton did not attempt to conceal his anger, Conoboy was taciturn to the point of insubordination and Braggan was scathing about almost everything. Bob, allergic to confrontation, stood uncomfortably and listened.

'The amateur detectives have been in again,' Braggan said. He placed two shotgun cartridges on MacNaughton's desk, the red cardboard casings already disintegrating.

'Do we think they're the killer's?' said MacNaughton.

'They may well be. They're the right type. But the idiot who brought them in can't tell us exactly where he found them so they're useless.'

'Any chance of fingerprints?'

'Too damp. We need to stop these amateur idiots from picking things up.'

'I'll mention it at the press conference. It would have helped, of course, if it was our officers who discovered them first.'

'There's nothing to suggest these weren't left there after Wednesday,' said Conoboy.

'Are you suggesting someone's been up the Cuddies Strip since, shooting a 12-bore shotgun? With half of Perth out there sightseeing?'

Braggan broke the ensuing silence. 'I'd like to discuss Marjory Fenwick, sir.'

'Go ahead,' said MacNaughton.

'She told us, quite explicitly, that the boy had a pocketbook on him that night. "He showed me it," she said.'

'Yes.'

'We found the pocketbook in Kerrigan's room yesterday.'

'Could she have been mistaken?'

'She was most definite.'

'It might have been a different pocketbook,' said Bob.

'Why would a boy have two pocketbooks?' said Braggan.

'He got one for Christmas, Marjory told us. Perhaps he already had another. Wanted to keep the new one for best.'

'She described this one.'

'She might have just assumed it was that one and described it from memory. She would have been interested in the contents, not the pocketbook.'

'Marjory Fenwick never seems interested in anything much. Anyway, we also found his inhaler and the chain and pendant. How do you explain that?'

'She wasn't certain about those. She only said it was a possibility he had them.' Bob stared at Braggan. Conoboy watched with wry admiration. Well done, Robert, he thought. Sticking up for yourself.

'Haven't you got a beat to walk, City boy?' said Braggan. He turned to MacNaughton. 'I believe there's more to her than meets the eye, sir. I've never been comfortable with her story. Too much of it makes no sense. Chasing her. Stripping her naked. It's not typical behaviour.'

Conoboy exhaled heavily. Marjory Fenwick was the one innocent in this whole affair and here they were, wasting time investigating her. It was madness. 'I see no reason to disbelieve her, sir,' he said. 'Her story has been consistent throughout …'

'The Procurator Fiscal didn't agree,' said MacNaughton.

'The Procurator Fiscal suggested there were inconsistencies in minor details like the description of the killer. That is understandable. If anything, we would prefer that. Repeated statements that sound too familiar are suspicious. As though they've been rehearsed. But Marjory has always sounded like she's genuinely seeking to remember what happened. And in the explanation of the main events she has been entirely consistent. Remember, Dr Murphy agrees she was attacked.'

'The virginity thing bothers me,' said Braggan.

'Why?' said Conoboy. 'How is it relevant?'

'If she's been lying about that, what else has she lied about?'

'You don't know she is lying.'

'Dr Murphy's statement strongly suggests it.'

MacNaughton raised his hand. 'The Procurator Fiscal has already instigated a further medical examination,' he said. 'I agree with Braggan that we need to consider the girl very carefully.' He pointed to Conoboy. 'Have you anything useful I can present at today's press conference?'

'Investigations are ongoing.'

MacNaughton slammed his fist on the desk. 'Enough,' he shouted. 'Have something constructive for me to say. Is that clear?'

Cononboy and Bob exchanged glances. They both rose and left the room. Bob fixed his helmet on his head and said goodbye to the inspector and walked into afternoon sunshine. He headed for County Place and the police box, his new favourite refuge.

Marjory Fenwick and Annie Maybury strode the last few metres to the top of Callerfountain Hill.

'Made it,' said Annie.

'That was steeper than I expected,' said Marjory, puffing heavily.

'But worth it. Look at that view.'

Marjory turned in a circle. 'Which one's Kinnoull Hill?' she asked.

Annie looked around and pointed. Kinnoull Hill was proud and angular behind Perth, to the north west of them. To the east the Strathearn valley paraded in its finery, the river Earn looping through its centre. Kirkton of Mailer and Woodhead of Mailer farms lay at the foot of the hill, golden fields rippling in the breeze. Sunshine lit the valley. The noises of harvest filtered upwards, horsemen calling to their horses, stookers following behind, the bustle of human activity.

'I just love it up here,' said Annie. 'It's like you're above everything, away from it all.'

'I know. Down in town, everything's so claustrophobic. It's like I'm suffocating. Mum won't let me out alone. I'm in the house all day. The only people I ever speak to are the police, asking me the same questions over and over.'

'It must be awful.'

'I just want to be a normal girl. If I go out in Perth, everyone gawps at me. "There she is, that's the one." I'm like a zoo exhibit.' Her tightly permed hair waved in the wind, wisps blowing into her eyes. She wiped them away and thrust her hands into her coat pockets. 'It's little Princess Margaret Rose's birthday today,' she said. 'She's five. She's going to have a lifetime of that to look forward to. Always on show. Poor mite. What a life.'

'Aye. I'd hate to be famous like that.'

139

'Her whole life is going to be mapped out for her. What she'll do. Who she'll marry. How she behaves. Every moment. When will she ever become herself?'

'What do you want to do with your life?'

'I really don't know. Mrs Conoboy asked me that, too. I've always just expected to work in the factory and then get married and have children and be a housewife.'

'That doesn't sound so bad.'

'I'm not saying it is. But is there anything else?'

'I suppose it's up to you to decide.'

She stared out over the valley. 'I'm not sure I'm up to making decisions yet.'

Annie took the smaller girl's hand. She seemed little changed from when they'd been at school, younger than her years, vulnerable.

'Are you doing anything on Sunday?' she said.

'I never do anything anymore.'

'Bob's taking me out for the day to Crieff. Would you care to come?'

'PC Kelty? Are you sweethearts with him?'

'Not yet. But I'm hoping.'

'I wouldn't want to be a gooseberry.'

'We're not real sweethearts, so it would be grand. To be honest, Bob will probably be relieved. He's very shy, really.'

'Yes.' Marjory laughed. 'Mum calls him the blate bobby.'

'He's not had an easy life. His mother died in childbirth. His father killed himself when Bob was fourteen. It was Bob who found the body. He was sent to live with his gran. That's when I got to know him, at Hillyland School.'

'I don't remember him.'

'He was two years older than me, so that would make him about four years older than you. You probably wouldn't have noticed him.'

'Maybe not.'

'He hardly spoke for the first two years. He lived inside

himself. He always looked terrified. It's only in the last year or so he's stopped doing that.'

'Poor man.'

'So he might find it easier if you came too. Will you?'

A smile lit up Marjory's face. 'I'd love to.'

*

John McGuigan sloped up the marble entrance of the Sandeman Public Libary and queued at the counter. He handed over two books, one on fishing and the other on Scottish history, and waited until the suited assistant located the cards on the Browne issue trays and handed him two manila library tickets. Mr James Oram, they said. 6, Pomarium.

'Ta,' said McGuigan. He climbed a large stairway, imposing, twelve-feet wide, turning one-hundred and eighty degrees and leading to the reference library on the first floor. He pushed open heavy wooden doors and entered a silent room filled with bright August sunshine. Around the corner was the newspaper room and he took a copy of *The Courier* from the rack and sat at a wooden bench and spread it out. He turned to the local news. *Perth Murder: New Girl Witness.* He read of Elizabeth Gray and her sighting of a man in the whins on the night of the murder.

'Well spotted,' he said. He read about the escalating tension in Abyssinia, the difficulties for the government, the latest incursions of the state in Germany into the personal lives of its inhabitants. Ten minutes before the library was due to close he returned downstairs to the non-fiction room and selected a history of Perthshire he'd read twice before and a book on country lore. He joined the queue at the counter and in turn handed his books to a tall assistant, one he hadn't seen before, a young man with a face much scarred by acne. The assistant looked at the tickets McGuigan offered and

141

then looked up at McGuigan.

'Are you Mr Oram?' he said.

'Aye.'

'What address?'

'6, Pomarium. Like it says.'

'I live in Pomarium. I've never seen you.'

'Keep myself to myself, ken?'

'I'm sure Mr Oram's an older gentleman.'

'That'll be my faither.'

The assistant waved to the librarian watching from the enquiry desk. The queue behind McGuigan grew restless. McGuigan looked nonchalant.

'Mr Oram?' said the librarian. 'Would you mind coming to my office?' McGuigan was escorted back upstairs and they crossed a wide landing to the staff quarters. McGuigan was guided into a book-lined office facing onto Kinnoull Street. The librarian rounded an impressive teak desk and sat facing him. He placed his elbows on the desk.

'You are not Mr Oram, are you?'

'No.'

'What is your name?'

'John McGuigan.'

'And why are you using Mr Oram's tickets?' The librarian frowned over metal-rimmed glasses. If he was trying to appear frightening it didn't work. McGuigan relaxed.

'I found them in the street. A couple of years ago. I've been using them ever since. Every fortnight.'

'And why don't you arrange a membership of your own?'

'I live in a tent. On Kirkton of Mailer farm. Would you give me a membership?'

'In those circumstances, no.'

'There you are then.'

'I shall have to notify the police.'

For the first time McGuigan betrayed some nervousness. 'Why?' he said. 'I've done no harm. I bring the books back

142

on time.'

The librarian reflected. The man before him was clearly a rough sort, a tinker no doubt, but he did not appear unintelligent. So many of that type gave the impression of being vacant behind the eyes and this lad was different. Maybe he deserved a chance.

'Very well,' he said. 'I shall not report you. I shall have to confiscate these cards, of course.'

'Can I have a card of my own?'

'That wouldn't be appropriate.'

McGuigan stood up. An instant anger boiled up inside him at the realisation his only access to reading had been terminated. He walked out of the library and onto Kinnoull Street. He lit up a cigarette and felt the anger grow and grow and he knew it would have to be released somehow.

*

'Mr Pritchard is in your office, sir,' said Bob. 'Wants to make a statement.' Bob had spent a couple of hours at the police box. He only had a handful of laundries still to contact, down in the borders, and he would have stayed longer to finish the job but he feared Braggan's temper if he disappeared for too long. Irritatingly, Braggan had made no comment on seeing his arrival.

Conoboy looked up wearily. 'Excellent, Robert. Let's see what light he can shed on our imponderable mystery.'

He introduced himself to Pritchard, an obese man with balding, greying hair, perhaps fifty-years old and a regular drinker, to judge by the veins on his nose and cheeks.

'I live on Queen Street,' he said, 'number sixteen. On the night of the murder, late, about eleven o'clock, I was takin' the dug for a walk ...'

'At eleven o'clock?'

'It's auld. Pishes and shites roond the clock. If I dinnae

let it oot at that time it stinks the hoose oot by morning.'

'I see.'

'The front door's sair in need of a bit oil and makes a hell of a noise when you open it. So I opened it that night and there was a man just ootside, walking past the hoose. He got a fleg fae the door and turned and scarpered back the way he came. At the corner he turned onto Murray's Brae but he must hae gotten another fleg because a few seconds later he was runnin' back doon Queen Street again. Like a whippet. Then he ran up William Street and disappeared.'

Conoboy made notes but he did not think Mr Pritchard's story was in any way significant.

'What I was thinkin was, if he came fae Buckie Braes by the Friarton quarry, the place he'd arrive at would be Queen Street, would it no'? And the timing would be richt. The murder was back o' ten, aye?'

'Around then.'

'It's aboot three miles fae Buckie Braes across country by Craigie Knowes to Queen Street. thirty, forty minutes. That would fit, aye?'

'What did he look like?'

'Aboot five-seven or eight. Dark claes. Dark coloured cap.'

'Did you see his face?'

'Nut.'

They asked a few more questions but garnered nothing further of use. Bob escorted Pritchard out of the station and returned to the office. 'What do you think sir?'

'It may be the man, Robert, but if it is, what good does it do us? All we know is he may be in Perth. We knew that anyway.'

'Yes, sir. I only imagined, given what the Acting Chief Constable said this morning, you'd be keen to present him with a new lead.'

Conoboy rose without replying. Because MacNaughton

had asked for something was a very good reason not to provide it.

'Would you like me to investigate it, sir?'

'Not for the time being.'

'As you wish, sir.'

Bob walked through the building to the toilets and sat in a cubicle and locked the door. Grey walls surrounded him. He placed his head in his hands and closed his eyes and tried to free his mind of thought. These little steps forwards, they were almost worse than making no progress. Hope, minimal hope, dangling before them like a torment. The inspector felt the same, he was sure. He froze as the toilet door opened and people entered.

'You still on for later?' said one, and Bob recognised the voice of Sergeant Braggan.

'Aye.' Bob couldn't make out the voice. Jones, perhaps?

'And you've got the wherewithal?'

'Of course.'

Bob heard the clinking of an exchange of money. Then he heard the sound of someone pissing into the urinal.

'Excellent,' said Braggan. 'Couple of new faces coming, too.' Whoever it was at the urinal finished and the two men left and Bob was left to ponder in silence.

*

Clothing continued to appear through the day, from as far afield as Crianlarich and Lochgelly. It was bundled up and Bob took it to Marjory in the afternoon. Marjory made no mention of Sunday, thinking it best that Annie explain it to him. She shook her head at each item she was shown.

'You wouldn't credit how much clothing there seems to be just lying about,' she said. Bob agreed and parcelled it up again. He knew he should return to the station but he couldn't face Braggan and his bullying. He cycled home

145

instead and left the bundle of clothing in the hall and checked on Gran. She was sleeping and he made her a potted meat paste sandwich and left it by her chair, then cycled out to Buckie Braes and walked to the Cuddies Strip.

He stood at the stile where Marjory was caught and surveyed the rough grass where she was raped. A heaviness came over him, a weariness at the trouble of life. He fought it, looked around, tried to appreciate the countryside, the rolling valley, its enclosing hills. Be positive, Bob. But darkness was never far away, ready to overwhelm his senses if he permitted it. Then the memories would begin again. The visions. Blood-spattered walls. The body of his father on the floor, shotgun. The end of childhood. Innocence lost.

'Hello.'

Bob gave a start and looked around. Richard Hamill was standing beside him. They shook hands.

'Grand day,' said Hamill.

'Aye.'

'Doin' some reconnaissance?'

'Just lookin'.'

'Are you making any progress?'

'Investigations are ongoing.'

'It's okay. I'm not fishing for information.'

'You seem to be up here a lot.'

'Yes. That identity parade on Thursday. It bothered me. I saw the girl, the pain in her eyes. Terror. No one should have to go through that.'

'No.'

'So I've been trying to help. I'm afraid you all think I'm a terrible nuisance.'

'No' really.'

'Oh, you do. It's okay. I don't mind. Coming here and looking for clues, it helps. That's all.'

'Helps what?'

'Me. To think I'm being useful. Most people think I'm a

waste of space.'

Bob gave a hollow laugh. 'Talking of which, I'd better be gettin' back.'

*

Further sightings were reported. The vagrant who threatened Mrs McCann in Newburgh approached another woman in a caravan but was beaten off by her Cairn Terrier. Fife police reported an extensive search of Sir John Gilmour's estate at Montrave after a coal merchant saw a tramp carrying a brown paper parcel and looking 'wild and bewildered'. Nothing was found.

In the afternoon, house-to-house enquiries in Queen Street offered corroboration of William Pritchard's sighting on the night of the murder. Vina Murray, ferocious in a black dress and white pinny, scowled at PC McNab as though what she was relaying was somehow his fault. 'There was some daft galoot runnin' aboot outside,' she said, 'makin' a nuisance of himself. I opened my windae to shout at him but he made off afore I had the chance'.

'Did you see where he went?'

'Up William Street and into the wee lane runnin' off it.'

'You're sure?'

'You can see it frae my bedroom windae. Not that I'm lettin' you in to see.'

'No, that won't be necessary.'

*

A thick fug of cigarette smoke hung over the back room of the Cherrybank Inn. The heat was stifling. John McGuigan stared at the half empty pint of ale in front of him, his fifth. And last. He was not a big drinker and it lay heavily in his stomach and made him dizzy. The room was beginning to swim. He closed an eye and tried to focus on the bar. He feared he might be sick and heaved himself out of his seat, grabbed his jacket and staggered outside. He sucked in air, three or four deep breaths, and immediately felt better. He swore and began to walk towards Buckie Braes. There was a young man coming towards him, dressed in a tweed suit and tartan tie, ready for a night in town. Probably meeting a girl. Having a good time. Bastard.

He knew he was going to hit the boy but it still surprised him when he did. As they crossed on the path he swung his arm and landed a heavy punch on the boy's left cheek. The lad wouldn't have even seen it coming. He collapsed to the ground and lay motionless and McGuigan walked on as though nothing had happened. He was sure he heard the crack of bone.

In the gloom of dusk he climbed through Buckie Braes and followed the dyke by the side of the fields until he reached the stile at the Cuddies Strip. He found the spot to where he had dragged Marjory. The spot where he chased Nellie last night. He looked around. There was no one to be seen. Hurriedly, he unbuckled his trousers and fell to the ground. He took a pair of ladies' gloves out of his pocket and with difficulty forced the right glove over his hand. He pulled out a blue gingham top, the one he had taken from Nellie's wash basket the day before, and he buried his face in it and smelled her on it and with the glove he masturbated to the memory of what he had done and the vision of what he was going to do.

And a sudden perfect plan formed in his mind. He would do it here.

Again.

Properly this time. All the way.

He came into the blouse.

148

*

MacNaughton exhaled deeply and stubbed out his cigarette. Conoboy sat listlessly. They looked up as the door opened and Lord Kellett walked in. He wore a grim expression and sat down without acknowledging either man.

'George Gray rang me from the Home Office late this afternoon. Their patience has run out.'

'We're leading a very complex investigation,' said Conoboy.

'I don't doubt it. And with considerable skill, too.'

'Thank you, sir.'

'Do you anticipate making any arrests?'

'Not at this stage.'

'Has any of Marjory Fenwick's clothing been traced?'

'No, sir.'

'Nor the shotgun?'

'We will begin harvesting the fields to the south of the Cuddies Strip as soon as possible.'

'This is a murder enquiry. Couldn't they have been harvested sooner?' There was silence. MacNaughton lit a cigarette. So did Kellett. 'What about the laundry mark on the handkerchief?' he said. 'Has that been traced?'

'No.'

Kellett turned to MacNaughton. 'That whisky bottle you keep in the drawer,' he said. 'Get it out.' MacNaughton produced a three-quarters empty bottle of Bell's and poured the remains into three tumblers. The men sipped slowly.

'I've been instructed,' said Kellett. 'I have made a formal request to Glasgow City Police for support. First thing tomorrow morning they will be joining us.' He swallowed another mouthful of whisky. 'I'm sorry, Victor, but we have to recognise their greater expertise in these matters. Once a secondment is agreed you will immediately hand over

responsibility for the investigation.'
   'Yes, sir.'

Thursday 22nd August

A Day of Takeover

Bob scanned Gran's expression to gauge her mood. He had come to recognise her cycles of behaviour and he knew that, in the days following one of her disappearances, she would shift from confusion to frustration and finally to anger. The anger would last a few days and she would mellow and become, once more, like the gran he used to know.

Then the cycle would begin again.

He could tell that anger was imminent. Her eyes were blank and her mouth was drawn back in a rictus. 'Whaur have you been?' she shouted.

'Makin' your breakfast.'

'For two days?'

'No, Gran.'

'Two days you've left me here on my ain.'

'I put you to bed last night, Gran.'

'Liar. You're a selfish little bastard. Just like that hoor of a mother of yours.'

He sighed. 'I'll leave your breakfast by the bed. I'm sorry, I need to get to work. It's going to be a long day.'

'How d'you think it is for me, stuck here day after day?' She shifted in the bed and winced and cursed.

'If only you could be happy,' he said.

She clattered her cutlery on the plate and sat back in the bed and Bob was taken aback by the intensity of her expression. 'Aye, son, I wasnae always like this.' She picked

151

up her spoon again and began to eat automatically.

*

The men from Glasgow were already there when Conoboy arrived.

'What time did they get here?' he asked Bob.

'Before eight, sir. Mr MacNaughton asked you to join them as soon as you arrived.'

'Naturally.' He hung up his mackintosh. 'Could you bring me a cup of tea?'

Bob grinned. 'Of course, sir.'

Conoboy unfolded *The Courier* and turned to the international news. With the Geneva talks breaking down and war in Abyssinia inevitable, the Cabinet had returned from their various holidays and met for two hours the previous evening. Any war in Africa, next door to British territory, would most likely draw Britain into the conflict. Conoboy read the reports with despair. Violence, the remedy of lunatics throughout history. He looked up as Bob returned with his tea.

'What do you make of our guests?' he asked.

'Well,' said Bob, 'it's very interesting, sir. One of them is Assistant Chief Inspector Warnock.' He paused but Conoboy showed no sign of recognition. 'The Mills case, sir? In the papers last month?'

'Vaguely.'

'James Mills was convicted of murdering his stepmother in Glasgow in April and sentenced to death. The defence appealed, saying there were irregularities in the process. One of those related to Mr Warnock.'

'What irregularities?'

'Mills "confessed" to Warnock and that confession was used in court. But the defence alleged it wasn't a real confession. It was a conversation between Mills and

Warnock which Warnock then wrote up later.'

'That's not allowed.'

'Exactly. So it went to appeal last month and the Lord Chief Justice heard it and declared the verdict unsafe.'

'And this is the expert sent to help our investigation?'

'Yes, sir.'

'Heaven help us.' When he finished his tea he knocked on MacNaughton's door and entered an office full of false bonhomie. A small man rose and introduced himself as Chief Constable Sillitoe. The second man, taller, gruff and avuncular, rose and Conoboy knew the handshake would be painful. It was.

'Gentlemen,' he said, 'I greatly appreciate your assistance.'

'It's a devilish case,' said Warnock.

'Must be a terrible strain on your resources,' said Sillitoe.

'Indeed,' said MacNaughton. 'We're not one of the largest forces, despite the size of the county.'

Conoboy studied Warnock. There was no indication in his comportment that this was a man who as recently as a month before had been partly to blame for a miscarriage of justice. Had that been Conoboy, he would never have been able to face work again. Where did such confidence come from? Was it a good thing?

'We'll provide two men,' said Sillitoe. 'Watters certainly. Probably Lamping but I need to agree that with CID first.'

'Of course,' said Conoboy. 'We must always follow due process.' He looked at Warnock. Warnock said nothing.

'Now,' said Sillitoe, 'we are particularly keen to see the scene of the crime.'

'Crimes,' said Conoboy. 'The girl was raped, too.'

'Indeed. Is it far?'

'A ten-minute drive. Followed by a fifteen-minute hike.'

'Over rough terrain?'

'Oh no.' Conoboy turned to go. 'Once you're accustomed to it.'

On the Strip, half a dozen amateur detectives remained, bent over the ground at the spots where Danny Kerrigan was shot and Marjory Fenwick raped. A full sun made it hot work. The whins rustled, dry as dust beneath the trees. Casual chatter resounded through the usually quiet stretch, the questers joined in friendly rivalry.

Richard Hamill, most successful of them to date, was about to strike it lucky. Half an hour before he had found, close to the whins from which it was believed the murderer fired, another shotgun case. This was the third to be discovered, he knew, and it was thought that only three shots were fired. He had pocketed the case, intending to take it to the station in the afternoon. Now, he could see approaching a congregation of senior officers, their suit buttons gleaming in the sun. He recognised MacNaughton and Conoboy and could tell from their uniforms that the other two were equally senior. Outside help, he supposed.

'Are these all amateur sleuths?' said Sillitoe.

'Indeed,' said MacNaughton. 'They've been virtually camped out on the Strip since the murder. As you can see the grass is so long it's difficult to undertake a definitive search.'

'I imagine the whole area was cordoned off initially. To allow forensic search?'

'Of course.'

Liar, thought Richard Hamill.

'Why, what's this?' he shouted. He took the case from his pocket and leaned into the whins and rose up with it between his thumb and forefinger. 'Excuse me,' he said to the gathering of policemen, 'I think I may have just found something.' He slipped the case into MacNaughton's hand. 'That must be the third and final case,' he said.

'Where did you find this?'

'Right there. Right now.'

'That was a fortuitous discovery,' said Sillitoe. He stared coldly at Hamill. Hamill gave an ingenuous smile.

A cry came up from behind them, near the spot where Danny fell. Gerry Coburn, a lanky youth of eighteen, raised up with his hand in the air. 'I've found something,' he said. 'Just this second.'

'How remarkable,' said Sillitoe. He and Warnock exchanged glances, expressions masked into nothingness. The youth showed them his find, a fragment from a pearl button. Conoboy recognised it immediately.

'That's from Kerrigan's shirt,' he said.

'What an industrious group of explorers you have here,' said Sillitoe. 'If only we could harness those skills for official endeavours.'

Hamill glowered at Coburn, his moment of glory cruelly eclipsed.

'The farmer who owns these fields,' said Warnock. 'Does he live far from here?'

'Kirkton of Mailer,' said MacNaughton.

'Which is nearby?'

'A mile down there.'

'I wish to speak with him.'

'He's a feisty character.'

'As am I.'

William Brown was reaping the bottom field. His drivers and stookers took advantage of an unexpected break and watched the subsequent meeting curiously. MacNaughton made the introductions. William Brown appeared disinterested.

'The fields below the Cuddies Strip,' said Warnock. 'It is possible the killer concealed the murder weapon there.'

'Aye. And if he did we'll find it when we start the harvest.'

'That's what I wish to speak to you regarding. The harvest will commence this afternoon.'

'We've still got this field to finish. Tomorrow afternoon,

if it doesnae rain.'

'The harvest of those fields will commence at two o'clock this afternoon. Either your experienced farmhands will do it, or I will sequester your machinery and horses and my policemen will undertake the task instead. They will not be as expert as your men, of course, but they'll do their best. It's your choice.'

Without waiting for an answer he turned and walked away. The others followed. William Brown watched them go.

*

PC McNab made sure to avoid Vina Murray's house as he walked up Queen Street and turned onto William Street. The houses were compact and tidy. Women with babies on their hips stood in doorways and watched his progress.

'Have ye no' caught him yet?' shouted a gap-toothed, greying woman of around forty. 'We're scared to go oot, you ken.'

You'll be safe enough, hen, McNab thought. He was in his mid-twenties, possessed of a confidence greater than his ability warranted. He paused at the close leading off William Street and looked into it. Small and narrow, functional but falling into disrepair, it had stone steps turning up to the first floor entrances. The further he penetrated the more dilapidated it became. At the far end, shielded by the terrace, sunlight was a sparse commodity. Rubbish was lined against the outside of a semi-derelict building, sacks and boxes and assorted junk. An old chair, three-legged and tottering. A doorless cupboard. There would be rats, probably. McNab shivered.

Something moved and he recoiled, trying to make out any discernible shape among the detritus. Then he did. It was a man, reclining against the wall for all the world

156

like he was on a chaise longue in a fashionable west end sitting room. He was a tramp, filthy and unshaven and his eyes suggested he had succeeded the previous evening in acquiring a significant amount of alcohol.

McNab kicked his foot. The man shifted and groaned and looked up.

'What?' he said.

'Who are you?' said McNab.

'Who are you?'

'Don't be cheeky.'

'Sonny, I'm forty-seven. You're no' even shavin' yet. Dinnae talk to me about cheeky.'

'What's your name?'

'Frank Norie-Miller.'

'One more comment like that and I'll arrest you.'

'Stick it up your arse.'

PC McNab looked around. Already a crowd had gathered. There was laughter, jeering. Comments were made, scabrous, scandalous, slanderous. People hung out of windows to watch. He recognised a couple of urchins from James Street who customarily gave him cheek. Should they not be in school?

He grabbed the tramp and lifted him from the ground. The man stank. He cursed copiously and tried to shrug himself free but McNab's grip on his shoulder remained firm.

'I was doin' nothin',' he shouted. 'Arrested for havin' a kip, is it?' He played to the crowd as McNab marched him off, limping as though struggling against police brutality.

They were followed the whole way to the station by a crowd, initially forty or fifty, growing to three-hundred or more as they entered the South Street entrance and, once more, the roads of Perth were blocked by a crowd of men and women staring up at the County Police headquarters.

McNab approached the front desk. 'Sergeant, I've apprehended the man from Queen Street reported by Mr

Pritchard and Mrs Murray.'

'Stick him in the interview room,' said Strangeway, more concerned about the racket outside and the effect it would have on the guests recently returned from the Cuddies Strip. He closed the front door and went in search of Inspector Conoboy.

'What's all the noise, Sergeant?' said Acting Chief Constable MacNaughton. The Glasgow guests followed him into the hallway.

'McNab brought in a man for questioning, sir. The Queen Street sighting. There's a crowd gathered outside to watch.'

'Is this a credible sighting?' said Sillitoe.

'I believe so, sir. He was first seen in town on the night of the murder. The timings would be about right.'

Conoboy appeared, followed by Bob. 'Where is he, Sergeant?' said Conoboy.

'Main interview room, sir.'

Conoboy and Bob headed for the interview room and MacNaughton, Sillitoe and Warnock followed. The vagrant looked up as they entered.

'Blimey,' he said. 'All this for me?' He grinned. 'Morning Bob,' he said to Bob Kelty. 'Any chance of a cuppa? Two sugars.'

Bob closed his eyes. 'Morning Wattie,' he said.

'That's four times you've arrested me now.'

MacNaughton turned and walked out of the room, followed by the others.

'Tea?' said Wattie.

'Aye,' said Bob.

*

Richard Hamill walked along the path from Buckie Braes to Kirkton of Mailer. Sun shone and the valley stretched open and free all around, rising towards the Campsie Hills surrounding Perth. Three horses pulled William Brown's reaper towards the top field beneath the Cuddies Strip, their black and brown flanks rippling sleek in the sunshine, white-topped hooves measuring out a slow and steady progress. As he walked he scanned the ditch at the side of the path. Beneath a hawthorn bush he saw a shape that appeared unusual, an unnatural bulge in the long grass. He stepped across a muddy line of water and reached down. A clump of grass came away in his hand and concealed beneath was a piece of fabric. He lifted it out and shook it. It was a gingham blouse, apparently in good condition, almost new, but somewhat stained.

Well, he thought, that didn't get here by accident. He searched more closely around the spot and found a pair of ladies' leather gloves. He gathered them up and made his way back to Buckie Braes and into town.

*

Within the space of an hour three new bundles of clothing were handed in at the County Police station. A police officer from Dundee brought some men's clothing found in Lochee.

'I don't suppose it's related,' he said, 'but I thought I'd better bring it in anyway.'

Sergeant Strangeway thanked him and stowed it in the rear office along with the items previously handed in. When he returned to the desk an elderly woman dressed entirely in black was waiting. She had come especially from Broughty Ferry, she said.

'I found these in my shed. They're no' mines.'

Strangeway shook them out of the bag. There was some women's underclothing, old and faded and frayed, and a tramwayman's jacket, past any serviceable life. He took her details and added the clothing to the collection. Within the hour a man arrived with a bag of men's and women's shoes and a pair of men's trousers that were more hole than fabric. Strangeway gathered these, too, and took them into the rear. As he did, Sillitoe and Warnock approached.

'What is all this stuff?' said Sillitoe.

'Items brought in by the public and other police forces.'

Warnock rummaged through it. He pulled out the old trousers and shoes. 'What are you?' he said. 'A bloody jumble sale?' He threw them down and picked up the tramwayman's jacket.

'We're looking for a young woman's skirt and undergarments. Why on earth would you accept this rubbish?'

'Sergeant,' said Sillitoe, 'I think you need to remove this material and concentrate on more productive lines of enquiry.'

Strangeway bristled. Arrogant bastards. The fact they were right made it worse. He shouted for Kelty and ordered him to clear the piles into the yard.

Richard Hamill arrived at the station an hour later. He showed the sergeant his latest discovery. 'The blouse has got a label on it,' he said. 'Nellie Gammon.'

'Which rather proves it doesn't belong to Marjory Fenwick, doesn't it?' said Strangeway.

'But the way it was concealed is suspicious. And so close to the Cuddies Strip ...'

Strangeway cut him off irritably. He had no intention of accepting any further clothing today, not with those Glesga keelie busybodies watching his every move.

'Thank you,' he said, 'but it's clearly not related to our current investigation. If a crime involving anyone called Nellie Gammon is reported we'll be in touch.'

'What should I do with it?'

'If you give it a wash it might just fit you.'

Strangeway turned to the station duty log and flicked the page ostentatiously. He shouted for Kelty.

'We've had two separate reports from people on the Dundee train that they've seen what looks like a pistol lying at the side of the track near Friarton,' he said. 'Go with McNab and find it.'

*

At two o'clock, Robert Brown, son of William Brown, clicked his three horses and they started to drag the ageing reaper in the westernmost field beneath the Cuddies Strip. Beside him, his father operated the sheafing rake. A line of men walked behind, gathering the sheaves and forming them into stooks with four heads together in a pyramid shape. They progressed ponderously. It would take a week to complete both fields. Robert Brown lit a cigarette and shouted encouragement to the horses. His face was red beneath his flat cap. His waistcoat was tight around his stomach. The heat from the afternoon sun was intense. Wheat glinted gold and silver in the glare and the sky was an unblemished expanse of blue. Children's laughter drifted in the wind from Buckie Braes. A man walked along the path to the Cuddies Strip, his girl on his arm. Sparrows swooped in the air. A hawk hovered over the still ground. The sound of a motor car could be heard on the Dunning road, heading towards Aberdalgie. The lightest wind threaded through the trees.

*

Bob and McNab returned just before five. Bob was an alarming shade of red. He pulled out a handkerchief and unwrapped an ageing pistol, a point 22 in such poor condition it did not appear useable.

'They must have good eyesight, the folk who saw this from the train,' he said. 'It was in light grass on the banking. We missed it first time.'

161

'Good work,' said Strangeway.

Sillitoe, who much to the sergeant's irritation had been hovering all afternoon, picked up the weapon and inspected it carefully.

'Did you know it was a pistol when you went to look for it?' he said.

'Yes,' said Strangeway. 'Two separate people reported it …'

'What was the murder weapon?'

'A shotgun.'

'So why have you wasted two officers for two hours retrieving a pistol?'

'Well, it's not something we would want lying around. It might go off.'

'Granted. But did you have to use officers engaged in the murder enquiry? Could you not have passed it to the City boys?'

Kelty is a City boy, Strangeway wanted to say. He looked at Bob, who gave his usual self-deprecating smile.

Sillitoe didn't wait for an answer and Strangeway watched him depart. Fuck off, you arrogant bastard, he breathed.

*

The bus station in Leonard Street was new and still smelled of paint. There were fifteen or so bays but only two were occupied, one by a red bus heading for Stirling and the other by a Midland Bluebird going to Crieff and Lochearnhead. John McGuigan threw his cigarette end on the pavement and swung open the office door. An elderly man in a threadbare three-piece suit and a mismatching brown bunnet was standing at the rack of timetables, a look of perplexity on his face.

'I cannae make head nor tail of this. What time's the next bus tae Dundee?'

McGuigan gestured for him to move and took his place before the racks and turned the first three until he found the Dundee timetable. He scanned it, running his finger down the list of times.

'Half four,' he said.

'Hell. What am I goin' tae do till then?'

'It's no' my fault.' McGuigan turned his back on the man and flicked the racks over until he found the Glasgow timetable. He made a note of the first bus out on Wednesday morning. Ten past six.

Just right. The plan was unfolding.

*

At ten o'clock Marjory Fenwick let herself into Wellshill Cemetery. The police guard had been removed but the graveside was still roped off. She lifted the rope and bent beneath it and sat on the grass. The wreaths were beginning to wither. She spoke to Danny in a low and even voice, telling him the news of her day. She felt better, she said. Her various injuries were mostly healed and the physical reminders were receding. That made a difference.

'I'm looking forward to Sunday,' she said. 'It'll be good just to get out of Perth for a while. Become unknown again.' She sat for some moments. 'Danny, d'you think I'll ever be happy again?'

Course you will, Madge. You'll see. One day another boy will come along and he'll sweep you off your feet and you'll fall in love and everything.

'Would that be okay?'

Yes, gal.

'I'll always wish it was you. No matter who I'm with. How much I love him. It'll always be you, Danny.'

I know, Madge.

'I love you.'

163

I love you.

Marjory cried into the dusk that was settling on the hillside. The lights of Perth shone in the distance but around her was calm, peace, solid rows of history reaching down and up and over this place of final refuge.

*

Bob watched the stars through the kitchen window, Orion flickering above the terrace opposite. He played *Banish Misfortune* on his guitar, striking the notes softly so as not to wake Gran. The music soothed him. Allowed him to think. Although he felt badly for Inspector Conoboy, he didn't mind that the Glasgow police had taken over. It made things easier. Ever since he had joined the police he felt a fraud. He knew perfectly well that Conoboy had made it happen. Bob wasn't there on merit. He was acting the part rather than being a genuine policeman. People like Brannan and Strangeway, for all their difficult ways, they were the real thing. Bob was an imposter.

But now the investigation had been handed to another force and the Perth force had been reduced to bit-part players. They were all imposters now. What was real, anyway?

Friday 23rd August

A Day of Renewal

The press conference began at nine. Seated alongside Conoboy and MacNaughton were Chief Constable Sillitoe and Assistant Chief Constable Warnock. Lord Kellett completed the bench. Each stared ahead, solitary in company.

Oliver from *The Scotsman* gave a throaty laugh. 'The Glesga Keelies take over the Keystone Cops,' he said. He tapped the shoulder of Templeton of the *Tele*. 'You can use that for your headline if you want. No charge.'

MacNaughton banged the table to bring the conference to order. 'I'm very pleased to announce,' he said, 'that yesterday we were visited by the most senior officers from Glasgow City Police and as a result they have agreed to second two officers to Perth for the duration of the investigation.' He invited Sillitoe to speak.

'We have made available two highly experienced officers who have each been involved in several complex and serious murder investigations. They will begin work today.'

Templeton raised his hand. 'Is this a recognition of failure in the current investigation?'

'Absolutely not,' said Lord Kellett. 'It is not at all unusual for officers from one constabulary to help another, demonstrating the fine spirit of cooperation that exists among police forces in this country.' He glowered at Templeton and swigged from a glass of water. The glass shook.

Sillitoe continued: 'The Perth police have had a

tremendous task in sifting through information coming from all corners of Scotland. We saw for ourselves yesterday the extensive lines of enquiry being pursued. Many supposed clues have subsequently been found to be false but each must still be investigated and that takes time. There is every reason to believe this mystery will be solved and the murderer apprehended. Glasgow City Police are delighted to be able to offer support to make that happen sooner.'

'What will they do differently?' said Templeton.

'It's not a question of doing things differently, so much as providing additional resource. These officers have a degree of experience of investigating the depravity of the criminal mind, and they will offer a fresh pair of eyes. They will not be working independently except insofar as independence of action is unavoidable.'

Conoboy had heard that precise configuration of words the previous evening when the agreement was reached. He didn't understand it then and he didn't understand it now.

*

The Cuddies Strip was closed to the public at ten o'clock and the police entourage congregated at the spot where Danny and Marjory sat together before the crimes. In the field to the south-west the Browns were continuing the harvest. Detective Lieutenant Jack Lamping and Sergeant Harry Watters surveyed the Strathearn valley. Lamping was tall and rakish, a handsome man in his late thirties, his hair beginning to grey behind the ears. He wore a closely cropped moustache. Watters was shorter and older, in his fifties, with heavy spectacles through which he peered intently.

'Kerrigan and Fenwick left here when?' said Lamping.

'Just after ten,' said Braggan. 'They headed back into town.'

Braggan and Conoboy led the way and they followed the

166

youngsters' route. Black seed pods covered the broom like scabs. Periodically, they burst with a loud popping sound in the fierce heat. The whins were turquoise in the sun, the trees around them lush and proud. Rosebay willowherb and chunky thistles towered above the grass. Nettles and dead nettles were starting to go over. Hogweed, white and bullying, stood in clumps. Beneath the trees the ground was dry, soil powdery, scrub like tinder. The summer had been so dry whatever rain there was quickly drained into the soil. It smelled dusty. The Strip narrowed to single file and dipped slightly, twisting left and right. Exposed tree roots criss-crossed the path. They reached a section completely enclosed by silver birches and oaks and beeches and a single blackthorn tree reaching into the sky. The peeling bark of the silver birches lent the place an ancient air. A sloe tree, glaucous blue, stood apart. The ground darkened and it turned cooler. A large oak, easily sixty-years old, dominated. Beyond it they emerged into light, the path widening into a small clearing. In the distance to their left they could see Letham and the westernmost edge of Perth. A southerly wind broke through the morning silence, delivering occasional snatches of the sound of the river Earn in flow, like a fragment of time passing from one present into another. The path narrowed again and to their right was a large clump of whins.

'That's where he hid,' said Braggan. He stood at the side of the path about ten yards further on. 'And this is where Kerrigan was shot.'

'Where was the girl?'

'On his right facing Perth. He turned back to face the killer.'

DL Lamping pushed his way into the whins and looked for the optimum spot to hide and stood poised, an imaginary shotgun raised to his shoulder. Watters positioned himself where Danny fell. 'Here?' he said. Braggan nodded.

'And the girl?'

Braggan positioned himself by Watters's side. 'Here. They had already passed the whins. The first shot went over them. Kerrigan turned back. He was hit in the face and chest.'

'And the girl wasn't hit?'

'No. Which I find extremely suspicious.'

Lamping and Watters squinted at each other across the Strip. Lamping kept pointing his imaginary shotgun and Watters followed its line.

'It's possible,' he said.

'There were shotgun pellets found in this tree,' said Braggan, pointing to a beech behind them. Again, the Glasgow detectives tried to track the line of fire.

'What happened after he was shot?' said Lamping.

'The girl was bent over Kerrigan when the killer came up to her. She thought he was a passer-by and told him to wait while she got help. She started to run back towards town and he chased her.'

'This way?'

They retraced Marjory's steps. The track was mostly even but a couple of sections kinked around large birches and the path was laced with exposed roots.

'Must have been hairy running on this in the dark.'

'It was a full moon so there would have been some light,' said Conoboy, 'but no, it wouldn't be easy.'

After another hundred yards they reached the stile at the end of the Strip.

'This is where she was caught,' said Braggan. Lamping and Watters looked back the way they had come.

'So she was raped here,' said Lamping. 'And afterwards he made off with her clothing?'

'Which also stretches credibility,' said Braggan.

'Unusual, certainly. And then he returned and shot the boy again.'

'And covered his face with a handkerchief.'

'After that, where do you think he went? Back this way?'

'No. The girl says she lay where she was for about half an hour. Which seems a very long time. She would have seen him if he came back. More likely he went to the opposite end of the Strip and crossed over the Dunning road and went through the trees west and south.'

Watters looked to Conoboy for confirmation.

'Yes,' he said. 'That is possible. Or he could also have cut through the fields. If he went through this field,' he pointed to his left, 'he'd end up back at the entrance to Buckie Braes and could have been in Perth in half an hour. Or he could have gone south-east, towards Callerfountain.' He shrugged. 'The truth is, it's so open round here there are eight or nine different routes he could have taken.'

'Seeing the lie of the land,' said Watters, 'I understand how it makes everything more complicated.'

'Do you think the girl's story is believable?' said Braggan.

'Well, you clearly don't.' Watters and Braggan exchanged looks. The older man thought Braggan dogmatic. Too sure of himself. It was a trait he saw often. 'You seem determined to convince us of your viewpoint from the outset, Seregant. But at this stage, I'll reserve my judgement, thank you.'

'I believe her,' said Conoboy. 'If you were going to make up a story it wouldn't be that one. For example, why would she make up the chase?'

'It doesn't feel like a usual rape scene, that's all,' said Braggan.

Conoboy turned away dismissively. 'Apart from domestic rape, Sergeant, which is all too predictable, there's no such thing as a usual rape scene.'

'And why would he let her run on for so long?' said Braggan. 'He could have caught her easily.'

Before Conoboy could reply, Watters intervened. 'Here's a tip for you, Sergeant,' he said. 'In investigations, follow your hunch by all means, but don't base your whole investigation on a hunch. If you think the girl's lying, prove it and then work out why and come back and tell us what she did instead. But, until you do, the boy was murdered and the girl was raped, exactly as she described it.'

He turned to Conoboy and gave a slight incline of his head.

*

'You were late home last night.' Mrs Fenwick bustled around the kitchen. Marjory sat motionless.

'You know where I was.'

'It's not right, a young girl being out alone at midnight.'

'I was at the cemetery. What's going to happen to me there?'

'It's an awfae world. Nowhere's safe.'

'I know all about safe. I know better than anyone.'

Mrs Fenwick sat beside her at the table. 'I just worry about you.'

'I know, Mum. But I'm fine in the cemetery. No one will bother me there.'

'It's morbid.'

'I need to get over this in my own way.'

The sound of the letterbox opening and snapping shut rang through the kitchen. 'Postie,' said Mrs Fenwick. She went to the door and picked up a single letter in a plain white envelope. 'It's for you,' she said.

Marjory snatched it, wondering whether it might be another postal order. Three halfpenny stamps were affixed in a neat row in the corner and it was postmarked Dundee the day before. She slit it open with her breakfast knife and pulled out a single piece of white paper. She read it in silence and handed it to her mother.

'Meet me at Perth General Station at 6.30 pm on Saturday night, Dundee platform. Refuse, then you know.' It was

170

signed, 'Man in Blue.'

'Oh Mum,' Marjory said. 'Is it real?'

'I dinnae ken, hen. We need to tell the polis.'

But, before they could, the police arrived. Mrs Fenwick greeted Inspector Conoboy and he introduced the Glasgow detectives. She looked at them suspiciously.

'We've had a letter,' said Marjory, her voice high and thin. She thrust it towards Conoboy as though glad to be rid of it. He read it grimly.

'What does it mean, "then you know"?' he said.

'I've no idea.'

Conoboy passed it to Lamping. He read it and snorted.

'It's a hoax,' he said.

'How do you know?' said Marjory.

'You get this sort of thing in cases that are in the papers. People get excited. Want to be involved.'

'But what if it's real?'

Watters took the letter and examined it briefly. 'Look at that handwriting,' he said. 'It's too neat. That was written by a woman.'

Lamping turned to Mrs Fenwick. 'We'll take it to the press. They'll publish it and half of Perth will be at the station tomorrow. Nothing will happen.' Mrs Fenwick gave a weak smile. 'Now, if you don't mind, Mrs Fenwick, we've got a few questions we'd like to ask your daughter.'

'Ask away.'

'We'd like to speak to her alone.'

'She's nothing to hide from me.'

'Of course she hasn't. But we're new to the case and we need to go through everything again. We needn't detain you. I'm sure you have much to be doing around the house.'

'I could do with speaking to you about this letter, Mrs Fenwick,' said Conoboy. 'Perhaps we could discuss it here while the detectives speak to Marjory in her bedroom.'

Mrs Fenwick tried to argue but saw the world conspiring

against her and sighed.

Marjory led the detectives to her room and sat on the bed and gripped her arms around herself. She stared at them, tight-lipped.

'I've told everything before,' she said. 'Lots of times.'

'I know you have, miss,' said Watters, 'and I'm sorry to make you go through it all again. We were up on the Cuddies Strip earlier. It must have been terrifying for you.' She looked at him bleakly. 'The place where you were attacked, so close to the stile. You must have hoped you might escape.'

'I wasn't really thinking anything.'

'After the attack,' said Lamping, 'you lay where you were for some time …'

'I couldn't move,' interrupted Marjory.

'Quite. Did anyone come past while you were lying there?'

'No.'

'You're sure?'

'Yes. I remember just lying there. There's a big tree on the path that runs up by the dyke.'

'Yes, I saw it.'

'I could see its outline against the sky. I lay there until it was so dark I couldn't see it any more. Then I moved. Tried to find my clothes. Then I went back to Danny.'

'Was Danny your first boyfriend?'

'Yes.'

'Are you sure?'

'Why do people keep asking me that?'

'Because when we find the man who did this – and we will, Marjory – when it comes to trial his lawyers will argue that he wasn't.'

'Why?'

'To discredit you as a witness.'

'Why?'

'Marjory, I have to ask this. Were you a virgin before that

172

night?'

She clenched her fists and squeezed her eyes shut, trying not to cry. 'How often do I have to answer this?'

'Please don't get upset.'

She snorted and sat upright, her lower jaw thrust forwards. 'You accuse me of being a strumpet and then tell me there's no need to be upset. People keep asking me if I was a virgin and nobody ever believes me.' She slumped back and stared blankly at the pattern on the rug by the fireplace. There was a hole where a falling lump of coal had burned through it. Its edges were crisp and hard and, when she was a child, Marjory used to lie on the carpet and circle the hole with her fingertip, feeling its sharpness, imagining the power of the fire that created it. She looked at the policemen, their doubt, their accusation. She would never be rid of this.

'Alright, love,' said Lamping. 'Go and ask your mother if we might have a cup of tea.' Marjory leaped up and escaped before they could change their mind.

'What do you think?' said Watters.

'This virginity question has to be answered.'

*

Bob let himself into the police box and sat on the rickety wooden seat. He had left a flask of tea first thing that morning and he opened it now and poured a milky concoction into a tin mug. He had only a handful of laundries still to contact and he would probably finish today. Then he'd have to find a new way to convince himself he was a real policeman. His notebook was heavily marked, the telephone numbers of each laundry in turn having been scored through after being eliminated. He had contacted laundries in Perthshire first, then Fife and Stirlingshire and Clackmannanshire, then north into Angus and Aberdeenshire. He had now spoken to almost every laundry in Scotland. None appeared to have a

173

numbering system like the one on the handkerchief.

'Kelso Laundry?' he asked as the operator connected him. The voice at the other end of the phone, distant and indistinct, confirmed it was and Bob explained the nature of his enquiry. When he had first embarked on this mission he had had to compose himself before each call, settling his nerves and rehearsing his speech. Now, he could speak fluently from memory.

'It was marked with what?' said the voice. She sounded English. Posh.

'M 1 dash 2.'

'In what colour thread?'

'Red.'

'Yes, that could be ours.'

Bob was barely listening, thinking instead about Gran's forgetfulness that morning, when she couldn't recall the name of Geordie the milkman.

'What?' he said when the woman's words sunk in.

'I'd need to see it to verify it. But we use that kind of notation. "M1" is the account and "2" would be the number of the cleaning batch. So that would be the second time we'd laundered for that particular client.'

'Can you tell me the name of the client?'

'Not until I've verified it, no. I'd need to see it. There are probably lots of other laundries that use similar notation.'

Bob could assure her, having spoken to most of them, that she was wrong, but he agreed that he would speak to his superiors and be in touch. He hung up and felt a surge of elation.

He had achieved something.

*

Annie bustled into the Conoboys' garden with a bundle of washing. The morning had been still but now a breeze was building and she wanted to take advantage. She reached for the washing line but gave a start and let out a scream.

'Mercy,' she said. 'You did surprise me.'

'I'm sorry,' said Bella Conoboy. 'I didn't mean to catch you unawares.'

'Are you quite alright, ma'am? Would you like me to take you inside?'

'I'm absolutely grand, thank you. Isn't it a lovely day?'

Annie looked at her in amazement. In the three years she had worked for the Conoboys this was the first time she had known Mrs Conoboy leave the house. Word had it she hadn't set foot out of doors since the war.

'It is indeed, ma'am. Should I fetch you a stool to sit on?'

Bella looked up at the sky and then at Annie. 'Do you know, that would be absolutely wonderful. Would you be a dear?'

*

Early evening in South Street and no one wanted to leave before the Keelies. Meaningless tasks were undertaken, work was done slowly, people walked to and from nowhere in particular in pursuit of nothing in particular. The Keelies sat and read. Statements, reports, newspapers, everything they could find.

Sergeant Strangeway answered the telephone. Sergeant Bowles at Methven reported a find of women's clothing on the playing grounds at the top of town.

'Could you describe them?' said Strangeway. They were an old woman's garments, he was told, dark and old-fashioned, heavily worn.

He glanced at the Keelies working in the adjacent office. The door was open. He spoke loudly. 'Thanks, Tam, but that doesn't sound like anything to do with our case. It's a young woman's clothing we need.' A pause. 'No.' Another pause, a louder voice. 'No, don't bring them in.' Exchange of pleasantries and the sound of the receiver being replaced on the handset.

'More clothing,' he said to nobody. 'I said we didn't want it.' Nobody replied.

He looked up as Richard Hamill walked in. 'I found this,' Hamill said, 'in the long grass on the Cuddies Strip.' He handed over a used shotgun cartridge, red, still smelling of gunpowder.

Strangeway thanked him, noticing Lamping and Watters approaching. 'Do you remember where you found it?'

'Twenty-three yards east of the murder scene.'

'Sergeant?' said Lamping.

'Another amateur sleuth has made a find sir. A shotgun cartridge.'

Lamping took it and examined it. He put it down. 'That's the fourth to be found, is it not?'

'It is, sir.'

'From three shots.'

'Yes, sir.'

On cue, the sound of gunfire resounded through the station. Strangeway and Richard Hamill ducked. Lamping looked startled.

'Take cover,' shouted Strangeway, remaining behind his counter.

Watters ran towards the source of the shot. He opened the door to the cells corridor and walked down it slowly, pausing at each cell in turn. The first two were empty. The third contained a drunk with his hands in the air begging not to be shot. The fourth held a man with a gun.

He was staring at it as though puzzled how it had got there. He turned it round and round in his hand. He stared at the wall opposite him, at the hole he had just made in it. Watters considered there to be no danger and stood in front of the bars.

'Give me the gun,' he said.

'Have it,' said the man, a young tinker lad arrested for stealing potatoes from Bryce's in Letham. He passed the pistol through the bars to Watters, who looked at it incredulously.

'Where the hell did you get this?' he said.

'In that room out there,' the lad said. 'When the sergeant was bookin' me the telephone rang. While he spoke to it I went in and saw the gun lyin' on a shelf.'

Watters looked at him with amazement and the lad misinterpreted his concern.

'I didnae ken it was goin' to fire. It looks ancient. I'd nae idea it would actually work. I just wanted to look at it.'

Strangeway took the gun. 'It was found yesterday,' he explained. 'On the railway line. We knew it was nothing to do with the case and put it in the museum.'

'The museum?'

'Through there. We keep all the old things we get handed in. We had a German rifle from the Great War the other day.'

'Why not give it to the drunk next door?' said Lamping. 'See if he can bayonet somebody.'

'I'll get a lock put on the door, sir.'

'Do that, Sergeant. And then get rid of any illegal weapons you're storing. It would be embarrassing to have to arrest yourself, wouldn't it?'

There was a cough behind them and they turned to see Bob waiting.

'Not now,' said Strangeway.

'It's important, sir,' said Bob. 'The Cuddies Strip is on fire.'

'Oh, for fuck's sake.'

*

By the time the police reached the Strip a swathe of whins from the stile westwards was ablaze, the flames reaching six feet in the air and pulsing in the wind. Within minutes another six feet of the Strip had caught fire. The smoke was thick, fire crackle filling the rural silence. Around a dozen people were already trying to stamp out the flames, using their feet on fresh outbreaks and jackets on the larger flames.

'Don't let the trees catch,' shouted Braggan. 'The whins will burn themselves out.'

They joined the existing firefighters and beat down the flames as best they could. The County Fire Brigade arrived at the Dunning Road end but without water in this remote spot they could offer no greater expertise than those already there. They joined the line and battled to stem the tide of flame. It took an hour to bring it under control. Grass and whin were destroyed along a stretch of three-hundred yards.

Included in the path of destruction were the scenes of Marjory's rape and Danny's murder.

'How did it start?' said Braggan.

A man, red-faced with exertion, collared with black smoke, raised his hand. 'It was me,' he said. 'I dropped a match on the ground and it must have still been alight because within seconds the grass was on fire. I tried to stamp it out but I couldn't and the flames got bigger and bigger. I shouted for help.'

'Just as well the amateurs were still here, eh?' said Richard Hamill, newly arrived by bicycle from the police station, hot and panting. His companions gave grime-blackened smiles.

'What would we do without you, Mr Hamill?' said Braggan.

'You'd have to find somebody else to arrest, for one thing.'

'Well,' said Lamping, turning to go, not wishing to look at the damage to his uniform, 'the good news is that you can all give up your amateur investigations now. There's going to be bugger all to find here now.'

*

McGuigan grunted as he hauled his body into the oak tree and draped himself across the lowest bough until he could get settled. He adjusted the telescope slung round his neck and stood nervously, gripping the trunk and pressing close to it. He climbed to the next branch and wedged himself against the tree and when he felt secure he put the telescope to his eye and focused. In front of him was the farmhouse and on the first floor a darkened window was directly opposite him.

About nine-thirty, as usual, the light went on in the room and he readied himself, telescope to his eye. After a moment, a shape appeared in the window, a girl, Isobel, the farmer's sxteen-year-old daughter. McGuigan's pulse throbbed in his throat. He unbuttoned his trousers and felt inside and gripped his penis, already hardening. Isobel stood still, presumably looking at herself in a mirror, and McGuigan admired her shape. What a bosom.

'Do it,' he said. 'Get 'em off. Get naked.' He masturbated furiously, steadying the telescope on his raised knee. Isobel disappeared from view for some minutes but this was normal and he knew she would return. He had seen her tits three times now and he was certain this would be the fourth. What was infuriating, though, was that from this angle he couldn't see below the waist. He really needed to be on one of the higher branches but none were strong enough. He tried to raise himself up but lost balance and felt himself wobble.

'Steady,' he said.

She reappeared and he squeezed himself as she paused before the mirror. This was it. He knew it. She unbuttoned her blouse and took it off and studied herself again.

'Do it, you fuckin' bitch.'

She reached behind and unclasped her bra and slid it off and stood sideways to the window.

'Turn round,' he said. This was the fourth time, to be sure, but he'd only seen nipples once and that was what really counted. 'Turn round.'

She fumbled with her waist and stepped out of her skirt. She bent over again and he knew she was taking off her slip and suspenders and stockings. Finally, she stood up and turned slightly and looked out of the window. She stepped right up to it and McGuigan stopped breathing as she stood in front of him, completely naked, a dark triangle of hair round her cunt. She pulled the curtains and she was gone, but McGuigan knew that image would remain with him forever. It was perfect, frozen and untouchable. He closed his eyes and conjured it into his mind and he masturbated until he came.

'Bitch,' he said. 'Slut.'

She was asking for it.

They all were.

Saturday 24th August

A Day of Consolidation

Muirton Park was full to bursting, only ten years old and one of the best football stadiums in Scotland. Bob Kelty weaved through the crowds towards the terracing behind the goal at the Florence Place end, his favourite position, but at the last moment he spotted Derek McNab and walked past with his head down. He settled for a position near the corner flag and counted down the minutes until kick-off. Laddies ran about, kicking stones, raising a stoor which hung in the air for several minutes. Wooden stands rose above the south touchline. Beneath the south stand was a small kiosk selling pies. Beside it stood Sergeant Braggan. Bob was surprised to see him, knowing he should have been on duty. Braggan was speaking to two men Bob didn't recognise, rough sorts, not the type Bob would have expected the sergeant to consort with. Braggan held out his hand and Bob watched as first one man, then the other, slipped a paper note into it. Braggan nodded and walked away. Bob had heard Braggan taking money in the toilets at the station the other day and now this. But, before he could ponder the meaning, cheers broke out from all corners and the teams ran on to the pitch, St Johnstone in their blue and white, skipper Harry Ferguson in the lead. The formidable Glasgow Celtic followed in green and white hoops, led by Scottish international winger Jimmy Delaney. Ordinarily, this would be a fixture for Bob to fear, because of the near certainty of a thrashing by one

181

of the best teams in the country. Under Tommy Muirhead, though, Saints had become one of the elite themselves. It was a golden era to be a Saints fan. Even the prospect of winning the Scottish Cup no longer felt ridiculous. The referee blew his whistle and the game commenced and Bob felt that familiar rake of nerves in his stomach. He hunched into his jacket and crossed his fingers inside his pockets and offered up silent encouragement. All around him, the crowd roared and cheered.

*

William Brown led his horses back to the stable at Kirkton of Mailer farm. The stookers lay with their backs against the sheaves of wheat and smoked. They were hot and damp, their muscles stiff with that delicious ache that comes when you know the work of the day is over. Two days in and the first field was more than half done. At this rate they could finish by Friday. Charles Elder, though, grieve for thirty years, warned of rain. The stookers looked at a sky of uninterrupted blue and chose not to believe him.

'So will he turn up tonight?' said Sandy Arnott. 'At the General Station?'

Graeme Peddie scoffed. 'Why would he give himself away like that? Half of Perth's goin' to be there.'

'Maybe he didn't think it would be in the paper. Didnae expect the girl to report it.'

'Of course she'd report it,' said John McGuigan. 'Anyway, if the killer wanted to see the girl he wouldnae send her a note first.'

'It sounds like he knew her,' said Peddie.

'How?'

'What does it say – "you know what"? How could she know what if she didn't know him?'

'Thon lassie has more to tell than she's lettin' on,' said

182

Arnott.

'Aye, if she's that innocent how come they never found her clothes?'

McGuigan closed his eyes and remembered stripping Marjory Fenwick naked. That was almost the most exciting part, the exposure of flesh, the uncovering of what was meant to be concealed. The ownership of it.

'Looks like we'll no' find anything in these fields,' said Peddie.

'I felt sure we would,' said Arnott.

'What did you think he was going to do? Just hurl his gun intae the field?'

'Aye. With all the wheat it would be well enough hid.'

'Until it was harvested.'

'Maybe he came back and picked it up.'

McGuigan lit another cigarette. 'Wi' all these sightseers on the Cuddies Strip all hours of the day?' he said. 'If the killer wanted to hide anything he wouldnae throw it intae a field, he'd hide it doon a hole where it winnae be found.'

Peddie picked at the soil between his splayed legs, at stray stalks of wheat left behind, a couple of small stones. 'Is that what you did with your gun?' he said.

McGuigan's face betrayed no emotion. 'Aye,' he said. 'It is.'

*

'City boy,' Sergeant Strangeway shouted. The football had not gone well and, with the size of the crowd trying to exit Muirton Park at full time, Bob had been fifteen minutes late for his half-shift. Sergeant Strangeway hadn't allowed it to go unnoticed.

'While you were out enjoying yourself on police time, some woman phoned you. From a laundry.'

'Aye?'

'Yes, Sergeant.'

'Yes, Sergeant. Did she want me to call back?'

'No, she just thought you'd work out what she wanted by telepathy.'

'Did you get her number?'

Strangeway snorted with exasperation. 'I'm assuming,' he said, 'she's not just phoning up to say your own laundry's ready?'

'No, Sergeant.'

'So, you've been phoning up laundries. Despite being told not to?'

'Yes, Sergeant.'

'Well, you'll make up that time as well as the half hour you were late today.'

'Quarter of an hour.'

'Are you arguing with me, City boy?'

'No, Sergeant.'

Strangeway handed over the telephone number with ill grace and Bob went into Conoboy's office and picked up the telephone and asked to be connected to the Kelso Laundry. A couple of minutes later he heard the connection being made and asked for Mrs McIntyre.

'Constable Kelty?' she said when she came on the line. As before, it was crackly and distant and Bob struggled to hear. 'I've been looking into our files regarding the "M1-2" marking. I now believe it is almost certainly ours.'

'Why?'

'The client to whom the item belongs comes from Perth. Or just outside.'

Bob's heart started to pound. He picked up a pencil and opened his notebook. His hand was shaking. 'Could you tell me the name of the client?' He listened intently, then closed his eyes, then frowned.

'Shit,' he said.

He was still seated at Conoboy's desk when the inspector

entered and hung up his coat and cap. 'Robert?' he said, surprised.

'Sir.' Bob rose, apologising.

Conoboy indicated for him to sit down again. 'What brings you in on a Saturday afternoon?'

'I had some time to make up, sir.'

'I'm sure you're doing far more than your hours. What have you been working on?'

'Well.' Bob paused. 'I do have some news, sir.' Conoboy sat down and lit a cigarette. 'The laundry, sir. I've identified where the handkerchief comes from.'

'Where?'

'Aberdalgie House.'

'Aberdalgie House? Home of Lord and Lady Douglas?'

'Yes, sir.'

'Shit.'

'That's what I thought, sir.'

'Leave it with me.'

*

Templeton of the *Tele* sat at the bar of the General Station, admiring Grace Cross's rear view as she poured a double measure of whisky. There was nothing like an A-line skirt to show off the attributes of a pretty girl. He checked her hand. No ring. He slid his off and put it in his jacket pocket.

'Ice?' she said.

'Raw.' He pointed to the copy of yesterday's paper. *Anonymous Note to Miss Fenwick*, the headline read. 'It was me who wrote that.'

'Really?' Templeton noted with satisfaction that Grace, previously a model of professional detachment, immediately softened. She leaned into him as she sat his glass on the counter. 'You must know all the inside story?'

She wore too much make-up but he could forgive her

that. It would wipe off. 'I'm called to the station every day for a briefing from the Chief Constable personally,' he said. He swallowed a large mouthful of Bell's and relished the heat sliding down his throat.

'I saw the killer, you know,' she said.

'I do know. On the Inverness train.'

She raised her eyebrows in mock approval. 'You really do know the case, don't you?'

'That was on Thursday afternoon. I was brought in on the Friday, when they realised this was going to be a big story. They needed the top man for the job.' He finished his whisky and angled the glass towards her. Grace took it and refilled it.

'On the house,' she said. She looked at the newspaper. 'This anonymous letter. Is it genuine?'

'Probably. The police are very interested in it.'

'I expected there'd be more of them here.'

'Oh, they are.' He tapped his nose.

'Undercover?'

'Correct.'

'D'you know who?'

'I'm not allowed to say.'

'I understand.'

Grace peered out of the window as though weighing up the congregation on the platform outside. She picked up half a dozen empty glasses and left them on the sink. She wiped down the counter.

'What time do you finish?' said Templeton.

'Nine.'

'Perfect. That would give me an hour to file my copy.'

She stood with her hand on her hip. 'And?'

'We could have a little drink in the Sally. I could tell you all about the case. The inside story.'

'D'you know who did it?'

'We've a pretty sound idea.'

The bar was filling up. Rose, Grace's fellow barmaid, coughed as she swished past to serve a couple of new arrivals. Three or four more were waiting. Rose's expression was not friendly.

'Nine?' said Templeton.

'Nine,' said Grace.

Outside, the concourse of the General Station was growing more congested by the moment. By six-thirty, hundreds lined the Dundee platform, with latecomers already having to make do with the Glasgow platform opposite. More daring individuals, young and cocky, perched on the two overhead bridges. The combined volume of five-hundred voices was audible on the South Inch a quarter of a mile away. Laughter and shrieks. Some brought sandwiches and ate meditatively, looking down the track. The station clock ticked down the minutes until seven.

The train, when it arrived, was five minutes late. A young woman with a baby in a pram struggled to get off and visibly shrunk when she saw the mob watching her from the platform. An aged couple, carnations in their lapels, followed. They, too, looked at the crowd with trepidation. They struggled to find passage through a gathering too large to allow for easy manoeuvring. Nobody else alighted. Nobody got on. The train stood at the platform for two minutes and with a toot of the horn it steamed on its passage eastward following the line of the Tay to Dundee.

The sense of anti-climax was palpable. Even those who hadn't truly believed the killer would arrive were disappointed. They watched for a few minutes longer until their final hopes of excitement were eclipsed, then dispersed into Perth for an evening of drink and discussion and disputation.

*

At the appointed time of the sender's rendezvous with Marjory, a full case conference was in progress in police headquarters. Inspector Conoboy was nominally its chairman but other than bring the meeting to order he said nothing. MacNaughton, too, was reserved. Detective Lieutenant Lamping, the youngest man in the room, was positioned in the middle of the conference table and it was clear he was the focus of the debate.

'By now,' he said, 'I think we can be confident we are looking for a local man, almost certainly living or hiding somewhere in Perth. Mr Pritchard may well have spotted the man on the night of the murder. The vagrant who was arrested may not have been the same person. There's nothing to say Pritchard's evidence is wrong. The Cuddies Strip is not somewhere you stumble across by accident and the killer must have been there for a purpose. That purpose would appear not to have been pre-meditated, at least as far as Kerrigan and Fenwick are concerned. They didn't plan to go there that night …'

'Unless Fenwick did,' said Braggan. 'It was her decision not to go to the pictures. She persuaded Kerrigan. Perhaps she'd already agreed with a lover to be at the Strip at that time.'

'For what reason?' said Watters.

'To be with the new lover. Get rid of the old one.'

'There's easier ways to ditch your boyfriend.'

'Has anyone investigated her background?' said Lamping. 'Other boyfriends?'

'One name comes up a few times,' said Braggan. 'Hamish Holland. Aged twenty-seven. Family friend. We have some reports of him taking the girl home from dances.'

'Who is he?'

'Works as a farrier. He seems a bit of a jack-the-lad.'

'Nobody else?'

'No.'

'Look into Hamish Holland a bit more. How well does he know Fenwick? What does he do in his spare time? Friends. Any debts? History of trouble or violence? And I want more information on Fenwick as well.'

'Could I raise the handkerchief?' said Conoboy.

'Usually it's a white flag,' said Lamping. He laughed at his own joke. Nobody else did.

'The handkerchief used to bind Marjory's hands,' Conoboy said. Hostile faces confronted him. His instinct was to retreat but he would not. 'Constable Kelty has been pursuing that line of enquiry ...' Conoboy saw a look of anger cross MacNaughton's face. 'In his own time. And he's traced the "M1-2" mark to a Kelso launderers. They have confirmed it is one of theirs. And they have confirmed the identity of the owners.'

'And?' said MacNaughton.

'Lord and Lady Douglas. Aberdalgie House.'

MacNaughton swore. Lamping and Watters watched in silence. MacNaughton stared out of the window at the charcoal sky.

'That's that, then,' he said. 'This is why I warned you not to pursue it. It was never going to lead us to the killer.'

'I thought I'd pay a visit to Aberdalgie House tomorrow ...'

'You will do no such thing.' MacNaughton's voice grew louder. 'Lord and Lady Douglas are highly connected. They're friends of Lord Kellett. They're more than likely to become involved in local politics now that they're back from South Africa. They're friends of Frank Norie-Miller. If you think we're involving them in a tawdry murder case ...'

'Just routine enquiries, sir.'

'That's an order, Conoboy.'

*

189

Marjory opened her wardrobe and stared inside. The closer she got to her rendezvous with Annie and PC Kelty the more nervous she was becoming. Despite her protestations to her mother, she still felt overwhelmed in public. It was bad enough being ferried to and from the police station but at least, then, she was always in transit, able to retreat into shadows and anonymity. The idea of being normal still seemed impossibly distant.

She took out her new suspenders and knickers, bought with the two ten-bob postal orders. Crisp and fresh. That was what she wanted. A new start, an escape from memory and history. She pulled her blouse from its hanger and laid it across her chest and looked in the mirror. Dark green and modern, with a shallow V-neck and an elegant bow, it made her look older. Sophisticated. She longed to wear it, to become that person, the person who wore sophisticated green blouses, the person who wasn't fearful, weary Madge Fenwick.

'Let me be happy. Just once.'

*

Conoboy looked up when he heard the knock at the door. 'I imagined you'd be going out with the lads,' he said. 'Saturday night.'

Watters shook his head. 'Too old for that game.' Conoboy offered him a cigarette and they decamped to armchairs beside an unlit fireplace. They both stared into it.

'This isn't an easy situation for any of us,' said Watters.

'No. But we must make the best of it.'

'I'd like to say, from what I've seen so far, everything you've done in this case has been exemplary.'

'Clearly not everyone agrees.'

Watters exhaled heavily. 'Politics,' he said. 'It's not enough to do a good job. You have to be seen to be doing

190

a good job. Some of these idiots in the Home Office, they seem to think you should be able to solve every crime in a couple of days. They don't understand.'

'Well,' said Conoboy. 'People are rightly apprehensive with a killer on the loose.'

'We'll find him.'

'I do appreciate your support. Both of you.'

'Lamping's a good detective. But he's very ambitious. He's here to advance his own career.'

'I got that impression.'

'I'm not.'

'No?'

'I'll be retiring in a couple of years. I'm ready for it. I had a case last year, a murder, young woman, barely eighteen. Her boyfriend beat her senseless. Because of an apple. She ate his apple. He killed her for it. You can't get things like that out of your head, you know? I think about that girl. What she had in store in life. What she could have been. Done. She was a bright lass by all accounts. From a good family. *Nobody* deserves to die like that but she really didn't. It shouldn't have happened.' He stared at Conoboy. 'It's an illness,' he said. 'In the world. The French are rioting. The Dutch will be next. Their government's already gone. As soon as they devalue their currency the mobs will be on the streets. The Yanks have had to bring in the dole. Everywhere you look there's unrest. And where you have unrest you get Mussolini and Hitler and Mosley. It'll end in war. Maybe that's what we need. To purge the system.'

'It wouldn't work,' said Conoboy. 'Surely we learned that at least from the last one?'

'We never learn. That's the trouble.'

*

In the staff room upstairs, Lamping studied his face in the

191

mirror. He stroked his moustache. 'Saturday night,' he said. 'Where's the best place for a pint?'

'MacNaughton doesn't like us drinking in the local bars,' said Braggan.

'He's not here.'

'Good point.'

Lamping, Braggan and Strangeway decamped to the Salutation and sat in the back room amid a fug of smoke and heat. The sound of a couple of fiddlers escaped from the front.

'Teuchter music,' said Lamping dismissively. Drunks sang out of tune. Men shouted, women screamed.

They ordered a round of heavy that disappeared almost before Braggan had paid for it. The second, bought by Strangeway, went as quickly, as did Braggan's third round. The conversation grew more raucous. Lamping talked about previous cases. Axes, cleavers, even a Gatling gun featured. He spoke of Glasgow life.

'Most of the trouble's caused by micks and spicks. A lot of wops, too.'

'D'you get many niggers?' said Braggan.

'A few. They're easy to manage, though. Thick and lazy.'

'Bit like our tinks. I haven't much time for Hitler, but he's got the right idea about that bunch.'

'Aye,' said Lamping. 'And he's shut down the freemasons' lodges.'

'That's not so good,' said Braggan.

'Depends which foot you lead with.' Lamping smirked and swigged from his drink. A morose-looking man entered, blue and white scarf round his neck. Lamping spotted it. 'Anyone ken the fitba score the day?' he said.

'Three – two to Celtic,' said the man.

'Grand.'

'You a Celtic fan?' said Strangeway.

'Rutherglen boy. Funnily enough, if I hadn't been called

up here I'd probably have gone to the match.' Braggan said nothing about having been there and silence ensued. The bar was full but the atmosphere was strangely muted. 'Is this Saturday night in Perth, then?' Lamping said.

Braggan looked around as though he was an anthropologist viewing it for the first time. 'There's Templeton of the *Tele*,' he said. 'Arsehole.'

'The newspaper guy?' said Lamping. 'I hate journalists. Pricks.' He watched as Templeton leaned towards Grace Cross and stroked her wrist. 'That's an attractive wee piece he's got with him, mind,' he said. He picked up his glass and strode towards Templeton's table. 'Evening,' he said.

Templeton's eyes flashed when he saw one of the Glasgow bigwigs standing in front of him. 'Detective Lieutenant,' he said. He turned to Grace. 'This is one of the experts from Glasgow I was telling you about. Detective Lieutenant Lamping, can I say how impressed I was with your explanations this morning. You set everything out very clearly.'

'I have to,' Lamping said. 'To make sure you paper boys understand it.' Templeton smiled unconvincingly. Lamping turned to Grace. 'I expect he's been telling you all about the case?'

'Aye.'

He rolled his eyes. 'Well, take it from me, hen, he knows hee-haw about it.' He gave Templeton a stare. 'Isn't that right, newspaper boy?'

Templeton tried to answer but no words came out.

'Tell you what,' Lamping said to Grace, 'why don't you come over and chat to me and the lads and we'll give you the real story?'

'We were just going,' said Templeton.

Grace paused for a moment, uncertain, and then she stood. She picked up her sherry glass. 'Alright, then.' She turned to Templeton. 'Ta ta,' she said. 'Thanks for the drinks.' And she followed Lamping across the bar.

Templeton fixed a smile on his face and endured the five minutes it took him to finish his beer before he got up and left without acknowledging anyone. Strangeway and Braggan and Lamping and his new conquest watched him go.

*

The house was in darkness when Bob Kelty let himself in at just after ten. 'Gran?' he shouted. He went into the front room and she was sitting in her armchair, a shawl over her shoulders, a cigarette between her fingers.

'What time d'you call this?'

'Sorry. I had to go back into work after the fitba. The murder …'

'I still need my tea, you ken. Am I supposed to sit and starve while you're gallivantin' playin' sodjers?'

'Police, Gran. D'you need the toilet?'

'Of course I do.'

He gripped her arms and lifted her from her chair and she clung to him as he guided her outside to the toilet. He swung open the door and backed her in and closed the door again. Stars shone from a clear sky, the Plough directly overhead. A week before that same sky had been alive with the Perseid meteor showers. He lit a cigarette and kept the match in his hand until the head had cooled and then he placed it in his trousers. Tonight would be difficult, he knew, with his day out tomorrow having already caused an argument at breakfast.

Back inside, he reheated some boiled beef and placed it on a tray on her lap.

'That looks vile,' she said. 'You've taken your cookin' skills fae your mother. She was useless as well.'

Bob ignored her. The only frames of reference Gran had left were his parents. Everything else in her life, husband of

194

thirty years included, was forgotten. One day her memories of Bob's parents would disappear into the same void. And, after that, Bob himself would follow. 'Who are you?' she would say. He waited for it every day and each time it didn't happen it gave him the strength to carry on.

'I do what I can,' he said.

'It's no' awfae much, is it?'

She hunched over the plate and began to spoon beef into her mouth. She had no top teeth and she part-sucked the meat, part ripped it with her gum and bottom set. She had probably been handsome, Bob thought. He had only ever known her as a fierce woman in black, determined to stand up to whatever fate threw at her. Now, finally, fate had won. She was not yet seventy, but everything about her seemed ancient. What joy she had derived from life had long since dissipated, along with her memory and her sense of community. Life had been reduced to a shell of eating and shitting, waiting and sleeping.

'Mind I'm goin' out tomorrow,' he said.

'You didnae tell me that.'

'I did. This morning. I'm goin' out with Annie.'

'That trollop.'

'She's not.'

'Tryin' to lead you astray. It's your money she's after. An' you're that green you'll fall for it. Just like that useless faither o' yours.'

'I'm goin' at ten. I'll be back around five. I'll leave you some lunch and do tea when I'm back.'

'Dinnae fash yoursel' aboot me, son. I'm on the way oot, and thank God for that.'

*

Night advanced, crisp and clear. Gordon Lamping and Grace Cross disappeared down Water Vennel behind the police station in South Street and Lamping fumbled with her clothing and pulled up her skirt and felt for her knickers and pulled them aside. Grace could hear something rustling behind them. She imagined rats. She gripped Lamping tightly and tried to persuade herself this was worth it.

In the small, sloping bedroom of his bed and breakfast Harry Watters lay smoking, pondering Conoboy and the investigation. Why was he here? What could he do differently? Could he make a difference?

Bob Kelty sat on a bench in his back garden in Jeanfield Road and smoked a pipe. It was his new possession, purchased that week from Rattray's on the Old High Street. He stared at the sky, at the shallow gas lamps, at the shade and occlusion of the night. The football had been a disappointment. So near and yet so far. Still, tomorrow he was going out with Annie Maybury. This was where his life might start.

Victor Conoboy smoked a cigarette and looked up at his wife's window. The light inside was extinguished and he pictured her turning in bed, settling her grief in place after another day of not being a mother. He thought of Tom. He thought of the grandchildren who would never realise their fate. What happens to all the unknowns, the spirits who should have inhabited a life that could never be conceived? Tom Conoboy and Danny Kerrigan, young men both in perpetuity. Where were they? Where would they be when there was no one left to grieve for them? Where do any of us go?

Upstairs Bella Conoboy stood behind her bedroom curtain and looked down at her husband. She looked at the sky. She looked at the world.

In Westhill cemetery, Marjory Fenwick lay stretched on Danny Kerrigan's grave and spoke in a quiet and slow voice of her sense of loss and loneliness. She couldn't articulate her feelings, not properly, but they existed all the same. And they hurt. She was going out tomorrow and she had invested

196

more hope in the occasion than she knew was sensible.

'You're a silly lassie,' she scolded.

But she wanted to be silly.

Without it, how could there be hope?

Sunday 25th August

A Day of Rest

Bob, Annie and Marjory got off the bus on Crieff High Street. They walked downhill to Comrie Street and on as far as the war memorial and turned down Milnab Street. On their right a large mill dominated. On their left a high embankment held the railway line to Comrie. They reached the entrance to Lady Mary's Walk and entered a wooded walkway. Sudden coolness offered relief from the hot morning sun. Ahead of them a tunnel through the viaduct allowed passage beneath the railway.

'That smell,' said Annie. 'It's like aniseed.'

'Sweet cicely,' said Bob.

On their left the River Barvick merged with the Earn, dark water flowing cold and dense. The path narrowed and climbed sharply and twisted left to accommodate a large oak that was tilting at forty-five degrees towards the river. The path narrowed even more, to single file, and began to fall away alarmingly.

'You'll need to be careful here,' said Bob. He turned to the girls and at the same time reached for the trunk of the tree and missed it and lost his balance and found himself falling eight feet down into the river and he braced himself against the impact. He landed shoulder first, instinctively raising his right arm to protect his picnic hamper. He sank beneath the water until he was almost completely submerged and after a few frantic seconds he rose to the surface and steadied himself while his feet searched for the solidity of the riverbed. He planted himself on the rough stony bottom and raised up and stood, waist deep in the water, and looked at the girls. He held out the picnic hamper.

'Still dry,' he said.

The looks of horror on the faces of Annie and Marjory gave way to relief and then to laughter. Annie scrambled down to the riverbank and reached for his hand and guided him back to the path.

'You daft galoot,' she laughed. "'You'll need to be careful here', he says and then flies headfirst into the river.' She helped him out and he stood dripping on the path.

He felt foolish but he looked at Marjory's face and saw with satisfaction that some of the tension had fallen away. She had the prettiest smile. 'It was a bit hot so I decided to take a wee dip to cool myself off,' he joked.

They made a second attempt at the path, this time without incident, and walked on, Bob leaving a trail of water in his wake. Sounds of laughter floated towards them. On a small, sandy beach by the riverbank families were picnicking, children in knitted swimming costumes scrambling in and out of the water and running up a steep embankment behind. A huge boulder, fire-blackened on one side, dominated the middle of the beach. Bob tilted his hat as they passed. Pleasantries were exchanged. His wetness went unremarked.

Beyond, the path opened into a wide avenue, bounded on both sides by lines of trees combining to form a natural canopy over the path, wide and high. There was nothing here of the pressing closeness of the Cuddies Strip. Nothing to fear. The ground beneath was soft with the accumulation of years of leaf-fall. It smelled fresh. The Comrie train rumbled past on the railway line running parallel, clouds of steam pulsing into the sky. Annie and Marjory waved and a number of passengers, day trippers and family visitors, waved back.

'People carve their names on these trees,' said Bob,

showing them a series of initials and names and dates inscribed in the barks of beeches and oaks the length of the walk. Every tree seemed to be engraved with the folk history of Crieff.

'Could you do ours?' said Marjory excitedly. It was the first time she had spoken unbidden.

Bob smiled. 'I believe we could,' he said. He took out a small red penknife and carefully began to score their initials into a beech tree on the right of the path, nearest the railway. BK, AM, MF, Aug 35, it read.

'That'll be there for ever,' said Marjory.

'Maybe not forever,' said Bob, 'but it'll see us out.'

'Oh Bob, don't talk morbid,' said Annie.

'That isn't morbid,' said Marjory. 'It's lovely to think that, long after we're gone, people will see that and wonder who we were.'

'They'll invent stories about us,' said Bob. 'How we lived our lives. What we did.'

'We all grew very rich,' said Marjory. 'And lived to the age of one-hundred and three. And had lots of family who loved us very, very much.'

'Wouldn't that be the dab?' said Bob.

After a mile of the wooded walk the view opened up again. Large rocks scarred the Earn, causing the water to spume and foam around them while, elsewhere, it flowed fat and smooth. They stopped at a bench overlooking the water. Bob was slowly drying out but his tweed jacket was beginning to smell musty. He spread his arms and legs in the sun and lifted his head towards it. Annie unwrapped sandwiches of cheese and ham and potted meat. The shells of the boiled eggs were already cracked after Bob's altercation with the river and they peeled and ate those first. Marjory poured tea from a flask. They sat and watched the river. Opposite, beneath the trees, a heron stood and watched them.

'This is the life,' said Bob. 'Perfect peace.'

'You must get a lot of hustle and bustle in the police,' said Marjory.

Bob said nothing for some moments. He chewed his sandwich. 'Aye, it's fine,' he said. 'Most of the time.'

'It must be exciting right now. In a way.'

'I dinnae ken how I feel about it, to be honest with you, Madge. I want to play my part in catchin' the man, of course. It would mean everything to all of us. I dinnae see eye to eye with most of my colleagues, but one thing I do ken is that we're all desperate to catch this man.'

'But?'

'But. We're face to face with evil here. No gettin' away frae that. An' it's no' somethin' we see in Perthshire. I'm no' scared of it. But I dinnae ken that I want to deal with it.'

'I wouldn't want anyone else to go through what I've gone through.'

'Exactly. Which is why I want to catch him.'

'You will.'

'Aye. I know we will.'

'Anyway, we're not here to talk about me.' Marjory turned to Annie and squeezed her hand. 'Are you two going to start courting proper?'

Annie gave a nervous laugh and looked at Bob. Bob gave a nervous laugh and looked at Annie.

'Because I haven't come all this way to chaperone the pair of you if nothing's going to come of it.' She pulled herself upright as though rearranging her dignity and the others laughed. 'Besides, you're grand together. Anyone can see that.' She stood and walked to the end of the bench. 'Move up,' she said and Annie slid across the bench until she was next to Bob. Marjory sat back down again. When she caught Annie's eye she gestured down to Annie's hands and then across to Bob's. Annie took Bob's hand and they sat like that in silence, two lovers falling in love while their chaperone smiled and stared ahead and wondered whether love might one day come again for her, too.

Picnic completed, they walked on and it was obvious that Marjory was limping. 'It's these stupid shoes,' she said. 'They're new. They're killing me.'

'We'll go steady,' said Bob.

In time they came to a small, dank tunnel under the railway line and walked uphill into a clearing in the woods where a neat little cottage, two-up, two-down, sat in hushed isolation. A little boy, no more than three, was sitting on the doorstep drawing lines in the soil with a stick. He gave them a shy wave and Bob waved back.

'What a beautiful place,' said Annie.

'You wouldn't want to have an emergency, though,' said Marjory. 'It's miles from anywhere.'

A woman appeared from the garden with a basket of washing. 'Come on, Archie,' she said. 'Inside, now.'

They walked uphill and by the time they reached the Laggan farm Marjory was trailing behind, limping badly.

'I'm sorry,' she said, 'but it really hurts.'

'Can I have a look?' said Bob. Marjory sat on a drystone dyke and removed her shoe. Bob could see beneath her stocking a large blister on the heel.

'That looks sore,' he said. 'It'd be best to burst it, or it'll happen by itself and all the skin will come off. Would you mind taking off your stocking?' He turned away and ostentatiously began to examine the hedgerow behind her. Smells of meadow sweet and privet and sweet vernal grass filled the air. Marjory lifted her skirt and peeled down her stocking. When she was ready Bob peered at Annie's hat and took a hat-pin from it.

'Hey,' she said.

'You'll get it back.' He lit a match and held the hat-pin in the flame, rolling it round and round until it was so hot he could barely hold it. He bent down and took Marjory's foot and gently pressed the pin into the edge of the blister three times. With her stocking he smoothed the blister until all the air was removed but the skin remained intact. He cut a square from his handkerchief with his penknife and layered it with docken leaves he had picked from the hedgerow. He pressed it carefully against the blister and told Annie to help Marjory put the stocking back on over it. He turned away again and when they were finished he eased her shoe back on, ensuring the handkerchief offered protection against the hardness of the heel.

'How's that?'

Marjory took a few tentative steps. 'Like new,' she said. 'I could go dancing.' She laughed loudly and then immediately stopped herself.

'Sorry,' she said.

Bob took her hand. 'Don't be,' he said. 'You cannae shut out happiness forever. Danny wouldnae have wanted that. Nobody wants that. You have to live your life.'

'I feel guilty.'

'There's only one person who should feel guilty.'

They strolled back into town, Bob and Annie walking hand in hand, Marjory content to enjoy the moment. At James Square, the Murray Fountain sprayed cooling water and they each stooped to take a drink. Two old men were playing draughts on a giant board laid out behind the fountain, laboriously shifting black and white chequers in turn.

'Aren't you the girl?' A man and a woman, mid-thirties, stood in front of them. They were in their Sunday best, the man sporting a straw boater. 'The Cuddies Strip?' Marjory turned away, gripping her arms around her waist, her face twisted into a scowl. 'I've seen your photograph in the newspaper.'

'You've made a mistake,' said Bob.

'I don't think so.'

Bob pulled out his police identity card. 'You've made a

203

mistake,' he repeated. 'On your way.'

The man blanched and his wife took his arm and tugged him. 'Come on, Albert,' she said and they marched towards the Drummond Arms.

'We'd best be getting back,' said Annie.

'Aye. I need to see to Gran,' said Bob. They walked slowly towards the bus station.

*

Back in Perth they escorted Marjory from the station to Longcauseway. 'Thank you so much,' she said. 'I've had a wonderful day. Really.' She gestured to her heel. 'And thanks to the doctor, too.' She ran up the tenement hallway and turned and waved and dashed upstairs.

'She's very brave,' said Annie.

'She certainly is. I hope the worst is over for her.' They walked to Annie's house at the foot of Feus Road and stood outside awkwardly.

'Thank you,' said Annie.

'Thank you.'

'No. I mean it. Thank you. For looking after Marjory. Being so kind. It was lovely.'

'Anyone would have done it.'

'No, they wouldn't, Bob Kelty. That's what makes you special.'

'There's nothing special about me.'

She leaned up and kissed him briefly on the lips. 'Oh yes, there is,' she said. She slipped inside her house and gave him a wave and closed the door.

Bob recorded the scene, memorised every instant of it, knowing he would never, ever forget it. He started to walk uphill.

Victor had spent the afternoon in his office, going over his files, looking for problems, shapes in the narrative, clues as yet unattended. The trouble was, he knew exactly where to look.

Aberdalgie House.

When he returned to his house on Rose Terrace in early evening Bella was sitting in her chair, the standard lamp casting yellow light from behind. On her lap was a brown photograph album. Victor hadn't seen it in seventeen years and, if asked, he would have ventured that it had been destroyed long ago in that painful unfurling of mourning that stretched from the armistice into the 1920s. He never expected to see it again.

And, more astonishing still, Bella was smiling. She went to the sideboard and poured a large sherry and handed it to him.

'What's this?'

She poured herself a smaller one and sat on the settee in front of the bookcases. She patted the seat beside her.

'Sit with me.'

Victor pulled a small table in front of the settee and settled the sherries on it and sat beside his wife. She rested her hand on his knee and leaned across and kissed his cheek.

'We have so few photographs,' she said. The album contained no more than thirty prints, mostly sepia, stiff family portraits in the main, posed in studios with the participants staring solemnly at the camera. Bella with a baby on her knee. Victor and Bella. The christening, baby Tom swathed in a long shawl. She turned back to their wedding photograph, Bella in white, Victor in police uniform. First Class Constable Conoboy, and what a dasher he was with that moustache, his uniform pristine, sharp creases, gleam of his boots. Victor's mother, Bella's parents, stout, all of them, late Victorian wealth before wars and illness and recession intervened. A generation more fortunate than the one that followed. It wasn't meant to be that way.

Victor held his breath because he knew what was coming, the last photograph in the album before pages of empty sets representing lost years and silence.

'Don't worry,' she said, as though reading his mind. 'I'm ready.'

She turned the page and a single portrait was revealed, an impossibly young man in military khaki, his foot resting on a wooden stool, a cane under one arm and his cap under the other. He had no moustache but in every other respect the photograph was like millions of others fixed in history during those four dark years, the only reminders of what was and could never be again, of what was thrown away. So many undone.

'He looks terrified,' Victor said.

'And proud,' said Bella. 'And happy.'

She sipped her sherry and they stayed like that for some moments, mother and father and son in formal pose, the present becoming the past, the past infiltrating the present.

*

'It was wonderful, Mum. Bob and Annie were so nice. He's a real gentleman. Kind and thoughtful. Look what he did to his handkerchief to make me a bandage for my heel.'

'I'm glad, hen.'

'Can I go and see Danny?'

'It's ower late. Maybe tomorrow.'

'Definitely tomorrow. I've so much to tell him. D'you know, this is the first time I've felt safe since it happened. I think, maybe, I might be able to escape all this after all.'

*

206

'I've had the grandest day. We had a rare dander down Lady Mary's Walk. It was the funniest thing when Bob fell into the river. But he was fine! And he didn't even let the picnic get wet. He was awfae nice with Marjory, too. You could see her coming to life as the day wore on. Even when that silly mannie said he recognised her, Bob just moved him on and that was that.'

'Will you be seein' him again?' said Annie's mother.

'I think so.'

'Well, you'll need to bring him hame so I can meet him.'

'You know Bob, Mum. You've known him for years.'

'Not as my daughter's man, I havenae.'

'You'll like him.'

'I'll be the judge of that, girl.' But Mrs Maybury had to force herself to look stern.

*

The smell of rain was musky in the air, hot dry earth mixing with the pulses of rainwater to create that unmistakable evocation of Scottish summer. John McGuigan lay outside his tent looking up at the sky. He lit his paraffin lamp and kicked off his boots and took the photograph of Marjory Fenwick from his pocket. He masturbated, slowly at first, then with increasing force as frustration kicked in. When he came it wasn't a good one. He opened the paraffin lamp and rolled up a piece of paper and lit it from the flame and held it over the photograph and watched the bitch's face disintegrate into ash. He lay back again and fantasised about Nellie, about what he would do to her on the Cuddies Strip. Taking her from behind, covering her mouth so she wouldn't scream, hitting her. That was a fresh embellishment to his fantasy, and an exciting one. Stripping her naked and tying her up. Punching her again. That stupid face, made for a fist.

Simpering smile. Dog eyes, trusting and idiotic. He'd see that look of terror in her eyes. She knows who I am now. She knows what I am. What I can do. And then he'd take her. Open up that cunt and use it and hurt her. He'd figure out how it worked. What happened. You can be bad with me, if you like. *If I like?* You think I need your fucking permission, you stupid bitch? Stupid cunt. Piece of meat.

He was hard again and this time the wank was slow and measured and the climax shuddered through his body and he grunted with pleasure.

He went inside and lay on his cot. He had received word that morning that his mother and stepfather were returning from the berries on Tuesday. Four weeks of peace and solitude were coming to an end. The tent was nowhere near big enough for three. There was no privacy, comfort.

Time to go. Which meant it was time to deal with Nellie. He grew hard again but it hurt too much to do anything about it. He imagined it instead. It was coming.

*

Nellie Gammon listened to her mother in the bathroom. She listened to the tap running and the click of her mother's teeth sliding into a glass and her mother walking across the hallway and the light going off in her bedroom. She got up and looked out of the window. Somewhere out there was John, in his tent, her bad boy who was going to teach her bad ways. Even when he was rough with her, that only showed she was important to him, didn't it?

'Make it soon, Johnny.'

*

'Well, that's a rum one and no mistake,' said Sergeant Hamilton in Perth City Police headquarters. He addressed

PC Morton because there was no one else in the station and he wanted to share it. 'Just had a telephone call from Mr Dunbar in Crieff. Complaining that a man was rude to him today.'

'Are they very thin-skinned in Crieff?'

'They certainly are. But the interesting point is the person showed Mr Dunbar a City Police identity card. PC Kelty.'

'Bob? Rude? That doesn't sound likely.'

'Perhaps not. But he also said that Kelty was in the company of the girl in the murder case.'

'Marjory Fenwick?'

'The same. Now why would PC Kelty be in Crieff on his day off with a material witness in an ongoing murder enquiry?'

'I couldn't say, Sarge.'

'Nor me. But I bet George Strangeway doesn't know anything about it.' He reached for the telephone.

*

Bob Kelty picked up his guitar and began to play it gently, a tune that came to him unbidden, strange and exotic, driven alternately by the melody strings and the bass rhythm of the E and A strings. He played it over and over. Then he played *Out on the Ocean*, slower than slow, like a meditation in sound.

What do you see? What do you hear? What do you feel? Take a step to your left, a step to your right, pitch yourself out of the present, the personal, the now. Another perspective. A different impulse. A million incidents leading up to this moment, and each one leading to something else again, and then again. Change. The rhythms change. The fabric, the weft. Take that step. What do you see now? What do you hear? Feel? Want?

Bob was coming to understand that there wasn't a single

world or a fixed present. Rather, existence was composed of billions of rhythms, each interacting with the other, each adapting and changing in response, the personal and the universal in concert, and everyone was attached to one of those rhythms and was propelled through their lives in a flux of unimaginable moments. And in this way history and truth were only human constructs to give the illusion of control over the randomness of it all. Comfort from order.

Until order broke down.

Monday 26th August

A Day of Revelation

Bob looked up from his breakfast with a jolt of surprise as Gran shuffled into the kitchen.

'You're up early,' he said. He went to the stove and poured tea from the pot into her china cup. She sat at the table and took the cup and twisted it until the handle was on the correct side.

'The rain woke me.'

'Aye. I suppose it had to break some time. It's been a rare summer.'

'We used to have better summers than this. Sunshine for weeks. We used to work on the farm all through the school holidays. It was grand.'

'Aye? I bet it was right hard work, too.'

'Och, laddie, you've nae idea. You young ains the day, you have it that easy.'

He piled bacon and a tattie scone on a plate and placed it in front of her. She smiled at him and sipped her tea. Bob smiled back but he felt a pang of regret. He was growing to hate the glimpses of the real Agnes Kelty that periodically emerged unbidden from the remnants of her diseased mind.

They were a reminder of what was lost.

'I love you, Gran.'

'Dinnae talk soft.'

*

Heavy rain thudded against the window of the conference room. Outside, the palings in front of the Sheriff Court were barely visible in the gloom. The room was dull. Cigarette smoke palled above the heads of the press.

'A great many lines of enquiry are being pursued.' Lamping wore a serious expression as he looked at the face of each man in turn. It was as though he was accusing them. 'Many have now been discounted. Others offer interesting potential but at this stage there remains no prospect of an arrest.'

Templeton stared from the front row. When Lamping was in full flow he interrupted loudly and persistently, drowning out the Glaswegian. 'It's been twelve days now. Have you at least managed to identify a motive?'

'We no longer think robbery was the primary motivation …'

'You told us that last week. I asked whether you had identified what was.'

They stared at one another across a no-man's land of wooden flooring and mutual antipathy. Each knew the other was thinking not about the murder but about Saturday evening. Triumph, humiliation. Gloating, revenge. History depends entirely on perspective.

'This is a complex …'

'Again, we've heard all this before. What about the handkerchief?'

'That has been identified and ruled out.'

'When will we hear something new? When will the citizens of Perth feel safe in their homes, in their streets, their parks and woodlands? Their shops?' He paused. 'Their bars?'

A rumble of discussion circulated behind Templeton, some of the journalists agreeing, others – mostly the older men – unimpressed by the intemperance of his words. The noise emboldened him.

'The Glasgow police were brought in on Thursday to a grand fanfare. Has the enquiry actually moved forward since then?'

Lamping bared his teeth in a grimace. 'As the gentleman from the *Telegraph* will no doubt be aware, once I decide to pursue something I carry on until I get it.' He stared at Templeton. 'Everything revealed and everything known.'

'Bastard,' mouthed Templeton. Lamping smiled.

*

'That seemed somewhat fractious,' said MacNaughton in his office afterwards.

'The story's slipping off the front pages, sir,' said Lamping. 'The journalists need to ignite a bit of controversy to sell a few more copies of their rags.'

'Was there something personal between you two?'

'Not that I'm aware of.'

'There seemed an edge.'

'I was only standing our ground, sir.'

MacNaughton looked out at the rain. He had a tightness in his chest that would not resolve itself. He picked up a memorandum written by Sergeant Strangeway the previous evening and handed it to Lamping and Watters.

'Where is Kelty now?' he asked.

'Gone to collect the Fenwick girl,' said Lamping.

'Do you want to speak to him when he returns?'

'With respect, sir,' said Watters, 'this feels like a matter for the County force. I think it would be better to wait for Inspector Conoboy to deal with it.'

'I suppose you're right,' said MacNaughton. He lit a cigarette and ordered them out and opened his bottom drawer. It was ten o'clock.

*

In the stairwell, Bob adjusted his cap and fiddled with his tie and his belt. The rain was steady and dense. Marjory gave a broad smile as she answered the door but immediately noticed his grim expression.

'What?' she said.

'I'm sorry, Madge. I have to take you to the station. I have an instruction from the Procurator Fiscal.'

'Why?'

'I dinnae ken.'

Mrs Fenwick hovered behind her, rotund and industrious and worried. 'What is it, hen?'

'Oh, the police want me again. More questions.'

They walked to the car and both were aware of invisible eyes watching, reproachful, inquisitive, interfering. The rain was growing heavier, the air hot and humid and unpleasant. Bob drove in silence.

By the time Marjory was seated in a small wood-panelled room on the second floor of police headquarters she felt sure something bad was going to happen. Didn't it always? Below, people were milling about and looking up, but not in the numbers of the previous week. Her legs were crossed at the ankle and her arms were folded on her lap. She was hunched and small. She tried to cling to memories of the day before. That wonderful little house in the woods. Wouldn't it be grand to live there? Hang the emergencies, enjoy the solitude.

An old man, short and fat, red-faced and unhealthy, entered the room, followed by a younger, taller man. Both wore white overalls over three-piece suits. They smelled of stale tobacco. Neither acknowledged Marjory as they arranged blankets over a table against the far wall. A cushion was placed at one end. Marjory watched in bemusement.

'Miss Fenwick,' said the older man at length. 'My name is Professor Mathieson. This is Dr Armitage. We have been instructed by the Procurator Fiscal to conduct an examination.'

'Of what?'

'Would you mind undressing, please?'

'Here?'

'Just your skirt and undergarments will be sufficient.'

She looked around the room. A teapot and empty cups sat uncleared on the desk. Copies of the *Evening Telegraph* lay on a chair. The room smelled heavily of cigarettes. An ashtray on the mantelpiece was brimming over. Another on a sideboard was almost full. The door was open and she could hear voices outside, laughter and shouts.

'Might anybody come in?'

'I shouldn't think so.'

'Could you close the shutters?'

'I'm afraid not. The lighting isn't very powerful.'

Marjory sat immobile. 'I don't want to,' she said.

'I'm afraid you have no say in the matter. It's on the instruction of the Procurator Fiscal. Let's get on.' He gestured towards her with both hands. The two men watched as she stood and unzipped her skirt and stepped out of it. She slid down her underslip. She began to unhook her suspenders.

'You can leave the stockings,' said Mathieson. 'Just the knickers.'

Marjory refused to cry as she bent and peeled down her silk knickers and laid them on top of her skirt and slip. She stood erect, protecting her private parts with her hand. She looked at the two men.

'Lie on the bed, please,' said Mathieson.

'It's a table.'

'Yes. If you could lie on it.'

She shuffled her bottom against it and hitched herself up. The blanket rucked beneath her. She rolled over and lay on her back, her head resting on the negligible cushion. Her feet hung over the edge. The ceiling stared down at her and she focused on a damp patch in the corner that looked like

215

an outline of Scotland. Go there, go there. Her feet were gripped and pressure applied until her knees rose in the air. Her legs were spread apart and the two men stood, one beside her, the other at the foot of the table, and stared down at her privates. Two fingers were pressed against her vagina, running up and down the labia as they sought entrance. They pushed hard and the labia parted and they found entrance and pressed deep inside her, and the fingers were spread and bent, probing against the inner walls of her vagina. One man examined. The other watched. She would not cry. The outline of Scotland grew indistinct. It grew hazy. It blurred into indistinction. It disappeared into a sea of wretchedness. Two fingers were inside her, knuckles outside, pressing, hurting. When they had done they were removed and the fourth violation in two weeks was complete. The men walked away, talking in low voices. Her knees remained aloft until she turned and faced the wall in silence and closed her legs tightly, her vagina as sensitive as though that alien presence were still there.

It always would be.

Escape? What escape?

'Get dressed.'

*

'Knock, knock.'

Conoboy looked up. Lord Kellett was standing inside his open doorway. He smiled and beckoned to him to enter and the older man shook his hand and sat in the chair opposite his desk. Conoboy offered him a cigarette and they both lit up and sat back.

'How is it?' said Kellett. 'With the Glasgow boys?'

'I'm sure they will be a great support.'

Kellett harrumphed. 'It's me who's supposed to be the diplomat.' They both laughed. Each thought the other looked tired. Each admired the other's dedication.

'Lamping,' said Kellett, 'in the conference, he talked about the handkerchief. Being eliminated. I was a bit surprised. I thought we'd stopped looking into that.'

'Kelty pursued it, sir. But it's a dead end. We're not pursuing it.'

'You didn't find where it came from?'

'We did, yes.'

'Where?'

'Aberdalgie House.'

'David Douglas?'

'Yes.'

'How extraordinary. And what does David say about it?'

'I haven't spoken to him.'

Kellett shifted in his seat. 'Why not?'

'Clearly, Lord Douglas is not the murderer. It's a red herring.'

'Is this MacNaughton's doing?'

'He suggested it was not appropriate for us to interview Lord Douglas.'

Kellett stood up. He walked towards the window and stared out at the street. He turned back to Conoboy. A vein throbbed in his temple. He ground his teeth.

'Of course David Douglas isn't the murderer,' he said. 'That's exactly why you need to interview him. Because the person who stole that handkerchief *is* the murderer, and we have to find out who that is.' He could see Conoboy's discomfort and shook his head. 'Look, Conoboy, I don't get involved in operational details. I have nothing to offer. You chaps are the experts. But I'll tell you this, if you don't go and interview David Douglas out of some misplaced respect for nobility it will be nothing short of a scandal. This isn't some tin-pot dictatorship where we run in fear of those in authority. Nobody in this country is above the law. I'm telling you, you must go and see David Douglas.'

'Yes, My Lord.'

217

'City boy!' shouted Strangeway.

Bob groaned.

'Take Miss Fenwick home and then get out to Bogle Bridge. Somebody bathing nude in the lade. That'll get you out of the way for an hour or so.'

Bob fetched Marjory from the staff room. She was distant and had been crying. He pressed his hand against the small of her back and she flinched. 'Are you okay?' he said.

She stood mutely, waiting for him to open the door.

'I'm sorry. I'm sure they were trying to help.'

'I don't understand how that could have helped.'

'Do you want me to drop you at the cemetery?'

They drove another couple of hundred yards before she spoke. 'It's Kinnoull Hill I want to be,' she said.

'Kinnoull Hill?'

'You know what they do at Kinnoull Hill?'

Bob said nothing. He studied her face, small and unhappy. 'Please be careful,' he said. 'Never forget, people love you, Madge. Even when they don't say so.'

She started to cry, softly and quietly. She pressed a handkerchief to her eyes. 'Just take me to the cemetery, please,' she said. Bob passed her house in Longcauseway and drove on to Wellshill. He stopped and opened her door and she jumped out and ran towards the cemetery gates.

'Madge,' he shouted after her. 'If you need anythin', let me know. Come and see me. Any time. Or Annie. Please.' She walked away without replying.

Bob was still troubled by the depth of her upset when he arrived at Bogle Bridge. He parked on the Dunkeld Road and walked towards the town lade near the Pullar's works. The man had been reported by Mrs Smeaton in Carter Street. 'Naked in full view of everyone.' As Bob turned onto Carter Street he saw the man immediately, sitting by the lade, pulling on his boots.

'What are you doin'?' said Bob.

'Havin' a bath.'

'You've been causin' complaints.'

'Tell them tae stop lookin'.'

'Could you no' go somewhere more private?'

'I would if I kent where sic a place was. I've just arrived. Three days travellin' frae Dunkeld. I was hot and my feet were sair and I saw this wee lade and it looked just grand. Look around ye. There's nae hooses. Anyone who saw anythin' must hae been lookin' right hard, ken?'

Bob was inclined to agree. 'Just keep your knickers on next time, then.'

'I would if I had ony.' He grinned at the constable. Nice-looking laddie, too soft for the polis. 'You wouldnae have any goin spare, would ye?'

Bob thought of the mountain of clothing piling up at the station. Despite the description specifying women's clothing, he knew it included men's underwear.

'Back of the station,' he said. 'Off South Street, near the river. Come by about six.'

'I was jokin'.'

'Nonetheless. If you want some. There's probably a jaicket'll fit, too.'

'Polis charity?'

'Let's say we've an awfae lot of stuff that could do wi' a good home. You dinnae ken any women, do you?'

'I wish, son.'

'Pity. If you did, I could probably kit her oot with a new outfit every day till Christmas.'

'Aye? How come?'

'You've just arrived in Perth, aye? You werenae here two weeks ago?'

'No' me. I was up in Sutherland.'

'Right. Stop flashin' your tadger for all the nosy gowks

tae see and be on your way.'

'Six o'clock?'

'Aye.'

*

'You know what I really hate about Perth?' said John McGuigan. He sat on a wooden bench at the foot of Buckie Braes. The trees overhead afforded shelter from rain that was still falling steadily.

Beside him Nellie Gammon was sitting forwards, her hands beneath her thighs.

'What I hate about this town is its houses.'

'Why ever would you hate the houses?'

'Because they're cold. Fat. They just sit there like puddocks, saying, "don't look at me," in that sort of way that makes you look. They're duller than the people who live in them. Everywhere looks the same. No life. No meaning.'

'But surely you want a roof over your head?'

'I have a roof over my head. My tent has two roofs. And if I get bored I can pack it up and walk away.'

Nellie wondered how it would feel to be so free. No ties. No responsibilities. No work. No getting up at six to light somebody else's fire and working non-stop until five. A life on the road? Wouldn't that be just the thing? Would it? She turned and rested her hand on John's thigh. She tried to ignore the way he flinched, as he always did when she touched him.

'Will you always stay in Perth?'

'God, no. It's so small. I want to travel the world.'

'The family in the big house are just back from South Africa,' she said.

'I know.' He gave a hollow smile. 'You told me before.'

'Yes, my bad boy.' She started to stroke his chest and he knew what would come next, the reach over, the caress of

220

his chin, pulling him towards her, the kiss. He kept his eyes closed. Then he felt it, the brush of her lips on his.

'Get off,' he shouted. He pushed her away and she sat back startled. The look of injury on her simple face infuriated him. He slapped her with the back of his hand, once, hard. She gasped and shrunk from him and covered her face.

'Stop pawing me all the time,' he said. 'It's suffocating.'

'I'm sorry.' Her head bowed, she began to sob.

'Stop that. I hardly touched you.' She looked up at him and gave a small smile. It made him sick. He wanted to be away from her, alone.

'Let's go,' he said.

'Already?'

'My folks are coming home tomorrow.'

'That'll be nice.' She was speaking automatically, as though she wasn't even aware of what she was saying. Jesus, do people get married to cretins like this? McGuigan made no effort to conceal his disgust.

'It won't. It'll be hellish. Tomorrow night, we'll go for a long walk. Just you and me.' He looked away so he wouldn't see her expression, that neediness, the pointless gratitude.

'Great.'

'We'll walk and walk and walk. Till it gets dark.'

'Great.'

Then we'll see what's what.

*

At six-thirty, Bob Kelty closed the rear door of the station, having offloaded two pairs of trousers, a pair of underpants and a donkey jacket on the tramp from Sutherland, along with a packet of Woodbine and a ten-bob note. The station was quiet in a lull between shifts and Bob wondered if he might sneak out to check on Gran. As he passed the boiler room he heard peals of laughter, three or four different men

221

probably, and he paused at the door and listened. He could make out Sergeant Braggan's barking voice and a couple of others he couldn't distinguish.

'Brought him all the way from Glasgow to inspect the girl again. I could have done that for them, saved all that effort.'

There was laughter again, raucous and harsh. Bob shifted with anger behind the door, half-minded to storm in and confront them. He didn't get the chance because, before he could move, the door was swung open and Braggan confronted him, cigarette in his mouth, playing cards splayed in his left hand.

'City boy. I hope you weren't spying on us. We don't do that kind of thing here.'

Bob was aware of his heart pounding, the fear of confrontation assailing his senses as usual. Through it, though, he felt his anger rising. This wasn't right.

'We don't run card schools either, Sergeant,' he said, pushing past Braggan and staring at two men seated round the boiler. They were the men he had seen on Saturday at Muirton Park.

'Just some pals having a quiet game in my break. Nothing wrong with that.'

'And how much do they owe you?' Bob stood directly in front of the two men, staring down at them. 'How much does he charge you to play? How much does he take you for?'

'Careful what you accuse people of, City boy. It's only a bit of fun.'

'Fun? My faither gambled for fun. Got himself into debt with three different bookies. That was fun. Then he put a shotgun in his mouth and blew his head off. For fun. I went to live with my gran and those bookies, they still chased us for their money. Gran, who's never owed anybody anything in her life. Won't even buy things on HP. And me. A fourteen-year-old laddie. So you think it's fun, aye? Well, gambling

222

ruined my life. If it hadn't been for my faither's gambling I'd still be on the farms, working with the heavy horses. Rather than the snakes in the grass here.'

'Steady, City boy.'

'Don't call me that. My name is Constable Kelty.'

'And I'm Sergeant Braggan. Just remember your place.'

Bob glared at him. He scarcely knew what he was saying. 'You might be a sergeant, *Sergeant*. But you'll get no respect from me.'

He turned and walked calmly out of the room and eased the door shut and leaned against the corridor wall, breathing heavily, his eyes closed. His whole body trembled. He turned and saw Sergeant Strangeway blocking the corridor. The sergeant nodded to him.

'I heard.'

'I won't apologise. I'll hand in my badge.'

'That won't be necessary.' He nodded to the boiler house. 'Even the finest orchard has its bad apples,' he said. 'But he'll get what's coming to him some day.'

'Maybe so, but he'll make my life a misery until he does.'

'Don't you worry yourself about Braggan. I've told you over and over, Constable Kelty, in this station you do what I tell you.'

Bob grinned. 'Yes, Sergeant.'

'However, I'm afraid your trouble isn't over yet. The Acting Chief Constable wants to speak to you. Now that you finally seem to have found your voice, let's see if you can talk your way out of this one.' He gave a rueful smile and indicated with a jerk of his thumb for Bob to move.

Bob composed himself in front of the Chief Constable's door and knocked and entered. 'You wanted me, sir?' he said to MacNaughton. Inspector Conoboy was seated at the edge of the desk and he looked up in surprise.

'Kelty,' said MacNaughton, 'I've had a complaint. About yesterday. Care to comment?'

223

'It was my day off, sir. I was in Crieff.'

'Who were you with?' Bob faltered. MacNaughton repeated the question.

'I was with Annie Maybury, sir, my sweetheart.'

'And anyone else?'

'Marjory Fenwick, sir.'

'You spent the day with a material witness in an ongoing criminal investigation? You must know that is improper conduct?'

'I'm sorry, sir.'

'That isn't sufficient Kelty.'

'I asked him,' said Conoboy. They both turned to him. 'It was my idea. Detective Lieutenant Lamping seems convinced the girl is hiding something. I asked Constable Kelty to take her on an informal trip to see if she revealed anything.'

'And did she?'

'No, sir,' said Bob. 'She was very quiet mostly. Never mentioned the crimes.'

MacNaughton studied Bob, and then Conoboy. 'Get out,' he said. Bob retreated with relief and when he was gone MacNaughton stood up. 'I don't believe you,' he said to Conoboy.

'You can either take my word for it, sir, or prove I was lying.'

'That's insubordination.'

Conoboy stood his ground.

'Get out.'

*

That evening, Bella Conoboy sat at the piano and played the strangest music Bob had ever heard. It was classical, but somehow as formless as jazz, floating in the air with no recognisable key or time signature. Hypnotic, repetitive, as

224

mournful as death itself but for all that it lifted Bob's spirits. A frangible beauty. Perfection in sound.

Bella's hands came to rest and the piano played itself into silence.

'What was that?' said Bob.

'Erik Satie. *Gnossienne Number Four*.'

'I've never heard anything like it.'

'Music of the senses. It takes you out of yourself. Do you play an instrument?'

'I'm in the pipe band. And I play piano – Gran has an old one. And guitar. And the fiddle, but I don't get to play it much.'

'Play me something.' She vacated the piano stool and indicated for him to take her place. Bob looked at Annie. He had never played in front of her before. She gave a smile of encouragement.

'This is a Scott Joplin tune,' he said.

'Really?'

'He's an American ragtime pianist.'

'I know he is. But I'm surprised you've heard of him. I have some of his records but they're hard to find in this country.'

'I listen to some odd wireless stations,' Bob explained. 'After Gran's gone to bed.' He readied himself and picked out a brief intro and started to play a slow and mournful tune, the *Bourbon and Tears Rag*, and as he played he was transformed into a different person, sloughing off the shyness that infested his daily interactions. Performance made him real, gave him confidence. For five minutes he made music, oblivious of everything except its sound and its texture and the joy of creation. When he finished he became self-conscious again and stared at the piano keys in silence. Music was easy, words were difficult.

'Wonderful,' said Bella. 'You have natural talent. A beautiful sense of rhythm. You syncopate very well.' She

225

turned to Annie. 'Do you play?'

'Oh, no,' said Annie.

'You must. Have Bob teach you. I have a feeling he'll be a natural tutor, too.'

Bob felt a rush of elation. Annie beamed at him and he picked at the lace of his boot. Bella rose and left the room and closed the door softly behind her.

'Inspector,' said Annie. 'Did I get Bob into trouble? Taking Madge out was my idea.'

Conoboy said no. 'There's no harm done, and if the child managed to get away from everything for a few hours you did a good thing.'

'But will it go against his record?'

'No. He was acting under my instruction.'

'Thank you, sir,' said Bob. 'You didn't need to do that.'

'I did. Our Acting Chief Constable is not the man he thinks he is. Although I shouldn't say that, of course.'

'Will he get the job permanently?'

'It's an irony that the murder case will probably decide that.'

'If we solve the crimes he gets the job?'

'More than likely.'

Bella returned and crossed to where Bob was still seated at the piano. In her hand was a violin case.

'Here,' she said. 'It won't be in tune. It hasn't been touched in eighteen years.'

Bob took it without a word.

'It was Tom's. He was never a great player, but he was enthusiastic.' She opened the case to reveal a fine violin, varnished deepest red, with a neck that was almost black. 'It'll need restrung, of course, but try it to see how it feels.'

Bob held the fiddle reverently. He raised it to his shoulder and plucked the E string. It was very flat. Bella played an E on the piano and Bob began to tune the fiddle gingerly, afraid the strings would snap. It took five minutes and, although now in tune, the fiddle still sounded dull. Bob played a few random notes as he flexed his fingers and then he began to play *The Faerie Boys of Leith* and *The New Way To Edinburgh*. Annie watched this new facet of her man in amazement, tapping her feet and thrumming the rhythm on her knees with her fingers. Bob cycled through both tunes twice and came to a halt.

Bella was holding Victor's hand. She gave a quick nod of satisfaction. 'Take it. It's yours.'

'I couldn't.'

'You will. It's a musical instrument. It needs to be played. It's cruel to keep it in silence. You're a much better player than Tom would ever have been.'

Annie reached out her hand for Bob's and he held it gratefully. 'Thank you,' he said to Bella.

'My only proviso is that I am allowed to hear you play sometimes.'

'Of course.'

'And you use it as a force for good.'

'I'll try,' he said, but he wasn't entirely sure what she meant.

'You'll understand one day,' she said.

Tuesday 27th August

A Day of Arrest

The shrill ring of the telephone in the hallway penetrated the whole house. Bob awoke in alarm, unable to imagine what it was. He had installed the telephone four months before when he started with the City Police but this was the first time it had ever rung. He raced downstairs and picked it up. The grandfather clock in the hallway said it was before half past four in the morning.

'I have County Police headquarters for you,' said a voice on the other end.

'Kelty? Sergeant Strangeway here.' Bob said good morning but Strangeway talked over him. 'You took the Fenwick girl home yesterday?'

'Yes.'

'Are you sure? Only she's not there. Her mother's just rung in, frantic. The child never came home yesterday.'

Bob's heart started hammering in his chest, a pulse throbbing in his throat. Fear of failure, never far from the surface, rose again. Madge. Madge.

'The cemetery,' he said. 'I took her to the cemetery. She sits by Danny's grave. She'll be there.'

'We've looked. Nothing.'

Bob replayed their earlier conversation, her distress, unhappiness. *Kinnoull Hill*, she said. *You know what people do there.*

'No Madge, please.'

'What?'

'I think I know where she might be, Sergeant. Leave it to me.' He replaced the telephone on its hook and sprinted upstairs and dressed and looked in on Gran. She was sleeping, her expression furious, fists clenched.

In early morning darkness he cycled towards Bridge of Earn but turned north before reaching the river. When the path became too steep, he jumped off his bicycle and left it and walked the remainder of the way to the top of Kinnoull Hill, his meagre torchlight offering scant illumination. It was about half an hour before dawn and the darkness was intense. Occasionally the moon appeared from behind shadow, throwing an insubstantial light on the scene, but otherwise there was nothing but blackness and wind. When he approached the top of the ridge he could see Marjory silhouetted against the sky at the cliff edge. He was out of breath, his thighs and calves aching, but he pressed on.

'Madge,' he said. 'Have you been here all night?'

She didn't turn around. She was sitting a yard from the edge. In front of her, Bob knew, was a fall of two-hundred feet onto granite rocks.

'You must be frozen.' He took off his jacket and draped it around her and hugged her to him. She neither resisted nor welcomed him and they sat in silence while life revolved around them. In inches, dawn approached, a halo fixing the horizon, gradually expanding and growing lighter, ever brighter until at almost exactly six o'clock it burst through and sunshine began to pulse into the Strathearn valley and it was revealed as though it had been newly created. The Tay flowed wide and grand towards the sea, railway line running alongside. Further on was the Earn, looping and turning eccentrically as though enjoying its last moments of independence before it merged with the bigger river. To their right was Kinnoull Tower, ragged and derelict. The fields below were empty. Soon they would be alive with reapers and horses, stookers behind, bringing in the harvest, ending the year.

'I'm sorry,' he said. 'About yesterday. I know what they did, now.'

'I don't want to talk about it.'

He stared ahead. 'I think we're getting close. Today, we're following a lead that might take us to him. He'll get what he deserves.'

She shook her head. 'I hope you do get him. But I'm not interested in what happens to him. I only care that nobody else has to go through this.'

'There was another girl attacked last night.'

'By the same man?'

'No. It was in Stirling. She got away. I thought of you as soon as I heard. And her. Poor lassie.'

She turned and took his hand and stroked it. 'You're very kind, Constable. You and the inspector. You've made this bearable, at least.'

'Well, I'm glad.'

A couple of minutes passed, silence, tension. 'I don't know if you know,' he said, 'but my father committed suicide when I was a laddie. I found the body.'

'Yes, I know. I'm sorry.' She looked at the sky. 'I wasn't going to jump, you know.'

'No.'

'Really, I wasn't. But once the idea is in your head ...'

'I know.'

'What upsets me most is that people don't believe me. They think I'm a trollop. That I've engineered this whole thing. People are so unkind.'

'Well, the thing about folks round here, we're inclined to look for the worst in other people.'

'But you're not like that.'

'No.'

'Why can't everyone be like you?'

'To be honest, because the place would fall to rack and ruin. I'm not very handy.'

She laughed. 'You're a very lovely man, Constable Kelty. Please can I come to your wedding?'

'Only if I can come to yours.'

'I'm a long way from that.'

'Aye. But the world turns, Madge. Things happen. Let them.'

*

In the small, hot interview room William Gow looked uncomfortable. He wore a necktie he was clearly unaccustomed to and repeatedly ran his finger round the inside of his collar as though seeking a release catch.

Inspector Conoboy opened his notebook. 'Why are you coming to us now, Mr Gow? It's been almost two weeks.'

'Well, it's no' my job tae find killers but you dinnae seem to be gettin' anywhere, so I thought maybe you might need some help.'

'We're most obliged. Please tell us your story.'

'It was aboot five o'clock. I saw this man up at the top of the Woodland wood, next to the Cuddies Strip. He was just standin' there for about five minutes wi' somethin' cockit up to his eye. I thought it was a gun. Then I saw him run doon the field and climb on the dyke and clap the thing to his eye again. And I saw it was a large spyglass.'

'Was he looking at anything in particular?'

'Well, I was walkin' towards him and when I was about twenty yards away I saw a couple lyin' in the grass.'

'Did you say anything to him?'

'I said, "can you no' see enough withoot the glass?" And he just laughed and put it doon. We started to walk together back towards Callerfountain.'

'And did you have a conversation?'

231

'Oh aye, we had a rare crack. He said he was frae Kirkton of Mailer. I said "how are you no' workin' the day?" and he said he slept in. "You're no' a ploughman, then," I said, "or you wouldnae be allowed to sleep in". "I'm no' a ploughman," he says, "but I work on the farm all the same."'

'Kirkton of Mailer farm?'

'Aye.'

'What else did you talk about?'

'Huntin'. I asked if there were many rabbits on the farm and he said aye. And partridges, too. I asked if he had a bird net and he said no, but he had a gun. I said your boss cannae know about that or he wouldnae let you keep it. "Naebody kens aboot it," he said.'

*

John McGuigan tied the canvas sack on his bed. He looked around the tent. Nervous excitement churned in his stomach, that delicious jolt of anticipation. He imagined it over and over, walking at dusk, the smell of summer air, the struggle, stripping her, hitting her, fucking her. This time there would be no mistake.

And by ten past six the next morning, before anyone knew anything about it, he would be on the bus to Glasgow. A man could get lost in Glasgow.

*

Aberdalgie House was set in woodland near the river Earn, a two-storey building in local sandstone. Sun glinted from the high windows. Conoboy and Bob were shown into a large, airy living room with a view through double glass doors over countryside and the distant Ochils. After five minutes a tall man in corduroy trousers entered. He held out his hand.

'David Douglas,' he said. 'What can I do for you?'

232

Conoboy handed him the handkerchief. 'Do you recognise this, sir?'

Douglas took it and turned it over. It was plain green on one side and patterned on the other. 'I do indeed,' he said. 'I was given this by an Indian gentleman in South Africa years ago. I never really liked it. Where did you find it?'

'It was used to tie the hands of the girl who was raped on the Cuddies Strip two weeks ago.'

'Good lord, what a thing. How could that have happened?'

'When did you last see it, sir?'

'Honestly, I have no idea. Possibly back in Africa.'

'Do you send your laundry to the Kelso Laundry?'

'Yes. We moved back to Scotland in May and sent everything there to be cleaned. We've been using them ever since because they were so good.'

'Have you had any break-ins recently?'

'Not that I'm aware of.'

'When your items were returned from Kelso, I imagine there was a lot of it. Where did you store it?'

'In the laundry. That's an outbuilding in the back.'

'May we see it?'

Douglas called for Mrs Moon and she escorted them to the rear of the house. Her expression gave the unmistakable impression that she disapproved of their presence. She unlocked the laundry door and they entered a long, cold room, whitewashed and spartan. Boxes of unopened laundry lay on a table at the rear. Mrs Moon showed them the laundry book and confirmed that a consignment had been returned from Kelso on the 14th of May. A green handkerchief was itemised.

'So, some time between May 14th and August 14th the handkerchief came into the possession of the killer.'

'Sir,' said Bob. He pointed to the window on the back wall. 'This looks like it's been forced.' Conoboy and Douglas peered up at the casement.

233

'It does,' agreed Conoboy. 'Nobody touch it. We'll arrange for the fingerprint experts to look at it.'

They went outside to look at the front of the window. Bob knelt and touched the ground. 'That looks like ladder marks,' he said, pointing to two small indentations about eighteen inches apart, directly beneath the window. They made a search of the vicinity and after a couple of minutes Bob found a ladder hidden in long grass.

They returned inside. 'Would you know if anything else was missing, sir?' Conoboy asked.

'Not easily. There's still things boxed up. I don't know what's where.' He stopped and walked across to the window again and bent and picked up a blue handkerchief bundled against the wall. 'That's not ours,' he said, handing it to Conoboy.

'Are you sure?'

'Positive. Look at it.'

It was moth-eaten and bedraggled, with dark staining that may have been blood. Conoboy stared it with satisfaction and put it in his pocket. A third handkerchief: first Danny's, covering his face, then the one binding Marjory's hands. And now this.

Possibly the killer's own.

He tried to contain his excitement. They were getting close. He knew it. 'If you don't mind, sir, I'd like to speak to your staff.'

'By all means.'

Conoboy and Bob set up an impromptu interview room in the study and the staff were brought in one by one. They were uniformly polite and helpful, answering every question promptly and fully. But none of them knew anything. Their honesty was evident, and so was their innocence. Conoboy and Bob both felt their excitement dissipate. The last maid arrived, composed and pretty, noticeably less nervous than her peers.

'What's your name?' said Conoboy.

'Nellie Gammon, sir.'

'You've probably already heard from the others why we're here.'

'Yes.'

'The laundry was broken into some time after the 14th of May. We know a handkerchief was taken. We suspect other items were taken as well. Do you know anything about it?'

'No, sir.'

'The burglar entered through the rear window, using a ladder to reach it.'

'Very resourceful, sir.'

Conoboy looked at her in surprise. 'This is a serious matter, miss.'

'Yes, sir.'

Bob watched her curiously. She wasn't at all like the others. There was no semblance of deference in her manner. She didn't seem shocked or surprised or concerned. Rather, the interview appeared to be a source of amusement.

'Have you seen anybody suspicious around the grounds?' Conoboy asked.

'No, sir. Nobody.'

'Are you sure?'

'Completely.' She sat forward as though she was bringing the interview to an end herself. 'Will there be anything else, sir?'

Conoboy shook his head and Nellie made to stand.

'Miss?' said Bob. 'Why do you think anyone would break into what looks like an empty building?'

'I couldn't say. Maybe he knew it wasn't empty.'

'And how could he have known that?'

'I don't know.' She shrugged. 'I suppose you're looking for a bad boy.' She gave another smile, vaguely insolent.

Intense irritation washed over Bob, but he was suspicious too. The girl was too cocky. It was a game to her. He vaguely knew her. She lived in Cherrybank and her father was a coalman. She wasn't that sort of girl. 'Miss,' he said, 'it is almost certainly the case that the man who broke into the laundry is the person who shot Daniel Kerrigan in the face at close range and murdered him and then chased and raped Marjory Fenwick on August the 14th. So, if those are the actions of a bad boy then I suppose you're right.'

The change was instant. Nellie's eyes glazed and her mouth fell open. She swallowed. She looked down at the floor and then up at Bob and Conoboy.

Bob spread his palms flat on the table. 'And having done it once, it's almost certain he'll do it again. So I'll ask you again, do you know who might have done that?'

The most important decision Nellie Gammon would ever make took no more than a couple of seconds to reach. She looked out of the window as she spoke, at the manicured lawn with rough countryside beyond. 'Yes,' she said. She turned and stared at Bob, her eyes tearing up. 'John McGuigan.'

'And who is he?'

'Farmhand. Kirkton of Mailer farm.'

*

Charles Elder smoked his pipe as he strode across the yard. Conoboy and Bob followed him.

'You have a John McGuigan working for you?'

'You could say that. Not that he does that much actual work.'

'Since when?'

'Last year sometime.'

Bob shook his head. 'When I asked for the names of everyone on the farm last week you didn't give us his name. Why not?'

'The McGuigans are tinks. They live in a tent up by the wood. They don't count.'

Conoboy cursed. 'Where is he now?'

'Nae idea.'

'Mr Elder, we're investigating the murder of Daniel Kerrigan. I would appreciate your cooperation.'

Elder stopped and turned. 'Did he do it?'

'We wish to speak to him in connection with the murder.'

'I thought so. He said he was up there that night.'

'And you didn't think to tell us that?'

'I've nae proof.'

Conoboy kicked a pebble in frustration. 'So where is he?'

'Mending some dykes with Peddie.'

'When will he be back?'

'Before five. He's no' a body tae put in extra hours.'

Conoboy looked at his pocket watch. It was not quite one. 'Tell him to come to the police station as soon as he returns.' He looked at Bob. 'Tell him to ask for Constable Kelty.'

'Aye.'

*

At four, Peddie and McGuigan strolled up the path towards the farmhouse, laughing. Elder picked up his walking stick and intercepted them. He sent Peddie to the stables to mix feed for the horses.

'The polis want to speak to you,' he said to McGuigan. He studied his face. 'Aboot the murder.'

'What about the murder?'

'They didnae say.'

'They're no' goin' to arrest me?'

'I've nae idea. Why, should they?'

McGuigan made no eye contact. 'No' me. I'm a quiet lad.'

'Aye, I dinnae ken aboot that. But if they were goin' tae arrest you they wouldnae just ask you to drop by and see them, I don't suppose. They'd come and get you.'

That seemed reasonable. McGuigan's first thought had been to make a bolt for it. But no. Keep your head, Johnno. They can't have evidence. Stay calm.

When he returned to the tent his mother and stepfather were already home. The kettle was boiling on a fire outside. He took it from the flame and shouted for them. His mother appeared from inside the tent.

'Is that you, son?'

'No, it's Benito Mussolini.' She reached up to kiss him but he stepped back. 'I'm away doon the polis station,' he said.

'What for? You havenae got in trouble again?'

He picked a blade of grass and chewed it. 'I'll see you later,' he said.

'Will I save you some tea?'

*

He arrived at County Police headquarters at six o'clock and explained to Sergeant Strangeway that he had come as requested.

'What for?'

'I dinnae ken.'

'Who were you told to ask for?'

'Some constable. Kiltie?'

'Kelty.'

'Aye.'

'That explains it. Wait here.' He had seen Kelty and Conoboy go into the inspector's office ten minutes before and he knocked on the door and announced their visitor.

Bob stood up. 'That, Sergeant, is the murderer of Daniel Kerrigan and the man who raped Marjory Fenwick. Put him in the interview room and place McNab on guard. The inspector will be ready to interview him forthwith.'

Strangeway faltered, then smiled broadly. 'Well done,

238

Constable. How did you do it?'

'The handkerchief marking.'

'Of course.' When he went outside, Braggan was waiting for him.

'What's up?' said Braggan.

'Oh,' said Strangeway. 'PC Kelty has just brought in the killer of Danny Kerrigan. And the man who raped the Fenwick girl.' He swept past Braggan and shouted for McNab.

'How?' said Braggan.

'Courtesy, conscientiousness, cautiousness, contentment, comradeship.'

'Eh?'

He turned back and faced him. 'Or, put simply, by being a good police officer, Sergeant. Working hard. You should try it some time.'

When Conoboy and Bob arrived at the interview room Lamping and Watters were already waiting. 'Gentlemen,' Conoboy said. 'You've heard?'

He opened the door and he and Bob strode into the room, followed by Lamping, Watters and Braggan. John McGuigan sat back in his chair, his left leg swinging from side to side. He was still grimy from work and smelled stale. Conoboy introduced himself and the others, speaking slowly and clearly. McGuigan stared at him and Conoboy tried to gauge his expression. There was fear, definitely, and uncertainty. But there was something else. Arrogance perhaps, or maybe simply confidence. This man thinks I have no evidence, he thought. And, at this stage, he was correct. The word of Nellie Gammon linked him to the robbery and the handkerchief linked the robbery to the rape. But that wasn't sufficient for a prosecution.

'Sergeant Braggan,' he said, 'go and fetch Miss Fenwick immediately.'

Braggan bristled and looked about to object but neither

Bob nor Conoboy nor Lamping nor Watters paid him any heed and after a moment's hesitation he slid out of the room unnoticed. Conoboy turned to McGuigan. 'Mr McGuigan, where were you on the night of August the 14th?'

'In my tent.'

'Alone?'

'Yes.'

'Were you anywhere near Buckie Braes or the Cuddies Strip that day?'

'No.'

'We have evidence you were there after five o'clock. You spoke for around half an hour with William Gow.'

'I don't know William Gow.'

'He told you he was looking to poach a couple of birds. You discussed the number of rabbits and birds on Kirkton of Mailer farm. Do you recollect that?'

'Kind of. I dinnae ken what day it was, though.'

'You also told Mr Gow you had a gun.'

'No' me. I couldnae afford that sort of thing.'

'Where is that weapon now?'

'I never had it.'

'So when we search your tent we won't find anything?'

'Only my parents.'

'Your parents?'

'Back from Blair the day. Bloody nuisance. There's not enough room for three in our tent.'

'Well, I suspect that is something you won't have to worry about for some time, Mr McGuigan.' Finally. Conoboy saw McGuigan's self-control waver, if only for an instant. Then the smirk returned.

'Tell me about Aberdalgie laundry.' The smirk disappeared again.

'What about it?'

'When did you break into it? Some time in May?'

'I dinnae ken anything about that.'

240

'What else did you steal apart from the green handkerchief?'

'Nothing.'

'Do you admit you stole a green handkerchief?'

'No.'

'The green handkerchief was subsequently used to bind Marjory Fenwick's wrists while you raped her.'

'No.'

'And when you finished you returned to Kerrigan and shot him again and placed his own handkerchief over his face.'

'No.'

'It's an old tinker custom, I believe. A mark of respect for the dead.'

'I dinnae ken.'

'But you do come from a tinker background, Mr McGuigan?'

'It's not a crime.'

'No. But murder is. And rape is. And then we found your handkerchief on the floor of the Aberdalgie House laundry.' He pulled the blue handkerchief from his pocket and laid it on the table. McGuigan stared at it impassively. 'Three handkerchiefs. All of them combining to link you to scenes of the crimes. John McGuigan, did you murder Daniel Kerrigan and rape Marjory Fenwick on the night of the 14th of August?'

'I want to see a solicitor.'

'We haven't charged you with anything, yet.'

'I'm saying nothing.'

'As you wish. We are arranging two identity parades. One with Miss Fenwick and the other with Mr Gow. I'm warning you now that if those result in a positive identification you will be charged with murder and rape. Is there anything you wish to say to that?'

McGuigan buried his face in his hands and breathed

heavily four or five times. When he looked up Conoboy and Lamping and Watters had left and Bob was watching him as though in the presence of evil.

*

Conoboy walked into South Street and looked among the men milling around for suitable candidates. Word quickly spread that the police were conducting an identity parade and within minutes the street was full. He was able to select six men of comparable stature and comportment.

'Are you goin' tae make an arrest?' asked a sharp-faced woman holding a morose baby.

'We anticipate developments,' he said. He took the men inside and told them to wait in the Chief Constable's office until Marjory arrived. He strode to his office and lit a cigarette and stared out of the window at the rear yard and the back of the council buildings. This was a moment of hope. He hadn't known many in the past twenty years. The door opened and MacNaughton strode in, newly arrived from a conference with Lord Kellett.

'Who are these people in my office?'

'An identity parade, sir.'

'For what?'

'For John McGuigan. Murderer and rapist. Miss Fenwick is on her way, as is Mr Gow.'

'Who?'

'William Gow, sir. He saw McGuigan peeping on a courting couple on the afternoon of the murder.'

'And who is McGuigan?'

'A tinker.'

MacNaughton's expression was blank. 'How did you find him?' he said, but he already knew the answer.

'Aberdalgie House.'

'I gave you express instruction not to go there.'

'Did you, sir? You might wish to reflect on that, given the circumstances. Should you recall differently I will, of course, back you up.'

'That's twice you've been insubordinate.'

'There have been more occasions, sir. You simply didn't notice.' He glanced in the direction of the locked drawer and stood up and straightened his tunic. He stroked his moustache. 'I expect you'll be needing some whisky now so, if you'll excuse me, I have an identity parade to conduct.'

'For your sake it had better be positive.'

'For everybody's sake. But especially for Madge Fenwick and the family of Danny Kerrigan.' He paused. 'Sir.'

*

Conoboy addressed the six men in the identity parade. 'Form up in a line. Facing the front.' They shuffled into position and watched as McGuigan was led into the room by Jones.

'Take any position you wish,' Conoboy said and McGuigan stepped into the row at the far left, nearest the wall where the light was weakest.

Conoboy instructed Bob to fetch Marjory and she entered moments later, fearful and nervous, her eyes shifting around the room. Her mother followed.

'Madge,' said Conoboy, 'I want you to take your time. Look at each man in turn and tell me if you recognise the man who attacked you.'

Marjory steeled herself and walked forward. She was not in control of her legs. She felt momentarily dizzy and stared at the floor to steady herself. She thought of Danny. *Don't faint here, Madge.* But what if he's there? *Point him out.* Is it that easy? *Easy peasy, gal.* She started at the right of the group and studied each in turn.

All the while, Bob studied her, her concentration, the way she bit her lip, the way her hands were fisted, the tension that

243

stiffened her body. He watched her pass the first six men and when she came to the last he watched as she gave a jump and let out a cry and he saw her eyes open wide with recognition. She stepped away in shock.

'What shall I do now?' she said.

'Do you recognise your attacker?'

'Yes.'

'Who?'

She didn't touch him but she stood in front of John McGuigan. She stared into his eyes and he stared back.

'This is the man.'

'You've made a mistake,' said McGuigan. 'I may resemble the man.' He gave a sardonic grin but it fooled no one.

Conoboy thanked Marjory and asked McNab to take her home. He told the men on parade to wait until Mr Gow arrived.

'You can move your position if you wish,' he told McGuigan. McGuigan remained where he was. The inspector instructed Bob to conduct the next parade and bring the prisoner to his office when it was concluded.

MacNaughton, Lamping and Watters were waiting in his office when he entered. He rounded them and sat and leaned across his desk. 'Miss Fenwick has made a positive identification,' he said.

'Congratulations, men,' said MacNaughton. 'A triumph of joint working between our two forces.'

'Thank you, sir,' said Lamping. 'I hope we've been able to offer support and assistance.'

'We couldn't have achieved this without it.' MacNaughton tapped a cigarette against his case. 'Could we, Conoboy?'

Conoboy drew out the silence long enough for it to become wholly uncomfortable. Finally, he spoke. 'I'm proud that Constable Kelty's perseverance and skill has been instrumental in catching a vicious killer and rapist,' he said.

They remained in purgatorial silence for some minutes until McGuigan was brought in.

'Another positive identification, sir,' said Bob.

'John McGuigan,' said Conoboy, 'I am going to prefer some charges against you. You are not required to say anything unless you wish to do so. Anything you do say will be written down and may be used in evidence. I am formally charging you with the murder of Daniel Kerrigan. I am charging you with the assault and ravishment of Marjory Fenwick. I am charging you with the theft of a pocketbook from Mr Kerrigan. I am charging you with the theft of items of clothing from Miss Fenwick. I must advise you that further charges are likely to follow, relating to housebreaking at Aberdalgie House. Is there anything you wish to say?'

McGuigan shook his head.

'You will be remanded in custody and will appear in the Sheriff Court in the morning. I must warn you that, given the gravity of the offences you are charged with, it is certain you will be detained in Perth Prison pending trial.'

He was led out and Conoboy stood and took his cap from the coat rack. 'I'm going to make a search of his tent,' he said, 'before his parents try to destroy any evidence.'

'You'll need a warrant,' said Lamping.

'There's no time,' he said. 'It's an emergency.'

'You can't. It's process. You'll blow the case when it goes to court. Assistant Chief Constable Warnock ...'

'I can and I will. If we delay we run the risk of evidence being destroyed. I will not permit that to happen. It's a matter of justice. Come, Robert.'

*

At ten o'clock, an hour after McGuigan had been charged, Conoboy and Bob visited his tent at Kirkton of Mailer farm. His parents listened impassively as Conoboy explained what had happened.

'He didnae do that,' said Mrs McGuigan.

'He's a good lad,' said his stepfather.

'I have to search the tent,' said Conoboy. They offered no resistance and stood aside as Bob bent low and pulled himself inside.

A single paraffin lamp offered little light. Most of McGuigan's possessions seemed to be in a canvas sack, as though he were about to leave. Bob rummaged through it and pulled out a vest, a pair of trousers and braces, two caps and a shirt. He put them back in the bag and threw it towards the entrance to the tent. He searched deeper into the tent and pulled out, in turn, a brown leather purse, a deflated football, a small alarm clock, a tube of lipstick, a large brown telescope and around a dozen snares. He pushed them towards the entrance and dragged himself out and showed them to the inspector.

'We shall need to remove these,' Conoboy said. Again, the McGuigans offered no objection and Bob loaded them into the back of the Wolseley.

'First thing tomorrow,' Conoboy said to Bob, 'take these items to Aberdalgie House. I'm certain they were taken in the robbery.'

'Yes, sir.'

'Bob?' Bob Kelty paused with his hand on the rear door. 'Well done, son. This is down to you.'

'No, sir.'

'Yes it is. You know that as well as I do. I was about to give up on Nellie Gammon. I thought she was just a silly girl. You saw it. You persevered. Without that McGuigan would still be free. Who knows what he might have done next? The Gammon girl would certainly have been in danger. You're a better policeman than you realise. Give yourself some credit.'

'Thank you, sir. I'm not sure that's true, or if it matters. But thank you.'

246

A midnight moon hung high over the graveyard. It was not cold. Marjory lay on the grave, her ear to the ground as though listening. She had just finished telling Danny the news and she lay in silence, hearing her own breathing, feeling a pulse rising in her ear.

She wondered what was happening to Danny's body. Was it starting to rot? How much flesh would be left? Would there be bones showing yet? Would it smell? It was the first time she had experienced such notions. Until then, when she had lain on his grave she imagined Danny as he was, still and unmoving, but identical to the last time she had seen him. Intact. For ever.

That night she dreamed of dark places and dark moments. The darkness crawled. It sucked. It smelled. She dreamed of decay and terminal loss. She dreamed of worms and maggots, of eye sockets black and empty, symbols of death suddenly writhing with life. She dreamed of black tunnels and bright passages, of capture and escape. She dreamed of violence and love, death and kisses.

She woke up exhausted.

And ecstatic.

Part Two

November 1935

Monday 25th November

A Day of Examination

At eight o'clock the Midland Bluebird stood with its engine idling at Perth Bus Station. The morning was cold and wet, a haze hanging overhead, obscuring Pomarium to the rear. One by one the witnesses at the trial of John McGuigan embarked. William McDougall from Hill Farm of Pitheavlis, who would confirm the time of the murder; Robert Barrie and Jamesie Stewart, who saw McGuigan on the Cuddies Strip; Arthur Hill, who could confirm it; John Spence, who encountered the frantic Marjory Fenwick after the attack; Constable Kelty and the Drummonds; Graeme Peddie and Charles Elder, workmates of McGuigan on Kirkton of Mailer farm; William Gow, who could identify him; assorted others with bit parts to play in the sad affair. Mr and Mrs McGuigan, the accused's parents, climbed aboard to silence and occupied a double seat near the front. Finally, Marjory and her mother took their seats, three rows behind and to the right of the McGuigans. The doors were closed and the entourage made its way to Friarton and onwards to the capital. They had to stop three times to allow Mrs McGuigan to be sick at the side of the road.

'We'll be late,' said Mrs Fenwick.

'I wouldnae worry, missus,' said Graeme Peddie. 'They winnae start withoot us.'

Laughter lightened the mood, but not for long. The strangest charabanc continued its journey.

251

The Justiciary Court of Scotland dominated the crossroads of the Royal Mile and Bank Street. Further down was St Giles Cathedral, the *Heart of Midlothian* adorning the pavement outside. Across the road were the office of births, marriages and deaths and the National Library of Scotland. Uphill, a quarter of a mile away, stood the castle. From as early as eight o'clock, before the witnesses had even departed Perth, an expectant crowd was gathering outside. Predominantly female and representing a full range of classes and types, they queued patiently. By nine-thirty there were in excess of two-hundred hopefuls, far more than could be accommodated within. Rain fell without cease. Discussion was muted. Edinburgh was grey of sky and mood.

When the witnesses arrived at the rear of the building on St Giles Street they caused a stir among that portion of the snaking queue lucky enough to be positioned there. For most, it would be their only interaction with the proceedings of the day. Marjory was identified from among the unknowns and endured pointing and shouts as she and her mother were ushered inside by a policeman.

'Here we go again,' she said. She was returned to those dark days of August, that pain, fear, despair. They had never truly gone away. Now, they were back.

Albert Russell, her counsel, greeted her in the hallway and introduced her to Geoffrey Cummings, his junior counsel. Marjory looked in wonder at the opulence of the open stairway, its size, the light illuminating it even on this dullest of days. All this, for criminals, she wondered. Russell led her to a small anteroom off the main court. It was functional in wood and brown varnish. Marjory's new, tightly fitting black coat made her appear even smaller than ever. A checked scarf was draped around her neck beneath a fur wrap, and a stylish black hat was cocked over her left eye. She looked like a child dressed as an adult. She looked too frail for the ordeal ahead of her, ill at ease. Her dark eyes stared at Mr Russell.

'This must all feel terribly daunting, Madge,' he said. 'But I will be there at all times. I will ask you questions as we've discussed before. Answer simply and truthfully. Don't offer anything that hasn't been asked for. But don't conceal anything.'

'What about the other lawyer?'

'For the defence? That won't be until this afternoon, I expect. We can discuss it over lunch. Mr Burnett will try to flummox you, but do the same thing. Answer simply and truthfully.'

Russell watched her carefully. He couldn't assess yet how she would react. Someone so young and naïve, she could easily buckle under the pressure, especially when Burnett started on her. He'd seen it often enough. The Harman case rose in his memory, his greatest failure, brought low by an eighteen-year-old girl who couldn't stop talking. Madge was seventeen, and a young seventeen at that. Like all youngsters, she was prone to flashes of anger when provoked. She would need to keep herself under control.

'Don't allow him to upset you. If you need reassurance, look at me.'

'Will he be there?'

'McGuigan? Yes. In the dock, flanked by two policemen.'

'Will he be able to see me?'

'He will. Ignore him. He can't harm you now.'

She was wringing her hands. She looked on the verge of tears, certainly close to panic. This early in the proceedings, it was a concern to Russell.

'It'll last six days at most. That's it. That might seem a long time to you now, but I promise it will go by in a flash, and then you'll be able to get on with your life.'

Get on with my life, Marjory thought. Three months on and normality seemed no closer. She was spared endless police questioning and she had returned to work but in all other respects had anything changed? She studied the wood panelling that covered the room. She liked its patterns, the regularity of it, the crisp straightness of its lines. It felt solid, real. I shall have something like this one day, in my own house. Cling to that, Madge. Dream. Russell offered her tea but she declined.

'I'll be needing to wee all morning if I do,' she said.

Russell clapped his hands. That was better. An attempt at humour.

'When do I go in?'

'I don't know exactly.' He looked at his court listing. 'There's two witnesses before you. The defence won't be interested in Darling the surveyor but they will want to pick holes in McDougall. Sow doubt in the jury's minds as early as possible. Probably an hour, I would think, but perhaps not as long.'

'The sooner the better,' said Mrs Fenwick.

For once, Marjory agreed.

*

Lord Chief Justice, Lord Aitchison, sat in his chambers and stared into the mirror as an attendant fixed his wig and adjusted his red cloak. The accused was a tinker. That would stand against him immediately in the eyes of the jury. Aitchison was alert to such matters. They got in the way of justice. He would address that early in the proceedings. The man deserved a fair trial and he would receive one.

'My Lord?' He looked in the mirror and saw the reflection of Alexander Rae, Clerk of Court, bristling and efficient as ever. 'I have a request, my Lord, from one of the lady members of the jury.'

'She wants to be permitted to knit?'

'No, my Lord. She has asked whether the ladies might remove their hats in court.'

'That would be most unusual. I would ask them to refrain from doing so.'

'Very well, my Lord. I shall let them know.'

Lord Aitchison shook his head and the attendant smiled. There was no need to let standards slip just because there were ladies involved.

*

Conoboy greeted Chief Constable Fraser of the City Police on the telephone. They discussed the pending court case.

'It's always difficult,' said Conoboy, 'when we have a major case at trial. The atmosphere in the station, it's tense. Everyone's mind is somewhere else.'

Fraser sympathised and wished him the best. Conversation turned to Bob Kelty.

'He's due to give evidence tomorrow,' said Conoboy. 'His first time.'

'Sergeant Hamilton has been coaching him.'

'I'm very grateful.' There was silence for a moment. 'I wondered whether, for the rest of the week, Robert might attend court. As part of his training. He might find it useful.'

'He might,' said Fraser non-commitally. 'He's come out of his shell a lot, but I still find it difficult to see a future for him in the police.'

'I rather fancy the next few days may decide that one way or the other.'

*

Court rose as Lord Chief Justice Aitchison swept in and took his seat on the King's Bench and settled his notes in place. A

255

tall and robust man, verging on portliness, he had a face like an Easter Island statue with an aquiline nose that appeared even larger beneath the wig, and a long, protruding jaw. His eyes were palest blue and deep, connoting intelligence. His expression was fierce. He exuded confidence. He sat unsmiling and observed his court. On his instruction the jury were called and sworn in, eight women and seven men. In the gallery, a veteran court watcher shook his head.

'More women than men,' he said. 'Reprehensible. I fear for a sound verdict.' Those around him, women included, inclined their heads in silent agreement.

A hush fell on the court as Lord Aitchison called for the accused to be brought forwards. A wooden door opened behind the dock and John McGuigan entered, followed by two police guards. He wore the same dark suit he had worn for the preliminary hearings in Perth Sheriff Court, but underneath he now wore a collar and tie. He surveyed the court with an insouciant smile and gripped the rail surrounding the dock tightly but otherwise betrayed no sign of nervousness. Lord Aitchison instructed the Clerk of Court to read the charges and Alexander Rae stood and spoke slowly.

'John McGuigan, you are charged that between May 14th and August 14th, 1935 you broke into a laundry adjacent to Aberdalgie House and stole a handkerchief and a number of items. You are further charged that on August the 14th, on a strip of woodland known as Cuddies Strip, you assaulted Marjory Fenwick and Daniel Kerrigan by shooting at them and you murdered Daniel Kerrigan and, B, you stole a pocketbook or wallet from Daniel Kerrigan. You are further charged that at a stile at the south side of the field adjoining the east end of the strip you criminally assaulted Marjory Fenwick and raped her.'

A palpable sense of anticipation circulated in the court. The gallery sat forwards. The jury appeared apprehensive.

256

Eyes turned constantly to John McGuigan but he stared ahead throughout, inhabiting his own thoughts, his expression calm and unconcerned. From McGuigan, eyes turned to the wooden case at the rear of the courtroom which contained one-hundred and six exhibits that would be produced in the course of the trial. The significance of a deflated football and a telescope was much pondered, scenarios invented for wider discussion at the next available break. Meanwhile, all thought, 'let it start.'

When it did, the first hour was a disappointment. John Darling, town surveyor, unrolled Ordnance Survey maps of the area and explained the terrain. The ground rose gradually to the south of Perth to a height of five-hundred feet. The highest point was Callerfountain Hill and it formed part of a ridge running along the north boundary of the Earn. The fields were bounded to the north by a wooded strip of rough ground called the Cuddies Strip. At the east corner of the strip was a stile giving entry to a pathway leading to the junction of Woodhead of Mailer road and the Dunning road. After going along the Strip one reached Buckie Braes, entered by a gate at the south. From there, Cherrybank was a short walk down a small glen.

'How far is it from the murder scene to the accused's abode?' asked Lord Aitchison.

'About one mile, my Lord, over the shoulder of Callerfountain hill.'

'And is it easily traversible?'

'It is. There is a path most of the way. The rest is light scrubland.'

It was important background information, but turgid stuff. The gallery wanted excitement. A few, intemperate enough to fall into conversation, were quickly silenced by a glare from the judge.

William McDougall, from Hill Farm of Pitheavlis, repeated his testimony about hearing shots at just after ten o'clock and fearing poachers on his land.

'Did the shots follow in quick succession?' asked Mr Russell.

McDougall slapped the edge of the witness box twice.

'That will be difficult to get in the official record,' said Mr Russell. The gallery laughed.

'Only a second or two apart.'

'And then was there a further shot?'

'Aye, ten or so minutes after.'

But no one was interested. They had come to hear the salacious details and a wave of excitement ran through the court as Marjory Fenwick's name was called.

*

Marjory took the witness box with greater confidence than Russell had expected and she stood erect and looked around the room. She gave a composed smile. Even when she looked at the dock she did not falter. Good girl, thought Russell. He started his examination and Marjory told the court she turned seventeen on March the 14th that year. She had been walking out with Danny Kerrigan since the New Year. She worked in the confectionery factory on Glover Street. An ordinary girl, in other words, like your own daughter or niece or neighbour. He asked her to describe the evening of August the 14th and she said that Danny arrived for her at 7 pm, as arranged.

'On that night, had you been unwell?'

'Yes.'

'Were you just getting better?'

'Yes.'

She said that Danny suggested the pictures. 'Shirley Temple was on at the King's,' she said, 'but I don't like her.' Laughter rippled through the courtroom. Russell looked at the jury and they, too, were laughing. Even McGuigan. Little details were important, he knew. They made Marjory real, a genuine girl with her own tastes and desires. He gave her an encouraging smile.

'So what did you do instead?'

'We went for a walk.'

'Where to?'

'Nowhere in particular. We were just walking.'

'You went out through Cherrybank to Buckie Braes?'

'Yes.'

'Did you stay there for some time?'

'Not in Buckie Braes.'

'Did you go right through Buckie Braes?'

'Yes.'

'When you reached the end of the Braes furthest from Perth where did you go?'

'There was a field and we went through it and came to the Cuddies Strip.'

'About what time was this?'

'I have no idea.'

'Did you pass any other people?'

'A couple passed us as we were going up the field.'

'Was any remark made?'

'They said, "Hello Danny."'

'Did you know either of them?'

'I didn't notice them much.'

'What did you do next?'

'We crossed the stile into the Cuddies Strip and about halfway down we stopped and sat on the grass.'

'Did he show you anything?'

'Photographs.'

'Photographs of what?'

'The one I really looked at was one of myself.'

'Was it one you had given him?'

'Yes.'

'What did he keep the photograph in?'

'A pocketbook.'

'Did you see the pocketbook?'

'I wasn't really looking.'

'When you were sitting together, was Danny kissing you?'

'Yes.'

'And embracing you?'

'Yes.'

'Were you actually engaged to be married to him?'

'No.'

'Had you been walking out with any other young man before Danny?'

'No.'

'Did any man interfere with you before that night?'

'No.'

Russell stroked his pocket watch and studied his book of notes. The pause was deliberate to allow the jury time to reflect. It also gave Marjory a moment to settle before her testimony became more difficult. She explained that they heard the chimes of the Perth Academy clock and realised it was late and began to walk back towards Perth. That was when the shot was fired.

'When the shot was fired, did something pass you?'

'Something seemed to whizz past my head.' She drew her hand across the right side of her face.

'From which side had the shot been fired?'

'The right-hand side.'

'Did you think it came from ahead or behind or just opposite?'

'Behind.'

'What happened then?'

'Danny said "Don't faint here, Madge."'

'And after he said that was there another shot?'

'Yes.'

'From which direction did it seem to come?'

'The same direction. It seemed to come from somewhere behind me and to the right.'

'What happened to Danny next?'

'He fell back. I bent over him and shouted, "Danny, Danny." There was blood on his face and chest. He was moaning, but not moving.'

Lord Aitchison had been impassive until now, sitting with his arms outstretched on the wooden chair arms. Now he sat forward. 'Before this happened,' he said, 'did Danny turn around?'

'Yes, in the direction the shot was fired.'

'I know this is difficult,' said Russell, 'but tell me what happened next.'

'I shouted "Help," and when I looked up there was a man beside me.'

'Was he carrying anything in his hand, as far as you saw?'

'No.'

'Could you describe what happened next?'

Marjory blinked once and swallowed before continuing. 'I told him to wait there till I got help. He didn't speak. I started to run along the path towards Perth. He was running alongside me. I got to the stile and tried to climb over it but I felt his hand on me. He pulled me off the stile and dragged me back. I cried out. He put his knee on me and I could hardly get a breath. It was while he was holding me that he tied my hands and mouth.'

She stopped and looked at the clerks in front of her, black-gowned bodies hunched over ledgers. They were the only people in the entire court room not staring at her. She turned to Mr Russell. He asked her to continue.

'He dragged me to the bushes and started to take my clothes off. He untied my hands again to get my swagger coat off and the he tied them again behind my back. And he took the rest of my clothes off.'

'What happened next?'

261

Marjory shook her head. For the first time she looked close to tears. 'Must I tell this in public?'

'I'm afraid you must, Madge. Don't be frightened.'

It took her a moment to compose herself again. She looked at her mother in the gallery. She looked at the dock. She looked at Mr Russell.

'He tried to take advantage of me. He succeeded. When he finished he went back towards where Danny was and I think there was another shot.'

'You think?'

'I am almost certain.'

'And did you see the man again?'

'No.'

'What did you do?'

'I lay there for some time. I was too shocked to move. I tried to get up but there was something tied around my ankles. I could feel it stretching and I managed to get loose. It was one of my stockings.'

'Had you anything round your hands?'

'A handkerchief.'

'How did that handkerchief get there?'

'The man who assaulted me tied my hands with it.'

'How did you manage to free your hands?'

'I pulled one hand out from the knots.'

'Did the handkerchief remain around your wrist?'

'Yes.'

'And you had something over your neck?'

'My suspender belt.'

'How did it come to be around your neck?'

'He tied it round my mouth. It slipped off.'

'And when you released your feet and hands what did you do?'

'I tried to find my clothes but the only thing I could find was my swagger coat. I put it on and ran back to Danny.'

'Had anything changed?'

'His handkerchief had been placed over his face.'

'What did you do next?'

'I told him I was going to get help. I ran across the field towards Buckie Braes.'

'Did you meet anyone?'

'Yes, a couple on Buckie Braes.'

'Did you know them?'

'No. He said he was called Spence. He was with his girl.'

'Were you crying?'

'Yes.'

'And did you ask them to get help?'

'I don't remember what I asked.'

'What did you do?'

'We went through Buckie Braes down to Cherrybank and Mr Spence telephoned for the police.'

'What did you do after the police arrived?'

'We went back to where Danny was.'

'Did anyone accompany you back?'

'Yes. There was a man called Drummond.'

'Was Danny in the same position as you left him?'

'Yes.'

'Did you remain there for some time?'

'Yes.'

'And then were you taken somewhere else?'

'Mr Drummond's house in Cherrybank.'

'At Mr Drummond's house you got some clothes?'

'Yes. Mrs Drummond gave me them.' She looked up into the gallery and located Mrs Drummond and gave a brief nod of her head. Mrs Drummond smiled back.

Russell called for exhibits to be shown and the clerks brought a swagger coat and suspender belt. Marjory, relieved to have a break from the constant questioning, identified them as hers. She was shown a handkerchief and identified it as Danny's.

'He had it that night in his top jacket pocket. He looked

263

ever so smart.'

'And this is the handkerchief which was over his face when you found him later?'

'Yes.'

She was shown the elastic band she had used to hold up her stocking. She was shown the pendant of her necklace. She was shown the strap of her underskirt. All belonged to her, she confirmed.

Russell thanked her. 'I wish to come now to the question of identification,' he said. The atmosphere in the courtroom, already tense, shifted further. The gallery turned, almost as one, to McGuigan.

'Do you recall on the 28th of August being summoned to the police office in Perth to look at a number of men?'

'Yes.'

'Tell us what happened when you went there.'

'They took us to a room, my mother and I. We stayed there for a little while and a policeman came and asked me to go into another room. When I went in there were some men standing in a line. I looked at them from one end to the other and when I came down to the last of them I seemed to recognise his face. I asked the inspector what I should do. He said, "Is the man who assaulted you here?" I said, "Yes," and pointed to him.'

'What was it about the man whom you identified that you recognised?'

'His face. His face came back to me.'

'Would you recognise him now?'

'Yes.'

'Is he in court now?'

'Yes.'

'Could you point to him?'

Marjory turned and pointed at John McGuigan.

'Have you no doubt at all about it?'

'No.'

Marjory forced herself to breathe slowly and deeply, the way Bella Conoboy had shown her. The longer Mr Russell's examination continued, the more relaxed she grew. As she had anticipated, the worst moment was when she had to describe her attack but once that was over she felt better able to control her emotions. She managed to look at her surroundings for the first time since she had entered the witness box an hour before. The judge fascinated her, in his red gown and white wig, with his stern stare and occasional interjections. He had a lovely voice. Strong but soothing. She fancied he was a kindly man beneath the stern exterior.

Her relaxed state was shattered, however, when she heard Mr Russell say he had no further questions. Immediately, Mr Burnett, counsel for the defence, rose. A short, wiry man with Brylcreemed, greying hair and small, round spectacles, he made a show of staring at Marjory. Moments passed, a silence too long for comfort. Mr Russell had warned Marjory he would do this, but it still affected her. Fear penetrated. Doubt followed.

Mr Burnett asked her the same questions as Mr Russell, but injected an inflection of incredulity. Without saying he didn't believe her, he managed to convey the sense. Marjory felt the last reserves of confidence draining from her. Finally, he rounded on her. He swiped his spectacles from his face and pointed them at her.

'Miss Fenwick, have you told us the whole truth about what happened on the night Daniel Kerrigan was shot?'

'Yes.'

'Buckie Braes and the Cuddies Strip are places where courting couples go. Are you aware of that?'

'Yes.'

'Had you been there before with Danny?'

'Yes.'

'You decided to go there that night?'

'No, we started walking and just landed there.'

'You didn't know where you intended to go?'

'No.'

'Do you know a man named Hamish Holland?'

Russell reacted with surprise at a name he had never heard before. He checked the list of witnesses the defence had itemised but he already knew there was no one named Holland on it. He felt a stab of trepidation as he looked at Marjory. Marjory, too, could not conceal her surprise at this non-sequitur. 'Yes,' she said, finally.

'Did you ever walk out with him?'

'No.'

'Did he visit you at the New Year?'

'Yes.'

'To see you?'

'No, my mother.'

'How old is he?'

'I don't know.'

'Is he a man about your own age?'

'Oh no. I think he is over twenty.'

'Have you ever been at dances with Hamish Holland?'

'No.'

'Have you been taken home from dances by Hamish Holland?'

'Yes.'

'Has he been at the house since the tragedy?'

'Yes, he came up one Sunday.'

Russell rose. 'Objection, your Honour,' he said. 'I fail to see the significance of this line of enquiry.'

Lord Aitchison scowled at Russell and then at Burnett. 'It's testing my patience too, I must confess,' he said. 'Mr Burnett, can you come to a conclusion?'

'Very well, my Lord. I will leave it at that for the moment.' He turned back to Marjory. 'Miss Fenwick, what way were you facing when the second shot was fired?'

Marjory was still flummoxed by the questioning about

Hamish. She went over it in her mind, trying to make some sense of it. He was a friend of her mother's, related to the family in some way that Marjory neither knew nor cared about.

'You were facing?' said Burnett again.

She forced herself to concentrate. 'My back was to the direction the shot came from. Danny was facing it.'

'Did the second shot appear to come from the same direction as the first?'

'Yes.'

'If that is true you must have been between Danny and the person who fired the shot?'

'Yes.'

'You were not hit at all?'

'No.'

Burnett looked round at the jury and then fixed his gaze on Marjory. Marjory felt a prickle of heat and knew that her neck would be blotchy and thanked her mother for insisting she wore the scarf. Burnett picked up his pencil.

'That is not what happened, is it?'

'That is what happened,' said Marjory heatedly.

Russell tried to hide his concern by sitting back in his chair and resting his arm over the vacant chair next to him. He tried to attract Marjory's attention but she was staring at Mr Burnett.

'Is it feasible that a man can be shot in the neck and chest at close range by a 12-bore shotgun and the girl standing right next to him, in the line of fire, was not hit by so much as a single pellet?'

'I can only tell you what happened.'

Burnett shook his head emphatically. Marjory looked at the faces of the jury, imagined she saw doubt, even scorn, in their expressions.

Burnett pressed on. 'As regards the assault upon you, did you resist to the utmost of your power?'

'No. I pretended I had fainted.'

Again, Lord Aitchison intervened and Marjory flinched. She was being assailed on two fronts now. 'This is an important point,' he said. 'Was that for your own protection?'

'Yes.'

Burnett thanked his lordship and continued. 'When describing your assault,' he said, 'you claimed your assailant held you down by placing his knee on your chest?'

'Yes.'

'How could he tie your hands behind your back with his knee on your chest?'

'I don't know, but he did it.'

'Do you seriously ask us to believe that?'

'It's what happened. That's all I can say.'

'Do you remember whether he tied your hands first or your mouth?'

'I don't remember.'

'You have told us your story very fluently twice, but you seem to have great difficulty about the details of it, Miss Fenwick.'

'I pray you are never in the same situation, sir, but if you are you will find that things happen in a blur. You remember the facts, but not the details. You remember the actions, but not the order they came in.' They stared at one another. Marjory refused to back away. She could not tell where that determination came from but she felt something deep inside her. It was Burnett who broke eye contact.

'You said the man had a black beard.'

'Not a beard, exactly. He was unshaven.'

'You said a beard.'

'I'm clarifying now.'

'You also said your assailant had a red face. Did the man you identified in the parade have a red face?'

'Yes. It was not awfully red but it was the same face.'

'Has the man you see in the dock got a red face?'

'Perhaps the passion is not on him now.'

The sound of ill-concealed laughter echoed around the court. Well done, Madge, thought Russell. Perfect answer. Marjory, thinking they were laughing at her, bit her lip and gripped the rail of the witness box.

'You do realise that the accused is on trial for his life?'

'Yes.'

'Keeping that very solemnly before your mind, do you say that the accused is the man who assaulted you that night?'

'Yes.'

'No further questions.'

Russell rose slowly. He still could not fathom the relevance of the questions about Hamish Holland and didn't dare ask Marjory about him. It was best to leave it. If Burnett returned to it later he could deal with it then. Overall, Russell was pleased with Marjory's performance. She had come across as polite and reasoned. She sounded, he felt assured, reliable. Believable.

And that was going to be the principal battleground of the trial. First skirmish, then, to Marjory.

'Madge,' he said, 'You told us the gunfire came from your right and from behind you?'

'Yes.'

'It was coming dusk, though, wasn't it?'

'Yes.'

'And you didn't actually see where the man who shot Danny was standing?'

'No.'

'So you were not in a position to tell whether or not you were actually in the line of fire? You just know that it was somebody behind you and to the right?'

'Yes.'

'No further questions.'

Lord Aitchison glanced up at the clock. It was after four o'clock. He thanked Marjory for her testimony and invited her to stand down and adjourned proceedings for the day, and after the longest two and a half hours of her life, Marjory stepped away. Her head was spinning. It would be days before she could stop replaying every moment, every exchange, every accusation. Exactly the same as in the days following the attack.

I didn't do anything wrong then, either.

Tuesday 26th November

A Day of Verification

Rain swept down from the castle to Holyrood, fat drops pulsing on the pavement before the Justiciary Court of Scotland. When Andrew Neiland arrived at 5.45 am to open the building, a man was huddled in the doorway.

'Good heavens,' said Neiland. 'You're early, Mr Roughead. They don't start for four hours.'

'I nearly didn't get a seat yesterday. I'm not taking any chances.'

'As long as you dinnae catch a fever.'

'Not me. I used to go camping in Mull when I was a boy. Cold and rain are nothing to me.'

*

Bob Kelty awoke exhausted. He had seen every hour pass that night. Even when he was asleep he was dreaming he was awake trying to get to sleep. The night was interminable. Now that it was over he wanted it to start again. He washed and dressed and went downstairs for a breakfast he wouldn't eat. He hadn't mentioned to Gran what was happening. She wouldn't understand and it would only upset her. When she disappeared the week before, it was six hours before she was found, halfway to Lochty on the Crieff road, heading for the farm cottage where she was born and where she spent the first ten years of her life. She was deteriorating by the day.

Rational conversation was almost impossible. It wouldn't be long before Bob could no longer cope. What happened then he chose not to think about. Instead, he thought of the day and the ordeal ahead. That offered no respite.

*

Marjory walked uphill from her bed and breakfast to the foot of Princes Street and strolled as far as Union Bridge. The rain had penetrated her coat and her fragile frame was growing colder by the moment. She liked it. It felt real. With no plan in mind she walked on, turning left or right at random, ending up in the old town, narrow streets with faded buildings looming over them. A man was approaching, middle-aged and dirty. He looked around continuously, a caricature of suspicious behaviour. Marjory glanced behind. There was nobody else in sight. Her pulse quickened as they walked towards one another. She thought of turning and fleeing. Then she thought against it. The man drew close.

'Hello darling, you're up early. All alone?' He planted himself in front of her, blocking her passage. Marjory examined him, dead eyes and alcohol-veined cheeks and nose. There was nothing to fear here. She would not be afraid.

'Just me and my cosh,' she said, gesturing with the hand inside her coat. She stared at him and refused to back away. The man stepped aside and she walked on.

*

Albert Russell studied the order paper detailing the day's witnesses. His plan was to place McGuigan in the vicinity of the Cuddies Strip and use each witness in turn to verify the testimony of the previous witnesses. Taken individually, his witnesses might lack credibility but his intention was that the weight of evidence would become overwhelming.

'Miss Gray is our best hope,' he said to Cummings.

'Except she can't identify McGuigan.'

'Doesn't matter. Her testimony isn't as strong as Gow or Peddie but she'll still come across better.'

Cummings agreed. 'We need her. She's the glue that binds all the sighting witnesses together.'

William Gow took the stand with the expression of a nun entering a brothel. Russell coaxed him through his testimony of seeing McGuigan spying on a courting couple and chatting with him for half an hour about guns and shooting, and of identifying him in the identity parade. Mr Burnett rose for his cross-examination.

'When did you go to the police with your story?'

'On the 27th of August.'

'But the crime occurred on the 14th. Why didn't you go to the police immediately?'

'That's their job. I didn't want to blame an innocent man.'

'None of us do. When you were chatting with Mr McGuigan, how did the subject of a gun come up? It's an unusual topic of conversation, surely?'

'Well, I've done a bit of poaching myself, like. I said to him I was up here to get myself a covey of birds.' There was laughter in the court and William Gow tried to determine whether or not to take offence. He looked at Russell. Russell looked away.

'You're a poacher?' said Burnett icily.

'Aye.'

'No further questions.'

Even before he called Robert Barrie, Russell knew he'd made a mistake in the order. Gow had been easily dismissed as a poacher and therefore unreliable. Now here was another. Further, Barrie was gallus and cocky. Burnett would tear into him. Russell asked his questions perfunctorily and when he finished Mr Burnett leapt to his feet.

'You say you saw someone walking towards the Cuddies Strip?'

'Yes.'

'And what did he do then?'

'He went in among the whins.'

'Where were you?'

'Mr Stewart and I were behind a dyke.'

'Why?'

'We supposed the man was the gamey.'

'And why would meeting the gamekeeper be a problem?'

'We were trespassing in his field.'

'Why?'

'We were just out walking.'

'Why not stick to the paths?'

'It was a shortcut.'

'And yet you said it took you an hour to walk from Callerfountain Hill to Buckie Braes. That's a very long time isn't it?'

'We werenae in a hurry.'

'So why take a shortcut?'

'Force of habit, I suppose.'

'You weren't out poaching?'

'No.'

'You didn't have a gun?'

'No.'

'Did you have any snares with you?'

'No. I wouldnae ken how to use one.'

'You probably wouldn't even know a rabbit if you saw one?'

'Oh, aye.'

Again, the sound of laughter reverberated round the courtroom. Russell sighed.

'No further questions,' said Burnett.

Lord Aitchison watched Barrie's retreating form, the ill-fitting suit, the squeaking shoes. 'Perth does appear to be replete with peeping toms and poachers,' he said. 'We will take a short break there.' The door behind the jury swung open and they filed out. The public gallery burst into activity, an explosion of noise and excitement. Albert Russell remained seated, staring at the desk in front of him.

'Can't wait to see your next witness,' Burnett said. 'A tinker, I shouldn't wonder.' He sauntered away, whistling. Russell and Cummings exchanged looks. Both reflected on who was next on the stand.

*

Arthur Hill swore on the Bible and said he was at Buckie Braes that night with his girlfriend. They met a couple of friends, the Dickson brothers, and stopped to talk to them.

'During that conversation,' said Russell, 'did you see anything unusual?'

'I saw two men crawling behind a dyke.'

'Where?'

'Coming towards the Cuddies Strip.'

Russell turned to the jury. 'That would be Barrie and Stewart,' he said. He turned to Hill. 'Did you see anything else?'

'I saw a man walking through the whins near the path.'

'At the Cuddies Strip?'

'Aye.'

Again, Russell explained to the jury. 'Remember,' he said. 'Robert Barrie and Jamesie Stewart saw the same person.' He turned back to Hill. 'And what happened next?'

'We started to walk up Callerfountain but had to turn around and come back before it got dark. We were crossing a field to the north of the Cuddies Strip when I heard two shots, one after the other. "That's some damned fool shooting rabbits at this time of night," I said. A few minutes later, when we were back on Buckie Braes, I heard another shot.'

'And you thought it was somebody shooting rabbits again?'

'Yes.'

Mr Russell thanked him and sat down.

Mr Burnett took his place and began his cross-examination. He was pleased with the way the morning was progressing and was confident about this witness, too. 'What were you doing there that night?'

'I was out with my girl.'

'On the Cuddies Strip?'

'In a field nearby.'

'Walking?'

'Some of the time.'

'And the rest of the time?'

Hill stared at the backs of his hands. 'Courting.'

'Are you engaged to this young lady?'

'No.'

'How long did you spend "courting"?' He said the word slowly, deliberately. Let the jury infer from it what they would.

'Half an hour?'

'Is that a question?'

'No. That's my answer.'

'And during that time, did you see any activity? For example, if a man had walked past you, directly past you, would you have seen him? Or would you have been otherwise engaged?'

'Otherwise engaged.'

'No further questions.'

Russell swore under his breath. He remained in his seat for some moments. The morning had been nothing short of disastrous. Two poachers and a jack-the-lad on the job. Their testimonies wouldn't stick. With half an hour until lunch, he called his next witness. His star witness, he hoped, someone who was neither poacher nor peeper nor Lothario. Elizabeth

Gray took the stand with a confidence that belied her age. She wore a powder-blue suit and matching hat and carried leather gloves. At Russell's prompting, she explained that she worked at the Oakbank dairy and described walking home and seeing a meeting of two men and a man and a woman on the Cuddies Strip.

Russell turned to the jury again. 'That will be Arthur Hill and his girlfriend with the Dickson brothers.' He addressed Elizabeth Gray again. 'What else did you see?'

'In the fields above the Cuddies Strip I saw a man creeping about in the whins.'

'What did you think about him?'

'That he was up to no good.'

'What did you do?'

'I didn't like the look of him so I hurried home.'

'That,' said Russell, 'is the third independent sighting of the man in the whins. John McGuigan.' He said he had no further questions and sat down.

Mr Burnett rose and walked to the despatch box. 'You thought he was up to no good. Did you actually see him do anything?'

'No.'

'Was he carrying a weapon?'

'Not that I could see.'

'Did you see his face?'

'Not up close.'

'Would you be able to recognise him?'

'No.'

'No further questions.'

'Lunch,' said Lord Chief Justice Aitchison.

*

Russell sat with Marjory and her mother over lunch. It was the first chance they'd had to talk since her testimony the day

277

before. He buttered a scone generously and applied a layer of strawberry jam. Mrs Fenwick was making inroads into a steak pie and Marjory nibbled a cheese sandwich, constantly dabbing her mouth with a napkin. Her eyes were so dark, Russell thought, they projected an almost unfaltering air of sadness. He felt sure it preceded the events that had brought them here.

'How do you fancy the trial is going?' she asked.

'We had the better of the morning,' he said. 'The defence will find it difficult to argue against McGuigan being at the Cuddies Strip that night.' That wasn't true, but Russell owed it to the girl to seem positive. He asked about Hamish Holland.

'Oh,' said Mrs Fenwick quickly, 'he's family, sort of. Cousin Jenny on my mother's side. She had a bairn.' She lowered her voice. 'A bastard. He was brought up by Auntie Elsie as her ain. He's a nice laddie but a bit simple.'

'Why did Mr Burnett ask me those questions about him?' said Marjory.

'I honestly couldn't say. Desperation, perhaps. They need to find a lover from your past.'

'Good luck to them.' She grimaced. 'What will happen this afternoon?'

Russell sat back and rubbed his hand over his belly. 'Firstly, we intend to demonstrate that McGuigan owned a gun. And then we will call the police who were there on the night of the crime. Kelty first.'

'Poor Constable Kelty will find that very difficult.'

'He will. And I must warn you that the defence will try to use his testimony to cast doubt on you.'

'Why?'

'It's about the only card they hold.'

'Questioning my character?'

'Yes.'

'It's a nasty world you inhabit, Mr Russell.'

Russell considered this for a moment but could find no argument against her. It was a nasty world all round. He feared for the future. He was glad not to be Marjory's age.

'Sometimes,' he said.

*

Graeme Peddie, the same age as the previous witness, Elizabeth Gray, suffered in comparison. Where she was poised he was cocksure. Her confidence was measured against his arrogance. There was no question that Peddie was enjoying himself too much. Juries noticed that sort of thing. They didn't like it. Russell tried to hurry through the questions.

'Where did the accused live?'

'In a tent.'

'Was that tent in a strip of wood some half a mile to the west of the farm steading?'

'Yes.'

'Did somebody else live in the tent with him?'

'His stepfather and mother.'

'Was he working on the farm?'

'Yes.'

'Was he a regular worker?'

'Some days he was out working, other days he was not.'

'Did you get to know him and sometimes visit him?'

'Yes.'

'You have been to the pictures with him and out walking?'

'Yes.'

'Have you ever been in his tent?'

'Yes.'

'More than once?'

'Yes.'

'Did you ever have any conversation with McGuigan about a gun?'

'Yes.'

'About how long before the murder was this?'

'A month.'

'What did you talk about?'

'Going poaching.'

'Did you know he had a gun?'

'He told me then. That was the first I knew of it.'

'Did he show you a gun on that occasion?'

'No, sir.'

'Did you have any conversation with the accused about a gun after that?'

'He showed me the gun about a fortnight after.'

'What kind of gun was it?'

'A double-barrelled shotgun.'

'Where were you when he showed you this gun?'

'Up at his tent.'

'Did you handle it yourself?'

'Yes, sir.'

'Was it loaded?'

'No.'

'How do you know?'

'There was no cartridge in it.'

'How could you tell that?'

'He took it down in two bits.'

'The shotgun broke into two parts?'

'Yes.'

'You are quite sure about that?'

'Yes. I saw it.'

'How did he come to show you the gun?'

'He just handed it over and said, "There's the gun."'

'On the Saturday after the murder, you were working with the accused in the morning. Is that correct?'

Peddie gave a broad smile, as though being asked to relate a favourite story. Russell glared at him but the boy took no notice. 'Aye,' he said.

'And did you talk about the murder?'

'We did. I said to him, with him having a gun, that he might have been up shooting and accidentally shot the man. He said, "I thought you'd be thinking that."'

'Did you ask where the gun was?'

'Yes.'

'Did he tell you?'

'He told me he had it hidden but didn't tell me where it was.'

'Did you ask why he had hidden it?'

'Yes. He said he was frightened for the police getting it. He had no licence.'

In the dock McGuigan jumped up with agitation and whispered to his brief. It was the first time he had shown any interest in proceedings since the trial began. Lord Aitchison stretched forwards. 'Did he tell you where he got the gun originally?'

'No.'

'Did you ever ask?'

'Yes. But he wouldn't tell me.'

Lord Aitchison made a note on his daily schedule and waved at Russell to continue. 'Did he tell you anything about his movements on the night of the murder?'

'Yes, he told me he had seen me. He was spying on me.'

Russell took a sip of water. 'What did you think he meant by saying he was spying on you?'

'That he was spying on us with his spying glass.'

'Had you ever seen him with a spying glass?'

'Yes. About two months before the shooting.'

Russell asked the clerk to fetch the telescope from the cabinet of exhibits and it was shown to Peddie. 'Is this it?'

'Yes. I know it because of these two cross marks on the leather strap.'

Russell turned to the clerk again and asked him to bring the blue handkerchief found on the floor of the laundry in

Aberdalgie House. 'Do you recognise this?'

'Yes. It belongs to John McGuigan.'

'How do you know?'

'I seen him use it lots of times.'

Russell sat down at the end of the examination and Burnett rose to begin his questions. 'When did you speak to the police about this matter?'

'The day after McGuigan was arrested.'

'Did you go to the police or did they come to you?'

'They came to me.'

'And did you give a statement straight away?'

'No. At first I never said anything. I was kind of taken aback. I went to see them later that night.'

'So at a time when it was public knowledge that a murderer who used a 12-bore shotgun was on the loose in Perth, you never thought to notify the police that a friend of yours, who lived less than a mile from the scene of the crime, illegally possessed such a weapon?'

'No.'

'And even when they came to interview you about the matter you still said nothing?'

'No.'

'And only later went to see them with this story of yours?'

'Yes.'

'I must put it to you that your story is not true.'

'It is, sir.'

But Peddie had the look of a startled rabbit. It was an expression that lacked credibility. Burnett waited for a moment to allow the jury to reflect on it.

'No further questions,' he said.

*

Russell had a burning dyspeptic pain in his stomach and he craved a glass of milk. He winced as he began his interrogation of Sandy Arnott, the Kirkton of Mailer farm joiner. At least the man presented a more professional demeanour than Peddie. He told of speaking to McGuigan the day after the murder with Charles Elder, the grieve.

'Mr Elder said to him, a bit joking like, "What's this you've been up to now, John?"'

'And how did the accused reply?'

'He said he'd been up the hill with his glasses and come down at half nine.'

'Could he know you had been talking about the murder?'

'No. He had just arrived.'

'So why do you think his answer referred to that night?'

'I thought it strange he mentioned the time he came down.'

Russell said he had no further questions and was relieved when Burnett waived the opportunity to cross-examine. He looked towards the judge, hoping there might be a brief adjournment. Lord Aitchison had decreed that court would remain in session for an extra hour each day in order to ensure they could be finished within a week. Russell was far from convinced this was a good idea. His concentration was flagging and from the faces of the jurors they were suffering similarly. And it was hot. Stuffy. But Lord Aitchison gave no indication of halting proceedings.

'I would like to call PC Kelty of Perth City Police,' he said.

*

The nondescript waiting room was empty apart from Bob, all the day's witnesses having previously been called to give evidence. A fog of cigarette smoke still hung in the air. Bob paced up and down. Empty teacups littered the tables but there had been no fresh brew since one o'clock. He combined the dregs from three or four cups and took a sip. It tasted horrible but at least it assuaged his thirst. He sat down and stood up several times in succession.

'PC Kelty?' The court usher appeared at the door, a red-cheeked man in clothes that were significantly too tight. 'You've been called.'

Bob laid the cup on the table with both hands to conceal the shake that had instantly overtaken them. He felt suddenly depressed, that lowering of mood that always afflicted him when he was about to confront something undesirable. Depression gave way to sickness, sickness to dizziness, dizziness to light-headedness. His ears rang. He acknowledged the usher and it seemed to him that his own voice was coming from across an ocean. The usher opened the courtroom door and guided him towards the witness box and Bob took the oath in a voice as loud and clear as he could muster.

'Speak up, please,' said Lord Aitchison.

Little Madge was watching him closely and he felt a surge of apprehension. Make things better for her. Do the right thing. He became aware of Mr Russell speaking.

'… own words what happened that night?'

Bob took a deep breath and began. 'We reached the scene some time just after eleven o'clock and Miss Fenwick directed us to the body. Danny Kerrigan's feet were on the footpath. His head and shoulders were on the grass on the north edge of the path. His right leg was extended and his left leg was fully bent and lying outwards across the path. The left arm was outstretched with the palm up. The right arm was bent at the elbow and the hand was half closed. There was blood on his fingers.'

He spoke quickly and plainly and by the time he had finished he could almost hear his own voice again.

'Was there a handkerchief over his face?'

'Yes. It was tucked in at the throat and went up to the eyes. It was spread right across the face, covering it.'

284

'Could it have fallen in that position?'

'No, sir.'

'Did you assume from what you saw that it had been deliberately placed there?'

'Yes, sir.'

'Do you know why this would have been done?'

'Yes, sir. It's an old tinker custom. A mark of respect for the dead.'

'And to your knowledge, is the accused a tinker?'

'Yes, sir. He comes from a travelling family.'

Bob went on to explain how he checked the pulse and concluded Kerrigan was dead and asked Spence to telephone the County Police. At this point Miss Fenwick complained of being cold and Mr Drummond took her back to his house. 'I waited at the scene for the County Police and an ambulance. They arrived around 11.40.'

'What did you do next?'

'When my colleagues arrived we made an examination of the woods, but we found nothing. Then we went to the stile and looked for the girl's clothing but again we found nothing. It was very dark and we only had two hand torches.'

In the gallery, Marjory listened in silence. That night had become an alternative reality to her. Each moment was so vivid it was etched unforgettably in her mind but, at the same time, the totality of what happened was clouded in uncertainty. She could only approach it obliquely. If she confronted it directly the individual moments would not come to her but, whenever she came at it aslant and then fixed on it, she found she could slip back into that time and interrogate it. She studied Bob's face. She could barely remember him even being there that night. He had said Danny was very badly hurt, but that was about the only thing she could recall. Poor Constable Kelty, she thought. She could tell he was even more nervous than she had been.

Bob noticed her watching him. For the first time he felt

able to look around the courtroom. It was full. The silence was intimidating. He focused on the front once more, the ushers sitting quietly and non-judgementally.

The man who rose to address him for the defence was small, with a neat moustache and Brylcreemed hair. Bob didn't think he looked especially threatening. Not enough to justify so many sleepless nights, anyway.

'When you first saw Marjory Fenwick, did you notice anything around her neck?'

'It looked like suspenders.'

'Did she explain how they got there?'

'She said her assailant did it to gag her.'

'In your opinion, would it have been tight enough to gag her?'

'I couldn't say.'

'Did you notice anything tied to any of her hands?'

'A handkerchief.'

'Did you notice anything about it?'

'It smelled of stick reek.'

'Stick reek?'

'It's the smell you generally find from travellers and those who stay in camps with wood fires.'

'You have an acute sense of smell?'

'I suppose so.'

'It's a wonder your superiors didn't think to turn you out to see if you could sniff out the murderer.'

'Actually, they did.'

Laughter rang round the court. Lord Aitchison allowed it to end. 'There must be a lot of stick reek in Perthshire,' he said. Bob recognised the patronising tone. All his life people had used it to put him down for his dialect and accent. Teuchter Boab.

Burnett continued his questioning. 'It was more the nature of the knotting that interested me. Did you investigate the way the handkerchief was tied?'

'I saw there was more than one knot.'

'You don't know how many knots there were?'

'I couldn't say whether it was one, two or three.'

'You said there was more than one knot?'

'There must have been or it would not have stayed on for the length of time it did.'

'So was it one, two or three?'

'Two or three.'

'Was it tied tightly round her wrist?'

'I could not say.'

'Loose enough for a hand to have been pulled through it?'

'I couldn't say.'

'Could it have been tied by Miss Fenwick herself?'

'I couldn't say.'

'You could. Is it possible that someone could tie a handkerchief round her left hand? A right handed person?'

'Yes, I imagine.'

'Did she mention whether any other part of her had been tied?'

'She said her ankles had been tied.'

'Did you see any evidence of that?'

'I didn't look.'

'Any bruising of any kind?'

'I didn't look.'

Frustration bubbled inside Bob. The way the questions were framed made it impossible for him to sound as if he knew what he was talking about. Burnett was deliberately making him appear confused, casting doubt on his evidence. And Bob could do nothing about it.

'Afterwards you went to the Drummonds' house and escorted Fenwick to the police station. Is that correct?'

'Yes, sir.'

'Was she coherent?'

'She was very upset.'

'Was she coherent?'

'She kept repeating herself. Going over and over it.'

'She told you she didn't know her assailant?'

'Yes.'

'Did she stress any special point about his appearance?'

'I remember her saying his cap was pulled down over his eyes.'

'She wouldn't be able to see his eyes then?'

'I couldn't say.'

'Presumably it would have that effect?'

'It might.'

'Did she say his complexion was ruddy?'

'She said his face was red.'

'And yet he had a cap pulled low over his face.' He turned away, creating a dramatic pause. He turned back again. 'Did she give you any story of the actual shot?'

'She said there was a shot that passed her ear. Another shot struck Danny ... Mr Kerrigan.'

'Did she say what they were doing when the shots were fired?'

'I can't remember exactly, but I think she said that they had been sitting laughing and joking and I think she said they had got up to go home.'

'Are you sure she did not tell you that the shots were fired while she and her boy were sitting laughing and joking?'

'I could not be sure of that. I can't remember the exact words she used and the way she used them.'

'So they might not have been walking?'

'I have no way of knowing.'

Lord Aitchison interrupted as Burnett was about to continue. 'During the time you were with Miss Fenwick that evening was there anything in her demeanour, her appearance or in what she said to cause a suspicion in your mind that she was making up a story?'

'No, my Lord. I would say she was genuinely upset.'

'That there was an invention in it never occurred to you.'

'It has never occurred to me.'

Burnett nodded as though Bob had said something significant and Bob tried to imagine how his words could be interpreted against him.

'How long have you been in the police force, Constable?'

'Approaching eight months, sir.'

'Do you take everybody you see on face value?'

'I like to give people the benefit of the doubt.'

'That's a very noble stance for a police officer. I'm sure, given the nature of the people you come into contact with on a daily basis, it must be severely tried at times?'

'Not as much as you might imagine, sir.'

Burnett gave him an incredulous stare, much laboured for the benefit of the jury. He turned and looked at them, then returned to Bob.

'Did you write her story down at the time?'

'No, I recollect it quite plainly.'

'Is that true, Constable? Only there seems to be quite a lot of testimony you can't offer an opinion on. Are you confident about your recollection?'

'Yes, sir. I can't offer an opinion on what Miss Fenwick thought or saw. But I recollect what I saw.'

'Although you could not have written anything down for some hours? And it all happened in darkness. You are still sure?'

'Yes, sir.'

'Have you ever said you were not sure?'

'No, sir. The only thing I was not sure of was whether he gagged her first and tied her afterwards, or tied her hands first and gagged her afterwards.'

'Did she say whether he tied her hands in front or behind?'

'She said in front.'

'And you are certain of that?'

'Yes, sir.'

In the gallery, Marjory jumped up in agitation. No, she thought. That's not right at all.

'And you're sure of your testimony?'

'Yes, sir.'

'Only, Miss Fenwick says otherwise. She was quite clear in her testimony that her hands were tied behind her back. So one of you is wrong.'

Constable Kelty, not having been asked a question, made no reply.

'No further questions,' said Burnett, slamming his notebook shut with a flourish.

Russell rose. 'Mr Burnett has made great play,' he said, 'of Miss Fenwick's varying descriptions of her assailant. Were you with her when she attended the identification parade?'

'Yes, I was.'

'And how did she react when she saw McGuigan?'

'She gave a start. It was obvious straight away she recognised him.'

'No further questions.'

Bob heard himself being dismissed by the judge. His thoughts were consumed by Burnett's questioning. He couldn't bring himself to look at Marjory. He followed the usher out of the courtroom and found himself back in the waiting room before he knew what was happening. Time rolled like lava flow and he was swept with it and he wanted to go back, to start again, to say everything differently, to prove that Madge was correct and McGuigan was guilty and the world was good and he was effectual.

But none of that would happen.

'I'm sorry, Madge,' he said.

Wednesday 27th November

A Day of Procedure

Six in the morning, sallow light in the living room, the colours of the furniture muted, almost sepia. Bella played Satie's *Gnossiennes*. The notes merged with the rhythms of her consciousness. Silence and consideration. Discord into harmony. Beauty from distress. In one hour Victor would depart for Edinburgh to give his testimony.

When he was gone she would telephone Annie and ask her to come. They would promenade round the South Inch in a clockwise direction. If it was fair they would sit beneath the statue of Walter Scott for ten minutes and watch the road traffic and the nannies with perambulators and the women with shopping. Engage. Communicate. She had tried, since the war, to ignore the world and its problems but she knew, now, that moral isolation was impossible. There was no difference between the world and the individual. Bella fancied that when Marjory's case was concluded everything would change and she would have to change with it.

'How do I look?' Victor strode into the living room, the embodiment of official aptitude in his freshly pressed uniform. Anyone would see in him a man in control of affairs. Bella saw deeper.

'Like a Chief Constable.'

He bent and kissed her forehead. 'I haven't felt this nervous about court in twenty years.'

'I know. It's because of the girl. She matters.'

'I spoke to Robert last night. The defence questioning was all about casting doubt on her evidence.'

'We knew it would be. They'll discredit her any way they can. They'll say she's unreliable. They'll say she's dishonest. They'll say she wasn't a virgin even though they have no evidence.'

'They do have evidence.'

'They do not. Two separate doctors have thrust their fingers inside her on three occasions to prove that her hymen was broken. That proves nothing at all. The hymen can break for many reasons, one of which is very heavy periods. Marjory suffers very heavy periods. These experts, they have proof of nothing. I've told Marjory to tell Mr Russell that, but I fear she won't have. Make sure you tell them.'

'I can only tell them what I'm asked.'

*

Conoboy felt in his pocket for sixpence and handed it to the newspaper seller and took a copy of *The Scotsman*. He read the headlines with satisfaction. *Abyssinia Advances. Sweep into Ogaden. 80 miles in three days.* Perhaps oppression could be resisted after all. Perhaps there was no ordained path.

'Interesting developments.'

He turned and saw Sergeant Watters walking towards him. 'Harry,' he said, and they shook hands warmly.

'Do you think the fascists can be beaten?' Watters asked.

Conoboy shrugged. 'Ultimately, probably not. But will Mussolini bankrupt his country in the process? Probably.'

'The world's changing. What we do now will shape everything for generations to come.'

'Are we ready for that responsibility?'

'We can't escape it. Watch out for New Zealand today.' Conoboy raised an eyebrow. 'General election. There's every possibility they could throw out the national government. An end to austerity.'

'If only we had done the same in ours last week.'

'There could have been worse outcomes. At least the Liberals were destroyed.'

Conoboy had voted Independent Liberal in the general election to compensate for Robert's missed vote. The boy was right. *Peace, trade, employment, social reform.* Those were fine priorities. 'I can't imagine Attlee will make a better Labour leader than Herbert Morrison,' he said.

Watters shrugged. 'Attlee's a pragmatist. He's what we need right now.'

They entered the court building, acknowledging the commissionaire's salute, and stood at the foot of the grand staircase.

'Ready?' said Watters.

'I am.'

'It's gone well so far, I hear.'

'I believe so. Lord Aitchison is a fair judge.'

'Tell that to my boss,' said Watters, smiling.

'Your boss should have followed procedure.'

*

'Could you describe what happened when you arrived at the Cuddies Strip?' Albert Russell leaned against the dais with his hand on his hip. He puffed out his cheeks as though readying himself for the day.

Conoboy told the court it was after one when he arrived at the scene. Sergeant Braggan picked up from near the feet of the deceased what they initially believed were three separate shotgun wads, but later realised were two, with one split in two. He found another embedded in Kerrigan's body. About fifty yards away Constable Jones picked up half a shirt button lying on a tree stump.

'Was there anything else there?'

'Three spots of blood on one side of the tree stump and a smear of blood on the other.'

'Can you describe this stump?'

'It was the stump of a small tree that had been roughly cut on the path of the Cuddies Strip. It projected about six inches above the ground.'

'The sort of thing someone running might stumble over?'

'Yes.'

'Was it you who took Marjory Fenwick's statement?'

'Yes,' said Conoboy. 'Early on Friday morning.'

'What was her appearance?'

'She appeared to have been very frightened. There was a bruise on her neck as if she had been held by the throat. There was a suspender belt round her neck tied with a double reef knot.'

'You are sure about that?'

'Quite sure.'

Russell asked for the suspender belt to be brought from the exhibit store and given to Conoboy. 'Please show us how it was tied.'

Conoboy tied the knot and showed it to the jury.

'This was tied round her neck in this fashion?' said Russell. 'If it were placed around her mouth would it have been tight enough to form an effective gag.'

'I believe so.'

'Did you examine the handkerchief around her wrist?'

'I did.'

'How was it tied?'

'It also had a double reef knot.'

'Could she have tied it herself?'

'I considered that at the time. It would be possible, but very difficult.'

'Would it have been possible for her other wrist to have been contained within the gap that remained?'

'Yes.'

Russell gave a theatrical nod and paced a few steps from the dais before returning again, creating a visual and temporal pause in his questioning. The jury adjusted their positions and coughs rang out from the gallery.

'Can you explain to the court the process which led you to connect the handkerchief with which Miss Fenwick's wrists were tied to the accused?'

Conoboy cleared his throat and swung his arms behind his back. 'In the course of our investigations,' he said, 'we discovered there was a laundry mark on the handkerchief. The mark was "M1-2" and it was made with red thread. We contacted all laundries, first in Perth and then in Perthshire and surrounding areas but were unable to identify the one from which the mark came. We then telephoned all laundries in Scotland and eventually contacted the Kelso Laundry. They confirmed the marking on the handkerchief was theirs.'

'To whom did it belong?'

'The Douglas family, residing in Aberdalgie House.'

'What did you do next?'

'We visited Aberdalgie House and showed Lord Douglas the handkerchief. He identified it as his. His maid showed us a laundry book which confirmed it was laundered by the Kelso laundry.'

'How could it have come to be at the Cuddies Strip?'

'There was evidence that the laundry room at Aberdalgie House had been broken into. Given that we knew a handkerchief taken in that robbery had been used to tied up Marjory Fenwick, it followed that the thief was the person who raped Marjory, and the person who raped Marjory was the person who murdered Danny Kerrigan.'

'Were any other items stolen in the robbery?'

'Mr Douglas was unable to say at the time. The family had recently returned from South Africa and much of their belongings was still boxed up. However, when we seized items found at the abode of the accused these were taken to Aberdalgie House and Mr Douglas confirmed they belonged to him.'

Russell nodded slowly, pleased with Conoboy's performance and slowing it down to give the jury time to consider. He sipped from a glass of water but before he could continue Mr Burnett rose and addressed Lord Aitchison.

'I think it is our duty to object to any further examination on these lines. My learned friend is apparently about to discuss evidence obtained during a search of my client's abode. The ordinary procedure in such circumstances is to obtain a warrant.'

The Lord Chief Justice frowned at him. 'Indeed?'

'In this case no warrant was obtained.' He turned to Conoboy. 'The police are not entitled to ransack a private dwelling.'

A wave of fear, hot and dizzying, flushed through Conoboy's body but before Burnett could continue there was a commotion in the jury box. Three jury members jumped out of their seats and hovered over another, a portly woman in a thick coat and black hat, who had collapsed to the floor.

'My Lord,' said Russell, spotting the disruption, 'Professor Mathieson is the next witness. He is a medical doctor. He will be in the waiting room.'

Lord Aitchison called for Mathieson to be fetched and adjourned proceedings. The jury was dismissed and the stricken woman was carried to a side room to be examined by the professor. Conoboy was taken back to the waiting room where he greeted Acting Chief Constable MacNaughton.

'Well?' said MacNaughton. 'How is it going?'

'We have a problem.' He outlined the defence's objection in a low and passive voice.

'You bloody fool. You might have caused a mistrial.'

Conoboy shook his head angrily. 'No. I maintain we have the right to investigate where we think there's a danger of evidence being destroyed. Not only a right. A duty.'

'Lamping warned you. He had experience of it.'

'Warnock was a different case. He called something a confession which wasn't. It was misrepresentation of the facts. I simply took steps to secure vital evidence before it could be destroyed.'

'Well, we'll see if the judge agrees.' He turned away as though finished with the conversation, then seemed to change his mind and rose and stood in front of Conoboy. 'And if he doesn't,' he continued, 'you can consider your career over.'

Conoboy sat with his hands gripped tightly between his knees and the two men remained in furious silence until Conoboy was called back to court.

'It was just a faint,' the usher said. 'She's fine now.' Conoboy nodded but he wasn't really listening. He resumed his position on the stand, feeling more like the accused than a witness. He was certain he was right, but he was equally convinced that Burnett would argue his actions were illegal.

Lord Chief Justice Aitchison marched back into court and settled himself on his bench. He gazed from above spectacles perched on the edge of his nose and turned to Conoboy.

'I understand you went to the tent occupied by the accused?'

'I did, my Lord.'

'On what day?'

'On the evening of the 28th of August.'

'Was that subsequent to his being charged with murder, rape and the theft of a pocketbook?'

'Yes, my Lord.'

'Had you applied for a warrant?'

'No, my Lord.'

'Is the practice of the police in Perth to apply for a warrant for a search in circumstances of that kind?'

'In ordinary circumstances of theft we always apply for

297

a warrant.'

'How did you get access to the tent?'

'The father and mother were there when we arrived.'

'Did you get in by the door?'

'Through a flap in the tent. It was a canvas erection.'

'Did they know who you were?'

'They did, my Lord.'

'And why you were there?'

'Yes.'

'Did they raise any objections to you making a search?'

'None whatsoever.'

'Did you tell them you were going to make a search?'

'Yes.'

'Did you ask their permission?'

'No.'

'What time was it you went to the tent?'

'Between nine and ten o'clock.'

'What time had he been charged?'

'About eight o'clock.'

'And you regarded it as essential in the interests of public justice a search should be carried out without delay?'

'I believed it should be done at once.'

'In the course of your search did you open any locked places?'

'No, my Lord.'

'Did you break anything open?'

'Nothing whatsoever.'

'I don't want you to say what they were, but you recovered certain articles from the tent?'

'Yes, my Lord.'

Lord Aitchison scribbled some notes in his folder and pointed to Mr Burnett. 'Outline your objection.'

'I submit that the main question is about the legality of the search that was made.'

Lord Aitchison inclined his head. 'If the police suspect

that some other person might destroy incriminating evidence are they not entitled to act immediately?'

'It is fundamental in the law that our own things are our private property.'

'Even if a delay might have the effect of negating the ends of public justice?'

'If circumstances require that a property should be inspected it should be done in the proper way.'

Conoboy followed the debate, feeling sick in his stomach. The logic of what he did seemed unarguable, but whenever Burnett spoke he could almost be convinced to the contrary.

'Mr Russell,' said Lord Aitchison, 'what is your view on the matter?'

Russell rose and cleared his throat. 'There is a common law right for officers of the law to apprehend without warrant. A charge of murder is one which would obviously be appropriate to that function given certain circumstances, such as pertained here.'

The judge drummed his fingers. 'I have no doubt the police were entitled to apprehend him forthwith and to search him forthwith. The only question is whether there was an element of urgency which would justify them subsequently searching his property without a warrant.'

Russell waved his arm vigorously. 'The accused was apprehended on a charge of murder and evidence which might have been available at his domicile might have disappeared if a period of more than an hour or two had been allowed to exist before the search was made.'

Lord Aitchison stared ahead, saying nothing. This was a matter which current case law was unable to answer. There was no precedent to which he could refer. He bristled with irritation at the impasse such uncertainty caused. 'If this is a good objection,' he said, 'then evidence which has been admitted may be inadmissible. Therefore, it is a very vital objection. How many articles found in the tent have already been put to witnesses?'

Russell flicked through his notes. 'Thirteen articles were removed during the search and all of them have been referred to in evidence already.'

'And all put to witnesses?'

'Yes, my Lord.'

Lord Aitchison sat back and scratched his cheek. 'There is in case law a case where a stolen letter was submitted as evidence although it had been taken possession of illegally.'

'That was a civil case, my Lord,' said Burnett.

'It seems to me the law about what can be done with a warrant and what can't is in a state of utter confusion and the sooner it is cleared up the better.'

'I think we would all agree on that, my Lord,' said Burnett.

'Very well,' said Lord Aitchison. He had made his decision and he knew this judgement would inform legal process for a generation. There were times when the law required strict interpretation and times when common sense had to prevail. Fundamental to his thinking was whether the accused had suffered any unfair treatment. James Mills, in the Glasgow murder, clearly had. Equally clearly, McGuigan had not. Lord Aitchison placed his fountain pen on the desk in front of him and addressed the court.

'Mr Burnett has raised a point of very considerable importance. He was quite entitled to raise it. Indeed, it was his clear duty to do so. He takes exception to evidence led by the Crown which was obtained through a search made by the police of the tent in which the accused lived along with his mother and stepfather. The ground of the objection is that this search was carried out and articles seized without a magistrate's warrant and therefore the search and seizure were illegal.

'At ten o'clock, two hours after the accused was charged, Inspector Conoboy went to the accused's tent. He found the tent occupied by the accused's mother and stepfather. He disclosed who he was, and what his purpose was. No objection was raised. On the other hand, no consent was asked. Now it must be obvious that in so grave a charge as murder it is of the first importance that a search of the tent which the accused occupied should be made forthwith. In the circumstances of the matter being, in the view of Inspector Conoboy, one of urgency, the police were entitled to act without delay and without having obtained a warrant from the magistrate. Even if I thought otherwise and had concluded the police had acted irregularly it could not in the least follow that the evidence thus obtained would be inadmissible. Irregularity in the obtaining of evidence does not necessarily make that evidence incompetent.

'In the present case thirteen articles to which objection would apply have already been put in evidence bearing labels showing where these articles were found to which no objection of any kind was taken, and it appears to me to be out of the question to exclude them now.'

He looked directly at Burnett. 'I have no hesitation in repelling the objection and allowing the evidence.'

Conoboy looked up at Marjory's perplexed face. He looked at McGuigan, who sat glowering at his counsel. He composed himself as Russell restarted his interrogation, asking the inspector to itemise which objects had been taken from the tent. Conoboy read out the list from his pocketbook.

'And did you take any of these items to Aberdalgie House?'

'We took the telescope, an alarm clock, a football, a purse and a razor.'

'Were they positively identified?'

'They were. Lord Douglas was able to show us his initials inked inside the purse. And he showed us the case from which the razor was taken. He confirmed all of the items belonged to his family.'

'Did Mr McGuigan explain how they had come into his possession?'

'He suggested he purchased them from a man he didn't know at Meikleour crossroads.'

'Do you consider that credible?'

'I do not.'

'We know the items were found in Mr McGuigan's possession. Do you have evidence that he was responsible for the housebreaking?'

'Yes, sir. There was evidence that entry had been gained through the rear window. We arranged for it to be removed and checked for fingerprints.'

'Were any found?'

'There were. They matched fingerprints provided by the accused while in Perth Prison.'

'You have no doubt, then, that the accused was responsible for the robbery at Aberdalgie House?'

'No doubt.'

'And in the course of that robbery a handkerchief was stolen which was subsequently used to bind Marjory Fenwick's hands?'

'That's correct.'

'No further questions.'

Whispered conversations were raised as Mr Burnett replaced Russell at the dais. The defence counsel gave Conoboy a sour smile as he settled his notes in place. He thumbed through them for some moments. Without looking up he began to speak.

'When did the officers from Glasgow join the investigation?'

'August the 22nd.'

'And why did they join?'

'To offer assistance. They have significant experience of murder enquiries.'

'Was it not the case that they took over the investigation

because the Perth police had made no progress?'

'It was not like that.'

'Did you have officers stationed at the Cuddies Strip to prevent the public wandering about until your investigations were completed?'

'On the first forenoon, but not afterwards.'

'On that first forenoon, you made careful examination of the ground?'

'Yes.'

'On the 15th of August some young men reported to the police station with items of evidence they had found at the site. Is that correct?'

'Yes.'

'That includes part of a necklace worn by Fenwick which you hadn't seen when you made a previous careful search?'

'We hadn't discovered it, no.'

'How was it lying?'

'It was among long grass.'

'Apparently these boys found it, although the police hadn't?'

'The grass had been trampled down a bit.'

'Could it have got there after your search was completed and the public were readmitted to the Cuddies Strip?'

'Yes, that's possible.'

'A number of other items of evidence were subsequently found by members of the public?'

'Yes.'

'Ignoring for the moment the question of why your searches did not pick up these items, the same doubt must apply to all of these items of evidence. Could they have been placed at the scene after the crime?'

'Yes.'

'Regarding the button that was found on the tree stump some distance from the body, do you agree that anybody had been proceeding from the place of the crime towards the tent

303

occupied by the accused, they would not pass that spot?'

'They wouldn't, no.'

'It's in the opposite direction.'

'It is.'

'It is also the case, is it not, that there is no evidence to link the accused to the Cuddies Strip?'

'The handkerchief ...'

'The handkerchief links *someone* to the Cuddies Strip. Absolutely no case has been made in respect of the accused, has it?'

'His fingerprints ...'

'The fingerprints, if they are genuine, would link the accused to Aberdalgie House.' He paused. 'But could they link him to the Cuddies Strip?'

'Not directly.'

'No further questions.'

Burnett swapped places and Russell settled his notes on the dais in front of him. 'Would it be the case, Inspector, that if anybody wished to keep under cover before going southwards from Cuddies Strip – in the direction of accused's tent, for example – then he would have gone westwards and past the tree stump on which the fragment of button was found?'

'That would be likely, yes.'

'No further questions.'

*

'What's it like? Being in court?' Annie and Marjory sat on Marjory's bed. The sound of Mrs Fenwick being busy filtered through the wall. Marjory kicked off her shoes and lay back on the bed and stared at the ceiling with her hands crossed over her stomach.

'It's exhausting. You're being stared at all the time. Talked about all the time. All those private things. Everyone hearing it. Strangers. People writing it down and putting it in the papers so that everyone else can read about it, too. I thought it would be hard but I never thought it would be this hard.'

Annie stretched back on the bed alongside her. She took the girl's hand and squeezed it and felt Marjory return the gesture.

'There was a bit today, when they started arguing all the legal details about searching that man's tent. I didn't understand a word of it but it was such a relief. You know? They weren't talking about me or Danny or that night. I could relax. I didn't want them to end. Just keep talking about that.'

'It'll be over soon.'

Marjory didn't reply. She closed her eyes. Mr Russell had warned her. Tomorrow. Tomorrow there would be the medical evidence. Those examinations.

Talking about the rape was one thing. She could accept that was the act of a monster, out of anyone's control. But talking about those examinations was something else. How could anyone explain that? Justify that?

*

Lord Aitchison settled in a voluminous armchair in front of a coal fire that was so hot he had to drape a blanket over his knees to stop them burning. Alexander Rae handed him a glass of whisky.

'Have one yourself, Sandy.' He invited him to sit in the seat opposite. 'A good day,' he said.

'We're still in danger of going over, I fear, my Lord.'

Lord Aitchison shook his head. 'Done by Saturday. I have a suspicion the defence won't call anyone.'

'No?'

'Burnett's approach seems to be to pick off the prosecution

305

witnesses. Discredit them. He won't want to run the risk of Russell doing the same to him. Let's face it, he only has one witness, and he's probably very reluctant to have the accused on the stand.' He sipped his whisky and stared into the fire. 'I wouldn't,' he said.

'It was a most complex judgement you made earlier, my Lord. Regarding the tent.'

'In one regard. It's a legal morass – when is it appropriate and when isn't it? But the police inspector – a most impressive man – presented a perfectly cogent case. Unarguable, really. There was only one outcome.'

*

Bella Conoboy was restless. The afternoon promenade had been a success. She had remained outdoors for almost two hours and felt no panic. Annie had been a tonic, chatting throughout, contriving an air of normality. But now, back at home, reflecting on the day, she was more unsettled than she had been for some months. It didn't help that Victor was silent and brooding. She wanted to discuss his day but couldn't until he raised it.

Victor, meanwhile, unaware of his wife's excursion and oblivious of her restlessness, replayed his day ceaselessly in his head. The things he said. Things he didn't say. He persuaded himself he had come close to destroying the case and although his actions were vindicated by the judge he could not deny the sense of failure that burned in him. Bella's silence served only to confirm it.

Thursday 28th November

A Day of Reputations

The sky was funereal, dampness clinging to clothes and faces. A deep chill penetrated. Snow threatened. It was not a morning to be outdoors. Half a dozen people were waiting in the rain behind William Roughead when Andrew Neiland arrived at six. He greeted the older man.

'They've agreed to sit until Saturday evening,' he said.

'Still won't be long enough,' said Roughead. 'We're only on the Crown's evidence. We've the defence case to hear yet and then all the summing up. Three or four days yet.'

'I hope you've a strong constitution, then.'

'Like an ox.'

By the time Neiland opened the doors, three-hundred people were queuing. Most of those who failed to gain entrance remained in hope of accessing the afternoon session. Discussion of the case sustained them through the vigil. Most anticipated a guilty verdict. Many, mostly women, distrusted Marjory. Theories mad and impossible were raised and debated.

'She's in this up to her neck,' said one woman. Others expressed their agreement.

'They say she knew McGuigan,' said another. 'They're in cahoots.'

'Nonsense,' said another still. 'Why would she identify him if she knew him?'

'He'd done what she wanted. This way she could get rid

307

of them both.'

'If she'd done that,' said a sturdy woman in black, 'he would have just told on her'. But her voice of reason was drowned out and she walked away and the group shuffled up to claim her space.

*

Albert Russell tied and re-tied his neckerchief in the mirror. Today was make or break. The case rested on being able to link the robbery at Aberdalgie House to McGuigan and then McGuigan to the murder scene. Linking him to Aberdalgie was easy but evidence connecting him to the Cuddies Strip was circumstantial, depending entirely on the handkerchief. To counteract that he wanted to ensure the jury was left with no possible doubt that McGuigan was responsible for the robbery. Create certainty about the first aspect and they would be more likely to take the leap of faith into the second. Fortunately, he had no doubts about Bertie Hammond.

'Detective Lieutenant Hammond,' he said. 'Please tell the court your occupation.'

'I work in the Fingerprint and Photographic Division of Glasgow City police.'

'How long have you done this?'

'Fifteen years.'

'Is it fair to say fingerprints have been your life's work?'

'It is.'

'You were engaged to take fingerprints from the casement window at Aberdalgie House. Is that correct?'

'It is.'

'And what did you discover?'

'They were a positive match with those on the prison form of the accused.'

'Have you any doubt?'

'No, sir.'

'Why not?'

'Sixteen ridge characteristics matched in the two samples.'

'What are ridge characteristics?'

'The inner surfaces of the fingers are covered by skin which has a particular ridge formation. The ridges have distinct peculiarities which vary between different fingers. The ridges may end abruptly or may divide. In my comparison of the fingerprints on the window and those submitted by the accused in prison, they were identical matches.'

'You say that there were sixteen ridge characteristics in agreement. How many similar characteristics is it necessary to find on a fingerprint in order definitely to say it is a fingerprint of a given person?'

'Sixteen ridge characteristics in a single fingerprint impression are generally regarded as sufficient to exclude every other person in the population of the earth. This is the result of a mathematical calculation.'

'Would you put it so high as to say it was impossible?'

'No one can say for certain until every person has been fingerprinted.'

'But is there any known instance or example of error?'

'There is no known example from the literature of the subject or my experience that two individuals have identical fingerprints.'

'So you are satisfied that the fingerprints left on the casement window at Aberdalgie House are those of John McGuigan?'

'Yes.'

Russell turned to Burnett. 'Your witness,' he said but Burnett remained seated.

*

The afternoon session began ten minutes early and the gallery was still shuffling into place when Mr Russell greeted his next witness. He gave him a welcoming smile.

'Mr Martin, you've given evidence in a number of court cases, I understand?'

'That is correct.'

'You're considered an expert in firearms?'

'Yes.'

'You were shown the wads and pellets from the bullets which killed Daniel Kerrigan. What can you tell me about them?'

'They were number five shot.'

'Did they come from a good quality cartridge?'

'On the contrary. They were undoubtedly cheaper cartridges.'

'Not something a professional would use?'

'I would say not.'

'You also studied the photographic evidence from the autopsy, I believe. What did you ascertain from that?'

'There were one-hundred and ninety pellet holes in the body.'

'And how many pellets are there on average in a number five cartridge?'

'There are usually two-hundred and thirty-four.'

'Did you form an opinion as to the angle at which the shot struck the deceased?'

'The shot struck the deceased from an oblique angle.'

'Does the actual spread of the shot indicate from which side it came?'

'The shot must have come from the right.'

'From how far was the shot fired?'

'From the tests I undertook, it would have been fired from a distance of approximately eight yards.'

Russell gathered his papers together with satisfaction and sat down. Cummings inclined his head towards him and congratulated him. The morning continued to go well. Professional evidence, professionally presented. Unequivocal, unarguable. They awaited Burnett's cross-examination.

'Mr Martin, you are a gunsmith, I believe?'

'Correct.'

'Not a scientist?'

'I have studied guns all of my life.'

'Miss Fenwick has told us she and Kerrigan were walking arm-in-arm when the crime occurred. Yet she was not touched by a single pellet. Can you explain how, if she were standing so close to Kerrigan, she escaped injury from the shot that killed the lad?'

'Quite readily. The pellets which are not in the body could only occupy a space of three by four inches over his shoulder.'

'What surprises me is that the one-hundred and ninety pellets reached Kerrigan without a single one touching the girl.'

'A spread only keeps a circle of over eight inches in diameter,. The victim has sustained all the pellets except about forty and the normal course those missing pellets would take is just over his shoulder.'

'I am asking you about the pellets which hit Kerrigan. Is it not surprising to you that these were not intercepted by the girl, who must have been between him and the shot if her story is true?'

Lord Aitchison shifted in irritation. 'Mr Burnett, you appear to be labouring this point,' he said.

'My Lord, this is a vital matter.'

'Very well.' He addressed Mr Martin. 'If the girl was in the direct line of fire would she have got some of the pellets?'

'Yes.'

'And if she was not in the direct line of fire might she have escaped the pellets?'

'Yes.'

311

'Now proceed, Mr Burnett.'

But Burnett remained seated.

'We will adjourn for fifteen minutes,' said Lord Aitchison.

*

Russell and Cummings sat in their office. Russell held a cup of tea, Cummings a glass of hot water. Cummings was an inconsequential man with a hunted expression, the sort of man who appeared to anticipate disaster at every turn. Now, though, he seemed relaxed.

'That was our morning,' he said. 'The weight of scientific evidence is with us.'

'It is. Hammond and Martin were brilliant. Burnett was floundering.'

'As the judge spotted. "You appear to be labouring the point."' They both laughed heartily.

'However,' said Russell, 'juries are more likely to be swayed by emotion.'

'Indeed.'

Both men could point to cases won in court but lost through the vicissitudes of the jury. Russell placed his cup in its saucer. 'The difficulty is that they will look for an excuse not to convict.'

'So we shan't give them one.'

Russell smiled. 'That's the spirit.'

*

Marjory flinched as Dr Murphy was brought into court. It was the first time she had seen him since his examination the day after the crime. Over the four days so far she had trained herself to negotiate discussion of the murder and the assault. She could – almost – listen to the testimony and divorce herself from the emotion, as though it had happened to somebody else. A different Madge Fenwick. But Murphy brought memories of acts she could not and would never be able to separate from herself.

'You inspected Miss Fenwick twice?' Russell asked.

'Correct. At around 1.30 am on the night of the crime and again the next morning.'

'From your examination, are you of the opinion that Miss Fenwick was forcibly assaulted?'

'The scratches and bruises are quite consistent with her having been used in violence.'

'You conducted an internal investigation?'

'I did.'

Marjory felt the eyes of the room on her, just as she had when giving testimony about the attack. Everyone listening to her most intimate experiences. Her greatest shame. She could taste blood in her mouth. She felt hot. She tried not to listen.

'Did you conclude she had been the subject of a sexual assault?' said Russell.

'She had.'

'She was raped?'

'She was.'

'Thank you.' He sat down.

Burnett remained seated for some moments. He knew the next two witnesses would determine the course of the trial. Medical evidence mattered more than fingerprints and shooting angles. 'We have no chance,' he told his junior counsel, Andrew MacRae, 'so long as it's McGuigan under scrutiny. Nobody's going to sympathise with a tinker.' Instead, they had to put the girl under pressure. 'Show her story to be false.'

He felt a delicious tension in his stomach and chest. He longed to begin. To perform.

He rose.

'Dr Murphy,' he said, 'as regards bruising of any kind, you found two merely superficial bruises over each of the shoulder blades?'

'Yes.'

'What appearance did they have?'

'Just a little reddening of the skin.'

'They were really hardly bruises at all?'

'Well, the skin was red and marked.'

'You found no signs of redness or anything else around her wrists and ankles?'

'None.'

'Does that not seem strange, given that she claims she was bound hand and foot?'

'It would depend how tight the bonds were.'

'Tight enough to restrict her movement, presumably?'

'I couldn't say.'

'You didn't see the handkerchief knotted round her wrist?'

'No. It had been removed by that point.'

'Knowing that she had been bound in that way, would you expect to see some bruising, particularly on the hand which she claims to have freed from the binding?'

'Not necessarily.'

Burnett forced a smile to conceal his irritation. 'But it would not be unexpected to see bruising in such an instance?'

'No.'

'Your examination of the girl was thorough?'

'Yes. Particularly the inspection the following day, when there was more time.'

Burnett studied the faces of the jury. They were blank. It was earlier than he planned but Murphy's non-committal responses were forcing his hand. He stared at Marjory, then turned back to Murphy. 'Might I put it that your view was that the girl was not a virgin?'

A few exhalations of surprise sounded around the public

314

gallery. Marjory felt as though she had taken a blow to the stomach. Her mother tensed beside her.

'I would not go as far as that,' said Dr Murphy. 'I would say that the signs were not consistent with virginity.'

The noises from the gallery grew louder. Lord Aitchison screwed up his face in irritation. 'This aspect of the case may be important,' he said. He addressed the doctor. 'What is your reasoning for suggesting this?'

'In my inspection there was no contemporaneous damage to the hymen. It had already been broken.'

'And that suggests previous penetration?'

'Yes.'

'Could penetration that night have accounted for it?'

'No. There was no fresh scarring.'

Lord Aitchison sat back. 'Thank you,' he said to the doctor. 'Mr Burnett, you may continue.'

Burnett considered. The judge's intervention was ideal, instilling an even greater sense of doubt in the jury's minds than he could have done. 'No further questions, my Lord.' Burnett closed his file and returned to his seat, satisfied. Stifled conversation escaped from the public benches.

Mr Russell retook the stand. 'Dr Murphy, the defence has made a great deal of the lack of markings on the wrists and ankles. In your experience, may you have pressure or violence applied to parts of the human body without leaving any overt signs?'

'Yes.'

'Take the case of a binding on the wrist with pieces of soft material like cloth or cotton or silk. Would you necessarily expect to find, three or four hours later, evidence of marks indicative of pressure which had been applied to them? Would that depend very much on the pressure that had been applied and the individual to whom it was applied?'

'Yes.'

'Therefore, it is not possible to extrapolate from a lack of

315

marks and suggest no bindings were in place?'

'That is correct.'

'Can you say definitely the injuries you saw were not self-inflicted?'

'Yes.'

Lord Aitchison intervened. 'Had you previously applied your mind to that?'

'I did think of that.'

'Are you satisfied she was assaulted?'

'Yes, my lord.'

Russell indicated he had no further questions. He gave a slight nod in the direction of Marjory, sitting white-faced in the gallery. The judge's intervention was helpful, leaving the focus at the end of Murphy's evidence on the injuries to Marjory, rather than the question of her virginity.

Next, though, was Professor Mathieson.

*

Marjory tried to eat her lunch but she could not force it down. She chewed mechanically but couldn't swallow. She thought she might gag.

'It's not true,' she said.

Mrs Fenwick patted her back. 'I know, hen.'

'But it's going to be in all the papers. Everyone's going to be talking about me.'

'It's a disgrace,' said Mrs Drummond. 'There was no need for that.' She snatched her handbag and marched towards the office used by the Crown prosecution team and rapped on the door. She walked in without waiting.

'Mrs Drummond,' said Russell, flustered, stubbing out his cigarette.

'Those questions,' she said. 'About the lassie. What were they for?'

'It was always likely, given what was said in the doctor's

316

report, that the defence would wish to pick up on the question of Marjory's virginity.'

'Why?'

'Her testimony is vital in terms of convicting McGuigan. They'll want to discredit her ...'

'But whether or not she's a virgin has nothing to do with it. That man killed the lassie's sweetheart and then he raped her. She did nothing. Anything she may or may not have done in the past is totally irrelevant.'

'I agree with you ...'

'But you won't stop it happening ...'

'I can't.'

'What kind of justice is it when a child gets raped and it's her reputation that's dragged through the court?' She towered over Russell, stout and formidable, clutching her handbag as though ready to wield it. Her voice could be heard in the corridor outside.

'I'm afraid it may get worse, Mrs Drummond,' he said. 'Professor Mathieson is likely to make the same observations. More forcefully.'

'And you're going to allow that?'

'I can't prevent it.'

'When do we get to hear all the rumours and scandal about the man who did this?'

'We won't. That's privileged information that will be withheld until after the trial.'

'So experts are allowed to make wild guesses about that poor wee lassie and drag her reputation through the mud, but no one's allowed to say a single word about a murderer and rapist? Justice is it?'

There was a knock on their door to alert the prosecution team that proceedings were due to recommence. Russell shot up with relief. 'Mrs Drummond,' he said, 'I honestly couldn't agree with you more, but the law is the law.'

'The law is an ass.'

'It has been said.'

*

Professor John Mathieson introduced himself as a pathologist at Glasgow University. He delivered his evidence on the body of Danny Kerrigan with a dry and dispassionate voice, borne of forty-five years' experience. In his opinion the shot was fired from between six and ten yards. Death would have been instantaneous. He went on to describe the experiments he conducted on clothing taken from McGuigan. There was little evidence of blood staining.

'One shirt and a cap showed staining but it was negligible. Greater staining was found on a handkerchief but it is entirely feasible that it might have come from the nose.'

Lord Aitchison sensed Russell was glossing over matters. The prosecution's case, he knew, was strongly circumstantial. There was nothing wrong with that providing sufficient corroboration could be presented. But a lack of blood was significant. 'In your considered opinion,' he said, 'there was nothing on the clothing of the accused from which any inference adverse to him could be drawn?'

'That is correct.'

Russell fumbled with his notes. He coughed.

'Mr Russell?' said Lord Aitchison.

'No further questions, My Lord.'

Burnett jumped up and took Russell's place.

'Professor Mathieson,' he said, 'you have said you examined the accused's clothing for blood and found only negligible traces. Does that include his trousers?'

'Yes.'

'You found no trace of blood around the area of the crotch?'

'No.'

'Did you specifically look for blood there?'

'Yes. I was requested by the Procurator Fiscal to do so.'

'Why?'

318

'On the night of the crime Miss Fenwick was menstruating. The Procurator Fiscal considered it likely that if the accused had come into contact with her then some menstrual blood would have been exchanged.'

'Yet you found none?'

'No.'

'I wish to address comments in your medical report on Marjory Fenwick, if I may. I understand the Procurator Fiscal requested a further examination of Marjory Fenwick on August the 26th?'

'He did.'

'What was the nature of that examination?'

Marjory sat frozen. She remembered. That room, cigarettes overflowing the ashtrays, the open door, the open windows, the blanket on a table, being forced to strip naked and lie on it and open her legs and be invaded.

Mathieson spoke in low and clear tones. 'I was requested to undertake a vaginal examination.'

'For what reason?'

'Dr Murphy's initial examination made a suggestion that the hymen may have been broken some time before the night of the crime. His tentative view was that the girl may not have been a virgin. The Procurator Fiscal wanted a further examination to try to provide greater certainty on the matter.'

'And what was your finding?'

'I was able to insert two fingers in the vaginal passage without difficulty.'

'Meaning?'

Mrs Fenwick was stiff by Marjory's side but Mrs Drummond gripped the girl's hand and squeezed it. Marjory could smell peppermint on the older woman's breath. She stared into nothingness, her eyes unfocused. She never wanted to focus them again.

'The breakage of the hymen was not new.'

'In your view, then, penetration had previously taken

placc?'

'Yes.'

'Can I be clear. Are you saying that in your view Marjory Fenwick was not a virgin?'

'That is correct.'

'Thank you, Professor.'

The courtroom settled back, digesting this testimony. Marjory sat unmoving. Mrs Drummond held her hand firmly.

Russell took his position again but before he could begin his re-examination Lord Aitchison addressed Professor Mathieson. 'You have great experience as a medical and legal expert,' he said. 'Is it within your knowledge that young women and girls sometimes pretend they have been criminally assaulted?'

'It is very common.'

'It is well known in the court of law and well known to you as an expert?'

'Children will often tell their parents of such.'

Marjory listened with incredulity. It was all she could do not to leap up. Mrs Drummond, as though intuiting this, pressed her hand again. Marjory felt tears forming and she opened her eyes wide to prevent them.

'In your experience,' said the judge, 'have you ever known a case in which a woman had her lover shot dead and went on to pretend she had been criminally assaulted?'

'No.'

'Neither in your experience nor in your course of reading or study?'

'I have no knowledge of such.'

'Very good. Mr Russell, your witness.'

Mr Russell stood up for his re-examination. He felt suddenly weary. An indolence overtook him, as it always did at the end of the evidence. Everything was done and nothing could be undone, everything presented and nothing outstanding. So much preparation, all the tension of the days of questions. And now it came down to this. Now the stage would be his and Burnett's for one final speech apiece. Evidence would be left behind and the performance would begin. And then they were in the hands of the judge and the jury.

It was ruthless.

'Professor Mathieson, you have given an opinion as to Miss Fenwick's virginity but let us be clear, that's all it is, isn't it? An opinion. There is no test to prove such a thing?'

'No.'

'Nor is there any reason that the fact of Miss Fenwick's virginity or otherwise should be germane to the question at hand.'

'Objection, my Lord,' said Burnett. 'That is a statement of opinion. There is no question for the witness to answer.'

'Sustained.'

'Very good,' said Russell. He looked at McGuigan in the dock and at Marjory in the court. He looked at the jury. They seemed tired, tense. There were still half a dozen witnesses listed but none of them had anything new to relate. The case was argued. The connections made. The trail from Aberdalgie House to a tinker's tent to the senseless death of an unblemished boy and the rape of an innocent girl on a strip of land normally reserved for love and romance. It was enough. He was done.

'My Lord,' he said, 'that concludes the evidence of the Crown.'

A murmur of surprise arose in the court. Even the court ushers looked up. Marjory turned to Mrs Drummond in confusion. The older woman shook her head.

'He'll know what he's doin',' said Mrs Fenwick.

Lord Aitchison looked at the defence benches, at the postures of Burnett and MacRae. He looked at the clock. 'Mr Burnett?' he said.

Burnett rose and addressed the bench without shifting his

position, his knees still bent, his head lowered towards his papers. 'My Lord, I do not propose to lead any evidence,' he said. He sat down.

Marjory scowled with incomprehension. 'What?' she said. 'Are they giving up?'

'I dinnae ken, hen,' said Mrs Drummond.

The Lord Chief Justice inclined his head slowly, as if there was nothing surprising about this sudden end to proceedings. 'There we are,' he said. He turned to the jury. 'Members of the jury, the full evidence of the case is now before you. John McGuigan is accused of three crimes: of the murder of Daniel Kerrigan; of the rape of Marjory Fenwick; and of housebreaking at Aberdalgie House. A fourth charge, of robbery from Daniel Kerrigan, has been withdrawn by the Crown. Tomorrow you will hear the summing up for the Crown and for the defence, following which I will guide you as far as I am able. Court is adjourned.'

*

Marjory could not hide her disappointment. She stood at the foot of the stairs looking through double glass doors into the gloom of an Edinburgh evening. She held her hat tightly in her hands, creasing the brim. She looked close to tears.

'I thought it was all over for a minute,' she said. 'That they'd given in.'

'No,' said Bob. 'They're just not presenting any witnesses themselves.'

'But why not?'

'Because they've no one who'll speak up for him,' said Mrs Drummond.

'But they did. The names are in the list.'

'They'll have changed their mind,' said Bob.

'Why?'

Bob said nothing. How could he? How could he tell

her that the defence thought their best asset was Marjory Fenwick and her murky past? 'We'd best get back to the bus,' he said.

'I can't take any more of this.' Marjory walked away head bowed. Bob followed and put his arm around her shoulder. 'Being talked about like that. It's unfair.'

'It was more than unfair, Madge. It was disgraceful.'

'So why did it happen?'

Bob shrugged. There was no possible answer.

*

Conoboy hurried after Russell as he descended the staircase of the Court of Justiciary and entered the Royal Mile. Fresh snowfall peppered the cold ground. The air was as grey as the buildings surrounding them. A heaviness hung over Edinburgh, slow and stolid like the city itself.

'We're nearing the end,' said Conoboy.

'Saturday.' Russell took out a silver cigarette case and slipped a cigarette into his mouth. Conoboy took one and pulled out his lighter and lit both cigarettes. They walked down Market Street towards the railway station.

'I got the impression yesterday court wasn't your forte,' Russell said. 'No offence.'

'None taken. You're right. I hate it. It's not how my mind works. I don't like confrontation and argument.'

'That must make it rather difficult to interview criminals …'

'That's different. That's easy. That's about finding the truth …'

'And court isn't?'

'No.' He laughed. 'Sorry, it's my turn to offend you now. But it's theatre, isn't it? Truth is important but it can be a casualty. The questions Burnett asked me. He already knew the answers. He simply wanted to sow the seeds of doubt. I

323

don't know, do solicitors believe what they say?'

Russell inhaled deeply and blew smoke out of his nose. He stared at the older man. 'Of course we sow the seeds of doubt. And so we should. Nothing is more corrosive to the truth than certainty. Certainty is the tool of dictators through the ages. But yes, we do believe what we say. I am convinced McGuigan is guilty. Mr Burnett is equally convinced that I haven't proved that sufficiently. It's his duty to argue against my certainty.'

'Solicitors' sophistry, Mr Russell. "Burnett is convinced I haven't proved the case." Perhaps that's so. But the real question is this: is he convinced that McGuigan is innocent?'

'I don't know.'

'Meanwhile, while you play linguistic games, that little girl is being hurt. Her reputation shredded. For what? For we participants in the justice game to pat ourselves on the back for our openness and fairness?'

'The law protects us from criminals, Inspector.'

'Perhaps so. But it can also make us criminals.'

'Only if abused.'

'When does sowing the seeds of doubt become an abuse of truth, Mr Russell?'

They paused at the gates of Waverley Station. Mr Russell raised his hat. 'I believe it has been a fair trial, Inspector.'

'Fair on McGuigan, certainly. Fair on Madge Fenwick?'

'I hope so.'

'With respect, Mr Russell, hope is not good enough.' Conoboy shook his hand and walked down the steps into the station. Albert Russell watched him retreat and turned and climbed towards Princes Street and the New Town.

Friday 29th November

A Day of Summation

Albert Russell spoke slowly, shifting his gaze from one juror to the next, waiting until he caught their eye and fixing on them for some moments. Making connections. He no longer felt any nerves. He no longer felt down. As soon as he began to speak he was in control. This was his court, his moment, his case.

His theatre.

'On August the 14th,' he said, 'a brutal murder was committed late in the evening in a strip of wood close to Perth. A young man of eighteen years, Daniel Kerrigan, was killed by a gun discharged by some lurking ruffian and as that young man's life was ebbing away within a few seconds, a man who, there can be no doubt, was the lurking murderer, committed a most revolting outrage upon the young girl who had been walking along with her young man when the gun was discharged.

'The question which we must determine is this – was the accused the man who committed these crimes, who killed young Kerrigan and who assaulted Miss Fenwick?

'The first stage of your deliberations must inevitably be occupied by consideration of the evidence of Marjory Fenwick. Do you accept the account given by Miss Fenwick in the witness box as a substantially true one? Supposing you were not to accept her statement, it would obviously have a most profound result upon any verdict you might reach.

'The facts of the crime are these: Miss Fenwick is going out for the night with Daniel Kerrigan. They have been keeping company since the New Year. Miss Fenwick's mother approves of Marjory walking out with this young man. That particular night they meet at seven o'clock. They go to the Cuddies Strip. They walk about four-hundred yards up the path and, as young people keeping company will do, they talk about things. There are affectionate exchanges. She admits they were kissing and embracing, and they were there for some time. He was showing her photographs, a most natural thing.

'Shortly after that they get up to go home because ten o'clock has struck. They start walking down the footpath side by side. Marjory has her hand in her coat pocket. Daniel Kerrigan has his arm around her waist.

'They come to a point about two-hundred and fifty yards from the stile. Like a bolt from the blue there rings out a shot. They both stop. Marjory turns to Kerrigan. Kerrigan says, "Don't faint, Madge."

'Then another shot rings out. Kerrigan falls back on the path. Miss Fenwick bends over him and says, "Danny, Danny". She sees blood on his face and shouts for help. She looks up. There is a figure standing beside her. "I am going for help," she tells him. The man says nothing. She starts running to the stile. She finds the man is running alongside her. She has just got one foot on the stile when this man gets hold of her and throws her to the ground.

'She cries out. He put his knee on top of her and she can hardly get breath. He ties her hands and mouth. She pretends to faint. He drags her to the bushes. He unties her hands to take off her coat, and then takes off all her clothing, then he ties her up again. She can do nothing. She is afraid. Her mouth cover slips off and she shouts for help. The man catches hold of her by the throat and nearly chokes her. Then he ties a suspender belt round her mouth.

'After his despicable deed, he ties her feet and goes off in the direction of where Danny Kerrigan was lying. There is another shot. Miss Fenwick struggles free, crosses the stile and runs down the field where she meets witnesses Spence and Miss Ewan at the fence at the end of Buckie Braes nearest to the Cuddies Strip.

'The story told by Marjory Fenwick in the witness box in this court is undoubtedly the story of an extraordinary occurrence. You heard this story subjected, quite properly, to a very searching cross-examination. You, ladies and gentlemen, saw Marjory Fenwick in the witness box and you can judge from her demeanour as to whether or not her evidence is to be accepted as reliable. You will see, however, time and again that specific points of her story are corroborated by the facts and circumstances, and by witnesses who have been called to this court. In every respect, she has seemed a credible and reliable and honest witness.

'Witnesses Spence and Miss Ewan corroborated her story about seeking help. Her first thoughts were not for herself but for Danny. Remember her words to Spence: "Oh mister, can you help?"

'Witness McDougall, who was working at Pitheavlis Farm, heard two shots at the time Miss Fenwick said, around 10.15.

'Witness Hill also heard a shot and placed the time around 10 o'clock.

'Medical and gunsmith experts have told that from the shot on the body and the way it had spread, that shot must have been fired somewhere between six to ten yards in distance, as Marjory Fenwick told us. Within ten yards of where Kerrigan fell there was an excellent lurking place in bushes as shown by photographs at the scene of the crime.

'In medical examinations, Miss Fenwick was found to be afflicted by scratches, contusions, abrasions. There was the

327

finding of the elastic band and the broken pendant which she had been wearing that night. All of these little things tend to corroborate Miss Fenwick's story. They could only be there if her story was true.

'On the other hand, if it were a story got up and invented, what possible motive might there be? It is difficult to figure one. I cannot see one.

'If her story is acceptable and confidently corroborated by independent facts and circumstances, then Danny Kerrigan was shot and Marjory Fenwick was assaulted in the way she has described.'

Russell paused and sipped from his glass of water. He studied the jury and liked the expressions on their faces. Some were nodding. All were listening. He looked at McGuigan in the dock. The accused stared back at him emotionlessly, as he had every day of the trial. It increased Russell's resolve. He continued, pointing at McGuigan.

'The second stage of your deliberations must then be, was the accused the man who did this?

'The first piece of evidence regarding that is that Marjory Fenwick swears on oath that he is. There has been no suggestion that Marjory Fenwick knew or was known to the accused. She identified him from a line-up of seven men. "This is the man," she said. Constable Kelty talked of a jolt of recognition when she saw him. Of course, if there was nothing except her identification to link him to the crime that would not be enough. You would not want to find a man guilty of murder based on the identification of one witness. Scottish law depends on corroborative evidence. Therefore, is there further evidence which independently of Marjory's identification links the accused to the crime?

'Yes there is.

'Here, I am going to detail a most extraordinary circumstance. I am referring to the handkerchief that was found around Marjory's wrist and was put there by her assailant when he was tying her hands.

'Earlier this year the Douglas family took up residence in Aberdalgie House, about half a mile from the scene of the crime. That house had a separate building called a laundry. The family, having been abroad, had all their clothing cleaned by a laundry in Kelso and it was brought to Aberdalgie and put in that laundry room. In the month of August, shortly after the abhorrent crimes on Cuddies Strip, it was discovered that various articles were missing from this laundry at Aberdalgie House and a housebreaking had taken place.

'Items from that housebreaking were subsequently found in the possession of the accused, including a telescope unusual enough to be considered almost unique and a purse which was inscribed in ink with the initials of David Douglas. It is impossible to conceive of two identical purses being identically inscribed. Again, then, it is undoubtedly a unique item.

'The witness Gow had no hesitation in identifying the accused as the man he had seen with that telescope on the afternoon before the crime was committed. You will have no difficulty, ladies and gentlemen, in holding it clearly proved that this telescope was in the possession of the accused, and the brown purse also.

'And, of course, there is the handkerchief that was found on the wrist of Marjory Fenwick. This bore a laundry mark, "M1-2," which identified it as having been serviced by the laundry in Kelso that laundered the possessions of the Douglas family. This handkerchief has a very unusual colour and pattern and Mr David Douglas has identified it as his.

'After the housebreaking, a blue handkerchief was found on the floor of the laundry near the window. It was found that the handkerchief did not belong to anyone in the house. Witness Peddie swore on oath that it was the only handkerchief he ever saw in the accused's possession.

'And should you have any lingering doubts there is the question of the fingerprints. The evidence of a scientific expert has demonstrated that undoubtedly the fingerprints of the accused were found on the casement window at Aberdalgie House. How did they get there? Only the hand of John McGuigan could have put them there.

'I suggest to you, ladies and gentlemen, that you will have no difficulty whatever in reaching a conclusion from the cumulative evidence of the telescope, the purse, the laundry mark and the fingerprints, that the accused broke into the laundry by the casement window. Further, he used an item from that housebreaking – the handkerchief – to bind Marjory Fenwick's wrists. An incontrovertible connection is thus made between John McGuigan and the dark acts of that August evening.

'If the evidence to date is sufficient to prove beyond all reasonable doubt that the accused was the girl's assailant, what about the shooting? Did he fire the shots? The man who assaulted Miss Fenwick was on the scene within a second or two after the deceased had fallen. Where did he come from if not the spot from where the gun had been fired?

'We know, from the evidence of Peddie, the Kirkton of Mailer farm servant, that McGuigan had a gun. We know he spoke of concealing it after the crime because he had no licence. It is not conjecture that McGuigan possessed this gun because Peddie saw it and handled it. There is no doubt, then, that the accused possessed a gun and had it within a very short time of the occurrence of the tragedy of August the 14th. He was seen at the scenes of the crimes earlier that afternoon. A figure which strongly resembled him was seen by no fewer than three sets of witnesses around the time of the crimes.'

Russell took another pause and breathed deeply. 'When you find that the accused can be identified through means of fingerprints and possession of stolen property as the man responsible for house-breaking at Aberdalgie; when you find that the handkerchief bound round the wrist of Marjory Fenwick within minutes of the shots which killed Danny Kerrigan was taken in that very robbery; when you recall that the shots which killed Danny Kerrigan were heard and the timings verified by different persons in the locality; when you go a step further and recall Marjory Fenwick has identified the accused by his features and his face as the man who assaulted her; when you bear all those factors in mind and conclude your deliberations then, ladies and gentlemen of the jury, the weight of evidence becomes incontrovertible.

'There can be no doubt that the killer of Daniel Kerrigan and the attacker of Marjory Fenwick were one and the same person. There can also be no doubt that this person was the same person who was responsible for the housebreaking at Aberdalgie House.'

He turned to the jury face-on. 'And there can be no doubt, ladies and gentlemen of the jury, that the accused, John McGuigan, is that person. I ask you to find John McGuigan guilty of housebreaking at Aberdalgie House, guilty of rape and guilty of murder.'

Russell closed his notebook and returned to his bench and sat down. He felt a flush of fatigue but, at the same time, a rush of excitement.

'We shall adjourn,' said the Lord Chief Justice, 'and reconvene this afternoon when we shall hear the summing up for the defence.'

*

Bob Kelty rested his elbows on his knees and sat forward as Mr Burnett rose to begin his address to the jury. The words of Mr Russell still rebounded in his head. It was a wonderful address. It made sense of what was an inexplicable set of circumstances. It laid bare the criminality and made clear

331

where responsibility lay. Over the months since the crime, Bob's faith in the criminal justice system had been tested. Mr Russell had renewed that faith. Now he waited to see what Mr Burnett would do.

Mr Burnett turned in a circle to inspect the entire court room. Then he focused on the jury. He paused for nine or ten seconds. He spoke.

'Ladies and gentlemen, you have heard Mr Russell's eloquent speech for the Crown, a speech in which I admit everything which could be said bearing on the guilt of the accused was said with perfect fairness.

'You have heard all the evidence and I am at this moment, with the heaviest heart, placed with the most difficult task that an advocate can be asked to discharge.

'You are sitting in the same box where a jury in the beginning of this century found Oscar Slater guilty of murder. You may not have heard of Oscar Slater but his story is a dark one in the annals of Scottish legal history. An innocent man, arraigned by circumstance, he was tried for a murder he did not commit and sentenced to life imprisonment. The accused is in the very spot where Oscar Slater sat to receive that grave judgement and where, nineteen years later, the verdict was overturned by the Lord Chief Justice himself when it was discovered that the original jury's verdict was unsound. Not through their mistakes but through circumstance. And it is circumstance with which we, all of us, you members of the jury, the officers of the court, counsels for the Crown and the defence and His Lordship the Lord Chief Justice, must contend. These are the decisions we must make. And these are the consequences of such decisions.' He paused again. 'It is, simply, a matter of life and death.'

Bob studied the faces of the jury, their set expressions, staring eyes. It was sobering stuff, to be sure. Such responsibility. He pictured Marjory, frightened, hoping for resolution. Make it right for her. Do it right.

'I question whether this court has ever heard quite so strange and inexplicable a story as the one which has been told you this week by Marjory Fenwick. We are not here to speculate or conjecture. The sole question for you is this: has the Crown satisfied you beyond all reasonable doubt ...' He stopped and repeated the phrase more slowly, pausing after each word. 'Beyond ... all ... reasonable ... doubt ... that the accused is the man who was guilty of the crimes with which he has been charged, and, in particular, guilty of the crime of murdering Danny Kerrigan?

'You are not here to say who is guilty of that crime. Only whether or not that person is the accused.

'There are three separate charges against the accused. These are, in a sense, interrelated, but you must consider each of the charges upon its own merits and consider whether there is sufficient evidence bearing on each one of them to return a verdict of guilty.

'To illustrate the matter, you might think that the accused was proved guilty of housebreaking at the Aberdalgie laundry, but it would by no means follow that this identified him in such a way as to become evidence in the more serious charge of murder.

'You must, therefore, take each charge in turn and satisfy yourself as to the strength of the argument set out by the Crown. There is no logical sequence of "if this happened, then that must also have happened". Such notions are pure conjecture. You must satisfy yourself, members of the jury, that your decision can be justified by the application of evidence. That is your duty.

'The most dramatic element in this whole case is the evidence, if any, afforded by the handkerchief which was found tied round Marjory Fenwick's wrist. This is a most sordid and terrible case but one cannot help feeling rather intrigued by the fact that a handkerchief should now be a clue of the utmost importance from the Crown's point of view.

'Because the simple truth is that there is nothing whatever to connect the accused with the handkerchief. It has not been proved that the handkerchief was ever in John McGuigan's possession. Indeed, I challenge the Crown to demonstrate that it was ever in the Aberdalgie Laundry at all. On what list or inventory is it declared? None at all.'

Bob sat upright and inhaled deeply. *Yes it was*, he thought. *I know it was. I saw it.*

'And there is no question that to a very large degree the Crown's case rests on that handkerchief. Have they adequately connected it to Mr McGuigan?

'What occurred on that night on the Cuddies Strip was a monstrous outrage against decency. Every one of us can agree on that. The ordeal that Marjory Fenwick underwent was real and terrible and utterly undeserved. You are entitled, in ordinary humanity, to make allowances for Marjory Fenwick and the evidence she has submitted, but you must not make allowances for Marjory to the prejudice of John McGuigan.

'Because, for all she underwent a terrifying ordeal, there remain serious questions regarding her evidence and her credibility as a witness.'

Lies. And now this. Now the attack on Madge's character. Bob felt an impotent anger.

'Miss Fenwick's story is indeed a remarkable one,' Burnett continued. 'So frightful is it, indeed, that if it be true it is almost incredible that any sane human should have behaved as the said man behaved in the Cuddies Strip. Can you believe that anyone but a madman could have been guilty of such horrible and revolting conduct as Marjory Fenwick suggests? It is not a facile question because there is no suggestion whatever in this case that the lad in the dock is insane. What could possibly possess him to undertake such acts?

334

'Again, that is not a facile question. A singular feature of this case is that, apart from sheer bestial, brutal lust there is absolutely no motive alleged. Marjory Fenwick and the accused did not know each other and had never met. There is no evidence that the accused and Danny Kerrigan knew each other. The ordinary motive of jealousy, which is at the bottom of so many crimes of this type, is completely out of the case and ever the lesser motive of robbery has disappeared. So what, I ask, was the motive?

'My learned friend, with his usual candour, said in the course of his address that if you do not accept the girl as a credible witness it must have a very profound result on your verdict.

'I respectfully agree with that observation. If Marjory Fenwick is not accepted by you as a witness on whom you can put reliance as wholly truthful, then the way to a result leading to to the acquittal of the accused is absolutely clear to you.

'I do not suggest Marjory Fenwick came here with a false story. Something very terrible indeed happened at the Cuddies Strip that evening. I should be the last person to criticise the evidence of a girl who went through the experience she must have gone through when Kerrigan was shot and to say to her "You are manufacturing and making up a story".'

Except you did. Bob breathed heavily, his hands fisted on his thighs. *You are.*

'What I do say is that, while the major part of her story, the shooting of Kerrigan, is true, the whole story as presented by her is not one that you can accept implicitly.

'You must remember that although she has told the same general story from the beginning, she was, when first seen, in a distressed, over-excited condition.' He removed his glasses and waved them theatrically, then reattached them.

'A man's life is not to be sworn away by the evidence of

an over-excited girl.'

Bob was concerned to see three of the jurywomen nodding. Albert Russell sat blank-faced beneath the judge, registering neither concern nor outrage. Bob felt both. He was grateful Madge wasn't here to hear this. There was something contemptible about Mr Burnett's words, the manipulation, the slyness of the insinuations, the deliberateness with which he tried to inject doubt in the minds of the jury.

'Miss Fenwick said that Kerrigan's words when the first shot rang out were, "Don't faint, Madge." Why on earth would he say that? It makes no sense.

'The account she gave of how she and Danny were standing when the shot was fired certainly does provoke speculation. How can it be that Marjory Fenwick was not hit? I do not say it is quite impossible for her to have escaped every one of the four-hundred and sixty-eight shots held in two shotgun cartridges, but it is almost incredible that she did. That she did means, at this very early stage, you do not know whether you are really getting the whole truth from Marjory Fenwick.

'And the story gets stranger and stranger from this point. She ran and found that the man was running alongside her until she reached the stile. Ladies and gentlemen, can you accept that? The man did not touch her, although he could have seized her at any moment. They ran like this for some two-hundred yards until they reached the stile. Then, and only then, the man seized hold of her. Is it normal behaviour for a murderer to let a witness run away and not apprehend her at the very first opportunity?

'No one saw the accused except Marjory Fenwick. Over a period of time her description varied. We were told he had "staring eyes" yet he wore a cap which would have made it all but impossible to see those eyes. Ultimately, her various descriptions coalesced into a general impression of a man in his thirties with a red complexion and a beard. Look at the man in the dock. Do you see any resemblance to the description Marjory Fenwick gave? None at all.

'Mr Burnett made a great play of the corroborating evidence. Let us consider some of that. Mr Peddie's told us a story of being shown a gun in the tent. That story is, I regret to say, quite ridiculous. It was singular that he did not go to the police but waited until they called for him, and even then he did not tell them his story. He couldn't, because he hadn't invented it by then. This is a young man who wanted to be in the limelight and his testimony is nonsense.

'Other people testified to seeing the accused. Mr Gow saw him at six o'clock. Very well, but the crime was committed at ten o'clock. Mr Barrie and Mr Strangeway believe they saw him. But what they were really looking for was the gamekeeper, in order to avoid him, to carry on their illegal poaching. Are they credible witnesses?

'The truth is, there is not one shred of evidence linking the accused to the Cuddies Strip at the time of the murder. There is not one logical reason why he would have committed such evil acts. The murder of a man, ladies and gentlemen of the jury, is the most serious crime to come before these courts. Remember, if John McGuigan is found guilty of this offence he will face the ultimate sanction. Is that something you would wish to impose on the basis of the evidence of a single handkerchief and the confused memory of a hysterical child?'

He stopped. Again he paused for another full ten seconds, allowing his words to echo in the silence.

Hysterical child.

*

Bob Kelty sat in Victor Conoboy's kitchen and peeled potatoes and dropped them into a pot of water. The events of the day reverberated in his head still. Annie jointed a chicken

337

and rubbed it with lard and set it on a tray and placed it in the range. She wiped hair from her eyes.

'Will you go to court again tomorrow?'

'Aye. For the verdict.'

'They're sure to find him guilty.'

Bob kept his doubts to himself. Part of him longed to tell Annie about it, the way Madge had been maligned, the lies, the innuendo. But he didn't know how to begin. He carried the pan to the range and set it on the gas burner. As he did, Bella Conoboy entered.

'Making yourself useful?' she said.

'Yes, ma'am.'

Bella asked Annie to help Victor with the fire in the living room. 'Forty years he's been trying and he still can't light a fire.' She sat at the table and motioned for Bob to join her.

'Annie tells me you're having doubts about the police force,' she said.

'Aye. I'm not sure it's for me.'

'No. The police isn't the right place for you. But, if you want my advice, stay there. At least for now. There's going to be a war within a couple of years. And if you're ill-suited to the police you're even less suited to the army. In the police you'd be exempt from conscription.'

'If there's a war we'll all have our part to play.'

'Yes. The part we're capable of playing. After the war we'll need people like you to bring folks back together again. That's your job, son. That's what you're good at.'

'I really don't know what I'm good at.'

'Being yourself. And that's enough.'

Saturday 30th November

A Day of Decisions

There were papers on his desk but it was too dark in the morning gloom to read them and Inspector Conoboy stared out of the window onto South Street. It would all be over in a few hours, judgement made, future foretold. He had intended going in by train but changed his mind. There was nothing he could do.

'Can I come in?'

Lord Kellett stood at the door, smiling. Conoboy beckoned for him to enter and slid his cigarette case across the desk. Lord Kellett took one and lit it with a silver lighter.

'Not in Edinburgh?' he asked.

'I asked Robert Kelty to go,' said Conoboy. 'Thought it would be good experience for him.'

'Yes,' Kellett said heavily. 'We must look to the new generation. I hope they're better than ours has been, Victor.'

'I fear they'll have to be, sir. With the world situation.'

'Fragile.'

'There will be war. You can't negotiate with madmen.'

'No. At least it won't be our war this time.'

'It'll be everybody's war.'

Lord Kellett pulled a hip flask from his jacket pocket. He offered it to Conoboy and the inspector sipped from it slowly, enjoying the burn of whisky sliding down his throat. He handed it back and Kellett swigged from it lustily.

'The interviews for Chief Constable will be held the

339

week after next,' he said. 'I've already advised the Acting Chief Constable that he will not be one of the candidates.'

'Really?'

'Fresh blood, I think.'

'That might be wise.'

'The Glasgow chaps, I asked them their views before they left. They said some harsh things. There was too much interference. Officers were given responsibility for things but MacNaughton kept taking over. That needs to change, they said. They're right.'

Conoboy considered for a moment. 'I don't think they helped a damn with the investigation, but they put things in perspective, in different ways. Watters was especially perceptive.'

'Yes, a good man. What about you?'

'Me, sir?'

'If you were to throw your hat in the ring, it'd be favourably received, I assure you. The Glasgow chaps, even the young turk, were very complimentary. You've still got a lot to offer.'

'Oh, I fear my end is nearing.'

Kellett sighed. 'Perhaps. It's a changing world. It's going to get harder. Harsher. People like us, Victor, we're old-fashioned. I'm not sure there's a place for us any longer. You're a gentleman, an honourable man. It's going to get ruthless. People like Lamping, they're the future.' He swigged from his hip flask again. 'But if we could hold back the thrust of the new, even for a few years, it might help. There's a lot the young ones could learn from you. Think about it. Please.'

An omnibus trundled past the window. Victor looked round his office, aware for the first time how spartan it was. It wouldn't take long to empty. Four photographs. None of which he would want to keep.

'I intend to resign on Monday morning, sir. I discussed it

with Bella last night and we decided.'

Lord Kellett sighed heavily. 'You're a much better officer than you realise. You will be greatly missed.'

'I imagine Sergeant Braggan will make inspector.'

'Not if I have any say in the matter. Sergeant Strangeway has alerted me to some alarming flaws in Braggan's character. Besides, if our replacements are to be more ruthless than us then they'd better be more intelligent, too. Ruthless and stupid, that's a frightening combination.'

'We've been there before.'

'We'll be there again.'

*

Marjory stood by the graveside. Her hands were thrust inside her coat pockets for warmth. There was no snow yet but by nightfall there would be. She looked forward to it. A cover. A mask. Something concealing the true nature of the world, if only for a time.

'Hello, my love,' she said. 'Today's the day. I'll tell you what I hope, and then what I expect. I hope they will know that he killed you. I expect they won't say so. I hope that life goes on. I expect that it endures. I hope the sadness will go away. I expect I shall grow used to it. I hope you are happy, or safe, or at peace. I expect you are beyond all that.' She faltered, looked around the empty cemetery. Trees stood like the dead guarding the road to the underworld.

'Mum asked me this morning if I wanted to go on holiday at Easter. To Carnoustie. The seaside. That was nice of her. I know she can't afford it. I don't know if I shall go.'

She wanted to explain her reasons but no words came and a minute passed. She started to cry. At first it was gentle, a few quiet sobs, tears tickling her cheeks. Then they grew louder, harder, and her body began to heave and she fought for breath with each new convulsion. She let out a wail, the longest, loudest, darkest sound that had ever passed her lips, and the terror and the pain and the melancholy and the heartache of the past three months intermingled and deepened and hardened and she felt herself subsumed by it, felt it wash over and across and around her protesting body. She felt close to panic, close to despair, close to destruction. She fell to her knees and buried her face in the wet grass and beat the ground with her fists and sobbed and cried and screamed until there was no voice left inside her and she was stilled and calm and broken and done.

*

Lord Aitchison surveyed the ushers before him, the Crown team and the defence, the jury to his left, the accused in the dock, flanked by uniformed policemen, the expectant crowd above and behind. Large windows surrounding the court offered little light. Beyond, snow was falling, life continuing the only way it can, moment by moment, inexorable, unaccountable.

Here, though, there was accounting to be done.

'Members of the jury,' he began, 'whatever difficulties and anxieties this case may present there can be no doubt as to the great gravity of the main issue you have to try.

'On the night of August the 14th of this year Daniel Kerrigan, a young man of eighteen years, standing at the very threshold of his life, was brutally murdered. It was a cruel and cowardly crime, committed as it was in the presence of the young woman with whom Kerrigan had been keeping company.

'The Crown alleged that Kerrigan was murdered by the accused John McGuigan and that it was McGuigan who, having murdered Kerrigan, committed the crime of rape upon Marjory Fenwick. There were two other charges in the indictment, a charge of housebreaking and theft from

342

the laundry at Aberdalgie House and a charge of theft of a pocketbook from the pocket of the murdered man. This last charge has now been struck from the case at the direction of the Crown's counsel.

'It might strike you as odd that when a man is charged with murder, other charges should appear in the same indictment. There was a reason in this case why that should be so. It was part of the case for the Crown that a handkerchief which was alleged to have been found on the wrist of Marjory Fenwick was a handkerchief stolen by the accused from the laundry at Aberdalgie House.

'It was necessary, therefore, according to our law and practice that the housebreaking and theft should be libelled in the indictment. If these had not been, the Crown could not have led evidence as to certain matters which they desired to prove as bearing on the charge of murder.

'Again, the reason for charging rape in the same indictment was clear. According to the Crown, the murder and the rape were part and parcel of one criminal enterprise. It would be necessary for them to consider the three charges in the indictment as a unity.

'It is my duty to try and assist you in your consideration of the case by giving you some direction on matters of law, and also by trying to help you focus the evidence upon the critical issues of the case.'

Aitchison surveyed the room again. Had he not sat in this court and presided over judgements fair and judgements false? Oscar Slater, sentenced to life imprisonment. James Mills, sentenced to death. Both of them reprieved. How many had not been so lucky? How many innocent men had suffered in this place, how many guilty escaped, freed by caprice or incompetence or fear? I may assist the jury, he thought. Who assists me?

'I need scarcely remind you that it is for the Crown to prove the charges set out in the indictment. It is an elementary rule of the law that the accused person is entitled to the doubt and that, of course, applies to all charges. The doubt must be reasonable, however. One can never achieve a mathematical demonstration of guilt. Furthermore, it is not necessary for the Crown to prove motive. You can never read the secrets of the human mind.'

He shifted his position until he faced the jury directly. 'There are certain cases in which human life is taken where it may be open to a jury to say that the crime committed is not murder but culpable homicide only. I am afraid I must give you direction as a matter of law that no such alternative is open in this case. If it is proved that the accused shot Kerrigan dead then the crime is murder. There is no middle course open upon the evidence of this case. The only possible verdicts on that charge are guilty, not guilty and not proven.'

Bob pondered the finality of that. Could human acts be broken down so absolutely? He stared at McGuigan. What was it inside him that made him do this? What impulse? Could he have controlled it? Could society? How could we ever know? Oh, wid a gift the giftie gie us. He returned his attention to the judge.

'In considering the charge of murder the first question you should address to yourself is: what weight is to be given to the evidence of Marjory Fenwick? That is a very vital question in this case. It involves two considerations.

'Firstly, is she an honest witness and secondly is she a reliable witness? You may get a witness who honestly thinks what she saw took place but her observations may be unreliable. You may get a witness who prevaricates or lies by omission or commission. In the case of Marjory Fenwick you must direct yourself to both questions.

'Members of the jury, if you are not satisfied with the honesty and reliability of Marjory Fenwick it would be unsafe to convict on so grave a charge as the murder of a man.

344

'There is no question that she told a very remarkable story. You must consider very closely whether it was a story honestly told. Accordingly, the first question is – Was the evidence of Marjory Fenwick honest evidence? If I had to decide that question, the first thing I would ask myself would be – What impression did she make upon me? What was her demeanour? Did she strike me as telling the truth? This is not easy. The most experienced judges are often quite misled by the demeanour of witnesses, but one thing you will probably think about Marjory Fenwick is that she was not a glib witness. Glib witnesses cause one to be on one's guard. In fact she may have struck you as being rather cautious and reserved, but she certainly was not glib or plausible.

'Did she strike you as a girl who was likely to invent a story? What is the probability of her story? It is said that her story is incredible, that it is unbelievable for a man to act as her assailant, whoever he was, is said, by her, to have acted. Of course, you will carefully consider it, but there are two observations I would like to make upon that.

'Members of the jury, don't forget that when you are dealing with crime of this gravity you are quite definitely in the region of the abnormal. People who commit crimes of this kind cannot be measured by ordinary standards. A man who was capable of shooting Kerrigan dead in the presence of that young girl when they were sweethearting together was a man capable of any crime. Don't forget that, and when you come to ask yourself whether the story is believable keep that present in your mind. There is no doubt that whoever committed this crime was a man of low and degraded mentality.'

Bob looked at the man in the dock. McGuigan stared ahead, unmoving.

'Now,' continued the judge, 'we must consider whether the story presented by Miss Fenwick was an invented story. Nobody, of course, suggested it was invented so far as the

345

shooting of Kerrigan was concerned, but was she telling a story? She was found without clothes other than her swagger coat. Do you think she took them off herself? Was she just playing a part? Her clothes were never found. Do you think she concealed them and, if so, why? There might be a very good reason why her assailant should have concealed them. If he took the girl's clothes away he might have supposed he had a better chance of getting out of the way, although if that were the case why would he have left her swagger coat behind?

'I said previously that young girls sometimes invent stories of criminal assault. I know that from my experience at the Crown office for four years. I have known it in not a few cases during my years at the Bar.

'You must ask yourselves this, what possible motive could this girl, whose lover had just been brutally murdered, have to strip herself naked and pretend that the murderer had criminally assaulted her? Was that likely to be an invention or was it the sober truth? You have seen the girl in the witness box. She does not strike me as a girl of a very alert intelligence. Do you think she simply made that story up and, if so, what was in her mind?'

Bob bristled. That was not only untrue, it was unnecessary.

'Ever since this case opened I have been turning the thing over in my own mind trying to think of some theory that would account for the girl taking off her own clothes and making a pretence and I confess I can find no theory that will account for it. It struck me it would be possible that she was trying to screen somebody but if she knew the person who shot Kerrigan and wanted to screen that person all she had to do was to say that she did not know who the man was and could not pick him out. How was it going to help her to screen the person she knew by taking all her clothes off and pretending she was criminally assaulted? Ask yourselves where the probability in this story lies. Do you think it likely that the story was just a bit of pretence on the part of Marjory Fenwick?

'Still dealing with the subject of Miss Fenwick's honesty, the next thing I would ask myself is whether there were circumstances that tended to corroborate her story. I have already referred to one – the fact that she was found without clothes other than the swagger coat. Mr Russell has pointed out, quite rightly, that certain things were found at or near the place which she alleged was the place of the assault.'

He halted his speech and asked the usher to bring him the broken pendant and the rubber band with which Marjory held up her stockings. He picked up the pendant.

'This is a poor thing, a piece of glass, no doubt, but it was a bit of jewellery she wore, and I have no doubt she was quite pleased to wear it. It was found three or four feet from the stile. Do you think that the girl just tore off her pendant and flung it away in order to make up a story? This rubber band, which comes from the confectionery factory in which she works, was found in a clump of trees some twenty yards from the stile. Do you think she put it there as part of the story she was making up? If she were to do something like that, why would she place it so far from the scene, where it might be overlooked?

'It has been said that Miss Fenwick is not to be believed, that she should be treated as discredited because she said in the witness box that she was a virgin and the doctors have said she is not. I want you to consider how far this gets into her evidence. In the case of the charge of rape it does not matter in the least whether the girl was a virgin or not except in so far as it might bear upon her reliability as a witness.

'It is all very well to say she is not a virgin, but not a single instance of unchastity was ever put to her in cross-examination. She had employment in a confectionery factory. No suggestion was made that she was a girl who walked the streets.'

No, thought Bob, *so why put such a thought in their minds now?*

'If the doctors are right, she appears to have made terrible mistakes in her life. However, you must seriously consider whether this would justify you rejecting her evidence. If you think she is wanting in frankness in that particular matter you would, of course, take that into account in weighing her story. But it is not necessary to hold that because she was not a virgin and refused to admit it her story should be discredited as an invention.

'There is no doubt the girl was assaulted. That is beyond doubt. The girl's story is that she was dragged before being stripped and then put on her back naked. Dr Murphy said that his impression was that the marks on her back were caused by scratching over undergrowth. Does the doctor's statement not go some way to corroborate her story?

'Coming to the point of identification it is perhaps important to consider what was the first description she gave of her assailant. To Mr Spence she said he was a small man, not much taller than herself, with staring eyes. Now, whatever various descriptions that girl has given, there are two features which she turns to in every description given – he was not a big man and he had large eyes.

'The really important thing is not the description the girl gave, but the identification itself. Very few people can give accurate verbal descriptions of even people they know. If Marjory Fenwick had said she was attacked by a man of six feet in height it would be necessary to discard her evidence but the description she gave is an approximation of the accused standing before you.

'In the identification parade Constable Kelty noted that she "gave a start" when she saw him. Again, was she acting? Or was it genuine? Constable Kelty struck me as a somewhat diffident but nonetheless estimable officer of the law. Is it likely that he would be deceived by such an act of dissemblance? The identification is very significant. It would, of course, be quite unsafe to convict of murder on Miss Fenwick's identification alone and you must consider whether there is any evidence that can properly be accepted as corroboration of the girl's story.

'You might not think it proved that the accused had, in his possession, a double-barrelled shotgun. You have the evidence of the witness Peddie that the accused had shown him a gun. Do you think that Peddie invented this story? You have the evidence of Gow as to the accused and his gun on the day of the crime. Was Gow just imagining what he said or was he truthfully repeating the conversation that took place?

'If there was a gun, it has never come to light. Why is that? Did the accused dispose of it because he had no licence, or for some more sinister reason?'

He asked the usher to bring him the handkerchief and tied it twice around his left wrist with his right hand and knotted it. 'You can see,' he said, 'that it is comparatively easy to tie this oneself. But if she did that, the question remains, how did she come into possession of it? We have evidence from Lord Douglas that the handkerchief belonged to him. We have evidence of housebreaking at his laundry, where that handkerchief would have been. If the handkerchief was stolen by the accused from Aberdalgie House and was then found around the wrist of Marjory Fenwick, then I am afraid you have got to face up to the fact that it is evidence of a most considerable kind against the accused.

'Whoever broke into Aberdalgie House stole the property. There is evidence from a very experienced police officer trained in identification of fingerprints, who has said the fingerprints found on the casement window and those of the accused are identical.

'It is clear the accused had the telescope and purse in his possession. What was the accused's explanation? That he purchased them at Meikleour crossroads. Could you believe that story?

'If the accused was the man who tied the handkerchief around the wrist of Marjory Fenwick and he was the man who stole the handkerchief from Aberdalgie, that brings the accused to the locus of the crime at the time of the crime. If you are satisfied the accused was that person, then the inference that he was also the person who fired the shot becomes inevitable.

'It is true there is no eyewitness, but it is true in a great many cases that you cannot get direct testimony. It is only by comparing circumstance with circumstance and considering the cumulative weight of evidence that guilt can be brought home. That is what we mean by circumstantial evidence.

'Here we are not purely in the realm of circumstantial evidence because you have the direct testimony of Marjory Fenwick.

'You have to take all these considerations as a whole. You have got to take Marjory's identification of the accused; his possession of a gun; the disappearance of the gun within two days of the murder; the evidence of three different handkerchiefs; and, talking all these things together you must solemnly direct yourself to which conclusion these things suggest.

'Now, ladies and gentlemen, that is a matter for you. I cannot relieve you of your responsibility in a matter of this kind.

'I cannot disguise from you the solemnity of the decision you have to make, especially when you come to consider the charge of murder. Whenever a jury has to make up its mind upon a grave matter of that kind, there is one rule and one rule only to follow. That is summed up, with a brevity and an adequacy to which I can add nothing, in the simple words of your oath: "You will truth say and no truth conceal." And now, members of the jury, I must instruct you to retire and consider your verdict.'

November snow fell on the streets of the capital, settling an inch or so deep, insulating the air from the noises of human life. The sky was dulled like slate. Lights from shops and public buildings barely penetrated the gloom. The cold raked Bob's skin. He shivered inside his coat. He lit his pipe and began to walk aimlessly in the direction of the national library. He became aware of a figure walking alongside.

'You gave evidence,' the man said.

'Aye. I was the first bobby on the scene.'

'William Roughead,' said the man, offering his hand. They shook hands and walked along.

'You must have been pleased with what the judge said about you?' Bob looked blankly at him. 'Estimable?'

'Did he?' In truth, Bob was so outraged by the judge's words about Madge, he completely failed to hear what was said about him.

'It's a fascinating case,' Roughead said.

'It is.'

'I've been at every murder trial in this court for thirty years.'

'Aye? You must have heard some terrible tales.'

'None as remarkable as this one.'

Bob bristled. 'Remarkable,' he had come to realise, is what people said when they were about to declare Marjory's testimony false.

'She's a couthy wee lass,' Roughead continued. 'I couldn't help liking her.'

'And did you believe her?'

'Oh yes. Without a doubt.'

'Will the jury?'

'No.'

'Why?'

'This is a capital charge. If the man is found guilty, he

351

hangs. That's a terrible responsibility. Juries don't like it. They try to escape it. They'll look for any reason to avoid finding a man guilty. The defence solicitors know that. Play on it.'

'Discredit Madge's evidence?'

'Her character. Her trustworthiness. It doesn't take much. Just the smallest seed. Take that nonsense about the so-called boyfriend, Hamish Holland.'

'Yes, I didn't understand that. Why did they mention him once and never again?'

'Sheer laziness. They'll have tried to find some skeletons in the girl's cupboard and failed. The only name they could come up with is this family friend. So just use it, leave the jury to jump to any conclusions they want.'

'That's utterly cynical.'

'Indeed. But they'll do anything that allows the jury to say, "yes, but …" and feel they are being honest and fair and even-handed.'

'So a guilty man will go free.'

'No. He'll be convicted of the rape.'

'Even though her testimony isn't trustworthy?'

'Not trustworthy enough to convict a man of murdering another man, no. But enough to convict of rape, yes.'

'That's a distinction I don't see.'

'Nor me. But neither of us are on the jury.' They walked past the porticoed entrance to the library. The bridge lay ahead, Greyfriars Bobby standing on his plinth, guarding his owner's grave. 'We *will* see justice today,' Roughead said. 'He will be convicted and serve time.'

'We might see justice today,' said Bob. 'But will Madge Fenwick? Will Danny Kerrigan?'

Roughead pondered for a moment. 'Kerrigan is beyond such cares, I'm afraid. And the girl? She's already experienced justice. She's been experiencing it ever since the crime happened. Justice isn't pain-free. It isn't without consequence …'

'But it shouldn't be without conscience.'

'Yes, it should, I'm afraid. Justice is neutral.'

'What's happened to Madge Fenwick this week hasn't been neutral.'

'No,' said Roughead. 'Wrong, isn't it?'

*

The jury deliberated for over two hours. They returned once and asked to inspect the handkerchief and suspender belt. When they returned the second time the foreman of the jury stood and declared a decision had been made on each of the charges.

'On the charge of rape,' said the Clerk of Court, 'how do you find?'

'Guilty.'

'On the charge of housebreaking how do you find?'

'Guilty.'

The court was silent. Bob pressed his palms hard together and held his breath. He stared at McGuigan, who looked expressionlessly ahead.

'On the charge of murder, how do you find?'

'Not proven.'

McGuigan smiled. Bob felt instantly sick. He looked over at Roughead. He pictured Marjory, waiting at home for news, hoping for a verdict which would vindicate her.

Justice is neutral. Consequence isn't.

Lord Aitchison allowed a moment for the verdict to resonate before speaking. 'You may sit,' he said to the foreman and addressed the jury. 'I should like to thank you for what, if I may be allowed to say so, I regard as a discriminating verdict.' The group of fifteen appeared more animated than at any time during the trial. Their comportment seemed lighter, looser, the burden of responsibility removed from them. Bob couldn't escape the disapproval he felt. Would he have done the same? Chosen the easy option? Denied justice?

Aitchison turned to McGuigan. 'I have in front of me your criminal record. This was kept from the jury to ensure you received a fair trial but I can reveal it now. You were convicted of assault in 1929 and later in the same year of housebreaking and theft. You were convicted in 1932 of housebreaking and in 1934 on four separate counts of theft.

'I am satisfied from your criminal record and from the convictions now recorded against you that you are a dangerous criminal. It is necessary in the public interest that you be detained for a very considerable time.

'In considering what sentence I shall impose on you I leave completely out of account the grave suspicion attached to you in connection with the murder of Kerrigan. You have been acquitted of that and I leave any suspicion that may be attached to you out of the case.' He shook his head imperceptibly and looked round at the packed courtroom before turning to McGuigan once more.

'Having regard to the gravity of the crimes of which you now stand convicted I sentence you to be detained in penal servitude for ten years.'

*

Bob crossed to the public telephone box outside St Giles Cathedral and asked to be connected to Inspector Conoboy. He watched the crowds bustling past, men and women adamant against the rain, determined to make home. The bustle of ordinary life, the everyday, the commonplace. Bob felt hollow, more downcast than he could have predicted. It was a partial victory only. It felt like failure.

'Conoboy,' came a voice on the other end of the telephone line. Bob greeted him and explained the verdict. There was a pause before Conoboy spoke.

354

'I hoped for better.'

'Me too, sir.'

'I wanted to go out on a high. I ought to tell you Robert, I'm handing in my resignation on Monday.'

'You and me both, sir.'

Conoboy sighed. He looked at Bella, frowning at her crossword. 'Are you sure? You'll have Annie to look after. And children, in time.'

'I've thought about it constantly, sir. It's really not me. I prefer to look for the good in people.'

'What will you do?'

'I'm going to teach music.'

'Can you make a living from that?'

'We believe so.'

'You'll be missed. You were a humanising influence.'

'No, sir. That's your wife.'

Conoboy paused for a moment. 'You may be right about that. The rest of us, we get caught up in the process. Lose track of the victims.'

'No, you never did. You're too hard on yourself. But as for the others, that's what I couldn't take. People like Braggan. He's a louse, sir. Sorry.'

'I couldn't agree more.'

'And the court case clarified it for me. This world isn't for me.'

'Again, you may be right.'

They said goodbye and Conoboy set the telephone on the receiver and passed the news to Bella.

'Go and tell the child,' she said. 'Before anyone else does.'

It was six o'clock when the Wolseley pulled up on Longcauseway and Conoboy stepped out and placed his hat on his head and climbed the stone steps to the first floor. He greeted Mrs Fenwick at the door and followed her into the living room. Marjory was waiting expectantly, knees drawn tightly together and fingers knotted.

'John McGuigan was found guilty of rape and housebreaking,' Conoboy told her. 'But the murder charge was not proven. He was sentenced to ten years.' Nobody spoke. The clock on the mantelpiece was loud in the silence, ticking the moments past.

'They didn't believe me,' said Marjory.

'They did. They convicted him of rape.'

'But not murder. My word was good enough to convict him of raping a woman but not enough to convict him of murdering a man. That's more important, after all.'

'It isn't.'

'It is. The judge said so.'

'The judge was wrong.'

'So was the jury. It doesn't change anything. They didn't believe me enough. I'm just a girl. Unreliable.'

'Juries,' said Conoboy, 'they tend to be conservative. Especially on a capital charge.'

'No,' said Marjory. 'That's not it.' She looked at him angrily. 'You have no idea,' she said. 'No idea what it's like to sit there and be accused of being hysterical, of inventing a story. Of not being a virgin.'

'I know.'

'You don't!' She slammed her fist against her thigh. 'You could never know. He's the one who was on trial. So why do I feel like I'm the one who's been convicted? To a life of tittle-tattle and mistrust? Answer me that!'

Sunday 1st December

A Day of Beginnings

'Gran,' said Bob. 'Mrs Maybury and Annie are here to see us.'

'Well, just you tell them to go away again. I'm no' even washed yet.'

'It's fine, Agnes,' said Betsy Maybury. 'There's nae standin' on ceremony here.'

'Who are you?'

'Betsy Maybury. Feus Road.'

'I mind you.'

'Course you do. We used to go to the picters.'

'Annie and I are just off out, Gran,' said Bob. 'For a walk round the Inch.'

'I'm goin' tae stay and talk to you, Agnes,' said Betsy.

'I dinnae need anyone lookin' after me.'

'Of course not. It's just that sometimes I get fair scunnered at hame on my own all day. I thought, maybe, I'd come roond and we could keep each other company.' Betsy gestured to Bob and Annie and ushered them out. She kissed Annie and nodded at Bob and returned to the living room. 'Now,' she said. 'Let's get that kettle on.'

*

There was no rain but residue of an earlier downpour remained on the grass. The ground was heavy, the air thick,

357

sky indistinct. The Cuddies Strip lay silent, nature in pause, trees bare, whins skeletal. Grass lay like a mat, flattened by rain, exhausted and still.

Bella Conoboy and Marjory Fenwick picked their way through this stilted landscape. The dyke ran at one-hundred and eighty degrees towards Kirkton of Mailer, alongside the giant beech, much diminished in its winter hibernation. Marjory pointed to her left but said nothing. They passed the scene in silence, heading towards a thicket of whin where the path narrowed and kinked.

'Watch for the tree roots,' said Marjory.

'They are somewhat demanding.'

'Try running across them in the dark.'

'No, thank you.'

They laughed and the sound acted like a release. Bella took the girl's hand.

'This is only the second time I've been here since that night,' said Marjory. 'I never thought I'd come here again, to be honest.'

'I know,' said Bella. 'And I understand how difficult this is but I wanted you to come, especially today.' They walked on, past an ancient oak and a slender birch.

'Why?' Marjory asked.

'Because nature heals. If you allow it. This is not a bad place. A very bad thing happened here, but that thing doesn't exist in this world any longer.'

'I don't understand.'

'It didn't happen here. It happened in the past.'

Marjory pondered for a moment. 'It happened in both,' she said. 'It did happen here.'

'But the here of that day isn't the same here as today.'

'I'm not frightened to come here, if that's what you mean.' She paused. 'After all, I know exactly where he is now.'

Bella trailed her hand across the bark of a beech tree. 'I

358

know you're not frightened. But are you leaving that night in the past, or are you still carrying it about with you?'

'I still think about it.'

'Of course. But does it dictate what you do?'

'No. I don't think so.'

Bella took her hand again. She stared forwards. 'You know, this is your second time here since it happened. This is only my second time out of the house in eighteen years.'

'Really?' Marjory couldn't conceal her amazement.

'My son was killed in the last weeks of the war. I didn't want him to go, but he lied about his age – he was only seventeen – and signed up with the Black Watch. He was killed in a minor skirmish at Arras on August the 14th, 1918.'

'August the 14th?'

'Indeed. The same date. Isn't that remarkable?' She gripped both of Marjory's hands and stared into her eyes. 'I've never discussed this with anyone. Not even Victor. It simply hasn't been allowed. I loved that boy more than anything in the world, in a way only a mother could understand. You'll experience it one day, dear, and it's a beautiful feeling. So losing him hurt more than it's possible to say.'

Tears fell down her face. 'The thing is,' she went on, 'I could never forgive him. For signing up. I'm a pacifist. I tried to instil those beliefs in him and he defied me. Betrayed me. And then he died.'

'I'm very sorry.'

'So ever since I've had grief and resentment at the same time. I've never been able to reconcile them. I've shut myself away from the world, lived a parallel life, not then and not now. Limbo, I suppose. In my world Tom's not alive but he's not dead either. Does that make sense?'

Marjory nodded uncertainly.

'I'm sure it doesn't. I'm sure you think I'm a crazy old woman. I probably am. But you'll understand one day, I promise.' She kissed her lightly on the cheek. 'Just don't lose half your life waiting for it like I have. What happened yesterday in court doesn't matter any longer. That man doesn't matter. Only you matter, my beautiful child. Your life. Your future.' She looked around. 'Was this where he died?'

'Just over there.' Marjory pointed to the path beyond a desolate stand of fire-blackened whins. Bella walked towards it.

'Hello Danny,' she said. 'I've heard so much about you. I wish I'd known you. Have no fear. You will be remembered. Your name will not be forgotten. Danny Kerrigan and Tom Conoboy. Loved forever.'

They stood in silence.

'Will you go to night classes?' Bella asked.

'I believe so. I discussed it with Annie. We may go together in January. I don't know that I shall be able to afford it, though.'

'Don't you worry about that. Either of you. I'll see you're paid up.'

'Oh, I couldn't do that.'

'Victor and I, we spend very little money. We have plenty in the bank and nobody to spend it on. It would give me great pleasure.'

'Thank you. For everything.'

And they walked back towards Perth, the old woman and the young woman, and the Cuddies Strip was left to silence. Ice-covered pockets of water on the rough ground, frost in the branches and snow on the whins and the grass. A thin sun hovered above. Stand and stare. Here was the spot where Danny Kerrigan fell, his blood clotting on the soil, his life ebbing into the void. Here was the spot where Marjory Fenwick encountered evil. The Cuddies Strip stretched for a mile from the Dunning road to the foot of Buckie Braes. To the north the river Tay flowed to the sea, to the south ran the Earn, fast and fat, energetic in contrast to the fatigue that

360

inhabited the land. Trees stood indolent against the lightest breeze. Granite air, insubstantial light. Narrow path worn deep by generations of feet. Fields above and fields below, Perth in the near distance, Callerfountain Hill, the farms of Pitheavlis and Woodhead and Kirkton of Mailer, Aberdalgie village with its house and its church and its bending road. Nothing stirred except the cold pulse of the Earn and a roe deer alert by the side of Woodhead wood. Everywhere else, silence. History and memory lay concealed behind the veneer of the moment. And all around, to east and to west, the Ochil hills stretched high and beautiful, forming the valley of Strathearn. Life within and beneath, life beyond.

Acknowledgements

I would like to thank the staff at the National Records of Scotland in Edinburgh for their assistance while I researched Cuddies Strip. Thanks also to the ever-friendly and helpful staff at the Local Studies and Archives departments in the AK Bell Library in Perth.

An early draft of Cuddies Strip was a winner of the Bradford Literature Festival Northern Noir Crime Novel competition in 2019. As a result of that, I attended a writers' residential course at Lumb Bank, former home of Ted Hughes, and I am grateful to Cathi Unsworth and AA Dhand, the course tutors, for their expert insights. The final version of Cuddies Strip is much better for their input.

I began writing seriously in 2005, when I joined Alex Keegan's online writing forum, Bootcamp. Bootcamp was not for the faint-hearted, but I owe pretty much all of my knowledge of writing craft to Alex's brutally honest and rigorous feedback. Thanks also to my fellow Bootcampers of the period. I am also grateful to Clio Gray for editorial advice which has greatly improved my writing, and Zoe King, my editor at Ringwood Publishing. Thanks also to the entire team at Ringwood, who have made me feel very welcome.

I was given invaluable information on the history of policing in Perth by Willie MacFarlane, former Honorary Curator of the Tayside Police Museum. All of the mistakes contained in Cuddies Strip are mine and not his.

I first became interested in the story of Marjory and Danny when I saw a photograph of Danny's funeral cortège on the St Johnstone Football Club web forum, WeArePerth. Thanks to "chips" for posting the photograph and piquing my interest.

Other Titles from Ringwood

All titles are available from the Ringwood website in both print and ebook format, as well as from usual outlets.

www.ringwoodpublishing.com

mail@ringwoodpublishing.com

Ruxton - The First Modern Murder

Tom Wood

It is 1935 and the deaths of Isabella Ruxton and Mary Rogerson would result in one of the most complex investigations the world had ever seen. The gruesome murders captured worldwide attention with newspapers keeping the public enthralled with all the gory details.

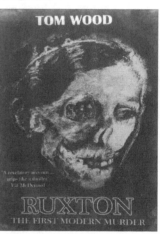

But behind the headlines was a different, more important story: the ground-breaking work of Scottish forensic scientists who developed new techniques to solve the case and shape the future of scientific criminal investigation.

ISBN: 978-1-901514-84-1
£9.99

The Ten Percent

Simon McLean

An often hilarious, sometimes scary, always fascinating journey through the ranks of the Scottish police from his spell as a rookie constable in the hills and lochs of Argyll, through his career in Rothesay and to his ultimate goal: The Serious Crime Squad in Glasgow.

We get a unique glimpse of the turmoil caused when the rules are stretched to the limit, when the gloves come off and and when some of their number decide that enough is enough. A very rare insight into the world of our plain clothes officers who infiltrate and suppress the very worst among us.

ISBN: 978-1-901514-43-8
£9.99

Murder at the Mela

Leela Soma

Newly appointed as Glasgow's first Asian DI, Alok Patel's first assignment is the investigation of the brutal murder of Nadia, an Asian woman. Her body was discovered in the aftermath of the Mela festival in Kelvingrove Park. During the Mela, a small fight erupted between a BNP group and an Asian gang, but was quickly quelled by police.

This novel peels away the layers of Glasgow's Asian communities, while exploring the complicated relationships between Asian people and the city.

ISBN: 978-1-901514-90-2
£9.99

Not the Deaths Imagined

Anne Pettigrew

It's here, the medical noir novel you've been waiting for! The sequel to Anne Pettigrew's acclaimed debut, *Not the Life Imagined.*

In *Not the Deaths Imagined* we again follow Beth Semple, now a dedicated GP and mother in Milngavie, as she aims to navigate Glasgow's busy medical scene.

But when she starts asking questions about a series of local deaths, Beth finds her life – and that of her family – is about to be turned upside down.

ISBN: 978-1-901514-80-3
£9.99

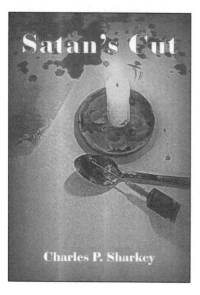

Satan's Cut

Charles P. Sharkey

Satan's Cut is a tale of crime and the criminal justice system set in the gritty, winter streets of Glasgow.

Inspector Frank Dorsey and his partner DC George Mitchell come across a dead body they believe to be linked to the Moffats, one of the biggest crime families in the city.

However, as they begin to delve further into the case, not all is as it seems, as the victim was sent a cryptic text message days before their death.

What does the message have to do with the case? How are the Moffats involved? And will Inspector Dorsey be able to crack it before another body shows up?

ISBN: 978-1-901514-72-8   £9.99

Who Jinxed Jesse James?

Alex Gordon

Jesse James – real name, Frank – shoots straight from the lip: the controversial gossip columnist makes a living sullying the reputations of the elite and, like his Wild West counterpart, is no stranger to infamy. He finds himself with no choice but to swallow his considerable ego and seek the help of his former colleague, freelance sports journalist and amateur sleuth, Charlie Brock. They soon becomes entangled in the mystery surrounding the identity of an enigmatic scribe - known locally as 'The Red Phantom'...

ISBN: 978-1-901514-71-1   £9.99